Circled Heart

Karen J. Hasley

Outskirts Press, Inc.
Denver, Colorado

Cover design by Krina Walsh at Visible Innovations

Outskirts Press, Inc.
http://www.outskirtspress.com

ISBN: 978-1-4327-5099-2

Outskirts Press and the "OP" logo are trademarks belonging to Outskirts Press, Inc.

PRINTED IN THE UNITED STATES OF AMERICA

Charles Nelson Crittenton
1833—1909

Katherine Harwood Waller Barrett, M.D.
1858—1925

Oh, though oft depressed and lonely,
All my fears are laid aside,
If I but remember only
Such as these have lived and died!

Author's note: All quoted poems are taken from the collections of American poet Henry
Wadsworth Longfellow (1807—1882))

And the last of all the figures
Was a heart within a circle,
Drawn within a magic circle;
And the image had this meaning:
"Naked lies your heart before me,
To your naked heart I whisper!"

With thy rude ploughshare, Death, turn up the sod,
And spread the furrow for the seed we sow;
This is the field and Acre of our God,
This is the place where human harvests grow.

Chapter One

I never thought, not once, that I would die that April night. Even as I looked over the railing into the churning, black, frigid water, the idea simply never crossed my mind. By the expressions and voices of the people around me, however, I could tell that many of my fellow passengers did not hold the same confident belief. They realized—and had begun to vocalize—our danger. But because I was always confident to a fault —"cocksure" my grandmother called it—and quick to think I had all the answers, I never believed any situation could get the better of me. A flaw in my character so I'd been told on numerous occasions, but a useful flaw for my purposes.

On that particular night it had been too cold to be out on deck and many people retired early, Grandmother included. I, however, was restless and unwilling to seek my bed too soon. Even as a child I'd deliberately resisted sleep, afraid of missing something exciting that might happen during the night hours. My grandmother had had to learn that although I was obedient to a bedtime, she could not bribe or coerce me to sleep until I was ready. That night my peculiar energy may very well have saved our lives, for if I hadn't stayed up late to finish a letter to a friend I'd left behind in London, I wouldn't have heard—felt, really—the gentlest of thuds as the great ship collided softly with something equally massive. The thud was followed by a slight shudder. That was all. But, prescient, I immediately put the letter down, pulled the first dress I could find over my head, reached for warm stockings and shoes, wrapped myself in my coat, and went to the connecting door that led to my grandmother's cabin.

She awoke instantly when I knocked, sat up in her narrow bed, and asked, "What is it, Johanna?"

"I believe something's happened to the ship, Grandmother. We should go up on deck." Never one to fuss, my grandmother mimicked my earlier actions, threw on a skirt and a heavy sweater over her nightdress, found shoes and coat, and as an afterthought before leaving her room dug out her wallet filled with cash and thrust it into her pocket. Through all her actions neither of us said a word.

A steward came down the steps as we went up. His face was white as chalk, his eyes wide and hair disheveled. I heard him begin to go from door to door, pounding to wake the inhabitants, calling for everyone to come up on deck immediately, panic just below the surface of every word he spoke.

People already milled about the deck, but the scene was remarkably calm. Except for the crowd the night seemed unremarkable, black and cold and lit by brittle stars. One lifeboat had already been lowered and another was nearly full, but most of the people I had met on the voyage had pulled away from the lifeboats giving the distinct impression they thought their use beneath them. Passengers in first class would not condescend to the indignity of clambering aboard a lifeboat and sharing its space with women and children who didn't speak English. One of the crew called out for order, but until the sixth lifeboat was lowered, he needn't have. Until then everyone remained calm and the orchestra still played.

Grandmother had moved a little ahead of me and stopped

to speak to Mrs. Astor, both women giving the effect of a leisurely boardwalk promenade, and I moved to the rail to stare out at the black Atlantic. The first lifeboats had disappeared into the distance only half full, but now that people understood from the groaning and listing of the ship that something serious had occurred, now that they realized there were not enough lifeboats for the mass of passengers crowding the deck, the mood on the deck changed.

"Women and children only!" the man by the lifeboats shouted. He waved a revolver in the air and shot twice. The action—not for defense as the papers later reported but to get people's attention—started a panic. Several people surged past me: a woman with a scarf on her head and a baby in her arms, an elderly man wearing thick glasses, a young couple grasping each other's hands, tears in her eyes and a terrified bravery in his. My grandmother turned to fix her gaze on me across the press of people and lifted an imperious hand to beckon me to her. Come along, the gesture said, we're getting in one of the boats. Now. She and I had been apart for two years but even wordless, I still understood her very well.

I turned to make my way through the crowd toward where she stood when a man reached out and grasped me firmly by the arm. I tried to shake him off at first, but he was insistent so that I had to turn to face him. Douglas Gallagher, I thought, who *would* pick the night the ship was sinking to seek out my company. I had noticed him early in the voyage, a man hard to miss, dark, polished and handsome, urbane and sophisticated, always perfectly dressed. I'd seen him once before this voyage, recognizing him from a very fine society ball in Chicago we had both attended two years earlier. He'd been dressed in black then, too, and dancing with a tall, slender woman whose hair had the sheen of liquid honey. Their striking appearance had left a lasting impression, and I recalled admiring him then as an attractive man. He remained attractive two years later, even standing on the shifting deck of a sinking ship. I had to look up at him, not as tall as the woman with honey-colored hair, and found him staring at me intently. Despite the sound of more gunshots behind us and the escalating roar of fear and panic from the crowd on deck, Gallagher maintained a casual posture, poised and sleek and slightly disdainful.

"You're from Chicago," he began without preamble.

"Yes."

"You should get to a lifeboat."

"I intend to."

He grabbed my hand and turned it palm up as he spoke. "My name is Douglas Gallagher and my brother is Andrew Gallagher, both of us from Chicago. Will you see that Drew gets these?" He dropped a ring and another small piece of jewelry into my hand, then folded my fingers over them. I didn't pretend to misunderstand.

"Yes. I promise. Is there anything you want me to tell him?" He shook his head, a bitter, odd twist to his mouth that I didn't think was caused by the situation at hand.

"No. What's your name?"

How humbling that I had been on this voyage with him for several days and he had not noticed me enough to inquire my name. Then I was ashamed of the brief and petty thought. He faced death in these terrible, frigid, dark waters, and I was put out that he didn't know my name!

"Johanna Swan."

"Thank you, Miss Swan." He turned me by the shoulders and pushed me away from him into the people surging toward the lifeboats. I stuffed the jewelry he'd given me deep into my coat pocket, then looked back briefly to see him take up his stance by the tilting railing. He actually lit a cigarette and his hands did not shake.

My grandmother, waiting for me impatiently, reached out, and pulled me over to her side. "Number sixteen is ours," she told me, "and it's time to get a seat."

Two young women with the look of sisters were in lifeboat number sixteen with us, both huddled together with their arms around each other, as well as an older woman with three grown daughters wordlessly pressed close to her side, and several women with young children. I heard a baby cry fretfully as we pulled away, the young steward in charge of the oars struggling to move us as quickly as he could. It was slow going, though, because cold and fear and inexperience made the poor boy fumble-fingered. All of us in the lifeboat were mesmerized by the sight of the big ship, unable to pull our eyes away even if we'd wanted to. We gasped in unison as we saw its prow slowly lift skyward and figures plummet from the decks into the ocean. The woman with the three daughters moaned, then put her hand up against her mouth to hold back any further display of grief and horror.

She has left someone behind on the deck, I thought, and knows he is lost. My heart went out to her. The young steward quit rowing altogether and sat watching the terrible sight, gaping at the spectacle before us. When the ship finally broke in two, a cracking sound echoed across the water.

"Pull farther away," I directed the crewman sternly. "We're too close. When it goes down, we could be dragged under with it." He ignored me, sitting immobile, staring at the great vessel that had been terribly miscalled and falsely publicized as "unsinkable." I moved closer to him and nudged him sharply. "Keep rowing. It's premature to stop." Still the steward sat there until I plopped myself next to him on the seat with enough force that the lifeboat swayed and one of the sisters gave a muted shriek. "Move aside, then. You're endangering the safety of all of us in this boat." He turned a dumb, wretched gaze on me, and I realized he had left friends behind on the ship, too, that he was as afraid and numb as the rest of us. Why should it be any different for a man, after all?

One woman handed her baby over to her neighbor and situated herself on the seat to take hold of the other oar, squeezing the steward between us.

Ready when you are," she muttered, and at my count of three we began pulling our boat away from the doomed liner, straining against the water, at first unsynchronized and clumsy but eventually finding our rhythm and rowing with all our might.

Because of my focused activity, I didn't see the great ship upend and slip decorously into the ocean's depths. Grandmother told me later it disappeared seamlessly under the waves like a warm knife sliding through butter. In the end it seemed the ocean liner had never been there at all. The other woman and I continued to row, oblivious to the muted sounds of weeping among the women in our boat, ignoring the whimpers of the baby, truly rowing for all our lives.

Finally Grandmother pointed out practically, "Johanna, I believe the danger of undertow is past," and I looked up and around. The night was black, bitterly cold, and still. Except for the few other rowboats we could barely see bobbing on the water, we might have been the only people in the world. My rowing partner and I stopped our efforts at exactly the same time and looked at each other across the drooping steward. Then she reached for her child and pulled him against her chest, burying her face in the babe's neck.

She has left husband and father behind in this watery graveyard, I thought. Poor baby, never to know his papa.

Perhaps something of their loss showed on my own face for Grandmother, never one to indulge in sentimentality, held out her hand and commanded, "Come and sit next to me,

Johanna. There's no use both of us taking a chill when we can keep each other warm."

Until the *Carpathia* arrived and began to retrieve the survivors, we remained numb and quiet. None of us spoke more than a few quiet words to any but our own immediate circle. We were in shock, I suppose. Once on board the rescue ship, bundled in blankets and sipping hot tea, a *Carpathia* passenger offered Grandmother and me his stateroom for privacy.

"I'm afraid it won't offer much warmth," he apologized. "The captain shut off all heat to the rooms in order to make speed for the rescue, but it's still warmer than the deck and you could rest on the bed there."

"We couldn't possibly take your room," my grandmother responded, ever polite but fully intending to take him up on his offer. He insisted, the courteous and requisite response to my grandmother's proper reluctance, and led Grandmother and me to his room. She lay down almost immediately.

"Come and sleep a while, Johanna. You'll accomplish nothing with all that pacing." I wandered around the room, unable to stop moving, not feeling tired at all but energized by a nervous force that I could not contain.

"I'm not tired, Grandmother."

As I spoke, I thrust my hands hard into my coat pockets for warmth and touched cold, unyielding metal there. The past hours had so consumed me that at first I had no memory of what was in my pocket. I fished out the items and stared at them as they lay in my palm, a man's ring heavy with platinum, onyx, and diamonds and a more delicate gold stickpin in the shape of the letter *G*. The pin, twinkling in the recognizable manner of expensive diamonds, was handsome and elegant, a reflection of the man who had given it to me for safekeeping and delivery. He was certainly dead now, slipping from the deck to tumble over the railing, stunned by the icy temperature of the ocean, hands reaching out in desperation, mouth open gasping for air and finding only water and then sinking, sinking— certainly dead.

I raised my eyes from the items in my hand, feeling suddenly deflated, my energy gone and replaced by dismay and grief at the loss of a man I had admired from a distance and now would never know.

My face, always transparent and incapable of subterfuge, caused Grandmother to say again, more gently and with less imperative, "But I am tired, Johanna, even if you're not, and your restless activity will not let me sleep. Come lie down beside me for a while."

I dropped the ring and stickpin back into my pocket and crawled in next to her, both of us, despite our layers of dresses and coats, still shaking from the hours in the cold. She slept first, I could tell from her breathing, and then, finally, I slept too.

Uncle Hal waited for us on the dock in New York when the *Carpathia* pulled into port. He stood among a large but restrained crowd that wordlessly searched the faces of the people standing at the ship's railing for their own loved ones. No one waved or called a greeting but instead maintained a somber mix of welcome and mourning. When Grandmother and I finally descended the gangplank, Uncle Hal came forward quickly and embraced his mother, a rare gesture that surprised them both.

"Thank God, you're safe, Mother." Then he turned and hugged me, too, saying, "I planned a better homecoming for you, Johanna."

"I can't find fault, Uncle Hal. At least I'm alive."

"The papers are full of nothing but the *Titanic*. Until you responded to our telegram, Kitty and Jennie feared the worst and didn't sleep a wink. Peter even came home from school until we had the good word that you were safe."

Grandmother asked, "Did you bring any of the family to New York with you?"

"No. Peter's back in school and I left Kitty and Jen at home, but they're anxious to see you."

"Not like this, I trust." Grandmother spoke briskly and fluffed out her worn skirts. "We could use a hot bath and a change of clothes, Harry, and sooner rather than later."

Uncle Hal and I both realized the small moment of sentiment had passed. Grandmother was her usual practical, peremptory self again.

"Of course, Mother." I felt slightly sorry for my uncle, a man of feeling who wanted to tell his mother he loved her but was not encouraged to do so. Standing on tiptoe, I kissed him lightly on the cheek.

"We're anxious to get home, too, Uncle Hal. Thank you for making the trip to meet us. I know that wasn't part of the original plan."

"Had to come," he answered gruffly. "Terrible thing to read about. Had to be sure you were both all right."

"As you can see, we are." Grandmother picked up her skirts and headed toward the closest cab. "But I can't promise we'll remain so if we have to stand in this breeze much longer. Come along, Harry, and stop dawdling." I linked arms with my uncle and we followed in her wake through the crowd.

"She'll never change, you know," I remarked casually. Uncle Hal gave me a sidelong smile.

"I know. Your mother could manage her, though, and I should have paid more attention at the time."

"Mother had a gift for dealing comfortably with people."

Uncle Hal helped Grandmother into the cab, then extended a hand to me.

"Yes, she did. I never realized it before, Johanna, but seeing you for the first time in two years makes me appreciate how much like your mother you are."

"She was a beauty, Uncle Hal." My tone was polite but skeptical.

"I didn't mean in appearance although you look more like her than you choose to admit."

He climbed in next to us and gave directions to the cabbie to take us to a well-known hotel. I wanted to pursue the subject with him, always eager to talk about my mother, but I felt tired and strangely lethargic, not at all my usual self. All I longed for was hot, really hot, water, fresh clothing, and a featherbed. I suppose my reaction was to be expected after the drama of the trip, but I was surprised at my lack of energy and disappointed in myself. I had spent the last two years at the Florence Nightingale School of Nursing, had in fact met the great woman herself just before she died, and I wished for nothing more than to emulate Miss Nightingale's vision and vigor. Yet here I sat, curled into a corner, a silent and weary lump of humanity. How humbling to realize that I was not the woman I wanted to be! Thinking that discreditable thought forced my mind to Douglas Gallagher, who for all the time we had socialized in the same rooms and eaten at the same tables had not noticed me enough to ask my name until an hour before his death. I reached into my coat pocket and fingered the cloth in which I had wrapped his two pieces of jewelry. A better way to keep them safe, I thought, than to let them bounce loosely in my pocket, but I missed the feel of cold platinum against my skin. A man named Andrew Gallagher waited somewhere in Chicago. Did he already know of his brother's death or would I be the bearer of both jewelry and grievous news? I started to ask my uncle whether he recognized the man's name, but we pulled up in front of the hotel then and I lost the inclination.

Hot water and clean clothes beckoned and they were all I could think about.

We left on the train for Chicago the next afternoon, even though I would easily and willingly have stayed longer in New York. I love the city, love any city really, but next to Chicago I've always been especially taken with New York City, such a teeming, busy place, so much to see and do that I could never be bored there. When Grandfather was alive, we had made the trip east at least three times a year. A highly regarded attorney, he had clients and business there, and knowing that I loved the place, always asked me along. Grandmother accompanied us, but disdained the city's smells and dirt and lamented my need to be out and about. Not for me the sedate carriage rides, the upscale restaurants, Fifth Avenue shopping, and a suitably refined theatrical production in the evening. That was my cousin Jennie's idea of perfection. I would put on unfashionable walking shoes and a sturdy coat and take to the sidewalks, invigorated by the profusion of languages I heard, by neighborhoods new to me, by the sights and sounds of the docks. Grandfather understood my dislike of being confined and my ill-concealed scorn for the strictures of upper class propriety, and he always rose to my defense.

"Leave her alone, Trudy," he would say to Grandmother, the only person in the world allowed to use that affectionate nickname. "Nettie was the same way, and Johanna is her mother's daughter."

"Yes, and look what came of it. Gone from home by the time she was twenty and dead before she was thirty-five. Is that what you want for our granddaughter?"

Grandfather's face always saddened at the blunt rebuttal, but he never argued past that point. They had lost my mother, their only daughter, too soon and at too great a distance, and he knew Grandmother felt the loss as keenly as he. Still, he

understood me better than anyone else and never tried to force
me into a mold I would not fit. I miss him to this day. Through
difficult years he remained my closest confidant.

"Are you rested this morning, Grandmother?" I asked once
we settled into our first-class train compartment. I took in with
appreciation the gray silk dress of such impeccable fit that she
might have had time for a dozen fittings to make it right. One
would never guess that the dress had appeared overnight, that
the elegant woman wearing it had spent a night in a lifeboat
floating on the Atlantic and the past few days in a cabin the
size of a closet, all the while dressed in her nightdress. Seeming
to read my thoughts—as she disconcertingly did more often
than I wished—Grandmother met my look with a twinkle in
her eyes.

"Yes, Johanna. It's remarkable how a bath and a change of
clothes affect one's attitude toward life." Then examining me
carefully, she added, without a nuance to her voice, "I wish you
had had time to find something more becoming than that suit,
but I know it was short notice."

"This is perfectly respectable," I responded indignantly.
"Everything the woman showed me was far too expensive attire for a train trip."

"You forget that all of the clothes waiting for you at home
are two years old at least, and if anything you're thinner than
when you left. I doubt much in your closet will fit you, whether
in fashion or not."

I settled into the train seat and smoothed the navy wool of
my skirt. I liked the look and the feel of it. When the woman
had brought the suit to my room last evening, I appreciated that
there was nothing pretentious about it, a tailored, serviceable,
and practical garment in a classic style and color. I would
get wear out of it for a long time. The matching jacket was
cut broad at the shoulders and unfashionably short, but as

susceptible to vanity as the next person, I liked to show off my small waist. I didn't have a lot of becoming features, so who could blame me for latching onto one and displaying it for all the world to see?

"Clothes can be taken in," was my terse response before I turned to look out the train window. I viewed the constricting skirts, the laces, flounces, and all those buttons that adorned gowns of fashion as a waste of time and money. That attitude was thanks to my father, who told me often enough that packages could be wrapped up as prettily as you pleased. It wasn't the outer wrapping that really mattered; only what was inside the box counted.

Hardly a day went by that I did not think of my parents, both dead on the same day over eleven years ago. I kept my grief at their deaths locked away in a private place inside me. The terrible dreams had stopped all on their own several years ago, replaced by gentler night visions. Time had softened the loss, and remembering the women in the lifeboat, the older woman with her daughters pressed against her and my fellow oarsman, who had wept into her infant's neck, I hoped time would do the same for them.

"I left Mother and Father's wedding picture behind on the ship," I volunteered aloud.

"Kitty and I have another copy," Uncle Hal replied quickly. If he was taken aback by my abrupt announcement, he didn't show it. "You can have that one."

I smiled at him. Uncle Hal, my mother's brother, was a kind and generous man, if inclined to take the easy way out more often than not. Too permissive with his children, I always thought, and ready to be permissive with me, too, if I would allow it.

"Thank you. I would appreciate that very much." Holding my small purse on my lap, I turned once more to the window.

Because I could not help it, I reached inside my purse to finger the two pieces of men's jewelry there, wrapping my fingers around the ring, its smooth surface already becoming a talisman of sorts for me. I had been gone for two years and was home again, but how could I know if the catastrophic return trip was an omen for my future? The cool surface of the ring soothed me when everything around me seemed to be changing, when I felt I was changing, too, but into what or who remained to be seen.

Levi, my grandmother's driver, waited for us at the station when we arrived in Chicago. "Madam," he greeted Grandmother, his attitude one of a man who had dropped his passenger off that morning and was now picking her up after a quick shopping trip.

"We have no luggage," Grandmother gave Levi a small smile, "and you've no doubt heard why."

"Yes, Mrs. McIntyre. May and I are glad you and Miss Johanna made it home safely. I trust you're both well." Levi didn't look glad, but he was cut from the same cloth as my grandmother, not given to showing emotion and always correct, so for all I knew, inside he was leaping with ecstasy. He held open the door of the automobile for us.

"Quite well, thank you." She patted the seat next to her. "Come along, Johanna. You may gaze off into space once we're on our way, but now is not the time."

"I was delighting in the prospect of being home," I answered mildly, climbing in as directed.

"Delight all you want—later. If we could make it home before the street lamps came on, I would consider myself fortunate. I am long past the stage of finding evening drives romantic."

"I have never found them romantic either," I agreed, but Grandmother surprised me with her reply.

"You will, Johanna, you will. There are a great many things you haven't experienced." I turned to meet her gaze. Affection there, a hint of a smile, and something almost wistful. So she had not been as unaffected by the sinking of the great ocean liner, the loss of life, and the grief of fellow survivors as she tried to pretend. She had been on social speaking terms with the Astors, after all, and apparently they both went down with the ship, so her sudden small wave of nostalgia should not have surprised me.

Instead of replying, I rested my hand on my bag and felt the hard metal of Douglas Gallagher's jewelry through the cloth. Grandmother was right. There were a great many things I had not experienced, but I was alive when so many were not, and if only for that reason, the future must be bright.

Labor with what zeal we will,
Something still remains undone,
Something uncompleted still
Waits the rising of the sun.

Chapter Two

The big house on Hill Street blazed extravagant light from every window.

"I see Kitty is here for our welcome," Grandmother remarked dryly but made no other comment. I think she was as relieved and happy to be home as I was but more skilled at hiding her emotions, and that evening Aunt Kitty could have built bonfires on the front porch without Grandmother's disapproval.

My Aunt Kitty came out the front door and down the porch steps as the auto came to a halt in the side drive. Levi held open the door as Uncle Hal handed Grandmother out of the vehicle.

"Gertrude, what an ordeal! You must have been beside yourself." Kitty gave her mother-in-law a feather kiss on the cheek, then turned to me. "Johanna, this will teach you to go gallivanting around the globe. You both could have been killed." She spoke with a light tone and kissed me, too, but as always with Aunt Kitty, I heard her implied criticism of my behavior, the loss of *Titanic* and its subsequent endangering of Grandmother somehow to be laid directly at my feet.

"Hello, Aunt Kitty. Many people were killed, but as you can see, Grandmother and I weren't among their numbers." I disembarked from the auto without assistance and looked past her to exclaim, "Jennie, is that you?!"

My cousin Jennie was sixteen when I left, a fair and pretty girl with a charming smile and a girl's slim figure. The past two years had turned her into a blooming beauty. She came forward, more her father's daughter than her mother's, and gave me a heartfelt hug.

"Hello, Johanna. It's been so dull without you. I've been anticipating your homecoming for weeks. That nuisance *Titanic* almost spoiled it all."

Her mother said her name with more indulgence than chastisement. "Jennie, that's hardly sensitive to what your grandmother and your cousin have had to endure."

My cousin linked arms with me and spoke over her shoulder as we walked up onto the front porch. "Nonsense. Look at them. Grandmother looks a decade younger and Johanna looks quite—" She paused and I waited, brows raised, for the missing adjective. Jennie caught my look, gave a gurgle of laughter, and finished, "—intelligent. Johanna looks even more intelligent than she did two years ago, and that was awe-inspiring enough then."

I wanted to tell my cousin that the sinking of the great liner was more than a nuisance, that I had seen people die, watched fathers and sons fall to terrible graves, heard wives and mothers and daughters moan with grief. I wanted to say that the handsomest man I'd ever seen had stood by a tilting railing and lit a cigarette not many minutes before he would slide into the ocean and that when I least expected it, I could hear his quiet "Thank you, Miss Swan," the words clipped and clear. But I spoke none of my thoughts. Because Jennie was Jennie, spoiled and charming and funny and endearing and not one to be weighted down with the realities of life, I gave her a poke with my elbow instead.

"I would rather be intelligent than incorrigible, devil child. Behave yourself and show some respect for your elders."

She laughed again and led me inside, saying in a low voice, "I am truly glad you're home, Johanna. I wasn't joking. It's never boring when you're around."

"Only because I drive your poor mother to distracted frustration with my lack of social skills."

"Yes there is that," she agreed with equanimity. "While you were gone, I had to bear the full force of her motherly advice and admonition. I begged Peter to come home more often but he abandoned me to her tender mercies." We went into the parlor where tea and sandwiches and an array of cakes were laid out. Something in her tone made me turn to look at her more intently.

"She is your mother, Jen, and as much as she and I disagree, I know she dotes on you and has only your best interests at heart."

"I'm not sixteen any more, Johanna, but Mother refuses to see that I've grown up."

I eyed her objectively before agreeing, "That is certainly true. The girl who waved goodbye to me at the train station two years ago has been replaced by a beautiful woman." I only stated the obvious. My cousin Jennie was indeed beautiful, glowing skin, sparkling blue eyes, golden brown hair, and a figure like the quintessential Gibson Girl with her small waist and graceful, slender neck.

Jennie didn't argue, respond with false modesty, or color with pleasure at the compliment. So, I thought, she's already used to attention and to flattery. I could understand why her mother might wish her back to fifteen again. That combination of face, figure, and temperament might be more than either Uncle Hal or Aunt Kitty could handle.

"Now, Johanna," said Aunt Kitty, seating herself on the

sofa next to Uncle Hal, "tell us about your stay in London and your chosen profession." She colored the last word with a touch of censure and a whiff of distaste. The women in our family, wives and mothers all, never made their living outside the home. They might volunteer to do good works, but they must never, never be paid for their efforts. I understood her message and as usual ignored it. Since entering my grandmother's household over eleven years ago, I had been something of an enigma to my aunt, and from the beginning she had feared my attitude and temperament might contaminate Jennie in the same way I might pass along a contagious disease.

"If I hadn't gone to bring her home," Grandmother interjected, "I believe Johanna would still be parading through the London streets marching for women's suffrage."

"Johanna, you didn't!" exclaimed Jennie with admiration.

I turned to give Grandmother an unambiguous but respectful frown. "I am a nurse by profession, not a suffragette." Grandmother eyed me, daring me to say more so that I couldn't help but add, "Anyway, it was a perfectly peaceful demonstration before the police got involved. Imagine billy clubs used on defenseless women, their arms twisted around behind them like dangerous criminals. And all because women wanted the right to vote, a perfectly legitimate and rational expectation."

"Johanna, you are even more my hero." At the admiring tone in Jennie's voice, I could tell poor Aunt Kitty wanted to lean over and press her hands over her daughter's ears.

"I'm not a hero at all," I admitted honestly. "I was marching along peacefully and then the melee started and I was pushed into an alley. It was clear our intended message was being lost in all the hubbub so I simply went back home."

"Johanna, I have just the idea. You can organize a march for women's suffrage in Chicago. I'll help you. We'll make the headlines of the paper and get our pictures on the front page.

I'll mess my hair and tear my dress and be such a sympathetic figure that we'll win the vote out of pity and guilt."

"We ought to receive the vote because we're intelligent human beings who can make sensible decisions without the condescension or the intervention of the male sex. There are very few things that differentiate women from men, and none of them is our brain."

"That," stated Grandmother calmly with a hint of humor, "must be something you learned in nursing school." At her words, Aunt Kitty stood abruptly, Uncle Hal following suit as if a string connected them.

"No doubt nursing school was an education for you in many ways, Johanna. We'll have to hear more about it later. Right now I'm sure the two of you wish to unpack and settle in."

"Oh, Johanna's not a settling-in kind of woman, Mother, you should know that by now." Jennie's eyes sparkled. "She's never bored and never boring, which is why I want to be exactly like her."

That night, crawling into my familiar bed, I recalled the look on my aunt's face at those words from her daughter and felt a stirring of pity for her. Aunt Kitty had a vision for Jennie and a plan, neither of which included suffrage marches or nursing school. I privately thought that Jennie should be in college, using her quick wit and bright mind to learn more about herself and the world around her, but that wasn't part of my aunt's plan either. Jennie was to marry well, marry someone with a recognized name and old money. That's what her mother had done, and Aunt Kitty intended Jennie to follow in her footsteps.

Over breakfast the next morning, Grandmother told me we were going shopping. "I know you don't generally favor shopping as a pastime, Johanna, but even you must admit we have a reason to invest in new wardrobes. Besides, your aunt thinks we should hold a party to celebrate your homecoming and you'll need something besides a navy wool suit to wear to the festivities."

"But Aunt Kitty isn't glad I'm home," I pointed out. "If she's planning a party, it's so my dark hair and pallid complexion will show Jennie's glow to even greater advantage." I caught Grandmother's reproachful look. "You know it's true, Grandmother, but I don't mind."

Grandmother didn't argue, only replied, "Jennie is a beauty without the necessity of comparison, Johanna. We'll leave for Marshall Field's after breakfast."

I regretted the words I had spoken, the result of my sharp tongue and too many years of crossing swords with Aunt Kitty, and I wished Grandmother had reproached me for my uncharitable comments.

When I admitted as much, Grandmother remarked, "That trait must come from the Swan side of the family. Your mother often disagreed with me, but she had the ability to turn every disagreement to her advantage without a single unkind word."

"That's how I remember her, too." After a pause, I added, "Remind me to get their picture from Uncle Hal. My bedside table is empty without them smiling out at me." I paused again before saying, "I've been thinking about the Swan side of the family lately," trying to watch Grandmother's face as I made the comment without appearing to do so.

"Thinking what exactly?"

"That I might make a trip west for a visit."

"Johanna, you've just arrived home. Take some time to settle in for a while." I pushed myself away from the table and rose.

"You heard Jennie. I'm not a settling-in kind of woman."

"First, you wanted to be a social worker and left for two

years to accomplish that. Then you wanted to be a nurse and crossed an ocean in order to do so. Don't you think you should decide what you really want to do with your future before you leave on another trip?" I knew that although she was careful not to criticize, Grandmother never liked my interaction with my father's side of the family. For the first time, I heard in her voice the same worried, almost jealous tone I sometimes heard from Aunt Kitty when she talked of Jennie. It was love that spoke so. I turned back to kiss Grandmother lightly on the cheek.

"Perhaps you're right," I conceded. "Does that apply to today's shopping trip, too?" She gave a little smile and returned to the newspaper she held.

"Those tickets are already purchased, Johanna. Levi will be waiting at the front door at ten sharp. Don't be late. It doesn't do to keep the McIntyre train waiting."

The planned shopping was something to be endured but not enjoyed. For as long as I had lived with my grandmother, I had coveted a flair for fashion. I don't recall that clothing and style ever mattered before I came to Chicago, certainly not to my parents, who lived simply and wore utilitarian clothes. My mother loved color, though, and I remember her tying her hair back with a bright ribbon. Then, seeing me eye the streak of blue with wonder, she removed the ribbon and fastened it around my neck with a flourish. But that one gesture did not display a love for fashion on her part, only a love for me. One would think that after so many years I would not still miss my mother so sharply.

The problem with fashion was that I had no one to pattern myself after, not Grandmother, with her choice of dresses from the last century, and not Aunt Kitty, who equated style with cost. For my aunt, the more costly a garment, the more fashionable it must be. Even when she sadly pronounced that

I did not inherit my mother's good taste, I knew I was a step ahead of her when it came to realizing that expensive fashion was not always smart or becoming. Fortunate Jennie could wear anything with flair; I knew I did not have the same gift.

I came back from our all-day trip with my usual assortment of practical skirts, shirtwaists and long jackets, very little lace, and not a ruffle in sight. Grandmother insisted on a new spring dress for me—"It's possible you will go somewhere besides the hospital in your lifetime, Johanna"—and I found a pretty, high-necked gown in lavender for the party Aunt Kitty planned. When everything was delivered the next day, I felt slightly guilty. Why should one person need so many clothes when others had only what they wore on their backs? But I stroked the lavender silk with pleasure and thought Mother would have appreciated the color.

At the end of that week, my cousin Peter came home from Harvard, bounding up on the porch and nearly running into me as I stepped outside the front door.

"Peter!"

I was very fond of Jennie, and I had the greatest affection for Uncle Hal, but I absolutely loved my cousin Peter. He was the most unspoiled of the family, fair-haired like Jennie but without her innate mischief that often bordered on malice, kind like his father but with an energy that my easygoing uncle lacked. Peter was spared all of my overbearing and stubborn traits, and he resembled his mother only physically. Peter had inherited all that was the best of us.

"Johanna, how terrible it must have been for you!" He put his arms around my waist and gave me a big hug that left me breathless. "We're so glad you and Grandmother are home safe and sound. Was it very awful?"

We went inside and sat down.

"Not so awful for me, but it was terrible for a great many

people. Now let's talk about you. How are your studies?"

He grimaced, but I knew the expression was in jest. Peter was bright and a good student and planned to be an attorney like his father. No one had to force him into the profession either. He loved the law. Someday I knew he would be a fine lawyer, the best in his field and much in demand.

"Grueling."

"Then why are you home? Surely it's not break time."

"I'm home for your party, Johanna. Mother commanded an appearance."

"That was thoughtful."

Another grimace followed by, "You know there's often an ulterior motive with Mother. She encouraged me to bring some college friends home with me. You know the kind: good family and—"

"—old money," I supplied, and we both laughed.

"Exactly. You'll meet them at the party. Sometimes I think I was only sent away to school to find a husband for Jennie."

"Is Jennie ready for a husband, do you think?" I meant it teasingly but his face sobered.

"Jennie's nineteen going on forty. She thinks she's Miss Sophistication but she's just a girl. Not like you, Johanna."

"Thank you, I think."

"You know what I mean. You have some experience in the world, good sense, and a feel for people. Jennie has no experience in the world and a very narrow perspective. I wouldn't exactly call her an innocent, though, so a husband might be what she needs to keep her out of trouble."

I would have continued the conversation, but Grandmother came to the door and Peter rose to greet her. Like all of, she favored Peter. Her eyes always lit up when she saw him, and he was as fond of her in return. I never detected anything false in his tone when he spoke to her or about her.

Later, after Peter left, I remembered I had been interrupted on my way out for a walk, so grabbing a coat, because the day was cool and the wind off the lake even cooler, I strode briskly around the neighborhood. As I did so, I clearly remembered my first glimpse of Hill Street and how enormous the houses had seemed to me, how palatial and luxurious. I imagined royalty must live on Hill Street because until then all I had known were small, rustic dwellings, where many people crowded into one or two rooms and did everything communally, where privacy was a luxury along with indoor plumbing and beds on legs. Chicago and Hill Street had seemed very foreign, and I had felt lost and anguished but too cautious and proud to let my feelings show.

Striding along the walk that late April day, I considered Hill Street the closest place to home I would ever know, loved the large, stately houses with their handsome front doors and green lawns, appreciated front porches and urns of freshly planted flowers. Probably too early for them to last, I thought, but I understood that by April in Chicago people longed for spring with impatient desperation.

Returning from my walk, I noticed an auto parked at the curb in front of our house and a man coming out the front door, pulling the door shut behind him. With a cry, I called, "Allen!" and ran forward, abandoning all dignity, tripped up the steps and fell into his arms for a warm hug.

Grinning, he set me down and said, "That was worth the trip, Johanna. I know you used to run for sport, but I've never seen you move quite that fast."

"Haven't I always run into your arms?"

"Not in recent memory, but I do recall one episode with a spider."

The memory made me laugh. "I wasn't exactly running toward you, more like away from that large, hairy arachnid. It scared the dickens out of me."

"Your years away must have mellowed you because I've never heard you confess to a fear of anything."

I pushed open the front door and took his hand. "I admit to a loathing for anything with eight legs, large or small, smooth or hairy. Come back inside. Were you going to leave without saying hello?"

"I stopped by to say hello, but your grandmother told me you were out for a walk, and I figured it would be hours before you were back. What have you done to your hair?"

I stopped to examine myself in the hall mirror. "Cut it as short as I could without scandalizing Grandmother. Is it awful?" I hadn't really given my hairstyle much thought before, but now, seeing it through his eyes, I was inclined to be critical.

He turned me away from the mirror to give me a sober inspection, finally telling me, "No, it's not awful, not at all. The style suits you somehow." Then, hands still on my shoulders, he added in a different tone, "I don't know of anyone who's had your share of adventures in life, Johanna. How are you?"

Five years before I had met Allen Goldwyn on the train to Philadelphia, I on my way to Bryn Mawr College and he traveling to Temple University, both of us away from home for the first time and sensing in each other a kindred spirit. We were friends since that meeting, good friends, and sometimes I wondered if we might not become more than friends, although nothing ever passed between us that would have led me to such speculation.

"I'm fine. I suppose it was an adventure but more a tragedy, I think." I shook off the memory of Douglas Gallagher shielding his match to light a last cigarette and patted the sofa cushion next to me. "Sit down and tell me what's happening in your life. Are you still with the same firm?" He nodded.

"Yes. I have the feeling I'll be offered a partnership in the company next year. They like everything I design and my clients seem to be pleased. You'll have to let me show you some of my buildings. They're springing up all over the city."

"I'd love that. I knew you'd be a success. You once told me you were born to build."

"You remember that?"

"It seemed poetic at the time, I recall."

"I'm not a very poetic man, Johanna."

"Not in words, but I have a feeling your architecture speaks to people."

"You're a kind woman but wait until I give you the grand tour before you say any more. I don't want you to have unrealistic expectations."

"About your work?"

"About me." He went suddenly quiet, a little half smile on his face, and I thought he had told me something besides the obvious with his last remark. "Now," he continued, "what about you? You finished your social work studies with honors from college, then crossed an ocean to attend nursing school. What's next?"

I hesitated. "I know this will sound odd, but I'm not quite sure." Allen looked at me with surprise.

"That's impossible. You are the most sure woman I know."

"I don't know if that's good or bad, but I'm going to take some time to think things through."

"That will make your grandmother happy. She told me earlier that she hoped you were home to stay."

"If she could, she'd have me live in this big house forever, grow old in the front room, take up needlework, and putter around the kitchen, but she knows me too well to believe that will ever happen. I have my mother's sense of adventure."

"Which is why Mrs. McIntyre wants you to stay close to home, I imagine."

I looked at him guiltily. Of course, that was true, and I should be less dismissive of Grandmother's concerns. She lost a dearly loved daughter and missed her as much as I did despite the intervening years.

Allen added, "She's not the only one who would like to see you stay close to home, you know." Surprised, I met his innocent gaze as he continued, "I'm sure your aunt and uncle and cousins all feel the same." Allen stood up. "I'm on my way back to work, but I'll see you tomorrow night. Your grandmother arbitrarily invited me to your homecoming party without, she told me shamelessly, even consulting you or your aunt." We walked together to the door.

"Grandmother always gets what she wants," I commented, but even as I said it, I thought of my mother buried in a cemetery an ocean away and knew it was not true.

Allen leaned to kiss me lightly on the cheek, a brotherly kiss with nothing but friendly affection in it, and said, "I am glad you're home safely, Johanna."

I waved to him from the open doorway as he left, then turned to find my grandmother watching me from across the hallway.

"Aren't you glad I insisted you buy that lavender silk dress?" she asked, too sure of herself for her own good, and before I could respond, added, "May's set supper and it's getting cold." I followed her into the dining room.

"You don't always know everything, Grandmother." She didn't dignify my remark with a response or a look, only let a little smug smile tug at the corners of her mouth as she sat down at the table.

I quickly settled back into the placid life of Hill Street except for the discomfiting matter of Douglas Gallagher's jewelry. The ring and the pin haunted me in a peculiar and inexplicable way. Rising in the morning, I always stopped long enough to open the lid of my jewelry box and stare at the two pieces lying on their velvet bed, sometimes touching the ring gently or picking up the stickpin and turning it so the diamonds sparkled in the morning sun that streamed through the window. I knew I could not keep the pieces but neither could I bear to part with them. Somewhere in Chicago a man named Andrew Gallagher went about his daily business, grieving for his brother and unaware that I had these meaningful mementos. I knew it wasn't right for me to hold onto them, but I couldn't help it. Something of the man was in the onyx and diamonds and gold, something of his cool poise and dark charisma, and I could not bear to part with the pieces he had entrusted to me. I would not betray his trust but I would delay it for while.

The loss of the *Titanic* affected me more than I was willing to admit to anyone. I seldom thought about the experience during the day, but at night I was provoked by dreams of men toppling from the deck like rag dolls and women weeping seawater. Douglas Gallagher inhabited my dreams, too, stared at me accusingly over the railing as I rowed away, or reached up a flailing hand—the ring gleaming in the moonlight—through the black waves, or called something to me as he plunged into the ocean, I straining, desperate to hear, and furious that I could not catch his final words. The ring and pin became part of the dreams, haunted—and comforted—me in a strange way so that I could not part with them. Not yet.

The night of my welcome home party I opened my jewelry box to reach for my mother's strand of pearls and the little diamond G twinkled up at me, begging to be let out of its plush prison. I felt suddenly guilty and ashamed of myself. I had no right to hold onto either it or the ring. The jewelry belonged elsewhere and I determined to go in search of Andrew

Gallagher and find him before the month ended.

The lavender dress that looked so beautiful on the hanger did not look beautiful on me, and I could only sigh at my reflection. It would have been perfect for Jennie's soft complexion and rosy lips but did not suit me. Too much coal in my hair and brows, eyes too dark, unbecoming freckles scattered across the bridge of my nose, and skin too warm a brown to wear such a cool, soft color. Although I gave lip service to nonchalance about my appearance, I had a strong streak of vanity, and how I looked mattered more than I cared to admit. How often had I been a dark foil for my cousin's fairness! And I knew as soon as I stepped into the parlor that I would be again.

Jennie was already there, wearing spring white threaded through with soft green, a vision of blue eyes and gold-streaked hair, astonishingly beautiful and definitely all grown up. But despite her extraordinary appearance and her air of sophistication, I could tell from her expression that I was important to her and that she was sincerely glad to see me.

There was no pretense about Jennie when she drew me into Grandmother's large front room and called to the people there, "Here is our guest of honor, Miss Johanna Swan, lately of London, England, and now back in Chicago to set the city on its ear!" She turned to me. "Come and meet Peter's friends, Johanna. And your friend Allen Goldwyn is here, too. I forgot how pleasant he was."

I looked quickly for Allen and found him by the punch bowl, watching me. He smiled and lifted a cup by way of greeting, looking handsome in his usual neat way, dressed in an evening suit that matched the color of his brown hair.

Peter detached me from Jennie and led me to two young men conversing with Aunt Kitty. "Johanna, may I introduce you to Carl Milford and Frank Mulholland?" he said by way of introduction.

"Which is which?" I asked with a laugh, extending a hand to the young man nearer me.

"I'm Frank Mulholland. How do you do, Miss Swan?"

"Johanna, please. For the past two years I was always called Miss Swan so it's music to hear my given name again." Frank Mulholland had sandy hair and eyebrows and pleasant green eyes, slimmer than Peter but similar to my cousin in his good-natured expression. "So you," I said, turning to the second young man, "must be Carl Milford." He responded with a little military salute.

"Indeed, Ma'm, if I must then I am and have been for the last twenty-two years. I'm delighted to meet the family paragon, though I admit to being even more intimidated now that I've met you."

"Really? Why is that?"

This young man was nothing like Peter or Frank. I would have assumed a few years past twenty-two, tall, good-looking and well aware of it, flirtatious and smooth, and I would guess possessed of a strong predilection for the ladies. I hoped Aunt Kitty watched him carefully when he was around Jennie. I didn't think it would bother him at all to seduce a friend's sister.

"So much intelligence in such a small package would intimidate any man."

"Not *any* man, Mr. Milford. Only one who recognized in himself a proportionate deficiency of the same quality." After a small pause all three young men burst out laughing.

Peter thumped Carl on the shoulder, saying, "See, I told you. No one gets the last word with Johanna."

Behind me, Jennie stated mildly, "I missed the joke," and stepped next to me. I was instantly forgotten by both of Peter's friends, who eagerly turned their attention to the new arrival. Their easy loss of interest didn't bother me. They were all younger than I and besides, the men's reaction was perfectly understandable. I drifted toward the punch table, stopping to greet friends of my grandmother and a few guests from my Aunt Kitty's side of the family. I didn't know them well, but if I were not appropriately cordial and attentive, I would certainly hear about it later.

Reaching the place where Allen still stood, I asked, "Do you know anyone here except me and my family?"

"Not a soul."

"I thought that might be why you took such an unobtrusive spot by the punch bowl, poor man. Are you sorry you came?"

"Not at all." At my questioning look, he added with a straight face, "Your aunt promised a buffet."

I laughed. "That's humbling but probably very true. Mayville's been cooking all day and you'd regret missing the feast. How do you manage to find three square meals a day while living the bachelor life?"

"My landlady takes care of that necessity, but I could cook if I had to."

"Which," I responded honestly, "is more than I can say for myself."

"You'll have to marry a rich man then, so you won't need to bother with tedious domestic duties."

"I don't have to marry at all, Allen." I responded with a smile to take any sting from the words. "An old woman I met in hospital in London once told me that only a very good husband was better than no husband at all and sternly warned me to stay clear of the blessed estate because mighty good husbands were few and far between."

"That seems unfairly cynical to males. Do you agree with her, Johanna?"

The conversation had taken an awkward twist, and I wasn't sure how to respond, so I welcomed Uncle Hal's entrance and his invitation to gather in the dining room.

"Here's your buffet, Allen. You were right to anticipate it. Mayville never does anything halfway."

"It's not like you to avoid a subject, Johanna. You didn't answer my last question."

"You're right. I didn't," I admitted, laughing, "and now I'm being summoned by my aunt, so I'm not answering it a second time."

Later in the evening Grandmother took my arm and drew me to a woman standing quietly to the side.

"I'd like you to meet my friend Kate Harwood Barrett, Johanna." The woman was perhaps ten years younger than my grandmother with white hair and clear, dark eyes.

"How do you do?" I took her extended hand and racked my brain for some faint memory of the name.

"No, Johanna, you've never met Mrs. Barrett before so you may relax." Occasionally I was grateful for my grandmother's clairvoyance because it saved me a great deal of mental energy. "Your grandfather handled the Crittentons' legal affairs for their Chicago venture, and I had the pleasure of meeting Kate when she was appointed to head their national mission."

"Are you affiliated with the organization that sponsors the Florence Crittenton homes?" I inquired.

Kate Barrett smiled. "Yes, for nearly the last three years. Apparently you've heard of us," a slight inquisitive lift at the end of her words.

"I took my degree in social work from Bryn Mawr. We studied your philosophy and mission."

"Which was—?"

"To provide a home for prostitutes and help them find useful work."

"Certainly that was the foundation on which Mr. Crittenton established the first home in New York thirty years ago. Now, though, I see a shift in emphasis. We have found that unwed mothers and other destitute women also need a home and practical skills. The future of our organization lies in expanding our social services, and I believe Mr. Crittenton would approve." Mrs. Barrett spoke decisively in a voice moderated with a southern softness. "Your grandmother speaks very highly of your credentials, Miss Swan. What are your future plans?"

I was embarrassed but answered honestly, "At the moment I don't have any. I suppose I'll try to find work at one of our local hospitals, Mrs. Barrett."

"Doctor Barrett," Grandmother corrected gently.

I looked at the woman. "Medical doctor?"

"I'm a doctor of obstetrics, Miss Swan, which is why, I suppose, I feel so strongly about the need to help indigent and unwed mothers. Are you aware there is a Crittenton Home here in Chicago?"

"No."

"The Anchorage Home is located on Indiana Avenue and run by a very good and competent woman named Hilda Cartwright. I'd like you to meet her."

"Why?" My grandmother gave a quiet sigh at my blunt question.

"Because you are an intelligent woman with very fine qualifications and your grandmother assures me you have a practical compassion as well. Such a combination could prove very valuable. The Anchorage has any number of do-gooders who volunteer there because, I fear, it gives them a faint sense of superiority. I'm sure they would vehemently deny that fact, but I was not comfortable with some of the people I saw there recently. You I would be comfortable with and your background in both social services and nursing is as perfect as it gets. Are you willing to at least see what we're all about?"

I confess, I was not immediately enthusiastic. The vision of a Gothic-style house with unfortunate, pregnant, abused, downtrodden, and abandoned girls locked in the attic held no attraction.

But then I met Kate Barrett's dark eyes, serious and challenging me to answer, and in spite of myself replied, "Yes. What about a Monday morning visit?"

"Monday is fine. I'll let Hilda know to expect you." She and my grandmother exchanged a look before she asked about London and we moved onto another topic. When a man stopped to introduce himself to Dr. Barrett, I drifted away with Grandmother.

"Thank you," I told her.

Because she always understood me, Grandmother immediately responded, "Kate Barrett is a remarkable woman and I knew Charles Crittenton. Richard considered him a good man and his organization highly respectable."

"Grandfather was an expert judge of character."

"Yes. He had a legal mind, sharp and uncluttered by excessive emotion. Unlike you, Johanna."

"I'm not sentimental," I replied indignantly.

"I didn't say sentimental. I said emotional, and you are that, whatever appearance you choose to show the world. I think the Anchorage might be a good place for you, somewhere you can put all your energy to valuable use. Might even give you dragons to slay."

"You think I need dragons to be happy?"

"You have always needed to feel challenged, the greater the odds against you and the more forceful your opponent, the better. Exactly like your mother." Her voice softened at the last word, unusual for her, and then she said briskly, "I see Kitty's cousins are coming our way to offer their good-byes. The evening must be officially over." We shared a smile and turned together to say good night.

When Allen approached with his coat over his arm, I walked

with him out onto the porch and down the front steps.

"I'm glad you came," I told him, "even if it was the buffet that drew you." He seemed more animated than usual, happy and boyishly good-looking.

"Not just the buffet," he responded. He looked past me at the large front window through which we could see people still mingling and chatting in the elegant front room. "I've always liked your family, Johanna, but now even more so since they saw fit to give you such a pleasant homecoming." He turned back to me and leaned to kiss me lightly on the cheek, another chaste and boring display of affection. He might as well have patted me on top of my head and handed me a lollipop. "I'm glad you're home. Perhaps we'll be able to see more of each other now."

Something in his voice seemed not quite right for a moment, a tentative or even mystified tone, and I looked at him quickly. There was nothing to be seen on his face, however, except his usual attentive and kind expression.

"I hope so, but I may have found something to keep myself occupied for a while." I told him of my planned visit to the Anchorage Home on Indiana Street.

"Does that work appeal to you?"

I shrugged and answered, "I can't say. I have completely unworthy notions of such a place but I'm going with an open mind. It is 1912, you know, not 1812. The times are different and people more accepting. Society has changed for the better."

"Is that what you believe, Johanna?"

"You don't?"

"I don't fool myself with your progressive ideas. People weren't very forgiving in 1812, and they're no more forgiving a hundred years later. Good night." He went down the walk and I turned back into the house, surprised and taken aback by the fervor in his voice. For a moment I felt foolish and childish, heard in Allen's tone a rebuke I didn't understand. I had never experienced even a mild chastisement from him before, and perhaps my surprise was proof of what he implied, that I was unrealistic and did not really know people at all. Jennie came to the door and called my name from the doorway.

"I'm coming." I turned to look at her, appreciating how the porch light flushed her complexion and gave sparkle to her eyes.

"People are asking where you disappeared to," she chided affectionately.

"Tell them into the night, Jen. Tell them I've run away to join the circus or take to the stage. Tell them I've gone to seek my fortune." She held the door open for me as I came back inside and put an arm around my shoulders for a quick hug as I passed her.

"You must have forgotten you already have a fortune. Stop speaking in riddles, Johanna, and come say good night to your friends. For the smart one in the family, you sometimes make no sense at all."

She said it all with a smile, her tone cool and practical and matter-of-fact. As I followed her into the front room, I was conscious of an odd reversal, Jennie suddenly decisive and mature and I childish and uncertain, an untried girl longing for something she could not name and did not understand.

—«◎»—

Monday I took the train to Indiana Street.

"Levi could very easily drive you," Grandmother pointed out with a touch of asperity as I pinned on my hat.

Hats were a necessary fashion evil that I always thought

looked ridiculous on me. Small straw boaters made me resemble a child ready for the seashore. Large flamboyant versions overwhelmed my short hair and small stature so that a good wind off the lake using the hat as a sail could surely lift me up and blow me all the way to my destination. In the mirror I wrinkled my nose at my reflection with its sharp chin and big eyes.

I could do no more about those unfashionable physical attributes than I could about the hat, so I jammed in a last pin and turned to say, "How would it look if I drove up to a home for destitute and desperate women in a chauffeured automobile? I'd be embarrassed. Besides, I like the train and the passing parade of people. I liked your friend Dr. Barrett, too, by the way, so thank you for the introduction, and don't wait on me for lunch. I may plan a couple of side trips along the way."

Since the first day I crossed my grandparents' threshold, Grandmother never protested my independence or expressed a worry. When I told her I was accepted by Bryn Mawr College in Philadelphia, she nodded and went back to the newspaper she was reading. When I informed her of my acceptance into the Florence Nightingale School of Nursing in London, she asked only when I would be leaving and how long I would be gone. It was more a matter of respect and trust than a lack of love or concern on her part. From the beginning she understood how to handle me with few missteps. Although a few of those had occurred through the years—on my part as well as hers—we never spoke of the altercations now, and I could hardly remember what all the fuss had been about. When Grandfather was alive, he had little patience for brawling women, as he phrased it. He argued cases in court, he said, and he was not about to come home to more arguments. Because Grandmother and I both loved him, we were always able to put aside our differences; and after a while whatever our issue had been quietly faded away.

The Anchorage Home was nothing like I pictured, not a brooding Gothic mansion with wrought iron railings and small, dark windows. Probably not a madwoman held captive in the attic, either, I thought, laughing at myself, although that remained to be seen. Instead, the house was neat red brick, the trim painted dark brown, windows showing frilly white curtains to the outside and the front yard surrounded by a pristine white fence. A perfectly domestic appearance, almost disappointing in its ordinariness.

A short, stout woman opened the door to my knock and gave me a frank look from head to toe. Because I appeared neither destitute nor despairing, she guessed correctly.

"You must be Miss Swan. Matron said to expect you this morning."

Inside, the hallway smelled like lemons and the wood and windows shone. The curtains I had seen from the outside hung crisp and clean, and fresh flowers filled a vase on a table by the front door. This could be anyone's comfortable home, I thought, and followed that with the immediate realization that it was someone's home, even if only temporary. Looking around, I felt inordinately glad that the environment was so bright and welcoming. If I were in trouble, pregnant, unmarried and cast out by my family, fleeing a husband who beat me, or widowed and poverty-stricken, alone and ill, any of the situations that befell a woman in a man's world, I would not be afraid to come here. It bespoke a woman's touch and said welcome.

Hilda Cartwright, *Matron* to the woman who first greeted me, came out a door at the end of the hallway and walked toward me. She was tall and walked with a slight limp, an innate dignity in her frank gaze, upright bearing, and sincere smile.

"Miss Swan, I'm Hilda Cartwright. Kate said you promised

to visit. Come into my office, please. Eulalie, would you bring Miss Swan a cup of tea? If you walked from the station, you had a bit of a hike." She stated everything calmly and I thought her temperament exactly right for the work she did. There was something reassuring about her voice and manner, a combination of tranquility and kindness that made one trust her judgment without knowing her at all.

Miss Cartwright's study was utilitarian at best, with plain curtains, an unadorned square desk, and shelves of books. Later I would find out that the room was a reflection of the woman, nothing ornamental about her either, every thought, word, and action directed to a practical objective.

She sat across the desk from me, examining me with her very fine gray eyes for a silent moment, then said, "You come highly recommended, Miss Swan, as a gifted student and a young woman of purpose. I spoke to Sally Gray, one of your college teachers, and she sang your praises to the heavens. I admit, however, that she also warned me about your stubborn streak, said you do not take correction well if you believe it to be unwarranted, and that you would rather make a wrong decision than no decision at all."

"She's right on all counts, but it's still humbling to have one's flaws enumerated like a shopping list. I had so much to learn then. I still do," I added at Hilda Cartwright's look, "but in my first year at college, I was almost beyond redemption, always opening my mouth and blurting out wrong answers and speaking without listening. Fortunately, Miss Gray saw that I meant well, took me under her wing, and with great patience taught me—as she called it—to listen between the lines. I have the warmest regard for Miss Gray. I hope she's well."

"Yes, very well. What do you know about the Anchorage?" The abrupt change of topic did not faze me.

"I know it's one of many Crittenton homes dotted across

the country, and that it offers shelter to unwed mothers whose families either cannot or will not care for them."

"Your tone speaks your disapproval."

"Not of the girls," I interjected quickly. "I would never hold their circumstances against them. It's the families with whom I have little patience, shipping the young woman off to an unfamiliar place to have her baby among strangers, then bringing her back and pretending she's been visiting Aunt Molly in Omaha."

"Sometimes that is the best course for everyone concerned, Miss Swan. The young woman picks up her life and the baby goes to a loving home, to parents who have longed for a child of their own."

"Sometimes," I agreed grudgingly, "but can you really tell me that every young woman willingly gives away her baby without feeling grief or rebellion at the action her family forced upon her because they did not wish to deal with public opinion and the unkind and hypocritical judgments society will make?" Hilda Cartwright did not answer my question, simply met my eyes and smiled.

"I see exactly what Sally Gray meant. The Anchorage mission began as a safe haven for prostitutes who wished to leave their lives on the streets. Following that, it grew into the conventional home for unwed mothers that you describe, but today under the leadership of Dr. Barrett it is evolving into something much more expansive and inclusive. We offer refuge to all women of all ages, Miss Swan, not just unwed mothers. We continue to have our share of those, of course, and it might surprise you that most of them are poor girls or young immigrants with little family support and no real home. We provide other options besides giving the child up for adoption. In fact, we encourage the mothers to keep their children and offer various means of support for them to do so. That's one of the many areas where I envision your assistance."

I was quiet, listening carefully. My plans for my future had not included this environment. Instead, I had pictured a gleaming hospital, something modern and progressive, where I would work with those truly ill. Yet the passion in Miss Cartwright's voice and her obvious dedication to the Anchorage and its mission were making an unexpected and favorable impression.

"We have women here who have fled brutish husbands and fathers but have no idea how to get on in the world. If we don't give them viable skills and help them find employment, they will be forced to return to an environment that could quite literally kill them. We have women who can hardly speak a word of English, lured to Chicago by unscrupulous men for lives of prostitution or demeaning labor, slave labor I call it, regardless of the fact that slavery was forbidden almost fifty years ago. The Anchorage offers protection, education, and encouragement, and we could use you, all of you, your skills, your education, and your temperament."

"If anything," I warned, "Miss Gray was too kind. I've led an unusual life and I am very flawed. Why do you think I would suit?"

She rose from her desk. "Follow me and I'll show you."

We went out of her office and down the hall toward the back of the house, stopping outside a pair of partially open double doors. Miss Cartwright put her finger to her lips and we stood there, shamelessly eavesdropping. From within I could hear a woman's voice.

"—judged by her quiet nature, Mrs. Stanislaw," the speaker droned. "Men who have worked all day in the rigors of the world prefer to be greeted with a smile and a soft hello. It would hardly be appropriate for you to hold one of the office jobs that modern women so enthusiastically pursue. That may be for women of a certain class, but you would be better served finding a husband or, lacking that, seeking domestic service."

Those words were almost too much for Miss Cartwright, who frowned and reached for the door to enter the room. She stopped mid-gesture, however, took me by the arm, and urged me back down the hall and into her office.

"That was Mrs. Fereon, one of several volunteers who need to leave. They disapprove of a woman working outside the home, regardless of her circumstance. They do not believe in advanced education for women, and they long for the old order of things, a caste system that's a relic of an old generation. They create rebellion with their unrealistic advice and then wonder why the girls are scornful and rude to them." Miss Cartwright spoke vehemently. "Unfortunately, I need a replacement before I can tactfully ask Mrs. Fereon to leave."

"And you think I'm suited to be that replacement?"

"You're young and straightforward and I believe our residents would listen to you. You don't appear to stand on pretense, and I can't imagine you've ever been pompous in your life. You've seen the world and you know what skills it would take for these women to survive in it. The Anchorage could use your services, Miss Swan." At my silence, she went on, "We can't pay you very much and it may not be what you planned for your future, but give us a year of your life and see what a difference you can make. You'll have free rein to set up educational and training programs and if, after a year, you decide it's not for you, so be it. You won't have lost all that much and I sincerely believe the Anchorage will have gained immeasurably. What do you say?"

I thought through her offer and all she said, then answered simply, "I say yes. I'll give it a year. Yes."

That simply I arranged my future, realizing as Hilda

Cartwright spoke that I might never again have the opportunity to make such a difference in people's lives. What had all my training been for, after all, the years of college and nursing school, if not for this time and place? I knew without a doubt that at this moment in my life, the Anchorage was where I was meant to be.

The holiest of all holidays are those
Kept by ourselves in silence and apart;
The secret anniversaries of the heart.

Chapter Three

B ecause I have absolutely no patience, once I made my decision I wanted to start immediately.

"Next week will be fine, Miss Swan," Hilda Cartwright replied, smiling. "You're just back from two years away from home and your return trip, I understand, was far from uneventful. It's perfectly understandable if you'd like to spend time with your family before beginning a new venture."

"Please call me Johanna, and I would prefer to start tomorrow. I'd like to sit in on everything you do and accustom myself to the routine, acquaint myself with the organizations you currently interact with, meet the women who reside here now, and try to understand their needs." I stopped abruptly, then grinned. "Now you see my flaws exposed and realize Miss Gray was right on target about me. Grandmother says I'm like a locomotive roaring down the track when I get an idea. Please forgive me. Of course, you may have completely different plans for my first days here, and I will start whenever it's convenient for you."

"Could we compromise and say Thursday, Johanna? That will give me a day or two to prepare Mrs. Fereon for her departure." Miss Cartwright had the guilty look of a little girl caught in mischief. "I'm too critical, I suppose, and too ready to dismiss her. She's been a volunteer here for many years, and

— 45 —

I know she means well."

"'She means well' are some of the most damning words in the English language, if you ask me," I responded bluntly, rising, "but I am the newcomer and too ignorant to criticize. Thursday it is. Could you and I spend some time together Thursday morning? I'll write out a few of my ideas and bring them with me. Then you can set me straight and tell me which ones are completely unsuitable."

She rose, too, and we walked together from her office down the hall toward the front door. I was once more impressed by the bright cleanliness of the foyer, the fresh lemon scent of furniture oil, and the crisp, starched curtains. Ahead of us, two women of very different ages walked up the stairs, deep in conversation. The younger woman, whose vivid red hair I could see from the back, had an arm around the other's shoulders and was talking to her in a low voice. For a moment the red-haired woman turned, threw a quick smile down to Miss Cartwright, and gave me a cooler but just as quick examination. Then she and her companion reached the top of the stairs and were out of sight. Miss Cartwright followed my gaze up to the retreating redhead and looked back at me.

"You'll meet Crea later in the week. She's invaluable to us."

"A staff member then?"

"Not exactly." Changing the subject, she added, "I'm looking forward to your presence here more than I can say, Johanna. You'll be a breath of fresh air and just what we all need. We've done things the same way for many years, but times are changing and we have to change with them. I believe you're the woman to help us do that. I'll look forward to Thursday morning."

I took the train home but got off downtown and took time to walk along the lakeshore before finishing the trip. As usual, the wind off the lake was much too cool for comfort, but I was possessed of a familiar energy that needed to be walked off. I loved new ventures and relished a challenge, and this opportunity appeared to offer both. To make a difference in people's lives, to be something and do something worthwhile, had always been my heart's desire, a legacy from my parents, whose example I could never fully emulate. Somehow, though, I knew they would approve of my plans. For years after their deaths, upon my return to the States and coming to my grand-mother's house, I had dreamed of my parents, usually lovely dreams although dark ones crept in now and then. Sadly, the dreams came with less frequency and lately I felt an odd panic, unable any longer to picture their faces in my mind or recall the sounds of their voices. I supposed that explained why the loss of their photograph as it sank along with the *Titanic* so affected me. Somehow, though, I seemed to have found them again there at the Anchorage, having retrieved a clear memory of my mother's passionate kindness and my father's relentlessly opti-mistic nature. A good omen, I thought, and felt both buoyed and comforted.

Grandmother did not raise an eyebrow when I told her of my decision, not even when I explained that I would take the train to work every day. Anticipating an argument, I contin-ued sternly, "I will not be chauffeur driven to the Anchorage in an expensive automobile. It would look ostentatious, and I wouldn't be comfortable."

Grandmother resettled her reading glasses on her nose and went back to her book, saying only, "You may ride a bicycle while wearing a hair shirt for all I care, Johanna. As your legal guardian, however—"

"For only two more years," I grumbled.

"As your legal guardian," she repeated without acknowledg-ing my interruption, "I am forced to warn you about becoming a snob."

"A snob! I am no such thing."

She still didn't look at me but pretended interest in her book as she spoke. "You are the one who is making appearance so important. It could well be that no one but you cares how you arrive at the front door. Beware of hypocritical elitism. I detected it among the anarchists, where the leaders pretended to a sympathy with the poor while their speeches sometimes betrayed a secret scorn for them. Poverty is not synonymous with stupidity, and it's foolish to assume that people are not smart enough to see through such a façade. That kind of superficiality is not worthy of you."

"You're being unkind," I retorted, stung by her words.

My tone made her look up. "I didn't intend to be unkind, Johanna. Anyone who knows you knows your intentions are benevolent. My words were meant as a friendly warning. Despite what we prefer to believe, human beings do not usually appreciate public charity or being the recipient of self-satisfying humanitarian gestures. Be careful not to patronize."

"Do I do that?" I was horrified at the idea.

Grandmother went back to her book. "I have never heard it in you, and I never saw it in your mother. Just be aware."

Her tone said she was finished with the conversation, but she had given me something to think about. The Anchorage was not the rarified and intellectual environment of college or as controlled and objective as nursing school. It was inhabited by living, breathing human beings, some desperate, some hurting, some undoubtedly angry and rebellious. Honesty was my greatest strength and at times my greatest flaw. I thought it would serve me well at the Anchorage, but it still would not hurt to follow my grandmother's advice and remain aware, not so much of my surroundings as of myself and my own motives.

That night as I readied for bed, I took Douglas Gallagher's

jewelry out of its case and held it in my hand, appreciating as usual the twinkle of the diamonds in the stickpin and the smooth, mirrored finish of the ring. I felt a strong, clear guilt as I did so. I, who prided myself on always keeping my promises, had yet to follow through on a pledge I made to a man rightfully anticipating death. I could not account for my reluctance but knew it to be wrong.

"I'm sorry," I said out loud. "I promised and I will follow through. You deserved better from me and I'm sorry." Ridiculous as it was, the spoken apology provided some relief. As soon as I became acclimated to my new position at the Anchorage, I would make finding Andrew Gallagher my top priority. Uncle Hal would be a big help because he had all the resources of Chicago at his fingertips and—prophetically as it turned out—I believed I was only a week away from finding Douglas Gallagher's brother.

The first week I spent at the Anchorage flew by. My initial Thursday morning meeting with Hilda Cartwright extended into the afternoon. Finally, both of us satisfied with my purpose and schedule, Miss Cartwright went to the door of her study.

"I'm going to find Crea so you can meet her. She'll prove indispensable to you." The matron returned with the redhaired young woman I had seen earlier in the week. "Johanna, this is Crea O'Rourke. Crea, Miss Swan is here to bring the Anchorage into the twentieth century. I believe you'll find her to be exactly what we need."

Crea O'Rourke was a lovely girl, her copper red hair, flawless porcelain skin, and deep green eyes all giving the impression of a china doll. She had a charming voice with an Irish lilt that made music of every word she spoke.

"Welcome, Miss Swan. Matron has spoken very highly of you."

"It's Johanna, not Miss Swan, if I may call you Crea in return. What a beautiful name!"

"Thank you. It's old Irish for heart." She quickly moved on to another subject. "I've told the ladies you were coming, and they're curious about what exactly you can do for them. These aren't college-educated women of society families. These are women who know what hard times are." Her tone held poorly veiled skepticism, if not hostility, and I couldn't blame her. I must have looked the part of a spoiled young woman trying to find an outlet for her boredom, but if that was what she thought and what her ladies expected, they would realize their mistake soon enough.

"I understand that, and I believe I can help in a number of ways. You—" I was interrupted by the breathless arrival of a woman in the open doorway.

"Matron, come quick. Flora's bad. It's not her time, but she's cramping something fierce."

Miss Cartwright stepped into the hallway to call Eulalie and send her for the doctor, and I headed for the stairs behind Crea, explaining to the young woman, "I'm a nurse and I may be able to help. Show me where Flora is."

Crea led me upstairs to a room that held several beds, one of which was inhabited by a girl of sixteen at most. She lay on her side beaded with sweat, her arms wrapped tightly over her rounded stomach. Even with her hair plastered to her head by perspiration and her face uncommonly pale, the girl was pretty, with fair hair and a clear complexion. As I stepped into the room, she moaned in pain and doubled up in a contortion, her knees nearly touching her chest.

I knelt beside the bed, brushing back the girl's hair from her damp forehead, and said, "Flora, my name is Johanna and I'm going to try to help you. Have you had any bleeding?"

Flora only looked at me piteously out of mute eyes and

moaned again. As I knelt there, I reached down my hand to steady myself and felt something against my knees, a glass object of some sort just under the edge of the bed. I brought it out for a closer look and then asked gently, "Did you drink this whole bottle of Mr. Peckham's Syrup, Flora?" She hesitated, then nodded and moaned again. I stood. "I'll need a large glass of water mixed with a heaping tablespoon of baking soda and a basin of some kind for Flora to be sick in. Mr. Peckham's Syrup needs to come up." Behind me, Miss Cartwright turned without a word and exited. Flora took my hand and squeezed it hard, whether in protest or understanding I couldn't tell.

"The stuff won't hurt you on the way up, Flora, but it will continue to cramp you like this if we don't get it out." Leaning closer to her, I said quietly, "I know what you thought you were doing, Flora, but Mr. Peckham's Syrup won't have any effect on the baby. All it will do, in the quantity you drank, is make you as sick as you feel right now. We'll deal with the baby sensibly when you're feeling better."

Crea, standing on the other side of the bed, met my look. "Do you really understand?" she asked obliquely.

"I think so. Desperation makes people do desperate things, things they wouldn't think of doing under normal circumstances if they could see any other way out of their situation."

"You don't blame her?"

"She's a child herself. How old is she? Fifteen?"

"Fourteen."

"I don't blame her, Crea, but that's why I'm here, to help women find ways out of desperate situations, to help them through those hard times you mentioned."

"I didn't know you were a nurse."

"When you get to know me, you'll find I'm a lot of things. A nurse is just one of them." We exchanged brief smiles before Flora moaned again and a woman appeared at the door with soda water and a large pan. After that we were busy, with nothing to smile about for the next hour or so. The doctor appeared just as Flora shuddered and retched one last time, then lay back down, exhausted and still very much pregnant.

"What happened here?" the doctor asked us.

Wrapping the bottle nonchalantly in a towel before rolling down my sleeves, I replied, "I'd guess some kind of food poisoning. She must have eaten something that didn't agree with her delicate condition. She and the baby will be all right." He came forward to examine Flora, and Crea and I stepped out of the room into the hallway.

"I'll take that," Crea told me, reaching for the basin.

"I can handle the slops as well as you," I responded tartly, "in spite of my college education and society family." My words made her grin.

"It isn't becoming in a woman like yourself to be so touchy, Johanna. You'll have to grow a thicker skin if you intend to spend more time at the Anchorage."

Holding my unpleasant burden out in front of me, I answered, "My skin is plenty thick enough, thank you, but my sense of direction could use some help. Where do I dump this?"

Laughing a little under her breath, Crea went ahead of me down the hall and then descended some steps that led to a small water closet.

"We have indoor plumbing" was all she said and opened the door with a flourish and a grin.

Sitting on the train on the way home, I decided I liked Crea O'Rourke and thought we might even become friends. She had taken the wrapped empty bottle from me without a word and disposed of it, coming to the front door later as I was putting on my coat to tell me, "The doctor says Flora will be none the worse for wear."

"Good. Who will watch her tonight?

"I will."

I looked at her curiously. "Do you live at the Anchorage, Crea?"

"It's my home."

"I didn't realize that."

"We're both women of mystery, then."

I laughed. "There's absolutely no mystery about me. I am exactly what you see, a woman plain and thin and stubborn. And thick-skinned." Crea smiled at my words, an honest smile that hinted she might be able to approve of me after all, and said good night.

That incident occurred Thursday and through the next week I met individually with all the residents of the Anchorage to introduce myself. I met Elena, a young, pregnant Greek immigrant whose husband had died their first week in Chicago, and Betsy, fresh from the Illinois farmlands and pregnant, too, unable to go home because her family wouldn't take her back. Yvesta, middle-aged with two blackened eyes from a brute of a husband, had her two children with her, both clinging to their mother's skirts and quick to jump at any loud noise. Kipsy, an orphaned girl who had taken to the streets for a living, was new at the Anchorage, twelve years old at the most and smart enough to see there was no future in a life of prostitution. Henrietta, who came with her newborn because her husband decided he didn't like married life and fatherhood after all; Ruthie, whose husband-to-be died in a fire leaving her pregnant and afraid to go home; and Mrs. McElhanie, sixty-five and nowhere else to turn, all lived there for the time being, too. And of course, there was young and pretty Flora, who hated the idea of being pregnant, hated the thought of a baby, and wanted her old dreams back. She longed to be an actress or a dancer on the stage with pretty clothes and face paint, surrounded by music and laughter and applause. Conception had come as a surprise to her.

"I didn't know that's how it happened," she told me defiantly. "No one ever explained it. If they had, I wouldn't be here now. I never wanted a family, and I don't need a man if this is what comes from having one around."

I looked at her gravely and suggested, "Let's look at your options. Are you certain you don't want to keep the child?"

"I don't want to *have* the child," she retorted, watching my face for any expression of outrage or disgust.

"I realize that—and I can appreciate it—but believe me, anything you attempt will endanger your own life more than the child's. Better to go through with the pregnancy and let us find a good home for the baby."

That was not the advice Flora wanted to hear, but recalling her misery after ingesting an entire bottle of Peckham's Syrup, she didn't argue, only glared at me with an expression of fury mixed with helplessness and fear before she flounced heavily out of the room.

At the end of my first full week, Hilda Cartwright stopped by my little office, hardly bigger than a closet, and asked if I recognized the name Grace Wilbur Trout.

"She's the head of the Chicago Political Equality League and is leading the charge for women's suffrage in the state of Illinois. Why?"

"I've known Grace for several years. The *Tribune* has invited her to speak at their offices tomorrow evening and she's going to do it. I warned her the invitation was no doubt made because it was a slow news week and the reporters will be hoping for something sensational, and I fear she may be facing an unsympathetic crowd. Would you like to attend or have you no interest in women's suffrage?" I remembered the London march I'd participated in, the outraged reaction from observers lining the streets, the feeling of unity with the women around me, the rhetoric, and the threats.

"I do have an interest and I'd very much like to come."

Saturday morning Aunt Kitty and Jennie stopped at Hill Street for a quick visit on their way to find a new dress for Jennie. She would turn nineteen in June and it would no doubt be the occasion for a major party with a band and catered refreshments and all the other accoutrements that my Aunt Kitty loved. Jennie, wearing a suit that somehow managed to accent her beautiful figure instead of hide it, asked me about my first week of work. I answered in generalities, careful not to betray the privacy of anyone at the Anchorage, the first rule of social services and one that had been vehemently repeated through my college years. Jennie was interested, listening intently and asking intelligent questions, but that did not sit well with her mother.

"Come along, Jennie. That's more information than you really need at your age. You have nothing in common with those women. They have one kind of life and future and you have quite another." Jennie made a face at me but stood obediently.

"Johanna's going to a suffrage rally tonight," she said artlessly. "I don't know why she gets to have all the fun." Aunt Kitty gave a disapproving little *tsk* in reply and Jennie flashed me a quick, mischievous grin.

She'll blossom some day, I thought, and have a mind and a will of her own once she gets out of her mother's shadow. I couldn't have been fonder of Jennie if she'd been my sister and thought that her quick mind, her spirit, and her classical beauty set her apart from other girls her age. Then I remembered Flora and Kipsy and Ruthie, all Jennie's age or younger but far removed from my cousin's life of privilege, and wondered how different their lives would have been had they experienced Jennie's advantages. I had realized years ago as I left the graves of my family behind and traveled to San Francisco that life was not fair or equal, but knowing did not keep me from wishing it were so.

That evening I asked Levi to take me downtown to the *Tribune* office and to return in an hour when I expected the presentation to be done; I am not always shy about using the privileges available to me. Hilda Cartwright waited for me at the doorway of the meeting room where Mrs. Trout was to speak and together the two of us made our way to the front row of chairs where two seats had been reserved for us. The room filled up quickly—mostly with men, I noticed—and I wondered whether Hilda had been right to believe this would be an unsympathetic and hostile crowd. If that were so, the knowledge did not appear to make a difference to the speaker.

Grace Wilbur Trout was an imposing woman, a stately and elegant brunette nearing fifty but with the animation and energy of a woman half her age. She took the podium comfortably after the brief introduction and spoke with intelligence and passion about the necessity for women to have the vote for the improvement of society and the good of the nation.

"That youths can vote on issues that affect their mothers while their mothers cannot vote at all is preposterous. How can we say that is good for society? If a nation implies that grown women are not informed or intelligent enough to make decisions at the ballot box, will that not cause young men to feel a natural scorn and disrespect for their mothers? Does not the inability of mothers and sisters to have their voices heard in elections create family disunity, and is that not the very effect suffrage opponents fear?"

"Wasn't any complaints heard before women like you stirred things up," one man grumbled audibly from the back of the room.

Mrs. Trout continued until another negative comment was

made: "Seems to me the family was doing just fine before all this hubbub started. Women shouldn't be interfering in men's business."

And still Mrs. Trout continued with her speech undeterred, calm and competent, intelligent and unflappable. I admired her perseverance and was outraged on her behalf at the rude comments that filtered through the crowd, nothing boisterous or overt so that I could tell the person to sit down and be quiet but always words spoken in a low voice that generated subdued laughter from those in the speaker's vicinity. I considered it a planned conspiracy to discredit Mrs. Trout and her message and would have preferred something more confrontational so I could respond in kind. As it was, all Hilda and I could do was sit quietly and considerately, give the speaker our full attention, and ignore the laughter that rippled softly but subversively through the room.

Mrs. Trout was a vigorous but disciplined speaker who ended with a flourish, "The struggle for social change has often been met with ridicule and scorn by small minds who live in the past and cannot think beyond the present. My challenge for all of you in this room is to step out of your constricted and complacent lives and look frankly into the future. Honestly ask yourselves if our present situation, where women are second-class citizens at best, is what you want for your daughters and granddaughters. We cannot stay bound to old ways from an old century. Now is the time to free the intelligence and the energy of your daughters and granddaughters so they may blossom into mature, responsible women, capable of making sound decisions for the family and just as capable of making responsible decisions to influence the progress of our state and federal governments!"

Her last ringing words fell into a deep silence. No one spoke or laughed or even coughed. She might as well have been speaking in a foreign language for all the response her stirring conclusion generated. Stubborn and arrogant men, I fumed, with your minds already made up before you even got here this evening.

As I raised both hands to applaud, a male voice from somewhere to my left called, "Well done, Mrs. Trout."

I turned to see a man several seats down in my row rise and face the podium. With his right hand he gave Grace Trout a small, charming salute and then methodically and purposefully began to applaud, a smile playing around his mouth as he did so. He's enjoying the attention, I thought, so why shouldn't I do the same? I took another quick look at his handsome profile, stood quickly, and applauded with him. From the corner of my eye, I saw the man turn to give me a brief, curious glance. For what seemed like an interminably long time, it was just the two of us standing and showing our public approval. Then Hilda stood with us, and a few other men and women in the room joined in. At least half the room remained seated and silent, but those of us standing made up for their bad humor with our prolonged enthusiasm.

Mrs. Trout smiled very specifically at the attractive, fair-haired man who had initiated the ovation, gave Hilda a nod and a smile, and made an elegant but silent bow to the room before exiting down a side aisle.

When the applause subsided, I asked Hilda, "Has Mrs. Trout met with such an ill-mannered reception before? I admit I was surprised by the open resentment that greeted her ideas. I thought she made good, practical sense and didn't play to the emotions as other suffragists are often accused of doing."

"I'd heard this group might be more antagonistic than usual, but I didn't expect the level of hostility that was displayed this evening," Hilda admitted. She turned to look past me and I followed her gaze to the tall, blonde man in the perfectly cut dark suit who had so nonchalantly—and so gracefully—voiced his approval of Grace Trout's speech.

Apparently oblivious to the disapproving glances around him, he slowly made his way from the room, one hand on the arm of a woman whom he maneuvered protectively through the crowd. When they reached the door, he leaned forward to say something close to her ear. The woman turned to look back at him and despite her extravagant, broad-brimmed hat, I caught a glimpse of rich brown hair and an impossibly red mouth. For some reason, that quick look gave me the impression she was not particularly pleased about something. Perhaps the press of the crowd made her uncomfortable.

"And who would have imagined that?" continued Hilda, her gaze still following the man.

"Imagined what?"

"That he would be the one to lead the defense. There's no doubt he made a public stand tonight, but I never imagined he had the slightest interest in universal suffrage. In fact, with his rather unsavory reputation for enjoying the company of women, I thought he would surely prefer the status quo. Well, life is full of surprises and I give him complete credit for the unpopular stand he took tonight. Perhaps all the stories about him are just so much rumor and innuendo."

"I didn't recognize the man, Hilda. Should I have? Who is he?"

"There's no reason you would know him, Johanna. I doubt you move in the same social circles, and he's always lived in the shadow of his successful older brother," adding thoughtfully, "until recently, of course, poor man. Considering your recent distressing experience, you can appreciate his situation more than the rest of us." With unsuspecting impact, Hilda concluded, "The man's name is Andrew Gallagher."

Our little lives are kept in equipoise
By opposite attractions and desires;
The struggle of the instinct that enjoys,
And the more noble instinct that aspires.

Chapter Four

Sunday afternoon I placed the stickpin and the onyx ring in a small envelope. Then I went downstairs to tell Grandmother I was taking the train and would be away for a few hours. She raised both regal eyebrows.

"Surely you aren't working on a Sunday afternoon."

"Many people work Sundays," I retorted. "It's only sacred to those who can afford it." At her continuing silent, steady look, I admitted, "No, I'm not working. I have an errand to run."

"The stores are closed."

"I know. It's not that kind of errand. I'm visiting someone on Prairie Avenue, which you must admit is as safe and distinguished as Chicago gets. Don't worry, I'll be home well before dark."

She eyed the envelope in my hand, perhaps guessing its contents. "Levi could take you."

"Thank you, but I prefer the train this afternoon."

I think she wanted to say more, to inquire or insist, but she didn't. Instead she instructed, "Be home by supper then or I'll worry" and returned to her reading.

The previous night I had responded to Hilda Cartwright's amazing identification of Andrew Gallagher with a quiet comment. "I met Mr. Gallagher's brother Douglas on the trip home on the *Titanic*."

"I wondered whether you had, Johanna," was her only response.

Finally I asked, "Do you know where Andrew Gallagher lives?"

"No, but I can find out and call you tomorrow with that information." If Hilda were curious about my query, she was too polite to voice her interest. "Is your grandmother on the telephone line?"

"Yes. She's a great fan of all the inventions of progress."

True to her promise, when I returned from church, Hilda called with the information that Drew Gallagher had very recently moved into his brother's house on Prairie Avenue. She gave me the house number and the closest cross street. "The person who gave me this information has dealt with Gallagher Enterprises for several years and is very reliable, Johanna."

I thanked Hilda for the information, joined Grandmother for Sunday dinner without commenting on the telephone call, and then went upstairs to gather the jewelry that I had already held onto far too long. Without being able to explain the sudden compulsion after so many weeks of inertia, I knew I had to go to Prairie Avenue immediately and couldn't have slept with that jewelry in my case one more night. Perhaps the urgency showed on my face and that was why Grandmother, after a studied look at my expression, gave no further argument.

Among the grand, tall houses of Prairie Avenue, the Gallagher house was distinct and immediately noticeable. Constructed of blush rose brick, the single-story house sprawled on the corner, and even in the dark afternoon now clouded over with ponderous clouds and imminent rain, the entire structure seemed made of light. The large windows that dotted the face of the house seemed to gather and hold the fading light, glowing in a way that had nothing to do with any illumination from within. Combined with the white trim around the windows and the large white door with gold knob and knocker, the house appeared to gleam.

I stopped too long to admire the building's clean, contemporary lines and was suddenly drenched by a looming cloudburst. As I stood on the front porch trying to shake water from my hat and coat, I grumbled to myself that dripping from a downpour was not quite the way I planned to commemorate the occasion. During the train trip and then on the walk from the station, I desperately—but unsuccessfully—sought the right words to use. Nothing I considered sounded appropriate, and now my unkempt appearance would add even more indignity to a meeting that deserved better. Despite my complete lack of any true knowledge of Douglas Gallagher, I felt he merited more from me, but it was too late. I stood on the front step, wet and growing cold from the unexpected afternoon May shower, the envelope of small treasures folded carefully in my cloth purse, suddenly inarticulate and reluctant to continue.

I took a deep breath and raised my hand to lift the knocker but at my touch and without any effort on my part, the apparently unlatched door swung open. At first I stepped back, embarrassed as if I had committed some huge social blunder. When I realized no one stood on the other side of the threshold, I leaned forward enough to call, "Hello," down the hallway. At the continuing silence, I stepped just inside the door and called once more. Although hall lights were lit against the gloom of the rainy afternoon, the house seemed vacant and still. Outside, the downpour continued, a rumble of rain on the roof and against the windows, and I thought that with the competing noise of the storm my greeting may not have been heard. I knew how improper it was to stroll uninvited and unushered through a stranger's house but couldn't stop myself, compelled by the need to deliver my precious cargo. As much as I had resisted the errand, I now yearned to be done with it. Certainly I would find at least a servant at home! I cautiously continued down the hallway, periodically calling hello. All the rooms I passed were dark and empty, but toward the end of the hall I saw an open door to a room clearly lit. I headed in that direction and stopped in the doorway to say hello once more, this time addressing the figure that stood on the other side of the room. The man didn't hear my greeting. His back was to me but I recognized the fair hair and tall figure of the man I had seen the previous night at the *Tribune* office. He stood immobile, staring out the windows of the graceful French doors that must have looked out on a terrace or a back lawn, although just then the view was obliterated by pouring rain. His motionless posture, hands in his pants pockets and not a muscle moving, indicated he was deep in thought. I hoped I was not interrupting a personal, emotional moment that would embarrass us both.

"Mr. Gallagher?" I queried with emphasis, and he turned quickly to face me.

Andrew Gallagher was handsome and surprisingly athletic in his stance for a city man, with thick, fair hair and light hazel eyes in a lean face. He could have been as old as thirty, although if the stories hinted to Hilda Cartwright were true, the rough edges of his face might have been caused by late nights and profligate habits. For a long moment he just stared at me, I think absolutely flabbergasted to see someone in the doorway.

"Mr. Gallagher?" I repeated. He gave his head a tiny shake, trying to clear it and bring himself back to reality, I thought with some sympathy. I knew I didn't belong there.

"Who are you and what on earth are you doing here?" His tone held such incredulity that I couldn't help but laugh.

"The look on your face tells me you think I am some kind of vision, but please don't elaborate. I got caught in the storm and am unfortunately and unbecomingly soaked. I can only imagine the kind of vision I must appear to be."

"Arthur's Lady of the Lake?" he responded promptly. "A mermaid perhaps?" He gave me a quick look from toe to head and added, "No, I don't think there's a flipper or a tail under that skirt. One of the Naiads then? That would make sense, anyway, this close to the lake." He had recovered nicely from the surprise of seeing me in the doorway and was being determinedly charming. His manner was as stylish as his fawn flannel trousers and the crisp white shirt he wore, sleeves folded back from his wrists and collar casually open at the neck. I thought him a man who knew how to use his innate attraction and good looks to advantage, a man who had learned it at such an early age that by now being charming came as naturally to him as breathing.

"None of those, I'm afraid. My name is Johanna Swan and I am woefully mortal. May I come in?"

He raised an eyebrow as answer, reminding me with a wry glance that I was already in with neither invitation nor announcement.

"Could I stop you even if I wanted to? I fear the deed is done, Miss Swan, but I appreciate your courtesy even if it is after the fact. Do you always wander aimlessly through the homes of strangers?"

"I tried to knock but the front door was open, and I called several times from the front of the house."

"Was it and did you? I didn't hear a sound."

"No, you were somewhere else. I'm sorry if I startled or interrupted you."

"You did neither of those things. I had a momentary lapse and was dwelling on the past in an unhealthy way. I blame the gray weather." His tone struck me as somewhat wistful, but he went on briskly. "You told me who you were, but you haven't answered my second question." I paused to remember what that question was and without warning gave a quick sneeze, which made him frown. "Are you going to catch pneumonia and die in my library?"

"Not purposefully," I retorted, "but if I do, you have my permission to drag my lifeless body out to the street corner and pretend you've never seen me before." Then I sneezed again and he came forward.

"Take off your hat and coat and sit down. I'll be right back." I did as directed and sat on a comfortable love seat, wondering how my noble errand had degenerated into this unusual exchange. Andrew Gallagher returned with a woolen shawl and placed it carefully over my shoulders, then shook out my coat and draped it just as carefully over the back of a chair. He picked up my hat, gave it a shake, too, and looked at it critically.

"You won't be able to salvage much of this, I'm afraid."

"Good. I never liked it. I wear hats because I must, but they're more of a bother than anything else. That one was always too much hat for me, anyway, so I won't miss it." He held the flattened object up and out in front of him, mentally measuring it against my head and face, and then nodded.

"Yes, I can see that. You should wear something with a smaller brim that doesn't obscure your face or overpower your figure." Mr. Gallagher put the hat down but continued to look at me intently. "I've seen you before, haven't I? How do I know you?" He sat down directly across from me, still examining my face carefully but dispassionately.

"I followed your lead last night after Mrs. Trout finished speaking." At first I could tell he was completely at a loss and then recognition made him nod.

"I remember. You were the woman who stood and joined me in applause."

"Yes."

"It was just the two of us for a while, wasn't it?"

"It was just you for a while," I admitted, "but I was so annoyed with the crowd I didn't trust myself to do anything until I was sure I was composed."

"They were a trying group."

"Rude and arrogant, I'd say, but I suppose different people react differently to change and new ideas."

Silence stretched out between us until Gallagher said, "I'd be flattered to think you tracked me down to tell me how much you admired my ability to applaud, but even I am not that self-absorbed. So really, Miss Swan, why are you here?"

Under his watchful eyes, I opened my bag and brought out the small envelope. "Hold out your hand, please."

He did so obediently and without question, and I emptied the envelope's contents into his outstretched palm. We both stared at the two items that lay there, the solid ring and the stickpin that twinkled even in the rain-dimmed room. I raised my eyes and watched him look at the items, his face expressionless except for a muscle that pulled along his jaw. He closed his fingers tightly over both pieces. In a peculiar way he did not pull his hand back but continued to hold it out between us as an upturned, clenched fist.

"Forgive me," I said finally. "I should have prepared you, but I didn't have the words. I thought and thought about what to say and how to say it, but nothing seemed right. He wanted you to have these. He asked me to find you and give them to you, and I promised I would." Andrew Gallagher still did not speak, but he lifted his head and met my look, listening carefully, his own face smooth and free from any awareness except of my words. "I can't pretend I knew your brother at all. I saw him on board, but, of course, he didn't notice me and we never spoke before that night. He was very brave and calm, I thought, almost detached. He gave the impression nothing could hurt or bother him and seemed almost to scorn the whole situation. I asked him whether he had a message for you, but he just shook his head. Everything was confused and people had begun to panic, and I think he just felt the situation wasn't right for words."

"No." Drew Gallagher finally spoke. "It wasn't that. He knew we'd said all there was to say before he left. There was simply nothing to add." His tone made me think their last words had not been kind or amicable.

"I'm sorry." Whether for his brother's death or their unhappy parting, I didn't know, but I meant the words sincerely.

Drew Gallagher gave me a lop-sided and boyish smile, the kind of smile calculated to make a woman's heart give a lurch, reached out his other hand, and with an unexpectedly tender gesture, completely innocent and somehow affectionate, lightly flicked my cheek with two fingers.

"I can see that on your face. Thank you." Then he went on inconsequentially, "I own this house now, but it will never be mine, not really. My brother built it."

"It's the most beautiful house I've ever seen. It's almost magical. Even on a rainy day, it draws in light."

"Douglas built it for a woman. I wouldn't call her magical, but like the house she, too, drew in light."

"The tall woman with honey-colored hair." I spoke with certainty because intuitively I knew it to be true.

"You're the one who's magical, Miss Swan. How can you possibly know that?"

"I saw them together once, two years ago at the annual Sweethearts Ball that the city holds downtown every Valentine's Day. I was leaving for London in a few weeks and for whatever reason, the memory never left me. I remember how perfect they looked together. He was so dark and handsome and she was beautiful, dressed in dark green satin with a ruffle of cream lace at her throat and her hair fastened down the back of her neck. I recognized him right away when I saw him on board the ship and I looked for her, but apparently he was traveling alone."

"The woman was Katherine Davis, my brother's one true love."

Yours, too, I thought, catching something in his tone that made me believe both Gallagher brothers might have been smitten. I wondered if she had been the reason for their acrimonious parting.

Somehow reading my mind, he said, "I admired Katherine a great deal," stressing the verb. "She was an intelligent, confident, strong-minded woman, but my brother loved her and for completely different reasons."

"What happened?"

He opened his hand to look once more at the ring and the pin, then carefully set them, one piece at a time, on the side table.

"It didn't work out. My brother's demons got in the way."

"Demons?"

"All the Gallagher men have them," he responded lightly, rising. "It's a family trait." Taking my cue from him, I rose, too. The shawl slid from my shoulders.

"I see the rain has stopped so I must be going. Thank you for letting me dry out in your library." He held my coat for me and I slid my arms into it, then turned to take my still damp hat from his hands. He hesitated before handing it to me.

"I don't think you can salvage it, and I wouldn't if I were you." Gallagher made one last dispassionate examination of my face. "This advice is unsolicited and you may ignore it completely, but I wouldn't wear a hat at all if I were you. Not with that face." I flushed despite myself, not expecting such a rude and insensitive comment.

"Surely I can find a chapeau somewhere that would suit this plain face," I retorted sharply.

"Is that what you think I meant?" When I didn't answer, he shook his head. "Miss Swan, you have a remarkable face, transparent and uncluttered. There's nothing plain about it."

"You needn't try to placate me, Mr. Gallagher. I've known all my life that I'm not in the least pretty."

"That much is true, but I never said you were pretty. I said remarkable. There is a difference and you've got the better end of it. Keep your hair short exactly as it is and stop trying to keep up with fashion. Anything that hides all your soft black curls and those fine eyes is not right for you, regardless of the fashion magazines." This time, at my look, he had the grace to flush. "I told you I was offering unsolicited advice, Miss Swan, but I suppose I should have added presumptuous as well. Forgive me if I offended you."

I took the hat from him but made no move to put it on. "You didn't offend me. I've been told I have no sense of style, and that's absolutely true. I have stopped trying to keep up with fashion, in fact, not because I'm above it but because it's so incomprehensible to me. Why should what we wear matter at all when we have so many more important issues to deal with?" I smiled to show I held no hard feelings.

"Why indeed?" he responded with a reciprocal smile, then asked abruptly. "Do you have far to go? I could arrange a ride for you. My brother's auto and Fritz, his driver, are out back somewhere."

"Only to Hill Street and I'd rather take the train, thank you." I glanced past him to the jewelry on the table. Despite the fact that I had carried out Douglas Gallagher's expressed wishes, it was hard to part with the items I had physically and emotionally carried for so many weeks. Andrew Gallagher followed my gaze and then looked back to me with comprehension in his expression.

"Thank you for your kindness to my brother. Those items mean something to you, don't they?"

I tried to find the words. "Yes, but I can't explain why. I keep seeing him standing at the railing, taking out a cigarette and looking out over the water, nothing but a man taking a stroll on the deck before bed. He was trying to appear valiant, but he seemed so sad to me. I thought he was the loneliest man I'd ever seen. I suppose my keeping his personal items safe and close was my way of telling him he wasn't alone after all. Maybe that's why it was hard to give them up."

After a long pause, Andrew Gallagher smiled. "You are a kind and perceptive woman, Miss Swan. Are you sure I can't arrange for you to be driven home?" The companionable moment was obviously past.

"No, I'm quite serious about taking the train, but thank you."

He walked me to the front door and opened it for me. Outside the rain had stopped and the clouds had almost all blown off, showing clear blue patches of sky. Although cool, the walk back to the station was exactly what I needed following the unexpected intimacy of my shared confidence about Douglas Gallagher. I put out a hand.

"Good-bye, Mr. Gallagher."

He took my hand in his own. "Good-bye, Miss Swan. Thank you for caring about my brother. He made it difficult for people to do that while he was alive, so I'm glad you were there with him that night. Whether I like it or not, I have inherited the power of Gallagher Enterprises now and if you ever need anything, if there's anything I can ever do for you, will you promise to track me down and ask?"

"I can't imagine that would ever occur," I replied, thinking about my own inheritance and financial independence.

"Yes, but if there ever is, promise me you'll find me and ask me about it," he persisted, still holding my hand.

"I promise that if I'm ever in need of your aid, I won't hesitate a minute asking for it." My words seemed to satisfy him and he let go of my hand.

"I appreciate the concession and I'll hold you to it. You'll be safe enough going home, won't you?" He laughed at my expression. "Sorry. It was a momentary lapse. I can see you don't want or need to be coddled." At the bottom of the front walk, I turned briefly to give a small wave at his figure, which still stood in the open doorway. Then I picked up my pace and— hatless all the way—made it to the station in time to catch the train home.

That night out of habit I lifted the lid of my jewelry box and feeling strangely bereft, stared at the place where Douglas Gallagher's jewelry had lain for several weeks. After a moment I raised my head and purposefully stared at my reflection in the bureau mirror. Looking back at me was a thin face with too-prominent cheekbones, a straight nose sprinkled with freckles that showed up against tan skin, a mouth too full for fashionable beauty, and plain brown eyes, all surrounded by short black curls that I now decided made me look half my age. I had cut my hair because I found trying to subdue my unruly curls too frustrating and time consuming. Now, seeing myself objectively, I decided I should have grown my hair even longer. At least I wouldn't look thirteen. How Drew Gallagher could see anything remarkable in such a face was a mystery to me. I thought he'd been sincere at the time but had also been placating me with his undeniable charm. Like undoubtedly any number of women before me, I had chosen to believe his words because of the man's appeal, not because the comments held expertise. I was only human and no more immune to the attraction of the opposite sex than any other female.

In the following week I began several classes for the inhabitants of the Anchorage: new baby care for all the women in that situation, a class to teach typewriter skills useful in the burgeoning Chicago business environment, an English language class, and a very basic class on reading and writing for both Kipsy and Yvesta, who could do neither in English or any other language.

Flora scorned all our efforts, content to sit and stare out the window and wish the child in her womb somewhere else. She spoke of the baby's father once, defiantly.

"He was handsome and he made me laugh. He never promised me anything but a good time, and I don't hold this against him. I didn't want to be tied to one person any more than he did." She glanced down at her waistline. "And I still don't."

For no obvious reason her words made me think of Drew Gallagher, who was certainly handsome and able to make a young girl laugh and, if what Hilda Cartwright had heard was true, was also not one to promise a woman anything besides a good time. I didn't want to think of him enticing a young woman like Flora to behavior that she would pay for her whole life and then abandoning her. He might enjoy the company of women, but I thought I detected in him some shred of an intelligent conscience. He had readily admitted that the Gallagher men had their demons, however, so I was presumptuous to assume anything about him from the little time we had spent together.

That Friday afternoon, from my little office I heard a pounding on the front door and waited long enough to realize Eulalie was not available to answer it. Because Hilda was out, I went to the door myself and opened it to face a scowling, shaggy-browed man with his hand raised for another knock. He was only my height but barrel-chested with brawny arms and hands and very dark eyes and wore the pervasive smell of alcohol.

"May I help you?" I asked, standing squarely in the doorway. The man's open hostility, more than his smell and rough appearance, made me certain I did not want him on the premises or crossing the threshold of the Anchorage.

"I've come for my wife and children," he told me and moved to push past me. He looked surprised when I held my ground, but I am stronger than I look and certainly more stubborn.

"This isn't a prison. Our residents are here of their own free will. What's your name? I'll pass the word along and if your wife wants to talk to you, she'll contact you later," which obviously wasn't what he wanted to hear. He pressed closer, one shoulder at an angle against mine prepared to push me out of the way.

"I'll take them with me now."

Still not retreating, in fact, pushing back with my own shoulder, I spoke right into his face. "No, sir, you will not. You're trespassing." I turned my head as if someone stood behind me and added, "Eulalie, send someone for the officer on the beat. This man is threatening me." When I turned back to him, I added calmly. "I don't know who you are, but you're not welcome here. I suggest you leave before the police arrive because I will certainly lodge charges against you."

Clearly he was unaccustomed to a woman speaking back to him and his face grew darker. He put both hands on my shoulders to shove me aside.

Despite the panic and fear roiling in my stomach, I warned in an even tone, "Be careful. If you manhandle me, I guarantee you'll spend time in prison. Is that what you want?" Something in my unhurried, rational manner penetrated his alcohol-saturated state. He was still furious, but he brought his hands down to his side and stepped back from me.

"My family's what I want. They belong to me."

"They're not property, sir. They're people. If they want to talk to you, I'll assist them in sending you a message. What is your name?"

From behind me Crea called, "Right this way, Officer. There's a man bothering Miss Swan at the front door."

The swarthy man stepped back another step and growled, "I won't forget this."

"I won't either. If you cause any more trouble, I'll find out who you are and arrange to have you arrested. Don't think I'm above having you put in prison for a long time. Doing so wouldn't bother me in the least." He shot me another dark look and stepped off the porch, took a few quick steps, then broke into a run down the street. If I had to guess if we'd see him again, I would have said no. Closing the door, I leaned back against it, wiped suddenly damp palms on my skirt, and took a deep, still shaky breath.

Crea approached from the end of the hallway and I said, "You can send the officer away, Crea. The man's gone."

"I didn't have time to find a policeman, Johanna."

After a pause, I smiled faintly and responded, "Then it's a good thing he didn't call our bluff, isn't it?"

From the top of the stairs young Kipsy called, "You'd have handled him, Johanna. He wouldn't a stood a chance." A murmur of assent made me look up to see all the boarders standing at the top of the steps, eyeing me as if I'd just sprouted wings—or horns.

"I'll give you credit," Betsy remarked. "You never backed down. He was scared of you, plain and simple."

"More scared of the officer he thought was coming down

the hall," I retorted. Looking past her, I caught an expression that combined fear and panic on Yvesta's face, poor woman, who must have felt that man's fist more than once in a life I could not imagine. I had known from his first words that she was the one he wanted. No one else at the Anchorage had children with her.

Later she sought me out, her two little girls clinging to her skirts. "I should go with him," she told me. "He is my husband."

"Would you and the children be safe?" I asked bluntly. "He seemed very angry."

"He is my husband. How else can I live? I can't stay here forever." She wore the same expression of mute fear and help-lessness I had seen on her face earlier.

"We'll find a job for you, Yvesta, so you don't need to be dependent on him."

"What do I do with the children then?"

"There's a place on Halsted Street called Hull House. Have you heard of it?" At her blank look, I explained, "It's a clean and safe place run by a woman named Jane Addams that offers nursery and kindergarten care for neighborhood children. You can leave your children there for the day while you work."

"But who would give me work and what kind of work could I do?"

"What about something in an office?" Even as I said it, I knew that was a foolish idea for a woman who could not read and write. She knew it, too.

"That is not for a woman like me. All I can do is clean and cook and sew and who would pay for that?"

I knew there were manufacturers that paid women to sew, but last year's horrible story of the scores of women who plunged to their deaths in New York City's Triangle Shirtwaist Fire had reached the London papers, and I couldn't send

Yvesta off to such a place. She had the skills—I had seen her tiny stitches and straight seams—but I would need to be sure she was safe and treated fairly. Out of nowhere I heard Drew Gallagher's voice saying, "I have inherited the power of Gallagher Enterprises," and I suddenly had an idea.

With my hand on her shoulder, I encouraged, "Don't despair, Yvesta, and don't go rushing back to the life you left. Think of your daughters and what that would mean for them. I may have an answer to your question about who would hire you."

When I inquired from Hilda Cartwright, she responded, "Gallagher Enterprises? I don't know much about it. I've heard they deal in textiles and meat and own some banks on both coasts."

As soon as she said textiles, my mind was made up. Drew Gallagher had invited me to come to him if I ever needed his aid, and although my request was probably not exactly what he intended, in a roundabout way I needed his help. That weekend I composed a letter inviting him to visit Indiana Avenue at his earliest convenience and posted it first thing Monday morning.

Each heart has its haunted chamber,
Where the silent moonlight falls!
On the floor are mysterious footsteps,
There are whispers along the walls!
What are ye, O pallid phantoms!
But the statues without breath,
That stand on the bridge overarching
The silent river of death?

Chapter Five

Mr. Andrew Gallagher, resplendent in a fine wool double-breasted reefer jacket of tasteful gray, matching trousers fashionably turned up at the cuffs, an immaculate white shirt, and a silk tie in muted blue, appeared at the front door of the Anchorage the following Friday morning. With a hesitant knock, Eulalie interrupted my reading class with Kipsy and Yvesta.

"There's a man waiting for you downstairs, Johanna. I've left him in the hall by the front door."

"Are you sure it's safe for him to be inside?"

"I left him in Matron's hands, so I'm not worried. He said his name was Mr. Gallagher and that you especially request-ed—no, I think he used the word *commanded*—his presence. He showed me a letter you wrote and I recognized your handwriting."

"Good. You're right, Eulalie, Mr. Gallagher is safe enough, and he might have the answer to a question Yvesta asked me last week." I gave Yvesta a quick smile and added, "Is Flora still holding her own?"

"Yes, but the pains are coming more regularly and she's not liking that very much."

"I can imagine, but there's nothing she can do about it now. Tell her to hold on. I'll come up and see her in a few minutes. Have you sent for the doctor?"

Eulalie nodded and I excused myself. At one time I'd hoped the sight of her new child would soften Flora's attitude toward it, but I knew she still couldn't wait to give the baby up for adoption. Her complete lack of desire for the child was sure to make labor and delivery even more painful and frightening than usual.

Downstairs Andrew Gallagher and Hilda Cartwright conversed in the front hallway like old school chums catching up on alumnae gossip. Both looked up at me as I descended the steps. I went forward with extended hand.

"Thank you for coming, Mr. Gallagher." To Hilda, I remarked, "I see you've already met Mr. Andrew Gallagher, Hilda. You'll recall we saw him at Mrs. Trout's presentation at the *Tribune* office two weekends ago." If she was surprised to see him turn up in her hallway, she never showed it.

"Yes. In fact, I was just telling him that I admired his response to Grace's speech and wished more men were as enlightened."

"And I," interjected Drew Gallagher lightly, "was still recovering from the shock of being considered enlightened. I can't recall that anyone has ever paired that word and my name in the same sentence before."

Hilda gave an obligatory smile to his remark but went on, "However you downplay it, your gesture was appreciated by a number of us in the room who didn't have the presence of mind or the courage to do the same." She turned to me. "I'm on my way out, Johanna, so if you have business with Mr.

Gallagher, feel free to use my office. Yours might not do." She said a polite good-bye, and I led my guest down the hallway to Hilda's office.

Drew Gallagher sat down in a chair across from me, gracefully crossed one leg over the other, and asked, "Tell me, Miss Swan, where exactly am I?" I choked back a small gurgle of laughter, bit my lip, and resisted the very strong temptation to recite the street address. He gave me a stern look seeming to know exactly what I was thinking, but then, almost in spite of himself, grinned and added, "Do not play with me, Miss Swan. The presence of Miss Cartwright and her office—why wouldn't your office do, by the way?"

"It's in a closet down the hall."

"Your office is in a closet?"

"Yes, well, it's the best we can do right now, and I don't spend much time in it anyway. There's room for a little desk and a chair and that's all I need when I'm working on class preparation. I don't think two people would fit in it simultaneously."

"What classes are you preparing?" Gallagher had the disconcerting habit of listening intently when I spoke, giving the impression that for that moment he could see or hear nothing else. No one had ever shown me such undivided attention before, and its effect on me was a mixture of gratification and juvenile self-consciousness. I thought he did not miss much and forgot even less.

"Baby care, typewriter skills, English, and literacy right now."

He thought a moment before he replied, "Which brings me back to my original question: Where exactly am I?"

"The Anchorage Home for Women in Need."

"Are you one of those women and is that why I'm here?"

"No. Well, not exactly." He spoke no response, picked a nonexistent piece of lint from his trousers, settled himself more comfortably in his chair, and offered a faint, encouraging smile. A man clearly waiting for clarification and not about to ask any more questions. A man prepared to wait as long as necessary to be enlightened.

"The Anchorage is a place women come for sanctuary when they're in trouble, any kind of trouble. Right now we have unwed mothers, destitute widows, a woman hiding from her abusive husband, and a girl leaving a life of prostitution. The Anchorage offers safety, protection, medical services, the rudiments of an education, and above all, hope for the future. Safety and hope are two basic rights of human beings, after all, and why should a woman's past keep her from knowing a safe present and a hopeful future? That's why you're here." At his blank look, I went on, "You offered me the power of Gallagher Enterprises, and I'd like to take you up on that offer." As I spoke, the animated interest in his face faded into a bland expression of courteous boredom.

"Miss Swan, if you can be patient, I'll write you a check as soon as I return home."

"Oh, I don't want your money. Is that why your face got all shuttered? The Anchorage is supported by very generous contributions from a number of highly placed women whose husbands have more money than they know what to do with. I have my own money, besides, or I will have when I'm twenty-five, so please be assured that I have absolutely no designs on your inheritance." I could tell my use of that word sobered him, made him remember how he came to have the kind of wherewithal that would make me seek him out.

"Then what?"

I guessed the abrupt bark of a question originated more from the unexpected memory of his brother than from impatience and explained, "Yvesta Stanislaw is an older woman with two small children. She can't read and write, her English is far from perfect, and she needs work." He started to speak, but I held up a peremptory hand and rushed on. "Yvesta is hard-working, strong, honest, and reliable. She's escaped an unbearable life, and right now the only future she can see is to go back to it, go back to a man who beats her and her children and drinks away the few pennies she manages to save. I won't have it. I realize she can't do anything really sophisticated, but she can clean and sew, and I know Gallagher Enterprises is in the textile business. I thought you might have an opening for a seamstress at one of your locations. If not, maybe she could clean at one of your banks or offices. You must have someone doing so now. Why not Yvesta? Of course, I'll need to approve the conditions in which she works, and a day job would be better because she could leave her children at Hull House. Still, if she must work at night, I'm sure we can work out arrangements for the children. It's a small thing I'm asking of you, Mr. Gallagher, but it would mean so much to Yvesta."

He never hesitated. "All right."

"All right what?"

"All right, I'll find a job for her somewhere. Isn't that what you wanted me to do or did I miss the point entirely?"

"No, I just thought it might take longer to persuade you."

"I am a relatively intelligent man and I recognize when resistance is useless. I—" He was interrupted by a loud rap at the door and Crea's voice.

"Johanna!" Crea stepped just inside the room, her face anxious and her tone urgent. "You'd better come. Something's not right with Flora's labor. She's scared and asking for you. Eulalie sent for our regular doctor but he's out, so she's gone in search of another one. Can you come? I don't know what to do."

"Of course, I'll come." To Drew Gallagher I said, "I'm sorry. Perhaps we could finish this conversation later."

He settled comfortably into his chair. "You're obviously

needed elsewhere and I'm in no hurry. I can wait a while."

"I don't know how long I'll be."

"Miss Swan, I'm all grown up and can take care of myself. Please don't give me a second thought." I smiled my appreciation and hurried with Crea out into the hallway, immediately following Mr. Gallagher's instructions to the letter by not giving him another thought until several hours later.

By the time the doctor arrived, I knew we had a problem. Flora's pains were coming regularly and close but the baby was not making progress. Something was terribly wrong and I looked up with relief when the doctor entered. He shooed Crea out to get clean cloths and hot water but asked me to stay, then did a quick, capable examination, finally standing to say grimly, "There's no time to get her to a hospital. I'll have to take the baby by incision. If I don't, we'll lose them both." Much later it was clear he would be at least half right. Life came into the world and life left it, all within a matter of minutes.

Crea took one look at my face as I followed the doctor out into the hallway and put a hand to her mouth. "What is it? What's happened? I heard the baby cry."

"Yes, it's a boy, but Flora's gone." My voice cracked, and I had to swallow hard to keep my composure.

"She can't be." Crea reached for the handle of the door to enter and see for herself, but I put a hand to her wrist.

"Don't go in, Crea. Not now. We couldn't save her. If the doctor hadn't done what he did, they both would have died. You know Flora was weak to start with, not eating as she should, no matter how much we scolded or encouraged her, and then she lost so much blood. We couldn't save her," I repeated.

"She never wanted that baby. She said she couldn't wait to have a life again and she couldn't wait to be done with it all, she said. It's not fair. It shouldn't have ended this way." Tears of fury pooled in Crea's eyes. "She was only fourteen and she learned her lesson. She had her life all planned out."

"I know."

"It shouldn't have ended this way." The words came out a wrenching cry that caused me to put both my hands to her shoulders.

"It shouldn't have, but it did, Crea, and it can't be undone. Now go tell Matron what happened, and let her know we have a newborn who needs a mother. I won't lose them both."

Only after Hilda took the baby downstairs, after Flora's body had been taken away and the room stripped and cleaned, did I think of how worried Grandmother must be. I called from the telephone in the downstairs hallway.

"Hilda Cartwright called me earlier," Grandmother told me, her voice sounding reedy and foreign through the earpiece. "What happened?" After I told her, she said calmly, "I'll send Levi for you." I started to speak but she continued, "Don't argue, Johanna. It's very late and you've done all you can do there. Hilda Cartwright has a great deal of experience with newborns, and I'd wager the wheels for finding that baby a home are already turning. Eulalie can keep an eye on the child through what's left of the night. Levi's on his way." She hung up, decision made, protest useless, Grandmother at her most authoritative.

At the moment, tired and sad and angry, I was glad someone else was making the decisions. All I could think of was pretty Flora, who wanted to dance and sing and live, especially live, and now was in a wagon on her way to the morgue.

Before I left, I went upstairs where several of the inhabitants, who had congregated on the landing, slowly drifted back to their shared rooms. Betsy, pregnant and alone herself, stared at me out of a pale face, something so vulnerable about her that I put an arm around her shoulders.

"Is she really dead?" Shock and a greater fear gave Betsy's

voice a breathy quality.

"Yes, but don't make yourself sick with worry. Flora was the exception. There's every reason to expect that your delivery will be perfectly normal. You're healthy and stronger than she was."

Betsy gave a weak smile before she went into her room. "Don't seem right, though, does it?" she asked rhetorically. "It ain't like we make these babies all by ourselves, so why should it just be us that runs the risks?"

Crea was nowhere to be found upstairs, but when I went to get my coat from my little office, I found her there, uncomfortably curled into my small chair, making me think she was waiting for me.

I realized that wasn't the case, however, from her first words when she saw me: "I thought you'd already gone home." Her red hair had come undone from its single thick braid and her shirtwaist was twisted and wrinkled. Despite the contorted sleeping position, I must have awakened her.

"I'm on my way home now." I went closer and perched on the corner of my desk to look at her. "You can't sleep here, Crea. Why don't you go up to bed?"

"Ruthie's there and I don't know what to tell her. She doesn't say anything, just looks at me, but I know she wants some words of assurance that everything will be all right, that she won't end up like Flora. She wants guarantees, but I don't have any to give her."

"I don't know of any guarantees in life, either, but the truth will be enough for her right now."

"What truth?" Her tone had that scornful bite I had heard the first day I met her.

"Tell her medicine continues to make great strides in all areas. Tell her it's never been safer to have a baby, that doctors and hospitals exist to protect her. Tell her we'll be here with her, and we'll stay with her until she holds that new baby in her arms. Tell her Flora's situation was rare, that around the globe women have thousands and thousands of babies without a hitch. You know the right words, Crea." As I spoke, her face smoothed out, some of her obvious distress fading.

"You have a way of talking that makes people want to believe you, Johanna. I can say the right words to Ruthie, but they won't sound the same as they do from you. I don't believe like you do that everything has a happy ending."

"I believe we have a hand in making our own happy endings when we make smart and thoughtful decisions."

"I wish it were that simple."

"I didn't say it was simple," I retorted, my tone too sharp. "I haven't found much in life that's simple, but I do believe in the power of choice."

"Sometimes you're at the mercy of someone else's choice, Johanna, and then none of your fine ideas matter and none of the rules hold." Crea spoke evenly, her only emotion a touch of bitterness as she concluded.

I wanted to continue the conversation, conscious that Crea was on the verge of sharing something with me that was private and apparently painful, but Eulalie interrupted us.

"Your driver's at the front door," she volunteered. "He said he'd wait, but it's been ten minutes and I thought you'd want to know."

"Thank you." To Crea, I added, "I wish I knew exactly what you were talking about, but I'm not changing what I said. It's always about choice, and just because you're robbed of it at one moment in your life doesn't mean you relinquish it from your future. Now go to bed, Crea. Ruthie's probably asleep by now so you can crawl in without having to mutter a single platitude." She rose, stretched, and trailed after me as I went down the hall to the front door, where Levi waited. As I turned to pull the door shut on my way out, I caught a last glimpse of Crea slowly ascending the steps to the second floor.

Anger there, I thought, and passion and regret and something else I could not quite put my finger on. Grief perhaps, but for whom or what I didn't know. Only Hilda knew Crea's story and she would not reveal it. I hoped that someday Crea would trust me enough to share her past of her own volition. She was young and bright, kind and pretty, with a future that should hold happiness, but something in life had subdued and disillusioned her. Flora and Crea, one lost and the other searching, weighed on my mind all the ride home.

Despite not getting to bed until the wee hours of the morning, I rose early on Saturday, one hand wrapped around a mug of hot coffee and the other clutching a letter that had arrived for me the day before. I did not typically go to the Anchorage on the weekends, but that morning I was there mentally from my first waking thought. I looked up as Grandmother entered the breakfast room.

"You didn't get much sleep, Johanna," she observed before she went to the sideboard to pour herself coffee, too.

As usual, a freshly brewed pot was waiting. Mayville Montgomery had been cook in the house well before the first day I ever stepped inside the front door. May had come to Chicago as a young Scottish woman over twenty-five years ago with six American dollars, the clothes on her back, and the good fortune to knock on my grandparents' door asking for work. It was a heavenly match in more ways than one. Levi Montgomery worked for my grandparents at the same time, and he and May ended up marrying and settling into the apartment over the garage. Even when raising their twin sons, both now grown with jobs at a local foundry, I never knew one morning when May did not have hot coffee and crisp toast waiting on the sideboard. She was devoted to Grandmother and tolerated me as long as I brought no trouble or grief to her employer. She'd set those boundary lines years ago and I did not begrudge May the right to draw them. I was the interloper, a withdrawn girl of twelve with bad dreams and an unjustified suspicion of the city, the house, and the family. We'd all been forced to adjust to change then, even May. Now I thought she not only tolerated me but might even be a little fond of me. With May you couldn't always tell, but I thought I caught a glimmer of affection once in a while. She worried about my being too thin and periodically plied me with pastries, so if I chose to attribute her solicitude to affection, what harm did it cause?

Grandmother sat down across from me, commenting casually, "I thought I recognized your aunt's handwriting," more of a question than a statement. She was always careful not to pry into my father's side of the family.

"Yes, it's from Aunt Mary."

"I trust everyone is well." My grandmother's attitude about my father's family and background in western Kansas was always enigmatic. Her tone became carefully bland, her voice expressionless, and her face a mask of polite interest. We never spoke of it, but I guessed she had not liked my father very much and blamed him for taking her only daughter to China. I wondered whether she feared my father's family might somehow take me away, too, tempt me to leave Chicago for the Kansas prairie. In the years I lived in my grandparents' house, I had resisted several invitations from my father's sister and brother to visit Kansas. I was a city girl for sure, but someday when the time and occasion were right, I would visit Blessing, Kansas, and meet the family I knew only through periodic photographs and letters and my father's remembrances. The time for that visit wasn't just yet, however. I didn't like the way my mentioning the idea drew Grandmother's lips together and tightened the skin around her eyes, a sign she definitely had an opinion about the idea but was too well bred to share it.

"Yes. Aunt Mary sent a picture of all my cousins." I handed the photograph across the table. Grandmother took it and looked at it politely before handing the photograph back.

"The little one favors your father a great deal" was all Grandmother said before picking up the paper, an indication that she was not in the mood for additional conversation. When she was like that, stiff and uninviting, I could have kicked her under the table out of sheer frustration. Not that I ever did, of course, but that morning the temptation, although brief, was sharp. She could have told me more about my father; she had to know more. But she couldn't bring herself to do that, couldn't quite forgive him all these years later for robbing her of her daughter.

Later, restless, unable to occupy either my hands or my mind, and still hurt and angry about Flora, I decided to take a brisk walk. The beautiful late May afternoon promised plenty of sunshine that hinted at the coming heat of the next months. Chicago could swelter, but then China had sweltered, too, so from the beginning I always welcomed the city's summer. For several years, until the feelings eventually lessened, the summer season always brought with it a peculiar familiarity and a consequent relief from homesickness and grief. With my thoughts dwelling on those earlier years, I hurried down the stairs, pulled open the front door, and nearly ran head on into Drew Gallagher, who stood with a hand poised for the knocker.

"Mr. Gallagher, what are you doing here?"

"Good afternoon to you, too, Miss Swan." If he meant the words as a gentle reprimand for my inelegant greeting, the effect was spoiled by the way the corners of his mouth twitched into an involuntary smile. "You may recall that we left our last conversation incomplete," he reminded me. "I thought

I should get my marching orders before making any further plans. You were in the process of telling me what to do." I stepped out onto the porch.

"That's not exactly how I remember it. How did you know where to find me?"

"Your tone indicates that I have made some kind of social gaffe, but may I point out that I, at least, waited to enter your house and did not wander aimlessly through rooms, peering into closets and under carpets?"

"I never did anything of the sort," I replied indignantly. "If you'd had your door properly closed and answered the bell in a timely fashion, I wouldn't have had to stoop to aimless wandering. Anyway, stop trying to distract me. How did you know where to find me?"

He returned an innocent, hazel-eyed look before explaining, "You told me you lived on Hill Street. I called the Anchorage and talked to Miss Cartwright, who supplied the number. You appear to be on your way out."

"I was going for a walk to blow away the mental cobwebs."

"May I join you?"

I eyed his clean, light suit, polished shoes, and brushed felt hat with skepticism. Everything about his appearance was perfectly in place and fashionable, pants creased exactly right and the brim of his hat turned just so.

"Of course, but you'll get wind-blown and be too warm with that jacket on."

He promptly removed his coat and hat and placed each on a pointed spire of wrought iron porch railing.

"Am I acceptable now?" His falsely meek tone made me laugh.

"You're more the fashion arbiter than I, Mr. Gallagher. Wear what you like." We went down the steps and the front walk side by side without speaking.

After a moment he said, "I believe I have just the place for your Mrs. Stanislaw, Miss Swan. Can she cook?"

"I don't have firsthand knowledge of it, but I'm sure she can. What do you have in mind?"

"Someone I know needs a live-in housekeeper, a woman to cook and clean and keep general order. Someone to answer the door in a timely fashion. She could keep the children with her."

"That sounds perfect. You're comfortable that her employer will treat her fairly?"

"Absolutely."

Something in his tone made me stop my walk to turn and stare at him. "Where exactly will she be working?"

After he rattled off an address on Prairie Avenue, I pointed out, "If memory serves, that's your address."

"Yes, it is. Before Douglas left on his extended European trip, he let all of his help go except Fritz, his driver. Fritz was enough to keep an eye on the house and the grounds in Douglas's absence. But I'm there now and Fritz and I aren't very good with domestic chores. We're at a loss as to what to do with all that shiny equipment in the kitchen. Your bringing Mrs. Stanislaw to my attention was timely." We started walking again.

"I'll take everything you say at face value because it's what I want to hear. Thank you. You won't be alarmed if Mr. Stanislaw shows up at your door, will you?"

"I didn't know there was a Mr. Stanislaw."

"I doubt he'll make an appearance, even if he could find Yvesta, but take it from me, he's easily cowed. Just stand up to him and he runs like a rabbit."

"You know that for a fact." A question in his tone.

"Yes," I replied grimly, "I do. He showed up at the

Anchorage recently, hardly any taller than I but a beefy man with large hands and shoulders. When I thought of him taking a swing at his wife and children, it was all I could do to keep from punching him myself. My tolerance for bullies is nonexistent."

"So the two of you had a face off? I don't need to ask who won."

"I don't think you ever really win with men like him. They show up like bad pennies when you least expect them, but I refused to let him frighten or intimidate me, and I told him I wouldn't hesitate to send him to prison on trumped up charges if that's what it took to keep him from hurting his family. I meant every word I said."

After a small silence Drew Gallagher commented, "Something in your tone made you sound remarkably like Katherine Davis just then. New women of the new century, I suppose."

I wasn't sure he meant it as a compliment and didn't know how to respond. Being compared to that beautiful, elegant woman I had once viewed from afar robbed me of a retort.

When it became apparent I wasn't going to reply, Gallagher went on, "When I last saw you, you were rushing off to help with a birth. Are you a doctor?"

"No, not a doctor. That never appealed to me. I've always been more interested in social ills than physical ones. My first chosen profession is social work, but I'm also a nurse. I was coming back on the *Titanic* from two years at the Nightingale School of Nursing in London."

"To what end?"

"An excellent question for which I have no answer. There was nothing beckoning on the horizon, so when the opportunity at the Anchorage appeared, I couldn't refuse. I had given thought to staffing a free clinic for poor women, so the

Anchorage seemed like good training ground."

"Have you always felt compelled to save the world?" I detected a touch of something not quite kind in his voice, something close to mocking. We approached a corner bench, where he sat down abruptly, forcing me to stop and look down at him.

"Not always," I answered lightly. "Have you never felt compelled to save at least one little corner of it?"

"Never."

"What have you done all your life then?"

"For several years I made it my goal to do nothing useful ever. I considered it a sacred duty to worry my parents and frustrate my brother. That is the sum total of my accomplishments." I didn't believe he was joking.

"I seem to detect a vague past tense in your comments. Have you changed your personal goals?"

"An excellent question for which I have no answer." He mimicked my own earlier reply but this time with no unkindness in his tone. "Life was much simpler when I was spending my inheritance on riotous living, and Douglas was constantly deploring my conduct. I inherited Gallagher Enterprises, which generate a great deal of money without my doing anything, and I suppose I could continue to squander the profits, but now that seems wrong somehow. It's Douglas's money and meant more to him than it will ever mean to me."

"Perhaps you could actually do some good with it." He stood abruptly without responding to my comment.

"I should be getting back. I have plans for the evening. When should I collect Mrs. Stanislaw?"

"Give me Monday to talk to her and come Tuesday." We walked companionably back the same way we'd come.

"By the way, did you bring a boy or a girl into the world last night? I should have asked."

"A healthy boy."

"That must have gladdened the mother's heart."

"The mother died," I said bluntly. "She was fourteen years old and she hated the idea of being a mother. Given the opportunity, she'd have swept that baby from her body and her life. Flora wanted to live. She had plans."

"I'm sorry." I turned my head to look at him as we walked.

"Are you? I wonder. Flora made a mistake and listened to a charming man. Then she paid for it with her life. We should all be sorry."

"Why does it sound like you're scolding me?"

"I'm not scolding you. Perhaps your conscience is just sensitive to my words. But it's hard to argue with one of the girls who said, 'It ain't like we make these babies all by ourselves so why should it just be us that runs the risks?'"

"Biology. Physiology." I made no answer, only looked my scorn at his flippant response so that he continued, "Are you telling me that your Flora was forced against her will to conceive a child?"

"No, I'm not saying that," adding defensively, "but that has been known to happen."

"Was she feeble-minded or handicapped in some way that she didn't understand the repercussions of her actions?"

"No."

"Then she knew exactly what she was doing. I may sound harsh, but your Flora made a bad decision to which there were serious consequences, of which she must certainly have been aware. It is the twentieth century now, Miss Swan, not the Dark Ages. Why is Flora's pregnancy the man's fault?" He had used my own beliefs about choice and decision in an argument that displeased me, and the realization turned my tone accusatory and pedantic.

"You're not understanding me, Mr. Gallagher. I'm not talking fault. I'm talking responsibility. As soon as Flora found out she was expecting, the man who promised undying faithfulness was nowhere to be found. He knew exactly what he was doing, too, and was surely as aware of the consequences as she, only he could leave the consequences behind and Flora couldn't. He should at least have been there with her even if he couldn't bring himself to do the right thing."

After a moment Drew Gallagher said gently, "Miss Swan, don't blame me for last night's sad happening. I was not the father of your Flora's baby."

"Not Flora's baby, anyway," I answered sarcastically without thinking and then stopped suddenly, aghast at my words. "That was rude and uncalled for, Mr. Gallagher. I'm not usually so offensive. I beg your pardon."

We silently reached the front walk and he went halfway up the porch steps to retrieve his coat and hat, then took an inordinately long time to put on his jacket before coming back down to the walk to face me.

"I'd like to say I enjoyed our walk, but I can't. You have a habit of giving me more to think about than I need or want, Miss Swan, and I can't say I like it. I'll send Fritz for Mrs. Stanislaw on Tuesday."

"Thank you. She'll be pleased and grateful as I am. And I really am sorry for my bad manners," I added once more, trying to sound penitent and meek.

"Your attempted humility is even more unsettling than your sarcasm, Miss Swan." He put his hat on at exactly the right, debonair angle, went down to the automobile that waited at the curb, and drove away without looking back.

Flora's baby was gone from the Anchorage when I returned there Monday morning.

"I had already lined up a young couple for the baby. From the beginning Flora made no secret about the fact that she didn't want it," Hilda told me. "Now her son has two wonderful parents who treasure him, a good home, and a future of comforts and opportunities. This couple is unable to have children of their own and were thrilled and excited at the prospect of a son."

"Somehow it doesn't seem right."

"It is right, though, Johanna. We never coerce our mothers to give up their children and make every effort to keep mother and child together, but if a girl chooses to do so for reasons entirely personal, why shouldn't a couple who have been deprived of children of their own have the chance to hold a baby in their arms and give it a loving home? In this particular case, I believe Flora's baby will be as happy in his new home with his new parents as he would have been with Flora. Don't sentimentalize the situation. We have to do what's best for the child."

I knew she was right and couldn't explain why her prompt action troubled me. We were a legitimate organization, not some white slaver or baby trafficker, and we were responsible for both mother and child. I suppose the memory of Flora lay at the bottom of my unease, Flora pretty and defiant and in love with life, now gone, almost as if she'd never been, leaving the baby as her only legacy. A baby she didn't even want at that. How baffling life was sometimes!

I felt the sudden need to share the good news about Yvesta's future and went in search of her, only to be baffled again by life's contrariness. Yvesta was not as delighted as I thought she would or should be.

"I don't know anything about living in a neighborhood and a fine house like that, Johanna. I won't be able to cook to please him. What if the children bother him? They're good children, but they make noise. He won't want them around. I saw him when he was here the day Flora died, and I don't think I'm what he wants. Look at me. I know you mean well, but I don't think it's a good idea." Her lips pressed together in a stubborn line.

"All right. What's your plan then?" I spoke calmly and waited for her response.

"Well—" I could see that she was searching desperately for an answer and finally had pity on her.

"Yvesta, I know you're uneasy about this, but it could be the perfect arrangement. You can keep your children with you instead of having to farm them out during the day and it's far enough from your old neighborhood that your husband won't bother you. If it doesn't work out, what have you lost? You can always come back here and we'll think of something else, but for now, please say you'll give it a try. Mr. Gallagher seems like a pleasant man and I've seen his house. It's large and it's my guess he truly would appreciate having someone take care of it for him. He certainly isn't inclined to do the housework himself. You're really doing him a favor."

From her look, I could tell she didn't believe that last remark, but her eyes had been fixed on my face as I spoke and whatever she saw in my expression must have convinced her.

"I'll try it a week and I'll do my best. Then he can send me packing if he wants."

I stood up and gave her a quick hug. "He won't, but if he does, you have a place to come back to, no questions asked."

After a moment of hesitation, Yvesta shyly added, "I don't want to disappoint you, Johanna, after all you've done." I was touched and uncharacteristically flustered.

"Don't be silly" was all I could think of to say and because I was embarrassed, I made an unconvincing excuse and went back to my office. That this woman who had known such a hard life should feel grateful for my little gesture of assistance made me uncomfortable. What seemed like a small thing to me had more import for her because so few people had ever extended her a helping hand. What a sad and humbling realization!

The next day, we all stood on the porch and waved as Yvesta and her daughters with their one meager satchel drove off in the back seat of Drew Gallagher's very fine automobile.

Mrs. McElhanie, slow and bent from arthritis, spoke for everyone when she said, "She'll be fine now—with honest work and her children with her. I'm sure she'll be just fine." She didn't sound as convinced as the words indicated, but everyone nodded anyway, wanting to believe someone had found a future that included a little hope, often a rare commodity for the inhabitants of the Anchorage.

That evening I came home to find an engraved invitation waiting for me on the table in the front hall. I noticed it immediately propped against a vase of fresh flowers, my name and address carefully handwritten across the front of the envelope. On the back of the envelope were the name and address of Allen's architectural firm and inside was an elegant invitation to a dinner and dance to be held in ten days, celebrating—so it said—the firm's most recent and most acclaimed construction, the Lancer Building. Festivities would be held at the Lancer Building itself. Handwritten at the bottom of the announcement were the words, *Please honor me by coming as my guest, Johanna*, followed by Allen Goldwyn's signature.

My heart gave a curious thump that would have been visible through my skin if anyone had been in the hallway with me, and I felt a rush of pleasant anticipation I hadn't experienced in a long time. I liked the idea of dressing up in something pretty and spending the evening with Allen, seeing new sights, dining on fine cuisine, and dancing to the latest tunes. It had been a very, very long time since I'd done anything really fun, and I was inordinately pleased, besides, that Allen Goldwyn wanted me to accompany him as his guest. I got along well with Allen, enjoyed his company, admired his talent, his intellect, and his quiet humor. I wasn't sure if there was anything more than friendly affection there, but friendship was enough to promise an enjoyable night.

I sent a quick response to Allen the next day accepting the invitation, then gave a critical look at my closet. I thought the lavender dress would do again, even though I knew it was less than becoming on me. When I mentioned the coming evening to Grandmother, she suggested I shop for something new to wear, and although I wasn't averse to the idea, I was honestly at a loss. I never paid much attention to fashion and didn't know where to start. Jennie had an innate sense of style, but I learned early on that it did me no good to copy her. The colors and designs that looked good on Jennie were never similarly becoming on me. I had assumed years ago that my form or face would not show to advantage, regardless of how it was packaged, and I still recalled the odd, almost adolescent, surprise I'd felt when Drew Gallagher had called my face remarkable. He'd meant it as a compliment and although I saw nothing remarkable in the mirror, it had been gratifying to think that someone somewhere did. My unbecoming streak of vanity again. Perhaps 'remarkable' wasn't the same as beautiful or even pretty, but it wasn't plain or common either, and I was not one to disdain an honest tribute.

"You're looking bright-eyed today," Crea told me the Friday of the dinner. She examined my face. "I'd guess you have special plans for the evening."

"I do. Does it show?" I asked with a smile.

She nodded, saying, "You have a face like window glass, Johanna. Everything shows."

"Mr. Gallagher told me very much the same thing once. Which reminds me, has anyone heard from Yvesta? She's been gone ten days."

"No, and that's no surprise. She was the only one who had doubts about her abilities. I'm sure she's already made herself invaluable. I do miss the children, though." Crea's face, crowned by that glorious red hair, dimmed a little as she spoke. "It's been much too quiet without them."

"They were quiet children, Crea. I don't think they ever spoke."

"They did to me. I told them stories and taught them the songs my mother taught me." Crea had never spoken of her family before.

"Where is your mother?"

"She died of typhus a few years ago."

"I'm sorry."

"I was twelve when she died, and she wasn't much older than that when I was born."

"Too young to have died."

"Yes, and not much joy in her life though she loved to sing. She taught me all the old songs of Ireland. She came to America as a young woman and someday hoped to go back home as she called Ireland. 'Tis green at home, Crea,' she said often enough, 'and nothin' like this place. We'll be goin' back some day. I promise.' We never did, of course. It's easy to forget over time, but I can still hear her pretty voice."

"Like yours, then, for I've heard you sing. You'll have a chance to teach your own children those same songs and stories some day. You'll make a wonderful mother." At my words Crea turned away, the animation in her expression disappearing as if someone had pulled shutters across her face. "I'm sorry," I said quickly. "I didn't mean to say the wrong thing. Please forgive me."

She shrugged and stepped back. "You didn't say anything wrong," but it was obvious I had. "You should leave now so you're not late for whatever—or whoever—it is you're looking forward to with such anticipation. Have fun, Johanna."

I thought about Crea all the way home, how the light in her eyes when she first spoke of Yvesta's children faded so quickly, how she lost her natural lively expression at my comments. I knew there was a history there, a painful history, and wished Crea trusted me enough to share it. She carried a burden inside that did not often show, but from what I'd sensed during our conversation, I thought it must weigh heavily almost all the time.

Grandmother came to my room just as I finished dressing for the evening. Framed in my doorway, she looked older and thinner, her face possessing an unhealthy pallor I hadn't noticed before. Then she stepped into the room and the look was gone. A trick of shadows, I thought, and dismissed the unsettling moment.

I had just pinched my cheeks for color because the lavender that turned Jennie's skin into blush porcelain only robbed me of what natural color I possessed.

When I faced her, she said, "I thought you might want to wear your mother's diamond earrings, but now I think they're not quite right with that dress." I looked at the earrings longingly, a dangle of light in her hand that reminded me of the sparkle of Douglas Gallagher's stickpin, but shook my head in reluctant agreement.

"I wish I could, but you're right, they're much too grand for this demure dress. I don't have anything in my closet that would do them justice. Thank you, though." I smiled at her, loving her very much at that moment—more for what she didn't say than for the offer of the earrings. No prying questions, no admonitions to be careful, no fussing, none of the things that would have driven me to distraction.

"You're welcome. You should have them, you know. They do no good in my jewelry box." I heard the bell from below and grabbed a shawl, giving her a quick kiss on the cheek as I passed her.

"As much good as they'd do in mine. I don't lead a wild social life."

"You could. You just don't want to." That made me turn at the top of the stairs.

"Jennie's the beauty of the family, Grandmother, not me." She looked like she wanted to reply, but May called up from the bottom of the steps that Mr. Goldwyn was waiting. "Don't wait up," I added, "I may not have much of a social life, but whenever I get the opportunity, I intend to take full advantage of it."

Allen had hired a horse-drawn cab for the evening, a change from Grandmother's motorcar that I found charming. The early June evening was pleasantly warm and unseasonably humid. I thought I could feel my hair springing into an abundance of curls as we rode but made a conscious effort to forget that I was neither elegantly sleek nor complimented by the color lavender. Allen didn't seem to mind, so why should I? I wasn't hideous, after all, was a good conversationalist and an excellent dancer, and I intended to enjoy the evening fully. I possessed good manners besides, and Allen knew I could be trusted not to embarrass him in front of his employers. There was, of course, that incident with Drew Gallagher where I had overstepped my bounds by miles, but although its memory still rankled, I consoled myself with the fact that this evening I was rested and in good spirits, nothing like my emotional state the day after Flora's death.

"Allen, it's a magnificent building! Did you have a role in its design?"

The Lancer Building stood in white splendor, the setting sun reflected in its rows of windows, the exterior design pristine and starkly beautiful. There wasn't a curlicue to be seen, nothing ornamental, no extra aesthetic anywhere, a simple and elegant geometric. Once inside, the abundance of white marble and the central foyer surrounded with clerestory windows filled the first floor with light and prompted my exclamation.

"A slight influence but nothing more," Allen replied. "Mr. Lancer asked my opinion about one or two details, but it's really his success. Speaking of the man in charge, let me introduce you."

Frederick Lancer, of the Lancer and Marlborough architectural firm, stood a few feet away in smiling conversation with a group of admirers. He turned to greet Allen and after our introduction asked, "How do you like your friend's building, Miss Swan?"

I looked at Allen in surprise before responding, "He said he had little to do with this wonderful structure."

"Allen is too modest. The windows, the color, the clean perpendicular exterior lines, even the tile outlining the wall mural were all Allen's contribution. He's a talented young man." Mr. Lancer gave Allen's shoulder a friendly pat before he moved away to another group of people.

"Why didn't you tell me, Allen? You don't have to be modest around me." He shrugged, clearly embarrassed by the attention.

"I wasn't being modest. The details Mr. Lancer described are basically cosmetic and fairly undemanding. I won't be satisfied until the whole building is mine, top to bottom and inside to out. Now come with me to the buffet table. I know you well enough, Johanna, to realize that small frame hides a healthy appetite." He successfully distracted me from further conversation about his vocation, but I hadn't missed the passion in his voice when he spoke about his desire for the whole building. I detected that fervent side of Allen only when he spoke of his work, but on those few occasions I thought him at his most attractive, a man with a clear enthusiasm and love for his vocation. That passionate Allen slipped through infrequently, but when I caught a glimpse of him, I thought he would be a man easy to love. I recognized in his expression the same fire I'd seen in my father's eyes when he spoke of his work, so for me such inner fervor struck a responsive chord deep inside.

As we filled our plates from the lavish buffet tables and found a place to sit, I heard a band strike up. After a moment, Allen pointedly looked down at my foot, the toe of which was tapping to the rhythm of the music.

"I can never keep up with you, Johanna, and I'm just letting you know in advance that I haven't mastered ragtime or the one-step."

"You don't expect me to sit those out, do you? You know I love the dance floor."

"I do know that but don't worry. There are enough gentlemen here this evening that I'm sure I can find you a willing partner for the dances at which I'm inept."

"Not this one, Allen. It's a plain old two-step." I stood, pulling him up by one hand. "Come on. You can't palm me off on unsuspecting strangers that easily." He let me steer him to the dance floor, which was set up in the middle of the marble foyer, then, smiling, took me in his arms.

"You win, but I warn you. I'm a plain man who builds buildings, Johanna. It's my hands that have the skill, not my feet." Allen was not falsely modest; he really wasn't a very good dancer, but he was good-natured about it and able to poke fun at himself.

"Vernon Castle is the only man I can think of who could keep up with you on the dance floor," Allen told me later in the evening. As the music of a tango began, he took my hand and brought me back to our table. "This one is out of my league entirely. Let's sit down and I'll bring you something to drink. It's warm and you must be thirsty."

I watched him move through the crowd that had gathered in size through the evening and which now comprised many of Chicago's most important business men, movers and shakers all. Men who brought energy to the city. Capitalists and monopolists and entrepreneurs circulating enough money in the Lancer Building that evening to buy and sell a dozen Chicagos.

As Allen disappeared into the crowd, I spied the familiar face and figure of Drew Gallagher across the room. He walked slowly with his female companion, the same stunning brunette I'd seen him with before, her hand tucked proprietarily under his arm. There was something so very stylish about Gallagher, a distinctive, casual elegance of well-tailored black and gleaming hair. When Allen returned with two glasses of lemonade, I asked him about Drew Gallagher.

"I knew his brother, or knew of him, but I couldn't pick Drew Gallagher out of a crowd. I've never met him. I do know that Wright was the consulting architect in the design of Douglas Gallagher's house and that Mr. Lancer was also involved."

"So that house is connected to your firm?"

Allen turned to look at me curiously. "Have you seen the house, Johanna?"

"Yes. I've even been inside it."

"How on earth—?"

"It's a long story, Allen, but the house was beautiful. I've never seen anything like it. Everything about it appeared airy and open and lit from within. What a wonderful accomplishment!"

"Mr. Lancer said that Douglas Gallagher was a man who knew exactly what he wanted and went first class all the way."

I remembered watching Douglas Gallagher on board the *Titanic* our first evening out and thinking the same thing about him. He'd seemed the embodiment of first class in everything, not just his accommodations but also in his expectations of service and even in the way he interacted with other passengers. I thought Drew had a similar inclination when it came to style and quality. The woman who accompanied him was a good example, but in some ways he was also his brother's antithesis. Where Douglas had appeared dark and intense and powerful, Drew cultivated a nonchalant and careless air, one that said he found the world around him interesting only for its ability to amuse.

"I want you to enjoy the evening, Johanna, so banish that pensive look from your face. You're too serious." Allen took my hand and pulled me up from my chair. "I hear a waltz and that's one step I've mastered. Are your feet up to the risk?" I laughed at that.

"You're too hard on yourself," I told him, but we both knew he had a realistic grasp of his dancing capabilities. "I love the waltz and would be perfectly happy if that's all the band played all night."

"Liar." We had crowded onto the dance floor so that I was pressed against him and had to look up at his face. A very nice face, really, with well-shaped features and clear eyes that were just then smiling into mine. I liked Allen Goldwyn very much at that moment.

"A little," I admitted, "but the company is worth a dozen tangos."

We danced the rest of the song without speaking, comfortable with each other and each other's steps. Later in the evening, Mr. Lancer came in search of Allen, begged my pardon for "borrowing" him a while, and left me sitting alone in a chair against the wall. As I watched the ebb and flow of people, Drew Gallagher sat down next to me.

"Miss Swan," he said by way of greeting.

I turned sideways to face him. "You are speaking to me after all. What a relief!"

"I'm not a man to hold a grudge."

"I wonder about that but never mind. Tell me about Yvesta. She hasn't returned so I have to believe the arrangement is working out."

"Yvesta is invaluable. I don't know how I ever managed without her."

"Really?"

"Really." His words caused a palpable relief that must have showed on my face. "You weren't truly worried about her, were you?" he inquired.

"Not exactly, not that she would come to any harm, I mean. But I feared that if it didn't work out, you'd hold it against the Anchorage, and I'd never be able to come begging for help at your doorstep again."

"Surely you jest, Miss Swan. We both know you wouldn't stop at my doorstep. You'd walk inside as if you owned the place." I tried to swallow a laugh.

"For a man who doesn't hold a grudge, you have a hard time forgetting my lapse in etiquette."

"It's just that there are so many lapses, Miss Swan," he murmured in return, "that forgiving and forgetting is taking longer than I anticipated." I couldn't swallow the laugh that time.

"Ouch. I suppose I deserved that." The band suddenly picked up tempo, and Drew Gallagher stood and held out his hand.

"I think you've been sitting out most of these rags all evening, Miss Swan. Join me?" I took a quick look past him, didn't see Allen anywhere in sight, and stood, too.

"I'd love to but won't your companion mind?"

"In the mystery that is woman, she left to freshen up and knowing her as I do, she will be gone for some time. Even if that weren't the case, it wouldn't matter. We have an understanding."

He had my hand and was leading me—pulling me, almost—along to the dance floor so that I had to wait until we stood facing each other to ask, "What kind of understanding?"

"Viola and I find mutual use in each other, Miss Swan, and please don't delve into that any further or even a progressive woman like yourself will find herself blushing. We enjoy each other's company without any commitment of faithfulness on either side."

"And that suits you?" We started the steps so there was just time for his brief response before the syncopations of the music took over.

"Perfectly." Drew Gallagher was the best dancing partner I ever had in my life, bar none, at any time and at any place. He made movement seem effortless, remained quick and light on his feet, never missed a step, never lost tempo, and always maintained a sincere appreciation for the music.

When the dance was over, I exclaimed, "What fun that was! You're very good, Mr. Gallagher, and you're not even out of breath!"

He gave me his unaffected, crooked grin, the one without pretense or affectation. "It was fun, wasn't it? And I return the compliment, Miss Swan. It's a shame your companion makes you sit all these out."

"He doesn't make me," I replied protectively. "He's a working man and hasn't had time to become as proficient in the recreational arts as you."

The band started up again, a new dance named the Half

and Half in an odd time signature that forced me to give all my attention to the music.

Not so for my partner, though, because despite the quick steps he parroted, "Ouch. I suppose I deserved that," and flashed me a quick, charming grin. I couldn't help but grin in return but had no time for more talk because I had to concentrate on the music and the steps. Allen wasn't the only person who hadn't had time to become proficient in the recreational arts.

When the dance ended, Drew Gallagher, not at all winded by the frantic pace of the Half and Half, looked over my shoulder and commented, "I see your young man on the sidelines but stay for one more dance. It's sedate and will give your pulse a chance to return to normal. You wouldn't want to return to your table breathless and with your hair all out of place." Involuntarily I put up a hand.

"My hair is always out of place, I'm afraid. I cut it because I got tired of fussing with it, but short or long, the curls refuse to be tamed. My mother had beautiful hair, but apparently that trait skips a generation."

He pulled himself away from me as we danced and examined me critically. "Don't change anything about your hair. It may not be fashionable, but it suits you and is very becoming."

I gave a small, unladylike hoot. "About as becoming as this shade of lavender."

"I agree with you there," he said calmly. "It isn't your best color."

"Lavender is a lovely color and very popular," I replied contrarily, a touch of defensiveness creeping into my tone.

"Not right for you, though." Because I held precisely the same opinion, I couldn't fault him for stating the obvious.

"I know," I responded with a slight sigh. "Unfortunately,

I've yet to find any color that's becoming."

"Stay away from pallid pastels and stick with the warm dramatic, Miss Swan. Those are the colors that will do you justice."

"Dramatic? What does that mean?" He was holding me closely enough that he could talk quietly and I could still hear.

"Black, crimson, deep green, cream, gold or—if you can find it—the unusual amber that's in your eyes. Any of those would suit." I was quiet, picturing the colors as he spoke, digesting how they would look on me. When the music ended and the band took a break, Drew Gallagher and I walked back together to where Allen stood.

"You know," I said, thoughtfully, "you may be right."

"I am right. I may be woefully inadequate when it comes to business, but I know women and women's fashions. You may trust me on that issue." I didn't respond to his comment but found it a telling remark.

After I introduced the two men, Drew Gallagher remarked lightly, "A pleasure, Mr. Goldwyn. Your firm does good work." He glanced over Allen's shoulder. "I see I am being summoned from across the room." Taking my hand briefly in his, he smiled. "Miss Swan, if you promise another Yvesta, you may come begging at my door whenever you like." Allen and I both watched him as he walked away to meet the brunette beauty who waited for him.

"What exactly did he mean by that, Johanna?" I didn't want to explain the details, not at that time or at that place and not to Allen, so I only shrugged.

"He once helped at the Anchorage and I believe he just offered to help again."

"Drew Gallagher? If rumor serves true, there's probably more than one woman who found herself at the Anchorage because of him." At my frown, Allen had the grace to look sheepish. "That was uncalled for and petty. I'm sorry. Forgive me?"

I felt unaccountably annoyed at his words, but I had practically said the same thing to Gallagher's face so how could I criticize Allen?

"There's nothing to forgive. I've heard the rumors, too." I took Allen's arm and led him back onto the dance floor. "I know you can handle this one," I assured him smiling and went easily into his arms to the strains of "Moonlight Bay."

It is the mystery of the unknown
That fascinates us; we are children still,
Wayward and wistful; with one hand we cling
To the familiar things we call our own,
And with the other, resolute of will,
Grope in the dark for what the day will bring.

Chapter Six

The next day Jennie and Aunt Kitty stopped by the house long enough to show off the dress Jennie would wear for her nineteenth birthday party.

"It's beautiful," I said with sincere admiration, "and it suits you, Jennie. All those flounces are so graceful and the rose catching the scarf at the front matches the color you have in your cheeks. You'll look like peaches and cream."

Jennie, for all her loveliness, was not vain and answered simply, "That was kind of you, Johanna. I wanted something a little more mature, but Mother said I was still the ingénue, her word"—Jennie gave a little grimace —"and I must stay in pastels and lace for another year."

"Don't rush things, Jennie," said her mother, overhearing the remark. "Nineteen is still young and you'll have plenty of time to indulge your flair for the inappropriate after you're married. Let your husband worry about you then." But Aunt Kitty spoke indulgently, obviously proud of her daughter and enjoying the stir Jennie's appearance caused whenever she went out.

"I may not marry, Mother. I may find a career and live on

my own or travel and see the world." I looked at Jennie with surprise, catching an edge to her voice I had never noticed before. Aunt Kitty either did not hear the same sharp inflection or chose to ignore it.

"Of course, you'll marry. One Johanna in the family is plenty."

Grandmother said, "Kitty," with a touch of rebuke, and my aunt colored slightly.

"I didn't mean anything unkind. We're proud of Johanna with her intelligence and her independence. I only meant that Jennie isn't cut from the same cloth."

I stayed quiet through the exchange but reached to squeeze Jennie's hand. "She's right, you know," I told her. "You're the beauty I'll never be and there's nothing wrong with matrimony. My parents had a wonderful marriage. If I could find a man who would make me as happy as my father made my mother, I'd marry him in an instant." Because I seldom spoke of my parents or of marriage, my comments were greeted by a surprised silence.

"Mother has my husband picked out already." Jennie glanced at her mother and then looked away, a disguised expression on her face I could not read, scorn or anger or perhaps she just teased. It was impossible to tell. I used to be able to read my cousin easily, but recently she'd developed a way of speaking and looking that masked her true feelings. I found the masquerade a troubling and unwelcome change from the fresh-faced girl I had watched grow up into a lovely young woman.

"Really? Who?" I turned innocent eyes to my aunt.

"Jennie is just being fanciful. I've done nothing of the sort."

"Carl Milford," supplied Jennie. "You met him at your party."

"Yes, I remember." I pictured him immediately, handsome and dark and too sure of himself. "Why Mr. Milford?"

"He's heir to a ship-building fortune. Mother fancies the beginning of a dynasty."

"Jennie." My aunt spoke as sharply as I'd ever heard her address her daughter, and no wonder. Jennie's tone had been uncharacteristically malicious and contemptuous.

Grandmother intervened to ask, "What night have you decided on for the party, Kitty?" The rancorous moment passed.

"The last Saturday in June."

"We're contemplating a dance band, Johanna," said Jennie, back to her mischievous self. "I know how you love to dance. Didn't you enjoy yourself last night?"

"I did, but how did you know about my evening?"

Jennie gave a graceful shrug. "You should know by now that there are no secrets in this family," but looking at her I thought for the first time that if there were secrets, they rested in my cousin. How odd to think of Jennie as anything other than ingenuous and innocent. Perhaps she was neither of those things. I'd been away for two years and a person could change a great deal over such a time.

"Johanna, the way you're staring at me, I must have grown a third eye," Jennie laughed, rising. "Come along, Mother. I think we've outstayed our welcome."

Walking to the door, I said quietly, "You know I'm here if you ever want to talk to me about anything, Jennie. I care about you, and I have no ulterior motives."

"I know that, Johanna" she responded just as seriously, "but you're the only one who doesn't have a plan for my future. Not that anyone's bothered to ask me what I want." Then she and her mother were down the walk and into the waiting automobile.

I looked back at Grandmother. "Jennie's grown up, hasn't she? I didn't realize the change until just now."

"Jennie's grown older," countered Grandmother, ever enigmatic, "but I'm not sure she's grown up all that much." When I asked her what exactly she meant, she didn't answer. Instead, she added, "I'm a little tired, Johanna. I believe I'll lie down for a while." At that moment Grandmother looked all her age and then some, and I felt a pang of concern.

"Aren't you feeling well?"

"Only tired, Johanna," she repeated with a faint smile and climbed the stairs to her room. Watching her walk away, I realized with a real shock how she'd aged. Her step was less firm and it appeared that going up the stairs was more of an effort for her than she cared to admit. Much later I would remember that afternoon: the changes I'd noticed in Jennie and Grandmother and my unexpected realization that people you thought you knew could transform into strangers right before your eyes.

Two new women arrived at the Anchorage the following week, one ill and the other pregnant. At the end of that same week Betsy, who'd been so affected by Flora's death, gave birth to a healthy daughter in an easy delivery.

When I stopped in to admire the new addition, Betsy said, "I'm glad to see you, Johanna. I was thinking of coming to find you only I ran out of time. Little Flora keeps me busier than I expected."

"Flora?"

"Yes. It didn't seem right that someone should live and die and be forgotten just like that. Now she's got a namesake."

"That was kind of you, Betsy."

"I liked Flora. I know she was difficult and acted tough as nails, but she wasn't. She was just a scared girl is all."

"I liked her, too, Betsy, and I think you're right about her."

After a pause, I asked, "Why were you coming to find me?"
Her face brightened.

"We thought you could help us."

"We?"

"Etta and me. We've had an idea." I sat down on the edge
of her small bed and listened as the words tumbled out. "Etta
don't have any plans for getting married. Well, she couldn't,
could she, even if she wanted to, since she's got a husband
already, even if he don't want nothing to do with her and little George? Anyway, we've been talking. We can't stay at the
Anchorage forever, but what will we do now that we've got
the babes? We thought and thought and then Etta said her and
me should join our resources. That's how she put it: join our
resources. Neither of us has a place to go and no family to take
us in, so she said why don't we find a room somewhere and
one of us work and the other stay home with the babies just
like a real family? I'm younger and stronger, and I don't mind
work. I did plenty of that on the farm. Etta's more used to a
baby around—her George is almost six months old—so we
decided I'd be the one to do the work and she'd stay home, at
least to start with. What do you think, Johanna? Why wouldn't
it work?"

"No reason I can think of," I responded with a smile.
Betsy's enthusiasm was infectious. "What can I do to help?"

"You found Yvesta a place. I thought maybe you could do
the same for me. I'm smart and strong and I don't complain,
Johanna. I'll work hard."

"I know you will," I told her, "and I believe I might be able
to help you." Drew Gallagher had come unbidden to mind
even before Betsy had finished sharing her plan. I'd enjoyed
sharing part of my evening with him recently and now that
we were once more on speaking terms, I felt no qualms about
sending him another letter asking again for his help.

Gallagher responded, not with a visit this time but with a note of his own, sent to my attention at the Anchorage. The message was short: *We can discuss your request over dinner this Saturday. I'll pick you up at eight.* That was all. He had a surprisingly neat and plain signature, no curlicues, no bold strokes, every letter legible. I was conscious of a pleasant feeling of expectation—he was an attractive, intelligent man, even if he enjoyed playing the dilettante—and decided lavender would not do for Saturday evening. The time was perfect for something more dramatic. Besides, I wanted something from Drew Gallagher so it wouldn't hurt for him to see that I had taken his advice. As enlightened as he apparently was, his male ego would still appreciate the fact that I had listened to him and followed his suggestion, which might make soliciting his help that much easier.

Saturday morning Grandmother was not up for breakfast, an occurrence so rare that I went upstairs to her room. I knocked and called her name, then went inside when I heard her voice. She was out of bed and dressed but propped in a cushioned divan in her room, her feet stretched out in front of her.

"Are you ill?" I asked, without even a good morning. Worry always made me abrupt.

"I'm not ill, Johanna, but I am, for whatever reason, exhausted. I asked May to bring my tea and toast up here this morning."

"You never have breakfast in your room," I accused. "You've always said food belongs downstairs."

"Rules were made to be broken. You of all people should understand that. I'm fine, only tired, so take that look of outrage off your face and go back downstairs and finish your own breakfast." Tired or not, she never lost the tone in her voice that made one think she'd been born to royalty.

"I'm not outraged, I'm worried. This isn't like you. Have you seen Dr. Truman lately?"

"Just last week."

"And?"

"And he agrees that when I'm tired, I should rest." That she was being evasive and would not share any details of the conversation made me even more uneasy.

"There's something you're not telling me, Grandmother, and I don't appreciate being kept in the dark. I am a nurse, you know. I might be able to help."

"Johanna, there are many things I don't tell you, and I can't believe that comes as any surprise to you. We are both adults. If there is something I feel you should know, be assured I'll share it. Now please go finish your breakfast. I hear Mayville on the steps and you're standing in her way." May, carrying a tray, walked past me and gave me a sideways look that told me she was as concerned as I about Grandmother's uncharacteristic behavior.

As May fussed with the tray, Grandmother said, "I saw a box delivered from the Emporium on the hall table yesterday, Johanna. It's not like you to purchase anything from so fashionable an establishment. Did you break down and order something new for Jennie's party?" I resisted the impulse to tell her I'd share with her when she did the same with me and shook my head.

"No, it's for another occasion. I can't imagine I could wear black to Jennie's party without being chastised by Aunt Kitty."

"Black?" My grandmother tilted her head just a little to examine me. "I've often thought black might be just the color for you."

"You never said anything."

"You never asked." She lifted a cup of steaming tea to her lips and our conversation was at an end.

Grandmother was right, of course. Drew Gallagher, too. That night I slid the black silk dress over my head and was amazed by my reflection. The sheen of the soft silk caught the light and instead of robbing my face of color seemed to darken my eyes and hair and turn my complexion to cream. I went closer to the mirror, literally open-mouthed. For a moment my mother had stood there, golden-eyed and beautiful, and although I was not the beauty my mother had been, I no longer looked the part of a plain daughter. Gallagher's word of choice—*dramatic*—was entirely appropriate and perfectly descriptive. Under the guidance of a very skilled sales woman at the Emporium, I selected a straight and simple under dress in black, gleaming silk, topped with an over blouse of black on black textured silk. The high-necked blouse draped elegantly at the throat and fastened at the shoulder with a simple pearl brooch that had been my mother's. I twirled slowly in front of the mirror, small matching pearls dangling from my ears, pleased with the result. Originally, I had wanted something unselfish from Drew Gallagher: assistance for the Anchorage and its inhabitants. Now I wanted something else besides, something personal and just for me. I wanted to see a look in his eyes that told me he thought I was attractive. Tonight I looked and felt as remarkable as he had once described me, and I was determined to have that comment repeat itself in the expression on his face.

I heard the downstairs knocker, took a final look at my reflection, grabbed my bag, and turned to surprise May standing in the doorway of my bedroom. Her eyes widened.

"Miss Johanna, you look more like your mother than I ever thought."

Suddenly shy, I asked, "Really, May? She didn't have all these curls, did she? I only remember her with her hair pulled back and the pictures don't show her with the kind of curls I inherited."

"No, your mother's hair was dark and straight and thick. Your father had the curls."

I stared. "I don't recall that."

"I think the curls embarrassed him, so he always kept his hair cut short, but I remember the first time your mother brought him home. He had the most beautiful curls I'd ever seen on a man." Seemingly embarrassed by her nostalgia, she changed the subject and announced briskly, "Mr. Gallagher's downstairs." I slid past her as she stood in the doorway and stopped to give her a quick, uncharacteristic kiss on the cheek.

"Thank you, May." I reached the head of the stairs when she said my name in a low voice, and I turned to look back at her. "Yes?"

"You be careful with that one downstairs. He's the kind of man to break your heart if you let him."

"I don't intend to let him, May, and I will be careful. But he's awfully handsome, isn't he?" I gave her a broad wink that brought a smile to her face.

"Handsome don't pay the bills, Johanna."

We were talking practically in whispers so we couldn't be heard downstairs, and I stepped back toward her long enough to respond, "No, it doesn't. You're absolutely right. But since I can pay my own bills, I'll just enjoy his company without worrying about his intentions."

"You're so sure his intentions are honorable?"

I had to laugh at that. "Oh, I hope not, Mayville. I sincerely hope not."

For a moment I knew I'd surprised her and then she gave a laugh, too, and made a shooing motion with her hands. "Johanna, you look like your mother but you're your grandmother all over again. Go on now." Complimented twice, I grinned and went downstairs.

Drew Gallagher had too much experience with women to

allow anything but a pleasant smile to show on his face when he first saw me, and I had to laugh at myself. Had I expected him to clutch his heart and fall to his knees, overwhelmed by my metamorphosis?

After his courteous greeting, he paused, then narrowed his eyes at me. "What devious thoughts caused that expression just now, Miss Swan?"

"What expression?"

"You have a disconcerting and nearly rude way of appearing privy to a joke that no one else shares. I've seen it before on your face. Is my tie crooked? Am I missing a button? Tell me now, please, before we go out in public."

I preceded him out onto the front porch. "Mr. Gallagher, I can't imagine that any part of your attire is ever less than exactly right for the occasion. That's not likely to happen with a man like you."

"Which means what?"

"I have never seen you anything but perfectly dressed and in control, but even if you weren't, I don't believe you'd care. You are a man with a great deal of confidence in his own opinions and his own taste. Regardless of what the world believes, you will always think you're right."

He took my elbow to guide me gracefully into the front seat of his automobile, commenting as he leaned closer, "That's the pot and the kettle if ever I heard it. Anyway, I was right about you wearing black, wasn't I?" Although I couldn't see the expression on his face, I was content with the words. He'd noticed after all.

On the way downtown, Drew Gallagher made easy small talk. "My brother loved this motorcar, but he never drove himself anywhere. Fritz always chauffeured him. I hope you're not bothered by the fact that I left Fritz behind."

"Not at all. I'm past the age of needing a chaperone. You drive with enjoyment."

"I admit that I like the feel of the wheel under my hands. I predicted early on that the automobile would be the invention of the century."

"More so than the airplane or the moving picture?"

"They have potential, too, but the automobile will open up the world for people, get them out of their everyday lives. It offers real freedom."

"This one does, anyway," I observed, running my hand over the interior. "It's the quietest vehicle I've ever ridden in and certainly the most luxurious."

"Douglas never did anything second class."

"A Gallagher trait, I'd say. You don't appear to be a person who'd settle for anything other than the best either."

"We were raised to believe that happiness could be bought, and Douglas, despite—or maybe because of—his pragmatic nature never doubted that."

"But you did?"

"I wanted to believe it was that easy, but I never saw the proof of it, not in my parents' lives and not in my brother's. In fact, with the years I've become more and more convinced that as trite as it sounds, money really can't buy happiness."

"I wonder."

We pulled up to the curb directly in front of a handsome red-brick building with the words *The Clermont* engraved in elegant script on a small sign over the front door. Drew Gallagher turned to look at me.

"You wonder what? If money can buy happiness? I'm surprised at that. You seem almost too altruistic and charitable for your own good, and I thought you would agree with the sentiment."

"I've seen too many poor and desperate souls, I suppose, so I know not having money doesn't make one happy either. Perhaps it's more about how you use your money than how much of it you actually have."

He started to respond, but his door was opened by a young man at the curbside who said, "Good evening, Mr. Gallagher. I'll take her from here."

When Gallagher came around to my side and gave me his hand to help me out, I murmured, "Thank you. I'm relieved to know he was talking about the automobile and not me."

He laughed and answered easily, "I've been looking forward to an evening in your company for several days, Miss Swan. I have no intention of sharing you with anyone else."

I ignored the remark and pretended I wasn't flattered by the comment, but inwardly I was surprised and warmed. May was right. If I wasn't careful, this charming man could very well break my heart. His words may or may not have been sincere, but I was as susceptible as any woman to flattery. Combining business with pleasure was more difficult than I anticipated.

The Clermont was larger than its exterior predicted with plain walls, fine oak tables covered with pristine white linen, and electric wall lights that gave the room an unusual muted glow. A man met us inside the front door, approaching with a faint smile to shake Drew Gallagher's hand vigorously.

"Mr. Gallagher, what a pleasure to see you! It has been too long. Please accept my condolences at your brother's tragic death."

"Thank you, Mario."

Perhaps sensing Gallagher's wish to change the subject, Mario smoothly continued, "I have your table ready for you and the young lady." He turned to me long enough to say, "Good evening, Miss. Is this your first visit to the Clermont?" At my nod, he smiled. "Then welcome, and do not hesitate to let me know if there is any service I can offer you this evening."

We followed him to a corner table set with gleaming silver and a small vase of delicate white flowers. Mario made a show of pulling my chair out with a flourish, offered me another compliment, and followed that with a small speech to Gallagher about his sincere desire to make our evening memorable. When he departed, I looked up and found my companion's gaze on me from across the table.

"The food here is superb and although Mario may tend to excess, he's very good at what he does, Miss Swan."

"I would never be so foolish as to doubt your culinary judgment and please call me Johanna."

"In exchange for Drew then."

"Never Andrew?"

"Never."

Mario filled our wine glasses after we reviewed the menu and placed our orders, and when he left, Drew raised his glass toward me.

"To business, Johanna." I wasn't sure if he was giving a casual toast or directing me to get to the point of the evening. "I know by the tone of the note you sent that you want something from me and you have devised a plan to get it."

I opened my mouth to defend myself, then closed it abruptly and waited another moment before I spoke. "Yes and yes. I do want something from you and I do have a plan, but I believe my request will be so reciprocal an arrangement that you will thank me for the idea." I went on to explain Betsy's desire to share arrangements with Henrietta. "You must have a place for a good worker somewhere, Drew. Betsy's young and bright and willing to work. She can do almost anything, sew, pack, slice, sweep, whatever, and she's motivated to support her daughter by working as much and as hard as she can. The best part for you is that she'll be more productive in her job because she won't have to worry about her baby during the day. The two women can take care of themselves and their children, earn a living, stay independent, keep off the streets, maintain their self-respect, and help add to your profits. Don't you agree it's a perfect plan?"

In his usual attentive way, he had set down his glass to focus on me and my words, listening carefully but without expression. When I was done, he didn't answer at first. Finally he stated, "If it were Douglas sitting here, he would tell you that he was a capitalist, not a social worker."

"If it were Douglas, I wouldn't be sitting here."

"You're sure?"

"Oh, absolutely. Until he spied me on the deck that last night, he hardly noticed me, didn't even know my name. He recalled I was from Chicago because he'd been introduced to Grandmother, and I was on deck with her. And you're not your brother anyway, so why digress? I know you own enough industry to need workers. Why not hire someone who comes highly recommended?"

"By you?"

"Yes, by me."

He had picked up his wine glass and was swirling the wine slowly as he sat looking down at the table, not speaking, hopefully pondering what I'd suggested. Mario, invisibly bidden, appeared to refill both our glasses.

After he left, Drew Gallagher said, "I'll think about it. I may have a plan of my own."

"What kind of plan?"

"I'll let you know." His tone told me he was done with the topic for a while, a circumstance that forced me to control my impatience. Drew noticed and smiled gently. "You can't always have everything you want right away, Johanna. The most valuable things are worth waiting for. You must have been your parents' darling girl and they spoiled you."

"I don't know what you mean by spoiled. My parents loved me and I always felt I was their darling girl, but they had a way of making everyone feel special so I don't think I was particularly spoiled. I always had chores to do and rules to follow. It never would have crossed my mind to think I should have any kind of exceptional treatment."

"You speak of your parents in the past tense."

"They're both dead."

"I'm sorry." I thought from his quick, sincere tone that he truly was sorry and I gave him a small smile.

"Thank you. They died when I was twelve, so it's been a number of years." At his serious look and continued silence, I surprised myself by volunteering, "They were murdered along with my younger brother."

My words startled both of us. I could tell he had not foreseen anything quite so stark, and I had not expected to share my most private and painful memories with him. I never spoke of my family's death, not even to Grandmother. Since coming to Chicago, the only person to whom I had unburdened my grief was Grandfather, and that was an unexpected and involuntary moment kept between the two of us. Before Drew could respond, Mario brought our dinners and for some time was occupied with arranging the table for the meal.

After Mario finished his fussing and left us alone, we ate quietly for a while until Drew asked, "May I ask what happened, or is it something you prefer not to talk about?" continuing our previous conversation seamlessly.

"It's true I don't talk about it, but that's not because it's too traumatic a memory for me to share, only that it's a private and personal matter. I often reminisce with Grandmother and Mayville and my Uncle Hal about my parents' lives but never about their deaths."

"Who's Mayville?"

"May's the woman you met at the front door, my grandmother's housekeeper, protector, and after Grandfather died, probably her best friend. When I first arrived in Chicago, May was already established as boss of the kitchen and the passing years have only entrenched her further. She's the reason I don't have one ounce of culinary ability: I was never allowed into her sanctum."

"Where was your home before Chicago?"

"Cho Chou, China, in the countryside just southwest of Peking."

"Why China?"

"My parents were missionaries."

Drew eyed the half-filled wine glass currently in my hand. "Apparently not Methodists."

I laughed. "No, Presbyterians—but very conservative Presbyterians. Until I stepped off the boat in San Francisco after leaving China, the only alcoholic beverage I knew of was a particularly strong wine called Shaoshing brewed by our rural population, certainly nothing that was ever served in our house. I remember catching its residual bitter smell on the breath of an old man and thinking people must be crazy to want to drink alcohol. But my grandparents were members of a much more liberal wing of the church, and when I turned seventeen and accompanied my grandfather on a trip to New York City, he introduced me to fine wine. I have been hopelessly corrupted ever since."

"Now that you mention it, there is something latently missionary-like about you," he remarked, observing me coolly, "but I can't quite put my finger on the quality. I'll have to give it thought. You don't look like a missionary's daughter tonight, though, not in that dress. It's immodest of me to say it, but I was right about you wearing black. The color is spectacular on you."

Flushing despite myself, I answered, "Thank you. I agree you were right. I would never have thought of wearing black socially, but that's because I associate the color with funerals and very formal occasions. I've had too many of the former and too few of the latter."

"What happened to your family then?" Drew asked abruptly.

"The Boxers killed them. We established a school to teach reading and writing and the basics of our faith. It was attended by both children and adults of the region. Father taught and Mother worked on health and hygiene issues with the local population. We were there over ten years and I believe had established credibility with the people. My father came originally from Kansas and was always a man of the soil, practical and generous, no fire and brimstone and nothing pretentious about him ever. He just loved helping people and most people saw his sincerity and responded in kind. Mother was—well, Mother was just Mother, lovely and kind and very strong-willed. They loved each other and loved the mutual goal they shared for doing good. My brother Teddy was four years younger than I. China was our home and the people of our village were our friends. Even when rumors of the Boxers' violence reached us, Father didn't believe it would affect us. Why should it? We were in a little backwater, quiet and out of the way, minding our business, helping people, and posing no threat to anyone. I remember my father suggesting to Mother that she take Teddy and me into Tung Chow for a while and I remember my mother firmly saying no. Families stay together, she said. You had to know her to understand how forceful and persuasive she could be. I expect she learned it from my grandmother. The two were exactly alike that way."

"Apparently a third generation is continuing the family trait."

I smiled. "I can't argue. I am like them both in some noticeable respects, but my mother was a beauty and my grandmother is very wise, so there are significant differences, too."

Mario appeared quietly at our side to whisk away our dishes and set a platter of fresh fruit and small pastries in the center of the table. He poured out small cups of strong coffee, asked if there was anything else we desired, and slipped away as unobtrusively as he arrived.

"I should have died, too. It was pure happenstance that I was invited to Dr. Hudson's for a musical evening. He was both a reverend and a medical doctor, who ran a medical clinic in Tung Chow. Dinah, his daughter, was several years my senior but she was still my best friend, and they had a piano besides. We were all supposed to go, but Teddy came down with a fever and Mother wouldn't leave him and Father wouldn't leave Mother. I wanted to go so badly I cried like a baby from disappointment, and Mother had pity on me. She allowed me to go by myself and said I could spend the night. I remember how excited I was and how grown up I felt, sleeping away from home for the first time. And that was the night the Boxers came into our little settlement, murdered my family and all the Chinese who attended the school, slashed their way through the compound with knives and clubs and burned everything to the ground. When word of the massacre arrived at the clinic, all the *yang kuei-tzu* in Tung Chow were evacuated to Peking."

At Drew's inquiring look, I translated, "Foreign devils. I thought at the time that leaving Tung Chow for Peking would be frying pan into the fire, but I was wrong. We waited out the siege and afterwards, Dinah was commissioned to accompany me to America. I never went back to Cho Chou. Later Dr Hudson sent me some pictures and a few personal items that survived the flames, but just like that everything familiar was gone, everything except my one friend Dinah Hudson. And when Grandmother met us on the dock in San Francisco, she kindly but firmly assumed the total responsibility for my well-being and loaded me onto a train headed for Chicago, so even Dinah was gone then." I paused, recalling that long train trip eastward and how desperately I had attempted to disguise my feelings of being totally lost and abandoned and how Grandmother had seen through me, even then. "That was over eleven years ago."

After a silence, Drew said, "The vast majority of people live out quiet and uneventful lives, but in your young life, you've been in the middle of two historical and renowned tragedies."

"And lived to tell about it," I added with a faint smile.

"Which explains your temperament."

"What about my temperament?"

"You come at everything full steam, Johanna, like a woman running out of time. Everything has to be done exactly as you say exactly when you say it. Mortality always seems to be nipping at your heels."

"I know," I admitted humbly. "Grandmother cautions me about the wisdom of moderation and my Aunt Kitty, less charitably inclined, says my headstrong impatience is a great and unbecoming fault."

"Your Aunt Kitty sounds like a woman of no imagination. She's completely and overwhelmingly wrong. I wouldn't let her opinion bother me too much, if I were you."

Looking at Drew Gallagher across the table, his fair hair burnished by the lights, a conspiratorial smile on his face and those warm, clear eyes meeting mine without a trace of affectation, I realized that I liked the man very much, blast it all. Mayville's warning was becoming more and more prophetic as the evening progressed.

"I don't. My Aunt Kitty and I have had different worldviews for as long as I can remember. To keep the peace we usually manage to avoid discussing anything more in depth than the weather." As I reached for a delicate pastry, I inquired casually, "You now know a great deal about me, but I am still in the dark about the Gallaghers. Do you have family, Drew?"

"None. Well, that's not exactly true. I have cousins on my mother's side somewhere in San Francisco, but I couldn't tell you their names. I was sent away to school on the east coast at an early age, and I never knew them."

"Your parents are gone, too?"

"Yes. My father dropped dead at his office one morning and a few years later my mother died in the great San Francisco earthquake."

"I'm sorry."

"By the compassionate expression on your face, you're sorrier than I ever was."

I put down my cup. "What an extraordinary thing to say."

"Johanna, between the two of us, could we agree to set aside the façade of society?" He looked unaccountably stern, frowning a little, the engaging man of five minutes ago completely gone.

"I'm not sure what you mean, but you certainly don't have to stand on ceremony with me. What façade exactly?"

Drew didn't answer my question but said, "My family life was nothing like yours, Johanna. My father was a man with a head for business, who generated a fortune as a relatively young man and preferred his office to his family. He made two sons with my mother, enough to continue the family name and be sure the money didn't go to strangers, and after that he had very little time or need to be home. My mother fulfilled her wifely duty quickly and with little fuss, bore two sons, and spent her remaining time filling our very large house on Nob Hill with items she didn't need. When the earthquake hit, she refused to leave her house and in a poetic sort of way died under a pile of very expensive rubble. I ceased caring about either of my parents at a young age. My father was cold and my mother pretentious." I thought that as I shared a private memory, so had he, and we were now even.

"I don't know what to say," I responded carefully. "Were you glad to be sent away to school then?"

"I was sent away because I was incorrigible and neither of my parents knew what to do with me. Douglas was the son who played by the rules, applied himself to his studies, and graduated with honors. He was focused and responsible. I, on the other hand, never graduated, and I'm proud to say I was expelled from some of the finest schools in the country."

I studied him wordlessly a moment, then remarked, "I don't think you're really proud of that fact, Drew, regardless of what you say, any more than I think that you really stopped caring about your parents. You can't shock me and you don't have to try. In my life I've seen some terrible things, so a rich and self-indulgent young man rebelling against his parents doesn't have much of an effect on me. It's normal for parents and children to love each other, of course, but I know that doesn't always follow. If you really didn't love your parents, it doesn't necessarily mean that's your fault. Is that why you were always in trouble?"

"Some kind of desperate plea for affection, you mean? You've been reading too much Freud, Johanna. I was lazy—still am, for that matter—and disinterested in anything that did not taste good, look good, or feel good. As a younger man, I learned to enjoy variety in women and that hasn't changed either. I've never contemplated a wife with anything other than horror. Because money had no meaning for me, I spent every cent I had and much that I didn't have on carnal pursuits, a perfectly happy and unapologetic prodigal. Douglas scorned my bad behavior, but he always bailed me out of trouble and debt. Every time he did so, he made me promise to behave myself, and as soon as he was out of sight, I was back in trouble."

"But why?"

Drew gave a graceful shrug. "Why not, Johanna? Who created the universal rules of behavior that I was expected to follow and who was I hurting by breaking those rules? It did no good to cite religious or moral codes to me because none of that made sense to me then any more than it makes sense to me now. Why shouldn't I be able to do exactly what I want?"

"An interesting philosophy," I responded mildly, "which explains why you were thrown out of several institutions of higher learning."

"My father gave up earlier, but Douglas kept cleaning up behind me until Yale." I popped a small cream puff into my mouth and wordlessly raised my brows in question. He went on, "The school officials took a dim and disapproving view of the woman in my room. A working girl from the city was not what I was supposed to be studying. We made a spectacle of ourselves that only the two of us appreciated and enjoyed."

"I told you you can't shock me, Drew, so you don't have to use a euphemism like *working girl*. I presume you mean a prostitute. You hired a prostitute and got caught with her in your room. Is that what happened?" His eyes darkened at my curt, slightly amused tone and the sense of sharing he had demonstrated disappeared.

"Yes. That's what happened," said abruptly with clipped words.

"I just wanted to be sure I understood. I hate to burst your bubble, but you may have been the only one enjoying the spectacle the two of you presented. Prostitutes do what they do to make a living, to keep from starving, to keep from being beaten by the men they work for, and to put food on the table for their children. I doubt very much whether there was much pleasure or appreciation on her part. You may have been expelled, but she probably went to jail. Did she?" I could tell he had never considered my question before because it took him a moment to answer and when he finally did so, it was with an obvious reluctance.

"I don't know."

"Ah, of course not. You had other things on your mind than what happened to that woman. Well, she's probably dead, anyway, so why bother considering her now? Prostitutes have a short life span compared to the rest of us. But it does give another perspective to your questions about why you shouldn't be allowed to do exactly as you please and whom you hurt by doing so, doesn't it?"

Drew Gallagher's face tightened, smile gone, mouth turned up slightly in a semi-polite sneer that expressed his scorn. I thought he was as angry as he had ever been in my presence, and I almost wished I hadn't been quite so blunt. I enjoyed the Drew that had been there ten minutes ago and hated to lose him.

"I had no idea the missionary's daughter was an expert on prostitution. I hesitate to speculate on the source of your knowledge."

"Oh, speculate away. The truth, however, is much less titillating than your imagination. Part of my nurse's training in London was spent working with the human refuse of the east end. Miss Nightingale was adamant that her nurses not be spared any of the truths of real life. And at the Anchorage right now is a twelve-year old girl who may never recover, either physically or emotionally, from her experiences on the street. Granted, your knowledge of prostitution may exceed mine in quantity, but I believe I make up for that in the quality of my understanding."

"You are a preachy woman." He snapped the words, intending them as insult, his tone mocking and purposefully hurtful.

Without thinking, I leaned forward and responded in kind, equally as blunt. "And you are an immature and selfish man." I stared back at him, our eyes locked across the crystal fruit platter. After a moment unbroken by word or blink, a corner of his mouth twitched.

"No fair," he murmured, "I used only one adjective." I sat back in my chair, the tension of the moment broken.

"You're right. Pick another one, then, and let me have it. I always fight fair and I never ask for concessions." I could see him pretending to think.

"Annoying."

"Preachy and annoying then. Fine. Now we're even."

"No, we're not even."

I examined his face, trying to understand his meaning. "You just said—"

"I know what I just said, Johanna. I'm not talking about trading insults. We're not even because you're right and I'm wrong." I was so taken aback that I must have stared at him. "Don't give me that skeptical look. I'm able to admit when I'm wrong, and I was wrong—wrong in my cavalier attitude, wrong to respond as I did to your observations, wrong to try to wound you."

I wanted to say something appropriate to the moment, tell him he was the most maddening, contradictory, thought-provoking, and attractive man I'd ever met, say that no man had ever admitted so humbly to being wrong in my presence and I found him completely adorable for doing so.

Instead of making such an unwise admission, however, I picked up my coffee cup and took a small sip before I responded, "Not so immature after all, then. I guess I was wrong, too." I gave him as open and clear a smile as I could and took another sip of coffee. We finished the meal in peaceful coexistence.

Later, sitting next to him as we drove home through the

dark streets, Drew said, "I'll see you in a week or so and let you know if I can do anything for your Betsy. I'm not making any promises."

"I know that. I didn't ask for promises."

"No, I don't imagine you're very interested in promises, only in the follow through. I'll bet that's how you read a book, too. Skip the wordy parts and get straight to the action section as quickly as you can." He laughed to himself and I said nothing. He was too close to the truth to comment.

When we arrived on Hill Street and stopped at the curb, Drew came around to my side, took my hand, and helped me out of the vehicle. For what seemed like too long he continued to hold my hand and we simply stood there facing each other, the auto's motor purring quietly beside us. I was conscious of being smaller than he and felt oddly feminine, a sensation with which I was not very familiar. Finally I pulled my hand free.

"You were right, too," I told him. The night was lovely and warm, and the moonlight illuminated the clouds in a way that made them look lit from behind by an incandescent bulb.

Strolling up the walk beside me, Drew stated, "It's about time you finally admitted it." He paused. "What was I right about exactly?"

"I am preachy and annoying," I answered meekly, "and I shouldn't have reacted as I did. It's not the first time I've heard that particular accusation made about my character. You have a right to your own opinion, and I'm sorry if I was rude." By then we reached the porch. Because I stood on a step above him, we were almost at equal eye level.

"Don't do that, Johanna."

"Do what?" I tried to read his expression but his face was in shadow.

"Back down. Apologize. Look and speak so humbly. I don't like it."

"I can't help it. I have to be nice to you."

"You don't *have* to be nice to me."

"Of course, I do. I want something from you. I'm not an idiot."

For just a moment he peered at me through the darkness, trying, I imagine, to gauge how sincere I was, trying to see if I was telling him the truth or even a portion of it. Then he gave a bark of laughter that sounded unusually loud in the quiet night and stepped away from me.

"You humble me, Miss Swan, you really do. Good night. I'll be in touch."

"Miss Swan again?"

"You deserve *Miss Swan* for that last remark."

"I suppose I do. Good night, Mr. Gallagher. Thank you for the evening. I enjoyed myself very much."

He was halfway to the curb before stopping long enough to turn and ask, "Being nice to me again?"

"Yes, but I really mean it. I did enjoy myself."

"You don't have to sound so surprised," he said lightly before he got into his automobile. I watched the beautiful, quiet vehicle pull away from the curb and went inside, deep in thought about the evening. May heard the door and stepped out of the front parlor as I started up the stairs to my room.

"You didn't have to wait up for me, May. I'm not eighteen any more."

"You're not as old as you like to think, missy, not when it comes to a man like that. How was the evening?"

"Lovely. We went to a very fine restaurant and had an enjoyable argument halfway through the meal. By the end of dessert, though, we were both in charity with each other again. All in all, it was a well-invested effort and time well spent."

"You talk like your grandfather sometimes." She came closer so she could look into my face. "I thought you favored that Mr. Goldwyn, but I believe this one tonight could give him a run for his money."

"I don't favor anyone," I answered too abruptly, then softened my words by adding, "Not yet anyway. I'm enjoying myself too much. How's Grandmother?"

"She got up for a while this evening and came downstairs. Said she was feeling better, but I don't like her color. Why don't you look in on her before you go to bed?"

I did so and found her sleeping soundly. Grandmother looked elderly and small in the big bed she'd shared with my grandfather for forty years. When I leaned to kiss her lightly on the forehead, she awoke and murmured my name.

"I'm sorry. I didn't mean to wake you," I said quietly.

Ignoring my apology, she asked, "Did you have a pleasant evening?"

"Very."

She gave a little yawn and closed her eyes. "Good. Now go to bed. I'd like to go back to sleep." She seemed to drift off again, but it may have been pretense; I couldn't always tell with her.

Back in my own room, I sat on the edge of the bed, reluctant to remove the black dress, reluctant to have the evening end. I really had enjoyed myself, enjoyed Drew Gallagher's company a great deal, appreciated that Gallagher charm and that Gallagher attention turned fully and solely on me. At one time I had imagined myself in the company of the dark brother, had wished it so. Now, however, the mental picture had altered, with a companion considerably fairer but equally as intriguing. Finally breaking the spell that held me deep in thought, I dressed for bed and hung the black dress out of sight. I still needed something from Drew Gallagher, and it would not do to sentimentalize him too much. He was right about my impatience with words and my predilection for action. As much as I enjoyed his company and his compliments, I would not be content until I had what I wanted from him.

So comes to us at times, from the unknown
And inaccessible solitudes of being,
The rushing of the sea-tides of the soul;
And inspirations, that we deem our own,
Are some divine foreshadowing and foreseeing
Of things beyond our reason or control.

Chapter Seven

Over the next weeks the Anchorage experienced a spurt of activity. The doorbell rang day and night, forcing me to have a serious discussion with Hilda about where to put the newcomers.

"Are you sure Mr. Gallagher will find a place for Betsy and Henrietta, Johanna?"

"Yes, but I admit I expected to hear from him by now."

Hilda chewed her lip in thought. "Even if those two beds open up, we'll still be cramped. We have to find a place for Mrs. McElhanie, Johanna. She's been here quite a while, and we try to limit the time spent at the Anchorage. It's only meant to be a place of transition, not a permanent residence."

I felt she was criticizing me and didn't know how to respond. "I know that," I finally said. "The classes will make a difference in the residents' ability to take care of themselves, but the results won't happen over night. I persuaded Ruthie to contact her family and once she has the baby, it looks like she'll be able to go home. Elena wants to go back to Greece, and I've inquired about transportation for her. I don't want her to have to ride third class." I had a vivid memory of the poor people traveling third class on the *Titanic*, trapped in the belly of the great ship and unable to make it up on deck. Not many had survived the catastrophe, and I did not wish that for Elena.

Hilda put a hand on my shoulder. "I'm not chastising you, Johanna. You've done wonders in the short time you've been here. I'll contact some of our benefactors and see whether I can arrange the necessary money for a one-way trip to Greece for Elena. Is second class acceptable?" Her eyes twinkled as I nodded a response. "But we're still short of space. The more people squeeze into Chicago, the more women will show up at our door. It's a worry."

Later that day Crea came to my office and began to speak in a way that made me wonder whether she'd overheard Hilda's and my conversation. "I've been here longer than anyone, Johanna, and I know it's time for me to leave. Do you know where I can find work? I'm not very good with a needle, but maybe I could learn to be one of those typewriters. I'm not afraid of hard work." I motioned her in and she crowded into my little closet of an office.

"Is that what you want to do?"

The scarf covering her red hair nearly slipped off when she shook her head in response. "No, but it doesn't matter what I want to do. I have to earn a living somehow, and it's obvious I can't stay here any longer. We had to put a bed in the hallway for the new girl this afternoon. I was earning my keep here for a while, but since you arrived, I'm not needed as I was. Matron's been more than kind to me, but it's time for me to be out on my own."

After her answer ran down, I persisted, "But what would you do if you could choose?"

With a slightly defiant look that indicated she thought I might laugh at her answer, Crea responded, "I'd be a teacher with my own class and my own classroom in my own school.

Children would call me Miss O'Rourke. I'd be surrounded by books and blackboards and desks and maps and everything else you find in a classroom. I'd be a teacher. If I had the choice." Despite her ironic closing words, there was no denying Crea's passionate sincerity.

"Then teach. Don't waste time and effort on anything else. Chicago has several fine teachers' colleges. Do what you want to do."

"It's not that easy."

"Why not?"

Her green eyes flared in temper. "You always make everything sound easy, Johanna, but you take so much for granted. You had a family to support you and money to do what you chose and if you failed, you had someplace to go back to where you were assured you'd be welcome. Most of us don't have those luxuries; I don't have those luxuries. How do you suggest I pay for an education while I'm also putting a roof over my head and food on the table?"

"I can't answer that right now," I replied mildly, "but I know it can be done. Anything can be done if you want it badly enough."

"I never finished high school. How could I even start college?" But amid the skepticism I was sure I heard faint hope in her voice.

"I don't know that either, but I'll find out." I leaned across my makeshift desk so that in the small room I could speak more directly to her. "Don't settle for anything other than your dream, Crea. Don't do it. You'll regret it all your life. Let me dig around a little."

"Johanna, there's no way even you could change the way my life has gone." I appreciated the "even you."

"I don't claim to be able to change the past, Crea. That's out of my hands. Whatever's happened in your life before this moment, good or bad, is unchangeable. But promise you'll give me two weeks to look into your future. That's why the Anchorage hired me, after all. Just keep earning your keep here for two more weeks. Promise?"

"You've a smooth tongue, Johanna. You ought to be Irish," Crea grumbled, her brogue thick and musical. She met my gaze and frowned. "All right, then, two weeks, but you must tell Matron I'm staying only because you're making me. She's been good to me, and I don't want her to think I'm taking advantage of her kindness."

"I'll tell her."

She turned in the doorway on her way out. "I wish I could be like you, Johanna, but it's too late for that."

"You don't need to be like me, Crea. Why would you want to be? You're Crea O'Rourke, not Johanna Swan. Be proud of that." I thought her face grew sad for just a moment, but perhaps I was mistaken, for she responded to my advice with a disdainful *tsk* and left abruptly without another word.

The following Friday, Drew Gallagher showed up unannounced at the Anchorage. He rose when I entered the front room where he waited.

"You're looking awfully pleased with yourself," I observed, taking him in from his fair hair to his polished shoes.

"I am awfully pleased with myself. And good morning to you, too, Johanna."

"I ceased standing on ceremony with you some time ago. Didn't you notice?" He grinned.

"Yes, I recall." His gaze swept over me from head to foot. "I was anticipating another metamorphosis but your color is not very remarkable today."

I may have flushed slightly as I said, "Thank you for that sensitive observation. It's clear you haven't the slightest idea what it's like to work for a living. I've been here since daybreak this morning because one of the girls is due, and between teaching classes and giving medical check ups, I may look a little worn."

"I didn't mean your personal color," he replied mildly. "I was referring to your clothing. You must really think I'm a clod, Johanna."

"I don't think anything of the sort."

"That's right. I remember now. Not a clod, only selfish and immature."

"I took the immature back."

He laughed at that. "Yes, you did. I recall that now, too."

I looked down at my straight, unadorned tan skirt. "You're right, of course. This shade is unremarkable and probably unbecoming, but I haven't completely ignored your advice to try more dramatic colors. Tomorrow night I'm wearing apple red, a color I never thought I could get away with, and it looks wonderful."

He didn't acknowledge my comment, only asked, "Aren't you at all curious about that self-satisfied expression you so astutely observed on my face?"

"I'm very curious. Have you brought me welcome news?"

"Come with me and see. Can you take the time?"

I nodded, heading for the door. "The doctor just said the pains were a false alarm and my afternoon class can wait. Let me tell Hilda I'm leaving. Where are we going?"

"It's a surprise," he called after me. "Just tell Miss Cartwright we're on Anchorage business."

We traveled into the city, down several smaller streets, and into a heavily populated industrial district. Fritz, the Gallagher chauffeur, drove us as Drew and I sat side by side behind him.

"By the way, Johanna, Fritz is quite taken with Yvesta." Drew lowered his voice. "I wouldn't be surprised to see a wedding in their future."

"Yvesta already has a husband," I pointed out.

"I'm not sure that really matters to either of them, and from what you've told me, Fritz as an illegal father would be better for the girls than their real father, regardless of the law. Besides, Fritz could use the stabilizing influence of a wife in his life."

I couldn't help but hoot at that. "You're a fine one to be lecturing Fritz on the stabilizing influence of marriage."

"I believe my feelings are hurt."

"I doubt it. You enjoy your single status more than any man I've ever met. I wonder how you can talk to Fritz about matrimony with any kind of a straight face and clear conscience." When he didn't respond, I turned and surprised an expression on his face that almost did look hurt or if not hurt, at least pensive. I felt I must have spoken too flippantly and as the auto pulled to a halt in front of a square, red brick building, quickly moved the conversation onto safer ground. "Where's the surprise?" Drew didn't answer immediately but got out of the auto on his side and waited for Fritz to open my door so I could join Drew on the sidewalk.

"Right in front of you," he told me, smiling. I was glad to see that usual good-humored expression restored. The thoughtful, brooding look I'd surprised on Drew's face was out of character for him and made me unaccountably uncomfortable. The truth was that I wouldn't hurt his feelings for the world and was afraid I had.

I took a closer look at the four-story brick building directly before me. It sat surrounded by buildings similar in size and shape but set apart by its obvious and recent renovations. The front door was new and all the windows on the upper floors were clean and unbroken, apparently recently replaced, with an interesting clerestory line of windows added to the first floor as well. A gaily striped awning shaded the front entrance, which had been freshly painted to match the new sign that hung next to the door displaying the words *Cox's Fine Women's Garments* in elegant script.

Drew took my hand and led me forward, pulled open one of the front double doors, and stepped inside. A heavy wooden desk sat immediately at the threshold and behind it, as far as I could see into the dim exterior of the large, cavernous room, were rows of sewing machines, interspersed with several work tables.

"I'm installing electric lights. They're safer and brighter than anything else. In case of an emergency, I've made sure there are two emergency exits, one on each end of each floor. I'll have an elevator in by the end of June, but for now we'll have to take the stairs to the next floor." I followed him into a stairwell without comment, puzzled yet captivated by his enthusiasm, and we climbed to the second floor. That floor was divided into two large rooms on either side of a central hallway, everything freshly painted and cleaned. Natural light spilled into both rooms from the modern new windows I'd noticed from the outside.

"I don't understand what I'm looking at, Drew. Is this floor still for factory work?"

"This floor is for children."

I frowned at him. "You intend to have children working in this factory? That's unacceptable even if the law didn't prohibit it."

"Don't preach. You haven't seen everything yet. Are you up to two more floors?" He took the steps much more easily than I, once again reminding me that despite the impression Drew Gallagher gave of being a man spoiled by the finer things in life, he was in very good physical shape, not winded by the climb while I panted along behind him.

The top two floors were newly divided into small two and three-room apartments, each one with a tiny kitchen and one or two additional rooms. Communal bathrooms with indoor plumbing were conveniently located on each floor.

After taking a minute to catch my breath, I demanded, "All right, I give up. I thought I understood what you were showing me, but now I'm completely at a loss. I don't know if I'm in a factory or an apartment building."

"You're in both, Johanna." He grinned at my still uncomprehending expression and continued, "Have you heard of George Pullman and the town of Pullman he established?"

"'The World's Most Perfect Town,' you mean? I recall hearing that the papers dubbed it the noble experiment that failed."

"I don't know how noble it was, Johanna. I once read a description of it that classified the place as a "civilized relic of European serfdom." People not only had to live under the Pullman rules, they also had to pay the escalating Pullman rents to continue to live in the company town. Pullman deducted the rent from the workers' wages even when doing so cut their pay to the bone. Everything fell apart after the strike, and today the place lies in ruins."

"That was before my time, Drew, but I always thought George Pullman meant well."

"My point exactly. Pullman believed that poverty and uncongenial home surroundings did not encourage a content, productive work force, and I believe he was right." My face must have shown some kind of surprise because Drew smiled slightly and added, "I know it must seem incredible to you that I had moments of lucid intelligence as I bounced from university to university spending my inheritance on riotous living, but I actually recall being fascinated by a lecture about the Pullman experiment."

"I never meant to imply you weren't intelligent," I protested. Then, as I recalled all the changes he had made in the building, I turned away from him to look down the hallway again, finally making sense of the line of freshly painted apartment doors. "Is that what you've done here, Drew—created a great Gallagher experiment?" He remained quiet as I thought through everything I'd seen. "The second floor is for children, you said?" He nodded, still silent but closely watching my face, clearly looking for something specific in my expression. Finally I turned to face him. "It should work. Why wouldn't it? A self-contained city that goes up instead of out. Drew, I am so impressed with the idea. It's nothing short of brilliant but so simple, really, that I don't know why others haven't thought of it." I felt such a surge of excitement and admiration that for a moment I wanted to hug him. At the last minute I contented myself instead with a wide smile and instructed, "Now give me the details as you picture them."

He seemed to find whatever emotion he was looking for on my face and looked relieved, giving the distinct impression that my approval was necessary for success, a gratifying but unlikely idea because he must have been working on this plan before he ever met me.

"This is a place for women, Johanna, women like your Henrietta and your Betsy. I looked around for a company that was on the market to be sold and discovered Cox's literally right under my nose. Do you know the name?" I shook my head. "Cox's was once a very well-known manufacturer of women's night dresses, undergarments, and lingerie. I can remember my mother receiving the boxes engraved with the white signature name of Cox, so it was no second-rate company. Then the recession of the late nineties hit—the same crash that caused the demise of the city of Pullman—and Cox's never recovered. It limped along for the last fifteen years or so until Mr. Cox,

Senior, died, and Mr. Cox, Junior, was finally able to sell the place. Douglas started the acquisition before he left and when I found the papers of ownership on his desk, everything fell into place."

"You had the idea for a communal work place altruistically and out of the blue?" I asked with some skepticism. My question had the unusual reaction of causing the unflappable Drew Gallagher to color faintly, a phenomenon as curious as it was rare.

"Not exactly," he answered without explanation and then hurried on to say, "The women can work on the first floor and live in these apartments on the top floors. The second floor is reserved for childcare. Nothing's free, Johanna. This isn't charity, but I'll pay a fair wage and they can pay the rent and the cost of childcare out of that. I think there should be some kind of renters committee to oversee the apartments and collect the rents, and we'll need to find someone who can supervise the children."

Mrs. McElhanie, I thought instantly but didn't want to interrupt Drew's explanation.

"We'll need good security for the place, and I know there are other details to work out, but that's where you come in. Social work is your field, not mine. What do you think?"

I understood that for whatever reason Drew wanted my approval and I was eager to give it. He'd come up with an innovative idea and acted on it, and he deserved more approval than just mine.

"I think it's brilliant. Simply brilliant. To offer poor women a safe living and working environment for both them and their children reflects progress at its finest. As the business owner, you'll have a content, secure workforce that will be able to devote all their energies to work because they won't have to worry about their children, their home, or their livelihood. I don't know what to say, Drew. I am truly impressed." Watching him, I knew I'd said the right thing, and we talked about the Cox Experiment—as we quickly came to call it—all the way back down the four flights of stairs.

Back in the auto, Drew said, "I need another month, Johanna. Can you hold on at the Anchorage that long?"

"We'll have to somehow, but we're so crowded we've had to set up beds in the hallway. Still, Ruthie's going back to her family and Elena's going back to Greece so that will free up some space." After a pause, I asked, "Whatever made you do this, Drew?"

He looked at me. "You're surprised."

"Well, yes, I am. By your own admission, you don't have much interest in either commerce or the plight of poor women. Now suddenly you've become an entrepreneur of both."

With a wry twist to his mouth, he answered, "I like to be different, Johanna, and I sometimes get an unnatural pleasure out of acting in ways that run against the norm. My reaction to Mrs. Trout's speech is one example of that quirk. I often do the unexpected simply for effect."

"Somehow I don't think that's what the Cox Experiment is all about, but I could be wrong."

He agreed easily. "I'm glad you realize that because yes, Johanna, when it comes to figuring me out, you could be very wrong about me and my motives." Smiling, I settled back in my seat to enjoy the remainder of the ride.

"With all due respect, Drew, your motives don't concern me one way or the other as long as I get what I want."

He gave me an amused look. "Perhaps they should."

"Why?"

"Maybe my motives are the exact opposite of noble and altruistic. Maybe I don't give a damn about poor women. Maybe I simply want something, the same as you." He waited for a question I was not about to ask and when I remained quiet, settled back in his seat, equally quiet. After a while, ignoring that I had refused his challenge to question his motives, Drew continued to make plans with business-like composure. "I can employ eighty women to start with. How many can the Anchorage supply?"

"Twenty easily in the next four months but I doubt eighty."

"Then if I put an employment ad in the local papers, are you willing to hire the workforce? I'm not inclined to wait four months to get started. Once the word is out, my guess is women will come in droves, and I've done my part by supplying the building and the work. I have no intention of sitting through meetings with hundreds of women, some of whom will probably not even speak English. That would be your field."

"Yes, it would be and I can do that. I'll meet the applicants at Cox's and make the selection. Just let me know what day and time. How many women do you think can live on site?" The trip back to the Anchorage passed quickly as we discussed the details, and I was surprised when Fritz pulled to the curb. I wanted somehow to let Drew know how grateful I was, but when I tried to tell him, he brushed me off, seemingly tired of the topic.

When he came around to stand next to me on the sidewalk, I said, "I can tell you don't want me to say any more about the Cox Experiment, Drew, so I'll only repeat that it's a brilliant idea and I'm pleased to be a part of it."

He shrugged, then asked abruptly, "What's the occasion for wearing red?"

I stared at him. "I beg your pardon."

"You said you were wearing apple red tomorrow night, and I wondered what happy occasion prompted that selection. You brought it up," he added defensively; my expression must have shown a certain incredulity at his question.

"I brought it up hours ago," I pointed out, "but you're right, it is a happy occasion. My cousin Jennie turns nineteen tomorrow, and her parents are hosting a gala reception for family and friends in her honor."

"Your Mr. Goldwyn will probably attend."

"Allen? Yes, I invited him and he is coming. He's been my friend since college and has become a friend of the family as well. Are you angling for an invitation?"

"If I were, would I get one?"

"Well, I—"

"Never mind," he said, grinning, "I can see you're trying to figure out a way to say no graciously so I'll spare you the effort. I'll be out of town for the weekend and couldn't attend even if your cousin Jennie and I were best friends."

"I'm not sure Aunt Kitty would allow you to get near Jennie. She has her daughter's future all mapped out, and I'd be surprised if it would include you. You have a fortune, of course, but Aunt Kitty's standards are very high."

"Ouch. You've done it again, Miss Swan. It's a wonder I have any self-confidence left at all after spending time with you. Fortunately, the friend with whom I'm sharing the weekend is very good for my ego." He hopped in the back of the auto without another word and it pulled away, the beautiful coupe as smooth and sleek as its owner.

Trudging up the walk, I was dismayed to find that the idea of Drew Gallagher spending the weekend with a friend, undoubtedly a woman friend, probably that brunette with the crimson mouth, made me quite cranky.

Eulalie met me at the door. "I thought you were the doctor, Johanna. There's a baby coming after all, and I'm glad you're here."

I hurried upstairs to help with the delivery, and it wasn't

until the train ride home later that afternoon that I thought of Drew Gallagher again. I had to admit I found him attractive but unpredictable and contradictory, too, a man who, with a glance or a smile or a tone, knew how to make a woman feel she was the center of his world. I tried to compare him with Allen Goldwyn but couldn't bring the two men side by side in my mind. Allen's quiet creativity had appealed to me from the start, and I always felt safe and comfortable with him. I seldom felt comfortable and never exactly safe with Drew Gallagher, but with my unfortunate contrariness I wished Drew were coming to Jennie's party. His presence would brighten the occasion in a way Allen's never could. The realization should have made me feel guiltily disloyal to my old friend, but I was conscious only of a vague regret without a hint of guilt anywhere.

Levi drove Grandmother and me to Jennie's party the next evening. Grandmother still looked unnaturally pale and I tried to insist she stay home, but she would never consider missing Jennie's birthday. Still, when I came to her side as we ascended the steps, I gently tucked her hand under my arm and instead of protesting, she gave me a grateful look and leaned against me for a brief moment. Considering her usual independence, that small gesture was enough to increase my concern.

"We only have to stay a little while," I murmured, "and not at all if you're feeling unwell."

"Thank you, Johanna. I'll let you know if I need your nursing services." A tart response as usual, but I detected an unexpected vulnerability in her voice that made me give her a quick look. By then a maid had opened the front door and Aunt Kitty descended on us in all her striped-satin glory, a woman pleased with her surroundings and anticipating the evening with enormous satisfaction.

After ritualistic cheek kisses, Aunt Kitty turned to Peter, who stood in the doorway of the study.

"Peter, your grandmother's here." As an afterthought, she added, "And Johanna." My cousin came forward and planted heartier kisses on both Grandmother and me as his mother continued, "I need to check with the kitchen, dear. Help Gertrude and Johanna find their way to Jennie and then to a comfortable table." To us she added, "We're eating out on the lawn. Wait until you see how lovely it is. The evening and the lake are both perfect. And Jennie, too, of course, even if I am her mother."

Aunt Kitty was in high color, very lady-of-the-manor, and very happy. She was never more pleased with her life than when she had the opportunity to display her beautiful lakeshore home and her handsome family. The combination of the two that evening brought her to euphoria. Peter came to stand between Grandmother and me so we could each take an arm.

"Mother's been like this for days: beside herself with anticipation." Turning to Grandmother, he asked, "Would you like to sit outside or in, Grandmother? You don't have to see the lawn right now if you'd rather not. I'm pretty sure it's not going anywhere." Peter was his typical pleasant, thoughtful self, more like his father every day.

We ended up outside on the lawn, which, as Aunt Kitty promised, was beautifully landscaped and set with small canopied tables. Large candles under crystal globes sat on marble pedestals and dotted the lawn everywhere, their flames flickering in the warm, dusk air. With the lake as a darkening backdrop and the opposite western sky in its last stages of indigo and deep rose, the scene seemed magical. After Peter left to find refreshments, I heard Jennie before I saw her. She was surrounded by a small cluster of young men, all standing under a gaslight on the terrace, and her laughter carried clearly.

"I don't want to be followed anywhere, thank you, so please don't. I see my grandmother and my cousin Johanna and I must go say hello." An undecipherable low male voice responded and Jennie laughed. "What nonsense, Frank! Have you been dipping into the punch already?" She detached herself from the huddle of admirers and walked in our direction, her progress interrupted periodically by other people on the lawn who stopped her to extend greetings. Jennie was always gracious and courteous, but lately I'd detected a noticeable edge to her manners, an impatience with the demands of polite society, and a recognition that the necessity for prescribed propriety was slightly ridiculous. But perhaps I attributed those feelings to Jennie only because my own attitudes often reflected the same.

My cousin leaned down to kiss Grandmother.

"You look lovely, Jennie," Grandmother told her and put a hand to Jennie's cheek, an unusually tender gesture.

Jennie was touched by both the action and the words and replied with warmth and obvious sincerity, "Thank you, Grandmother." She sat down with us at the small table.

"You look wonderful, Jen," I agreed. " Not too much the ingénue at all."

Jennie, dressed in pale peach chiffon and a long string of pearls doubled around her neck, grinned and with her usual generosity said, "I thought my dress was becoming until I saw yours, Johanna. That red puts every other woman here to shame. It's fabulous on you. Have I ever seen you wear that color before?"

"I've turned over a new fashion leaf. The pastels are gone—the dramatic is in. Next to you, though, I'm still the plain cousin. I'd resent anyone else, Jennie, but because it's you, I don't mind. You're a beauty."

She was, too. Her striking hair, golden but interwoven with contrasting strands of rich, burnished chocolate brown, was piled onto her head in loose, soft curls, and her flawless skin seemed to reflect the creamy peach of her dress in a muted glow. With sparkling eyes, an adorable nose, and a perfect bow of a mouth, it was no wonder she'd been surrounded by a throng of admirers. Like moths to a flame, and who could blame them?

Jennie turned toward the terrace doors. "There's your friend Allen, Johanna. He looks lost, poor man." She stood up and crossed the lawn in a moment, took Allen's arm, looked up into his face, and said something that made him smile. Then she drew him over to us.

"There you are, Mr. Goldwyn. I've found you a familiar face. Grandmother, are you up to a walk inside? Father was asking about you." Just like that, Allen and I were sitting companionably alone. I had to admire Jennie's style.

"I wondered if you'd come," I told him. "Was it the lure of the buffet again?"

Allen looked briefly puzzled. "Buffet?" Then he remembered my earlier welcome home party and smiled. "Food," he said, "had nothing to do with it."

"What then?"

"The company," he answered, adding, "You look very nice tonight, Johanna. Is there something different about you?" I had the quick, uncharitable thought that Drew Gallagher would have noticed the dress and the color right away.

Then, because I was ashamed of myself, I answered, "No. It must be the candlelight," and quickly shifted the conversation to Allen's work.

The evening passed pleasantly, despite the absence of the promised dance band. Because the lakeside cooled quickly once the sun set, the guests on the lawn slowly drifted inside where conversation continued to swirl through all the rooms. I lost track of Grandmother and Allen and wandered into a room where Jennie was seated at the piano, surrounded again by a small crowd of adoring young men. Carl Milford sat very close to her on the piano bench, his shoulder against hers, both of them trying to read from the same sheet of music and laughing at the result. Jennie was very gay and flirtatious, careful not to favor any one young man over another, turning to speak to someone behind her before leaning to whisper in Carl's ear. She was a social natural, had always been, regardless of her recent veiled disdain for the proprieties.

Coming up beside me, Peter commented, "What do you think, Johanna? Can you see my sister fitting in with the Milfords of Boston?"

"They'd be fortunate to have her." I watched the laughing scene at the piano. "Is he trustworthy with Jennie, Peter? Somehow I don't have a lot of confidence in Carl Milford's honorable intentions. But he's your friend and you know him better than I."

"Not really my friend, Johanna. Mother asked me to make his acquaintance and if the opportunity presented itself, to invite him home sometime, and I didn't have the energy to question or protest. Like the sheep I am, I simply did what I was asked. I don't think he's a bad sort. Spoiled, of course, with too much of a temper, but if you're worried about Jennie, don't be. She can handle herself quite ably. Jennie would only be seduced if she wanted to be."

I turned to look at Peter with surprise. "Do you really believe that to be true?"

"I know that to be true. You still see my sister through the lens of childhood, but Jennie's all grown up and when she chooses, she has a stronger will than either of us. No one can make Jennie do something she doesn't want to do. No one. I love my sister but she scares me a little." From the expression on his face, Peter didn't appear to be joking.

I wanted to continue the conversation but Carl Milford

began playing "Happy Birthday" on the piano, and everyone in the room joined in the tune. When Carl finished playing, he turned to Jennie for her reaction and she surprised everyone, including Carl, by leaning forward and kissing him on the mouth. Definitely not the ingénue any longer, I thought, and watched Aunt Kitty scurry from the doorway with offers of birthday cake, more interested in distracting than serving her guests just then. Peter moved easily toward the door, following his mother's lead, and as people began to exit toward the display of cake in the dining room, I was conscious of a small tableau that remained around the piano: Carl Milford with his face very close to Jennie's, holding her gaze with his dark, provocative eyes. Sandy-haired Frank Mulholland to Jennie's side, his eyes wistfully fixed on Jennie's face, apparently surprised by the kiss and clearly wishing he'd been the one next to her on the piano bench, Jennie herself no longer laughing, meeting Milford's look head on and unafraid, something daring and dangerous in her sparkle. And of all people, Allen Goldwyn standing partly in shadows against the far wall, as intent on the little scene as I.

Aunt Kitty came to the door and called Jennie's name—a maternal scolding put on hold but sure to take place later, I thought, recognizing the subtle inflection of her tone—and the picture dissolved. Jennie slid off the bench and took Frank's arm, leading him out of the room. Carl Milford followed them, smiling slightly beneath his dark mustache, and after him Allen with his hands in his pockets and a distant expression on his face, a man puzzling out the answer to a mystery. I stood there alone, watched the little parade exit, and knew that I had just seen something important—though not sure what or why.

Later in the evening as Jennie opened an embarrassingly tall stack of presents, I caught a glimpse of Grandmother across the room. The expression on her face alarmed me. She appeared bewildered, gazing around the room with what appeared to be confusion and uncertainty. Jennie made a laughing comment about the box she was trying unsuccessfully to open and the guests laughed with her. I stood, anxious to get across the room to Grandmother, certain that something was wrong. Grandmother, agitated, stood, too, but only for a moment before she collapsed in an inelegant heap on the floor, her hand reaching for her heart and her mouth contorted, gasping for breath.

I pushed people rudely to the side as I crossed the spacious room. By the time I reached Grandmother's side, those standing closest to her realized what had happened and were calling for Uncle Hal. He came quickly to kneel next to me as I loosened Grandmother's collar and felt for a pulse at the base of her throat.

"Johanna?" He looked at me helplessly.

"Call the doctor immediately. She has a pulse but it's light and fluttery. Move everyone out of the room, and ask Peter to help me lift her onto the loveseat." Uncle Hal left quickly and turning to the silent, staring people who crowded around us, I ordered curtly, "We need privacy and quiet." Aunt Kitty stood among the staring guests, all of them shocked into quiet immobility, and it was Jennie who took over, calmly herded people out of the room, assured them everything would be all right, thanked them for their concern and their presence that evening, and tactfully suggested it was time for the party to end. Peter and I resettled Grandmother's figure, more frail than I remembered it or thought it should be, on the couch.

"Bring me a cloth and a basin of cool water, Peter. There's nothing to be done for her except make her comfortable until the doctor arrives." Grandmother's breathing was shallow but regular so that I did not fear her imminent death. From the obvious sag of the right side of her mouth and the way her right arm hung limp and unresponsive, I was almost certain she'd had a paralyzing stroke.

Later, the doctor's brief examination confirmed my fears. "I can't as yet tell the extent of the damage," he said. "Only time will tell that. She'll need bed rest and care to get her strength back, and then we'll see what can be done."

Aunt Kitty, back to her usual, managing self, moved toward the door. "I'll get a room ready. Of course she'll stay with us."

Grandmother's left hand, resting in mine, tightened. I looked quickly at her face to find her eyes open, staring at me, sending a mute but unmistakable message.

"No," I stated firmly. "She wants to go home. She wants to be in her own bed in her own house. Thank you, Aunt Kitty, but call Levi and tell him to come for us immediately. Have him tell May to get Grandmother's room ready for her."

Aunt Kitty protested, as did Uncle Hal, although less stridently, but I would not be deterred. After Aunt Kitty scolded me for being stubborn, ungrateful, and uncaring, she capitulated and left to make the call, and I looked down at Grandmother, who still watched me steadily. Another clear but unspoken message passed between us before she closed her eyes and remained peacefully unconscious the entire trip back home to Hill Street.

No one is so accursed by fate,
No one so utterly desolate,
But some heart, though unknown,
Responds unto his own.
Responds, - as if with unseen wings,
An angel touched its quivering strings;
And whispers, in its song,
"Where hast thou stayed so long?"

Chapter Eight

When Grandmother finally awoke, she lay partially paralyzed, unable to move the right side of her body. In
addition, any words she tried to speak came out unintelligible
and jumbled. I might have thought her mental capacity impaired except for the steady, intelligent look I detected in her
eyes and hoped it was not simply wishful thinking on my part.
Initially, we used two ways to communicate. I would ask yes
and no questions and she would blink either once or twice, depending on the answer. If I sat next to her, she would use her
left hand to squeeze my hand in answer using the same code.
That was how I knew she could hear and understand what was
happening around her. The stroke had impaired her ability to
communicate orally and to move, but the grandmother I knew
and loved still lay alert within that inactive body.

The doctor told us if there were recovery, it would take
time. Later, sitting next to Grandmother's bed, I said scornfully,
"The fact that he said if there's a recovery shows he certainly
doesn't know you very well. Or me either for that matter." I

leaned down to kiss her lightly on the forehead. "I know this is difficult for you, but I'll be right next to you all the while. You know that, don't you?" Two blinks for yes before she closed her eyes to sleep.

Monday evening, Mayville directed me roughly, "You go get some sleep, Johanna. I'll sit with her. There's cards on the hall table of people who've been by and two telephone messages for you. And your Uncle Hal said he'd stop over this evening. Go on now. You're not the only one who cares about her, you know."

I slept through until Tuesday morning without interruption, apologized profusely to May, and gathered up the messages that waited for me. Allen Goldwyn sent flowers accompanied by a card asking about Grandmother's health, and Hilda Cartwright sent a note telling me not to worry about a thing at the Anchorage. Drew Gallagher, apparently oblivious to the high drama playing out on Hill Street, notified me that the employment announcement would go into the paper this week and asked if I could be ready next Monday to interview prospective workers.

For just a moment I felt crushed and overwhelmed, but after taking a deep breath, I went upstairs to sit with Grandmother. Her color was better and while still unable to speak clearly, her words seemed more coherent and sensible.

"I've decided to quit my work at the Anchorage, Grandmother. I want to be here with you. The doctor says your recovery is predicated on healthy interactions, daily exercise, mental stimulation, and good nutrition. I can give you all of that, and I want to." A pause, then one deliberate blink. "What do you mean no? I'm a nurse, remember? After you're better, I'll go back to the Anchorage or I'll find something equally as challenging. Right now I want to be here with you." She blinked once again. Puzzled and a little frustrated, I asked,

"Do you want Mayville to care for you?" Another single blink. We stared at each other until I finally frowned. "I haven't the slightest idea what you want me to do. You can be very difficult you know." The left side of her mouth gave a slight twitch and then she blinked. Twice.

I don't know where the idea came from, only that I awoke with it early Wednesday morning and wondered why it had taken me so long to think of it. When Mayville came to sit with Grandmother, I dressed to go out.

"I'll be at the Anchorage this afternoon," I explained to May and stepped outside into a hot July day, the first step I'd taken outdoors since last Saturday. I had planned to have Levi drive me, but the clear afternoon was so pleasant, I decided against it and walked briskly to the elevated station, enjoying the pleasure of being out and alive.

Hilda met me as I entered the Anchorage. "Johanna, I was so sorry to hear of your grandmother's illness! How is she?"

"Better, but not good yet, if that makes any sense. What have I missed here?"

"Nothing we couldn't handle, but I admit you've spoiled all of us. I know there was a time you weren't with us, but I can't remember how we managed." She paused. "Have you come to say good-bye?"

"No, I've come to talk to Crea."

Crea, who was coming down the stairs as I spoke, said, "And here I am. We've all missed you, Johanna, and we're not the only ones. Your Mr. Gallagher came by yesterday to speak to you and when I told him I hadn't seen or heard from you in days, he seemed very disappointed. More like a beau than a business associate." Her mischievous expression was teasing and welcoming. I thought she really had missed me.

"I'm sure Drew Gallagher has been called many things by many people, but I can't imagine that beau is one of them. I know why he was here, though, and that's why I need to talk to you." Crea followed me down the hall into my little office. "I have a proposition for you, Crea." She looked curious but wary. "You need a job and I need help caring for my grandmother. You need a place to live and I have room to spare. You want an education and I have contacts at the Chicago Teachers College. There. Doesn't it seem made to order?"

"What in the world are you talking about, Johanna?"

"My grandmother has had a stroke and she needs care to get better. I'm well suited and perfectly willing to be the one to give her that care, but for some reason she doesn't want it from me. That's what made me think of you. She and I live in a house that's much too big for two women. I was hoping you'd be willing to move in with us and be a companion for my grandmother, help her with her meals, make her do her exercises, read to her, keep her active and stimulated. The doctor says that with that kind of attention, she might possibly regain her strength and faculties. If you're agreeable to the idea, I could still work at the Anchorage without worrying about her. In exchange, I offer room and board and a reasonable stipend, but best of all, every month I'll put money into an education fund for you. When Grandmother's better, I'll arrange for you to start at the north side Teachers College. The rest will be up to you, Crea, and will depend on how hard you're willing to work to see your dream come true. Only you can make that happen, but I'm willing to help you get started. What do you say? Will you make the deal? Will you take the chance?"

Crea O'Rourke, with her green eyes unwavering on my face, never hesitated a second and didn't miss a beat. With one firm, clear word, she answered, "Yes."

I took Crea home to meet Grandmother the next day, which happened to be—appropriately for Crea, anyway—Independence Day. I felt more nervous than I cared to admit.

Even disabled, my grandmother remained a woman of strong opinion and excessive independence and there was always the possibility that she would refuse the offer of Crea's help. But when Crea said hello and sat down next to Grandmother's bed, something intangible passed between the two women, an unspoken message from eye to eye, and I knew the arrangement would work.

Mayville was another story, however. She was jealous about the house and even more jealous in her care of Grandmother.

"We don't know anything about her," Mayville snapped, "and you want to leave her alone in the house. Who knows what she'll get up to when no one's around. The Irish always have plenty of pocket space."

"Don't be rude and unkind," I retorted. "I'll vouch for Crea personally. Honestly, Mayville, sometimes I don't know what to make of you. Do you actually think I'd bring someone who couldn't be trusted into this house?"

"No one can care for Mrs. McIntyre like I can. I should be the one up there."

"You can't be two places at once unless you're the Divinity. If you think I'm going to make the meals while you're tending to Grandmother, you're deluded. You've tasted my cooking so I shouldn't have to explain further. You have plenty to keep yourself occupied, Mayville, and what good would it do any of us for you to exhaust yourself running up and down stairs a hundred times a day?"

By the expression on her face, it was clear she remained unconvinced, and I gave up all argument. May was stubborn, but she'd come around once she had time to think through my words. Years ago she didn't accept me immediately either and I had been family. Crea would undoubtedly take even longer.

When I shared the situation with Crea, she shrugged. "Mayville's attitude doesn't bother me, Johanna. I've experienced my share of hostility before and I've survived. Just so you know you can trust me."

"I don't have a concern about that," I answered sincerely. "I'm just delighted we can be of mutual assistance."

"You like working at the Anchorage that much?"

"Not just the Anchorage," I explained, "though that's part of it. I like the idea of making a difference in people's lives. I'm excited about the Cox Experiment that Drew Gallagher is willing to fund. I want to be a part of enlightened progress."

"Do you really believe there's such a thing as progress?" Her question made me look at her with surprise and curiosity.

"I do. Medical improvements, scientific discoveries, and increased social tolerance are happening all around us. It's an exciting time to live." At her skeptical expression I added, "But I can see you don't agree."

Her answer sounded uncannily like Allen's comments the night of my homecoming party: "People don't change, Johanna, so what good is all that so-called progress? People don't change on the inside and that's the only place progress really matters. To me, the more times change, the more they stay the same." Without giving me a chance to answer, she went on, "I'll take the train home tonight and start here in the morning."

"Levi can come for you," I volunteered. "You shouldn't have to lug all your belongings on the train."

Crea gave a small, wry smile. "All my belongings fit into one duffel, Johanna. That won't be a problem."

"I'm sorry. I didn't think."

She must have seen that I was annoyed with myself because she smiled and remarked, "I've noticed that about you a time or two, but that's when I find you the most likable. Too much thinking spoils your effect." Her comment made me laugh.

"I'm not sure how to take that, so I'll just let it lie. At least let Levi drive you back to the Anchorage this afternoon. It's getting late, and I'd feel better knowing you got there safe and sound."

After she left, I went upstairs to sit with Grandmother for a while. Seeing her white-haired and frail lying in the big bed caused my heart to give a lurch, and I was beset with an emotion that I at first identified as pity. Gertrude McIntyre was so independent a woman, so strong and so private, that having her helpless and dependent seemed inherently wrong. The more I sat there with her, however, the more I understood it wasn't pity I felt. Quietly holding her hand in mine as she slept, examining her aging, elegant face and the long braid of white hair that fell over her shoulder, I realized how dearly I loved her.

"I've lost too many people," I said quietly. "I'm not ready to lose you, too. Not now. I don't know why you didn't want me to care for you, but I'm confident Crea will do as well as I. She doesn't talk about it, but she's had some kind of grief in her life that's made her strong and sensitive to other people's pain. I like her. I hope you will, too. I wouldn't do anything to endanger you, Grandmother, and I hope I'm doing the right thing and what you want me to do."

I wondered if Grandmother heard me because she stirred in her sleep, and I thought she might awaken. She didn't, but— my imagination perhaps—I believe the hand resting in mine briefly pressed my fingers. In lieu of anything more definite, I accepted the feather-light gesture as her agreement and approval.

Once Crea arrived the next morning and was introduced to the geography of the house, I resisted the temptation to run interference between her and Mayville and left to spend the afternoon at the Anchorage. With any luck at all, the house would still be standing when I returned despite the presence of two strong-willed women, three if you included Grandmother, who should not be discounted simply because of a physical incapacity.

I came up to the front walk of the Anchorage at exactly the same time Drew Gallagher pulled up to the curb in his motorcar. He drove himself and I waited there until he turned off the motor and came around the auto to stand beside me.

"I was sorry to hear of your Grandmother's illness, Johanna," he said without introduction. "How is she?"

"Better than she was. Thank you for asking. She had a stroke that left her partially paralyzed, but I believe with time and attention she'll regain her strength."

"That's hopeful."

"Yes, it is. Has my situation thrown the Cox Experiment completely off schedule? I can still be available Monday."

"Are you sure?" He studied my face with disconcerting seriousness. "You don't look your usual high-spirited self."

"I admit it's been a difficult week, but you'll have to trust that I know my limitations."

"I believe you, but that's not quite the same as trusting you."

"You don't trust me? I'm shocked."

He laughed and fell into step beside me as I started up the walk.

"Why on earth would that shock you when you've told me on numerous occasions that you're only interested in what you can get from me?"

I stopped abruptly. "I never said that. Exactly."

"Johanna, has the past stressful week impaired your memory? Shall I quote chapter and verse? You've let me know more than once that you don't care a damn about me as long as you get what you want."

"I may have implied that—"

We stepped into the front hall, Drew following closely

enough behind me that I could hear his low laugh. "'Implied' suggests some degree of subtlety, Johanna, which you must agree is not your strong suit." I turned to face him and he held up a hand. "There's no use looking at me like that. I have a right to my own opinion."

"Even if it is wrong," I muttered, making him laugh again.

"Obviously my opinion must be wrong if it differs from yours, but even if it is wrong, it's still my opinion. I'll just hang on to it for a while. Now where can we talk about Monday's plans?" There wasn't much to talk about because he had it all arranged: employment advertisements posted, sewing machines and work stations in place, electricity and water hooked up, even a telephone line on the second floor. "By the time we have a work force in place, the apartments and the second floor will be plainly furnished. Nothing fancy, you understand, just the basics."

"Your basics will be more than many of these women have ever seen, Drew. None of us is asking for luxury."

"Luxury would offend your Puritan conscience, Johanna, so I knew better."

"I wish I had such a conscience," I confessed somewhat ruefully. "The truth is I've come to enjoy many of the finer things in life and would hate to be without them. My father was raised on the Kansas prairie and often spoke about his pioneer parents and their struggles to make a home and a life. I'm afraid I'm not made of the same stuff as my forebears, too much a city girl and too fond of the bright lights."

"Maybe you're just too hard on yourself."

I shrugged, not wanting to pursue the topic. Truth was, I believed that in some indeterminate way my current situation would be a disappointment to my parents had they lived. My father came from humble roots and worked a long line of menial jobs to pay his way through school. My mother left her big house and well-to-do family behind to live in a two-room shack in a country that eventually killed her, and she did it all cheerfully without complaint. There was none of that willing self-sacrifice in me and I knew it. I liked going home to a meal ready on the table, to a warm, safe bed, to a well-run house where clean, freshly-pressed clothes appeared in my closet and where the pantry was stocked without any effort on my part. I liked my independence and knew it was predicated on an inheritance I had not earned and did not deserve. What little I did for others was a small contribution. I had been given more than I could ever repay.

Drew said my name, calling me back to the conversation. "Where were you just now?"

"Lost in humble and healthy introspection."

"I wouldn't have said you were the type for self-abasement."

"Don't imagine you know me after so short an acquaintance," I lectured sternly. "Even a man as practiced as you in the ways of women is capable of being surprised."

"I couldn't agree more. Part of your appeal is your ability to surprise me. If you didn't usually combine it with either an insult or a lecture, I'd find the quality completely charming." Then he effortlessly brought the conversation back to the employment needs of Cox's Fine Women's Garments and we concluded our plans for Monday morning.

Over the weekend a steady stream of traffic kept Mayville busy at the Hill Street front door. Grandmother's friends dropped off greetings and the family came daily to check on her progress. Allen Goldwyn stopped by Saturday afternoon and as we sat comfortably in the front room talking, Uncle Hal, Aunt Kitty, and Jennie arrived. My uncle went upstairs immediately without asking, his own mother and the house of his childhood, after all, but it had taken only one look from

Grandmother's eyes when I mentioned Aunt Kitty to let me know that my aunt was not to enjoy the same freedom of movement as her husband. I headed her and Jennie off at the front door and herded them into the room where Allen still waited.

Jennie greeted him warmly. "Mr. Goldwyn, how pleasant to see you again! I was charmed by your kind remembrance to me on my birthday. The vase holds an honored place on my bureau. Even Mother commented on its graceful form, didn't you, Mother?"

My aunt raised both brows in frosty acknowledgment of Allen's presence and sniffed out a response, Aunt Kitty at her most condescending for some reason and taking it out on poor Allen. I gave her a quizzical look and then glanced at Jennie, who shrugged and continued to make conversation, encouraging Allen to talk about his job and his architectural designs. After a while, however, my aunt's disapproving posture could no longer be ignored and Allen said a polite farewell.

I walked him to the front door. "I'm sorry, Allen. I don't know what gets into Aunt Kitty sometimes. She doesn't mean it personally and she doesn't intend to be rude."

"Johanna, you—" Allen began and then stopped midsentence, changing his mind about whatever he'd planned to say. Looking into the hall mirror, he took longer than usual to put on his hat before he continued, "I'm sure she doesn't. Give Mrs. McIntyre my regards, Johanna, and if there's anything I can do for you, don't hesitate to ask."

Without thinking, I gave him a quick kiss on the cheek. "Thank you, Allen. You're a good friend."

"Not as good as you deserve." His tone was hard to decipher, sad and somehow weary so that I felt vaguely alarmed.

"Is something wrong, Allen?"

"Everything's fine," he answered, but I didn't believe him.

Before I could question him further, he opened the door and walked hurriedly down the front steps. I'd never known Allen to be moody or enigmatic, and this change in his usually pleasant demeanor troubled me.

When I returned to the front room, Aunt Kitty asked sternly, "Who is this young woman you've brought into the house, Johanna? I met her yesterday afternoon."

"Do you mean Crea O'Rourke? She's helping to care for Grandmother and she does a wonderful job." I answered too defensively, despite my intention to the contrary.

"Irish and from that place, I presume."

"If by 'that place' you mean the Anchorage, then yes."

Aunt Kitty fixed a hard stare at my face. "So there's no telling what kind of woman she is, and yet you leave her alone in the house? God only knows what she does while you're away. Really, Johanna, have you no sense at all? If you and Gertrude aren't murdered in your beds, you're still risking all the valuables in the house." At those words, I felt a hot flush start at the base of my throat and creep inexorably into my cheeks.

"I have complete confidence in Crea O'Rourke. I've seen her in difficult situations and know her to be compassionate and entirely trustworthy."

"She's Irish, Johanna," Aunt Kitty stated, considering that the words must explain everything.

"She may be Irish, but at least she's not a condescending and insufferable snob. I'll take the Irish anytime compared to that." Color rose in my aunt's face, too.

"Watch your tongue, young lady. Your disrespect proves what I've said for years, that you have been hopelessly and unfortunately spoiled. Despite my advice to the contrary, Gertrude has indulged your every whim regardless of how ridiculous, but now you are going too far. I can't walk into this house without running into people who don't belong here. If it's not the Irish, it's the Jews."

I looked at her blankly. "What?"

Jennie, watching the exchange silently, murmured, "I think she means Mr. Goldwyn, Johanna."

"A snob and a bigot, Aunt Kitty?" I flared, rising. "What nonsense you talk! Has anyone told you it's 1912?"

"Some things don't change," she responded, as angry as I.

Later, I considered the irony of my aunt's comment and how surprised she would have been to be in such complete agreement with both Crea and Allen on the subject. At the moment, however, I had to take a deep breath and mentally count to three before I could reply quietly, "Sadly, you're right. Some things don't change even though they should have years ago. Now if you'll excuse me, I'm going to look in on Grandmother. I'm sure you can see yourselves out."

My heart beat so hard I could feel it thumping against my chest. If I didn't distance myself from my aunt, I'd get into a screaming argument that would accomplish nothing. I was usually good at keeping my temper, but this time Aunt Kitty had pushed me right up to the edge. Uncle Hal met me on the stairs as I headed up to Grandmother's room.

He took a quick look at my face and asked, "With whom have you been arguing, Johanna? It's all over your face." When I didn't answer, he sighed. "Kitty, I suppose. She means well, Johanna, and she's as concerned about Mother as I am."

"Don't tell me you think Crea is going to murder us in our beds, Uncle Hal."

"Kitty didn't say that."

"Yes, she did."

We stood on the steps facing each other.

"I like Crea, Johanna. I've watched her with Mother and found her patient and persistent. Mother seems to like her, too."

"Even with her being Irish and all?" I asked sarcastically.

Uncle Hal grimaced. "Kitty comes from a different background and time than you, Johanna. You have so much compassion and understanding for other people, can't you spare any for your own aunt?" He took a look at my stubbornly set face and sighed. "Apparently not, at least not right now. Good-bye, Johanna. If you need anything, call." He started down the stairs and I continued my progress up, still too annoyed with my aunt to be able to entertain one charitable thought about her.

Crea, sitting next to Grandmother's bed, looked up as I entered the room.

"Your face looks like a thundercloud, Johanna. Who have you been quarreling with?" Grandmother slept calmly, her face peaceful and elegant in repose.

"My aunt," I answered in a low voice.

"Ah." She paused. "Was she stating her disapproval of me?"

"Yes. How did you know?"

"Your aunt is easily read, Johanna. She made it very clear that she doesn't approve of my being here, but I wasn't sure if it was because I'm Irish or because I came from the Anchorage."

"Both."

Crea nodded. "She has a right to her own opinion." Her words reminded me of my recent conversation with Drew Gallagher.

"Even if it's wrong?"

Crea laughed. "Yes, even if it's wrong." Then we talked about how Grandmother's morning had gone, how she was handling her prescribed exercises, and whether she was able to eat properly, topics that allowed me to regain my nurse's objectivity and usual equilibrium.

Later that evening Peter stopped by to see Grandmother

and again the next day.

"What a good grandson you are," I told him as I met him at the foot of the stairs Sunday afternoon. "You've been here three days in a row." A faint flush of color appeared on his cheeks and I thought I had embarrassed him, so I quickly added, "Of course, you are her favorite grandson so it's to be expected."

"I'm her only grandson," he reminded me dryly.

"That, too. Anyway, you know you're always welcome, Peter, and I was just teasing." He nodded and his unnatural color faded.

"It's hard to see her like that, isn't it, Johanna?"

"She'll get better, Peter. I know it. She's a strong woman, and we're going to give her the best of care. Did you meet Crea?"

"Yes."

"Then you know what I mean by the best of care. Grandmother will be up and dancing in no time."

"I hope so."

I walked with him to the front door. "I know so, Peter. Trust me."

"You're the most confident person I know, Johanna. Do you ever doubt yourself, ever find yourself up against a predicament you believe is too great for you to handle?"

"Never."

He grinned at my tone. "Lucky you, then." He said good-bye and went down to the curb where his own automobile was parked, the one his parents had given him the first year he went off to college. He was much more spoiled and indulged than I and yet completely unaffected by it, which was what made him so lovable. The best person in the family, the one and probably only fact we all would have agreed to without argument.

The following Monday became a day that lived on in my

dreams for years to come. I took the train and walked from the nearest station, arriving outside the Cox building well before nine o'clock. Time to spare, I told myself but stopped short at the cross street, amazed by the line of women that snaked down the street and around the corner. Fortunately, Drew Gallagher already sat in his parked vehicle at the curb, apparently waiting for me. When he saw me, he crossed the street in a few long strides.

"What did you say in the advertisement?" I asked. "What did you promise?" For a moment we both stared mutely at the crowd of women that continued to expand farther down the street.

"Fair wages, regular work, and safe housing." He attempted his usual nonchalance, but I could tell he was as taken aback as I.

"A holy threesome for sure, Drew. How many women can Cox's accommodate?"

"Eighty for the work and forty for the apartments, unless they double up." He gave me a helpless look. "Do you know how and where to start with this crowd?" In my usual contrary way, his discomposure put me at ease, even made me smile.

"By the time I reach the other side of the street, I will," I said and stepped purposefully off the curb. "If you wouldn't mind helping me get inside, I can take it from there as long as I can borrow Fritz for the day."

Drew took the lead and forged a way through the crowd, unlocked the door, ignored the murmur of emotion that swept down the line of applicants, and pushed me inside. When he exited once more for Fritz, I sat down at the desk inside the front door and pulled out a notebook and pencils from my bag. Once Drew and Fritz returned, I put Fritz in charge of the doors.

"One woman at a time," I told him. "She comes in through

the right side and exits at the back. Don't be threatened, ca-joled, or tricked. Desperate women will do any of those things and then some. Are you up to it?"

Fritz grinned. "Yes, Miss. I've had to learn how to hold my own these past weeks." He was thinking of Yvesta and smiling, so maybe Drew was right and it was love, after all.

Behind me, Drew asked, "Do I have an assignment?"

Surprised at his question, I answered, "You told me very specifically that you didn't have time to spend on this phase of the project. So no, there's nothing for you to do but go away and come back later when the line is down."

"And leave you here at the mercy of these women? What would that make me?" His tone was teasing, almost mocking, but whether directed at me or himself I couldn't tell.

"Smart and obedient, two exemplary but rare qualities in a man," I responded tartly. Then turning back to Fritz, I said, "I'm ready when you are," and the long day began. I didn't notice where and when Drew left because once Fritz let in the first applicant, who had been waiting in line since before sun-rise, I didn't have time for anything but the seemingly endless supply of needy women who came in search of work.

That day stayed with me a long time, especially through my dreams. For months afterwards, I awoke in the night, panicked by the vision of a mass of women on the shore of a small, crowded island, arms extended toward me, calling out my name in an ever-increasing din of desperation. In my dream, I stood exhausted and indecisive on the deck of a huge ship that remarkably resembled the *Titanic* and watched the crowd of women grow smaller and smaller as the vessel pulled away from the island. Angrily weeping, I began to search the ship for lifeboats, looking everywhere, yanking open doors and cupboards, asking for help from faceless people who promenaded the decks and invariably turned away from me, bored and annoyed.

"We can't leave them behind!" I cried and in the way of dreams, my attempt at speech always awakened me. I would lie in the darkness, at first disoriented and then conscious of a great relief that it was only a dream after all. That day at Cox's Fine Women's Garments affected me so strongly, I suppose, because I held the power of a better life in my hands and could grant it only to a select few.

We never made it to the end of the line of applicants and eventually had to send women away. Coward that I am, I made Fritz do it.

"I can't face them," I admitted. "Thank you, Fritz." Then I sat down gracelessly, tired and sad but triumphant, too. I believed I had selected the right women for the jobs, all of them hard-working and determined to better themselves.

Drew must have entered from the rear door because I didn't see him return. Coming up behind me, he asked, "Are you satisfied with the results of the day, Johanna?"

"I'll think too long and too often about the women we turned away, but yes, I am satisfied."

He moved around in front of me and reached down to take a hand. "Come along, Miss Swan. You look all in. We'll stop at my house where Yvesta has been working all day on a special dinner, and then Fritz can drive you home."

I didn't protest. At the moment, I was completely content to have someone else make the decisions. I had made enough for one day. We hardly spoke on the drive, but Yvesta more than made up for the quiet when she met us at the door.

"Johanna, I've been waiting all day to see you! When Mr. Gallagher said you might visit, I was so pleased I could have hugged him. Wait 'til you see how the girls have grown. Mr. Gallagher said they're to go to school in the fall. You were right to make me come."

"I didn't make you come," I protested, oddly hurt by the words.

Yvesta only laughed. "No one can stand up against you when you've made up your mind, Johanna, and you had already decided this was the place for me. I didn't have the nerve to argue much, but I sure didn't want to come. You were right, though, and I was wrong."

Drew interjected, "You've never admitted that to Fritz and me, Yvesta."

"Because," Yvesta responded, turning to start back down the hallway, "it's yet to be true about either of you." There was no rancor in her tone, only affection and humor. I sensed that Yvesta liked Drew Gallagher and was happy in her job, and the knowledge perked up my spirits.

"Come outside and sit on the terrace." Drew led me into the library, the room where I'd first seen him weeks ago, and out the French doors onto the stone terrace that overlooked a broad expanse of green lawn. The yard, backed by a brick wall, had the look of a spacious private park. After he left to find refreshments, I slipped off my jacket, ran a hand inelegantly through my hair, and plopped into the nearest chair. Drew reappeared with two glasses of wine, sat down next to me, and stretched out his long legs in a casual pose, both of us shoulder to shoulder and looking out at the empty lawn.

"Two years ago Douglas gave an Independence Day party here on the lawn. As was his style, everything was coordinated and luxurious, expensive caterers, big pots of red, white, and blue flowers," Drew waved an expressive hand out toward the yard, "tables with festive umbrellas draped in silk, and servants hovering everywhere. He'd invited his business and political associates and anyone else worth impressing, including his enemies. Maybe them especially. Douglas wore wealth so effectively that both his associates and his rivals sometimes wished him dead." I couldn't read Drew's tone and sitting as we were, I couldn't see his face either.

"And did his brother, too?" I asked. If my question startled Drew or offended him, he certainly didn't show it. Instead, when I glanced over at him, he appeared deep in thought.

Finally Drew said, "I did on occasion, Johanna, but only on occasion."

"Brothers sometimes quarrel, I'm told."

"You've been told right. In retrospect it seems he and I were always quarreling. He thought I was too irresponsible, and I thought he was too serious. Now I believe we were both right. Douglas didn't have much respect for me."

"Did he love you?"

That question did startle him. "Love me? I don't know. I never thought about it." He took a sip of wine, frowning to himself. "I don't think so. If Douglas loved anyone, it was the woman who refused him, and even that's debatable. Douglas enjoyed acquiring beautiful objects for the twin purposes of display and prestige. Acquisition was a game and being refused only increased his desire and his sense of purpose."

"Are you talking about the regal Katherine?"

Drew nodded. "I grant you Katherine looked regal, but she didn't have a pretentious bone in her body. I know for a fact that she didn't realize what a beauty she was. Douglas never understood that Katherine was much more interested in principles than appearances. For a while I worried that she would be drawn into a life with Douglas, and I knew that would never do. He had certain bad—habits—that would have ended up hurting her. Katherine was much, much too good for him." I was conscious of a prick of envy at the admiration in his tone and ashamed of the sudden and completely unwarranted proprietary interest I felt for Drew Gallagher.

To make up for my shabby feelings, I said quickly, "Don't be too quick to dismiss Douglas's affection for you, Drew. You're the one he thought of at the end, after all."

Drew didn't answer, and after a while he went on without reacting to my comment. "Now that I think about it, you're very much like Katherine, Johanna."

"Six inches shorter, unmanageable hair, a brown complexion, and a complete lack of elegance," I responded with good humor, "but if you say so, who am I to argue?"

He turned to look at me sternly and ask, "Why do you do that?"

"Do what?"

"Turn every compliment against yourself. Poke fun at yourself."

I started to argue that I never did that but stopped before I got out a word. Finally, I answered meekly, "I don't have any illusions about myself, Drew. I'm not hideous, but I'm no beauty, either, so I don't trust flattery, which is usually all superficial. I suppose I want to make sure that people understand I'm not taken in by it, but I can see it's a boorish way to accept a compliment, and in the future I'll try to be more gracious. Grandmother would say, 'A simple thank you would suffice, Johanna,' and of course, she's right."

Drew listened intently in the way he had that made you think you were saying words of enormous importance and then explained, "I didn't mean you looked like Katherine. Obviously there's a marked difference in physical appearance, though I'm amazed at how you see yourself. It's in attitude and temperament that I recognize definite similarities between the two of you."

"Do I say thank you now?"

He laughed. "You are incorrigible. No. A thank you is not necessary. I only meant that you and Katherine are both strong-minded women with a very clear vision of right and wrong. Neither of you is afraid to speak bluntly, but I give you the edge on that. No one takes me to task as forthrightly and as frequently as you."

"Ah, at least I excel at one worthwhile thing."

Drew laughed again and stood up. "Come along, Miss Swan. You're getting light-headed from hunger."

"No, from the wine on an empty stomach. If I don't eat something soon, I won't be responsible for my actions."

Drew held open the terrace door into the library and said in a low voice as I passed, "Don't tempt me, Johanna. The idea of you with your defenses down is very appealing." I stopped on the threshold and looked up at him, still standing very close.

"I'm flattered, Drew. Coming from you and considering the competition, that remark deserves another thank you."

"That must be the wine speaking," he responded lightly, stepping away from me to pull the doors shut behind us. But I knew in my heart the wine had nothing to do with it.

Over Yvesta's carefully prepared dinner of a light summer soup, crusty bread, and a fresh fruit tart, we discussed the day's activities.

"You look better," Drew told me from across the table. "I thought the day had affected you and not for the good."

"You were right. I hated being the godlike figure, the one to decide who should be chosen and who rejected. Everyone was so needy and there were so many sad stories that every hour just became more burdensome. One more person to refuse. One more woman to turn away."

"But also one more person to receive hope and one more homeless woman to have shelter."

"Yes." His words lightened my spirits. "You're absolutely right, Drew. I was thinking of it backwards. That doesn't mean I won't have bad dreams about it, of course, but concentrating on the positive helps."

"Do you have bad dreams? Somehow that doesn't seem to fit with what I know of you."

I felt warmth rise in my cheeks. "It's not something I talk about."

He ignored what must have been my heightened color and asked, "Have you always had nightmares?"

"Ever since I left China. Those particular dreams faded over time, but the *Titanic* disaster has bred its own new crop."

"Is Douglas featured in any of them?"

"Yes, but don't ask me details because I won't share them."

Drew put both elbows on the table and stared at me. "Bad dreams seem out of character for you, Johanna, so is there a touch of insecurity lurking behind that self-confident manner of yours? Could it mean that you're as vulnerable as the rest of us, I wonder?"

"I don't know what bad dreams signify, Dr. Freud, and stop looking at me in that smug way. See if I ever share another confidence with you."

"I won't tell a soul. I'm very trustworthy with confidences. Are there any others you'd like to disclose?" I scowled at him to discourage the line of conversation and asked about the factory instead.

"I told your new employees to show up next Monday for work. Will you be ready?" Drew took the hint and we spent the rest of the meal talking about the details of Cox's grand opening.

After supper I stood. "This was a treat, Drew. Thank you. I feel much better, but I must get home. I'll deliver Henrietta and Betsy and Mrs. McElhanie next Monday. After that, may I stop by Cox's once in a while if I promise not to be a nuisance?"

"You may come by anytime, even if you are a nuisance,"

Drew answered generously, making me laugh. He held my jacket and as I slipped my arms into it, his hands rested briefly and lightly on my shoulders. "Really, Johanna, come by anytime. I find I like the way I feel when I'm with you." I turned around quickly to try to catch his expression, which looked more serious than he'd been all evening.

"Scoldings and all?" The brief, intimate moment passed, and he walked with me to the front door.

"Scoldings aside," he corrected. He opened the front door where Fritz waited at the foot of the walk with the Gallagher luxury motorcar. "You're not going to protest the ride, are you, and tell me you think you should take the train?"

I shook my head. "I'm too tired to protest anything and the ride is both welcome and appreciated. Good luck with the opening, Drew."

"Thanks, Johanna. I have a feeling Cox's will be a raging success. Good night."

Once home, I checked in with Crea and then shared my day's activities with Grandmother, who had taken to waiting for our evening time together before drifting off to sleep. Despite the prophesied dreams, which started soon after—the desperate women calling to me from their barren island followed by my frantic, ineffectual search for lifeboats—that first night I slept peacefully uninterrupted.

When I awoke the next morning, rested and inexplicably happy, my first unrestrained thoughts connected my unusually happy mood back to the evening with Drew Gallagher. That initial, early morning realization had a startling and somehow annoying truth in it somewhere that I chose not to explore. Drew Gallagher already threatened to occupy more of my time than was acceptable, and I wasn't about to give him any help in doing so.

O summer day beside the joyous sea!
O summer day so wonderful and white,
So full of gladness and so full of pain!
Forever and forever shalt thou be
To some the gravestone of a dead delight,
To some the landmark of a new domain.

Chapter Nine

Life on Hill Street soon settled into a comfortable routine and July passed uneventfully. I arranged for Henrietta, Betsy, and babies to move into their new apartment home and personally accompanied Mrs. McElhanie to her small rooms on the second floor of Cox's, where she would reside just outside the nursery. She was embarrassingly grateful and would not stop thanking me until I told her she should direct her gratitude to Drew Gallagher.

"He's the one who spent his money on the building, set up the factory, and refurbished and furnished the apartments. All I did was recommend you to watch the children, and there may come a time you won't thank me for that, Mrs. McElhanie. I don't have that much experience with little ones, but I know they can tire a person out without much effort. You'll let me know if it's too much for you, won't you?"

The old woman straightened her shoulders. "I raised five babies of my own, Johanna, though where they've got to now, I couldn't tell you. I'm looking forward to being useful again. Besides," she winked, "their mothers are right downstairs so I'll know where to find help if I need it."

I went back a second time a week later to see all the machines up and running but didn't run into Drew on either visit, a disappointment, but I wasn't about to admit that to anyone.

Crea's presence in the house was a godsend. Grandmother listened to her and followed her instructions better than she ever would have with me, and when I came home one late afternoon at the end of July and found Crea sipping tea in the kitchen as Mayville prepared supper, I knew another battle was won.

"This is a cozy scene," I observed, coming in and plopping into a chair at the old butcher block kitchen table. An aproned May stepped away from the stove long enough to set a teacup in front of me. Despite the heat wave that had recently hit the city, the kitchen with its brick walls and northern exposure remained relatively cool.

"I should get back upstairs," Crea stated guiltily and moved to rise.

May finished pouring my tea and rested a hand on Crea's shoulder. "There's no need for you to go rushing off. Mrs. McIntyre was sound asleep fifteen minutes ago when I checked, and Johanna won't hold it against you if you rest a minute." To me, May added, "Miss Crea spent all morning cleaning every inch of your grandmother's room, besides giving her a cool bath, reading her the newspaper, and assisting her with her exercises. There's no call for her to jump up like a frightened rabbit just because you're home." May turned back to the stove so that I was forced to respond to her back.

"Of course, I won't hold it against Crea," adding indignantly, "And I didn't deserve that scolding, Mayville. I'm the one who invited Crea to join us and against the protests of certain people in this house as I recall." Mayville made a tsk-ing sound but didn't turn around.

I turned to Crea and mouthed the words *Miss Crea* to her

with a surprised expression. Obviously there'd been a change in opinion over the past weeks of which I had been unaware.

Smiling, Crea shrugged and rose. "I'm sure Johanna doesn't care one little bit that I've stepped away, but I'm not comfortable being gone too long, May."

After she left, May volunteered grudgingly, "I know I was against Crea staying here, her being Irish and all, but she's hard-working and kind to your grandmother. Mrs. McIntyre is in good hands when Crea's with her. She's got a way about her that makes a person feel at ease. And she's no shirker, I'll say that for her." High praise indeed from Mayville.

I finished my tea before responding, "I won't say I told you so, May, but only because I've been raised right." At Mayville's snort, I rose to give her an affectionate pat on the arm. "You know that's true. Anyway, I'm glad you're learning to like and trust Crea as much as I do."

Grandmother still slept when I looked in on her. "What did the doctor have to say, Crea?" I asked.

Crea, who sat next to the bed with a book open on her lap, answered, "Not much, Johanna, only that we should keep moving her right arm and leg and continue to encourage her to speak."

"Do you see any progress?"

"I'm careful not to exaggerate and offer false hope, Johanna, but yes, I do. This morning I wrapped her fingers around her coffee cup and for a moment she was able to hold onto it without my help. And when I read her an editorial about corruption in city government, she gave me a look and said, 'No surprise there,' the words very clear, followed by a grin that didn't seem lopsided at all. I think at that moment she was the woman she had been before the attack."

I sat down and looked at Crea across the sleeping figure in the bed, suddenly overwhelmed with hope, my eyes pooling with tears.

"I hope you're right, Crea. I'll love her any way she is, but I want that woman back, more for her sake than mine." I surreptitiously brushed a tear away with a forefinger, sniffed, and changed the subject. "Congratulations on getting past May's defenses, by the way. I'm impressed. How did you manage that in such a short time? I thought it would be half a year at least."

"The first week she gave me the cold shoulder at every opportunity, and I knew I couldn't live like that. So we had a serious discussion and decided we could coexist as adult women and that was that."

"I think there was more to it than you're telling me." When Crea didn't answer, I commented in mock accusation, "This house suddenly seems full of secrets," and was surprised to see a delicate color creep up Crea's cheeks. I thought I had somehow made her feel uncomfortable and added, "I really am glad you're here, Crea. You've managed to fit in so well that it seems as though you've been with us much longer than five weeks. It took months for May to accept my presence in the house when I first arrived. Obviously, you have a gift for getting along with people that I would do well to copy. "

"You're the one with gifts, Johanna. You've traveled the world, studied in England, and graduated from two well-known schools. Everyone who meets you talks about how intelligent and how fearless you are. I've never been outside the city limits of Chicago. My first automobile ride happened just a few weeks ago with Levi and I've never been on any kind of boat. And you know about my education. There's nothing about me to strike admiration." Her tone was wistful, not bitter.

"I was given a number of advantages, including family and education, that I didn't earn or deserve. If I had your start in life, I know I wouldn't be nearly as self-assured and persistent as you." Then, standing and stretching, I said, "Everyone's got strengths and weaknesses, Crea. That's what I think. The trick is to figure out which is which, build on the former and overcome the latter."

"Easy for you to say." A brusque retort but said with a smile.

"Easier for me to say than do, that's for sure," I agreed, "but I'll never stop trying to be better at what I do and how I act." After a purposeful pause, I said with a grin, "Of course, I have so much room for improvement that I'll be working at it 'til the day I die." I heard a low laugh from Crea as I left the room.

An August heat wave intensified July's stifling temperatures and oppressive humidity. I put on my lightest dress and took the train to Cox's, concerned about the effects of the heat on the women in the factory and the children on the second floor. The building was certainly hot, but the windows Drew had installed allowed a cross current of air to move continually through the work area so that while not ideal, the temperature was bearable. I found Betsy at one of the sewing machines and after lunch pulled her away into the alley for a quick chat.

Betsy said the work was all right, not hard but boring sometimes, and the apartment she shared with Henrietta, although hot right then, was "just about perfect."

"There's more room than either of us ever had before, Johanna, and we've done it up real nice. With Mrs. McElhanie and the nursery for the babies, both Etta and me can work straight off. Now that we're both earning money, we can put some away in the bank, in case of an emergency or for Christmas presents. We even thought maybe we'd take a trip somewhere. Mr. Gallagher made Ethel Poltis the floor supervisor. 'I'm putting a woman in charge to make sure things get done right,' he said. All the girls think Mr. Gallagher is just about the handsomest man they've ever seen and he seems real nice. If he wasn't your friend, I believe I might try to catch his eye."

"Mr. Gallagher has done a good deed setting up this factory, Betsy, but I'd be careful around him. I'm guessing he has a weakness for a pretty girl."

"You'd better listen to Miss Swan, Betsy. She's the moral voice of caution we all need to hear." Drew Gallagher, looking unfairly cool in a fawn beige suit that had neither wrinkle nor smudge, walked up behind us in the alley.

"We don't mind listening to Johanna, Mr. Gallagher. She never acts any better than anybody else even though she's probably smarter than all of us put together. Johanna hasn't steered any of us wrong, and she always seems to have the answers we're looking for." Betsy, not exactly sure if I'd been disparaged, sprang to my defense just in case.

Drew held up both hands. "I didn't mean to insult her, Betsy." The whistle blew, ending lunch.

"Well, all right then," Betsy replied agreeably and with a brief wave went back inside to her place at the sewing machine.

"You really don't have to warn these girls away from me, Johanna. My tastes run to older, more sophisticated, and less vulnerable women." I decided not to acknowledge that remark, which he made lightly but with an undertone of annoyance I didn't miss.

Instead I commented, "I had to come down to see how everyone was tolerating the heat. I thought it might be unbearable inside, but while it's not exactly comfortable, it's livable. Your windows catch a breeze just right."

"Your friend Mr. Goldwyn's windows," Drew corrected. We walked along the alley toward the street, all the sounds and smells of a large industrial city around us, the heat trapped between the buildings and bouncing off the pavement. We reached the front of Cox's and stood under the awning for shade.

"I didn't know Allen had a hand in any of this."

"Douglas respected his architectural firm, and I considered it more than coincidence that Goldwyn was a friend of yours. If it hadn't been for you, I doubt I'd have become so involved in this project, so not using Allen Goldwyn's expertise would have been flying in the face of fate. He's a creative man with true talent." The compliment was generous and ungrudging.

"Yes," I agreed warmly, "Allen sees color, shape, and structure in everything, and he has an eye for perfection of form. He's happiest when he's building things." Then, changing the subject, I asked, "Are you content with the results of the Cox Experiment, Drew? You won't lose money on the arrangement, will you?"

"I've surprised myself because I enjoy commerce, Johanna, and I find I possess a previously unrecognized flair for business. It must be in the Gallagher blood, after all. So no, I won't lose any money on Cox's. There's always a market for ladies' undergarments and the ones we manufacture are fashionable and growing in demand. I expect I'll eventually make a comfortable profit. If I don't, I won't blame you, though, so don't worry that I'll send you a bill. I wouldn't want you to feel obligated to spend your life savings on failed lingerie."

His patronizing, amused tone made me retort, "My life savings, as you call it, will be enough to cover several experiments, so don't hesitate to call me to account. I'm willing and able to pay all my debts in full."

"Are you sure?"

To squelch the laughter I still detected in his voice I added haughtily, "You'll have to wait eighteen months, however, because I don't come into my share of the McIntyre fortune until I'm twenty-five."

"A real fortune, Johanna? I had no idea."

"It's from my Grandfather McIntyre's side of the family and appears substantial. Mother shared the original bequest with Uncle Hal and now Mother's share is mine. I expect I'll be rich in a few years."

More seriously than I expected, Drew told me, "Being rich may not be what you expect. I'll deny I said this but the well-intentioned use of money is a lot more difficult and time-consuming than I ever imagined."

I patted his arm. "Thank you for your counsel, but I already know that and have started plans for a trust to dispense the funds on worthy purposes."

"Be careful. One handsome fortune hunter could change your plans." The glint in his eyes made me wonder if he considered trying out for the role.

"If you're implying yourself, Drew, you can't be a fortune hunter. You already have a fortune."

"Maybe I'll have run through mine by the time you come into yours."

Through the open front door of Cox's, I could hear the steady hum of sewing machines, see boxes stacked just inside waiting for pickup.

"I doubt it. Whether you want it or not, I'm afraid you're destined for success." The idea seemed to surprise him and as he considered its implications, I added, "I need to go home, but I'm glad the experiment is working out, Drew. I wouldn't want you to regret the undertaking."

Without acknowledging my words, Drew volunteered, "Let Fritz run you home, Johanna. The automobile will be cooler than the train."

"That's true, but it's not saying much. The only place in the city of Chicago I have any interest in right now is the lakeshore. Unfortunately, half the population of the city has the same idea. You couldn't figure out a way to clear a beach for me, could you?"

"As a matter of fact," he responded thoughtfully, "I think I could. How does a small excursion on a yacht sound?"

"Don't tell me you have yacht!" Drew looked sheepish at the awe and amazement in my tone.

"It's not my fault, Johanna. I inherited it along with the house, the motorcar, and the business. It's nothing I would ever have bought for myself and I'll probably sell it, but until that happens, why shouldn't I take it out? What do you say? Or won't that missionary streak allow you to play a little hooky from the responsibilities you've piled on yourself?" He gave that lop-sided, engaging grin I found more attractive each time he flashed it. Standing on a hot city pavement with beads of perspiration forming on my forehead gave his proposal an immediate and legitimate appeal I could not resist.

"You give me credit for more conscience than I really have. How could I say no to being out on the lake? Only, may I bring a friend?"

I thought Drew's face lost some of its teasing expression. "Your Mr. Goldwyn?"

Surprised at the assumption, I answered, "No, not Allen. My friend, Crea O'Rourke. She's been a godsend helping with Grandmother, and she recently told me she's never been on a boat. It would be such a treat for her, and I know she could use a break from the heat and the work."

Drew was cheerful in agreement. "Miss O'Rourke it is. Fritz will pick the two of you up around noon tomorrow and we'll float the afternoon away." Then he asked, curiosity obvious in his voice, "You didn't ask to bring a friend along because you thought you needed a chaperone, did you, Johanna?"

I laughed. "I told you before, Drew, that I'm past the age of needing one. I tend to do exactly what I want, but even if all that weren't the case, no one would worry about my virtue or my reputation when I'm with you. From the company you keep, it's clear I'm not your type."

"You're certain of that, are you?" I met his look, intrigued by the half-challenging expression I saw there.

"I'm afraid so. Your Viola and I might as well live on different planets. Now if your offer for a ride home still stands, I'll take it and look forward to seeing you Saturday."

Drew stayed behind at Cox's, giving Fritz directions to come back for him later, so I had the luxury of solitude in the roomy, luxurious red leather back seat of the Gallagher Pierce Great-Arrow. I liked Drew Gallagher a great deal, probably too much for my own good, but I was not fooled or flattered by his comments and the way he had of looking at me and giving the impression I was some beguiling creature he'd just discovered. We both knew that was a practiced expression he pulled from his book of social tricks, listed somewhere between *f* for flirtation and *s* for seduction. I spent a while contemplating being seduced by Drew Gallagher, decided it would be quite pleasant for as long as it lasted but unbearable once it ended. Poor Flora lingered in the back of my mind, too, whose pleasure in a man's company, undoubtedly also pleasant while it lasted, had brought her to a solitary, sad end. I was all grown up, though, not a childish Flora, and I believed I could take care of myself. In many ways, Drew seemed a contradiction, and I enjoyed trying to figure him out, enjoyed his humor and verbal sparring, his quick wit, and the way he had of listening to me as if I were the only woman in his universe. I liked his flashes of honesty and his complete disdain for social pretense, bigotry, and hypocrisy. More than all that, however, I occasionally saw something in him that appealed to me on an emotional level I had never experienced before, something vulnerable and thoughtful that surfaced only infrequently in tone or expression. Maybe that was all an act, too, though; how could I tell? Life had been a social game to Drew Gallagher for such a long time that I suspected all his actions were dubious, calculated, and done simply for effect. Still, he was the only man I knew with a yacht and the city was unbearably hot, so now was obviously not the time to examine his motives and my feelings too seriously. I could do that after the weather broke.

Crea's sole attempt at resisting the lake excursion was to ask whether she should leave Grandmother for the day.

"I appreciate that you've become fond of Grandmother, Crea, and you can trust that I've made satisfactory arrangements for her. Mayville is home, of course, and Jennie and Uncle Hal are coming for the afternoon. Grandmother enjoys their company. I bribed Peter to take his mother out of the city for the day so I can be assured Aunt Kitty won't show up. Grandmother's made such good progress in her speech that I'm afraid of a setback if my aunt spends any time with her. Aunt Kitty can have that effect on people." I recalled Uncle Hal's gentle chiding of my attitude toward my aunt and added, "I shouldn't have said that. She and I have never gotten along, but I don't need to be malicious or unkind."

"She is difficult," Crea commented, "but I feel sorry for her in a way. She's a fearful woman."

"Is that what it is?"

"Yes, I think so." Crea ignored the sarcasm in my tone. "Your aunt strikes me as a woman who lives with a number of phantom fears, the kind that hover in the back of her mind, unnamed and unacknowledged."

"You're more sensitive and certainly more charitable than I, Crea, and you deserve a day on the lake just on general principles." My remark changed the subject, but later I considered Crea's comment and decided she might be right.

Douglas Gallagher's yacht, like his house and his automobile, was the most handsome one of its kind I'd ever seen. I stood next to Drew on the dock and asked incredulously, "This is the Gallagher private yacht, Drew? It looks larger than several small countries I visited."

"I know," Drew responded complacently. He'd driven Crea and me himself, then left the roadster in the hands of a Yacht Club attendant. We pondered the docked vessel in silence a moment and when he finally spoke, I caught the honest amusement in his voice. "It's quite something, isn't it? My brother never shared its existence with me because he probably knew I wouldn't be able to take it seriously."

"I've never seen such a beautiful boat," Crea commented carefully. "Is it just my inexperience or is it unusually large?"

"It's not you, Miss O'Rourke. You don't have to have known my brother to appreciate his compulsion always to have the newest and the best and always to be one step ahead of everyone else."

I had shared the bare facts of Drew's inheritance with Crea earlier so she responded with quick sympathy. "I'm sorry I didn't have the opportunity to know him, Mr. Gallagher, and I'm sorry about his death."

Drew smiled at her sincerity. I thought he might respond with a flippant or casual remark, but he contented himself with a simple thank you, adding, "Won't you follow Johanna's lead and call me Drew?" From the start, Crea had been cautious around Drew, and she still seemed guarded in his presence.

"Yes, if you'll stop addressing me as Miss O'Rourke."

"It's a deal. Now, ladies, if you're ready, so am I. I admit to some excitement myself since it's also my maiden voyage on the *San Francisco*." I had missed the vessel's name until Drew said it aloud but then noticed the words written in bold, dark script on its side. I thought it a fitting name. The boat seemed as large as its namesake. Drew's gaze met mine and although I hadn't spoken the thought aloud, he grinned.

"I agree that it is, Johanna," he said, reading my mind, and for that brief, shared moment I found him completely irresistible. Then he took Crea and me each by an arm and led us on board.

After an hour out on the lake, Crea relaxed into the manner of a woman accustomed to wealth and privilege—and yachting. "I worried I might be seasick," she confessed to me privately, "but it's so calm and smooth, you hardly know you're on the water." She lay on a deck chaise, her face shaded by a large hat. Through a large, inelegant yawn, she murmured something about taking a little nap and closed her eyes.

I went in search of Drew and found him leaning over the railing at the prow, staring intently at the horizon. My approach startled him back from wherever he was daydreaming, and I apologized for intruding.

"I was contemplating sailing away and not looking back," he told me. I couldn't tell from his expression whether he was serious but guessed he might be.

Joining him at the railing, I said, "I can't imagine you have anything to run away from, Drew, but even if you did, I don't think running away from problems is the answer."

"No? What would you recommend then?"

"An abrupt about-face and a forceful stare. They work for me every time." He laughed and turned around, propping his elbows on the railing behind him.

"I'm sure they do, Johanna. Is your friend Crea enjoying herself?"

"Yes. Thank you for bringing us both along. Crea hasn't had much leisure or luxury in her life."

"How did you meet her?"

"Serendipity," I answered evasively. From his knowing smile, I thought he guessed that Crea's background included the Anchorage but guess all he want, I wasn't about to confirm or deny. Crea could talk for herself. I went on, "What a splendid boat this is! I'd guess there's enough room to fit the entire first floor of Cox's on board."

"It is big," Drew agreed. "Much too big for me, anyway. Enjoy the day because the *San Francisco* is going up for sale as soon as we get back."

"You can't be serious! Think what wonderful parties you could give, with lanterns strung along the railing and a dance band on deck!" The words conjured up a sudden and completely unexpected picture of the *Titanic* on its last night out. I remembered hearing music in the background when Grandmother and I first went on deck but couldn't recall when the music had stopped to be replaced by the growing hysterical murmur of frightened people. Drew was quiet until I looked up to meet his glance with a small smile. "Sorry. I was remembering something. Anyway, why sell the *San Francisco*? Wouldn't owning it please your friends and enhance your business relationships?"

"Sadly, I don't have enough friends to fill it for a party, and more importantly, I'm not Douglas, who no doubt would have known how to use the boat for both effect and profit. I don't have the talent or the desire to do so. The *San Francisco* has to go. I find its grandeur somewhat embarrassing."

"I'm surprised. You once admitted that you enjoyed doing things for effect."

"Doing things, not owning things, Johanna. There's a difference. Douglas was the collector, not me. Unlike him, I prefer women who enjoy my company more than my finances. Before Douglas's death, I didn't have to worry about ulterior motives because I was always on the edge of poverty."

"Is it different now?"

"Oh, yes. Where before women were warned away from me by their well-meaning families, I've now become a matrimonial catch."

"Poor you." The idea of Drew Gallagher walking down the aisle with some young thing put me in a bad temper that came out in my tone.

"It is poor me. Even if I'm honest and explain that marrying is not an option for my future, I detect a gleam in the woman's eye that says she knows better. When it comes to matters of love and marriage, the belief of members of your sex in their superior wisdom is annoying."

"Women have been groomed for marriage for centuries, Drew, and it's ingenuous of you to hold that against us. Unless society changes and offers women legal, economic, and political equality, the situation will continue exactly as it is. It hasn't been that long since women were considered property and to this day we can't affect the political process with our votes. Many women are deluded into thinking marriage is protection against poverty, loneliness, and back-breaking, never-ending labor."

"Do you agree that's a delusion, Johanna?"

I stopped to consider his words before answering carefully, "Not completely. Marriage is no panacea, but my parents and my grandparents were true partners in life, happy in each other's company. Somehow they found a way to live together in mutual respect and affection, so if I knew only their examples, I'm sure I'd be less skeptical than I am. But I've witnessed too much real life, I'm afraid, to be a whole-hearted romantic, seen too many women abandoned and destitute, bruised and beaten."

"Poor you." A gentle mockery as he repeated my earlier words.

I met Drew's eyes quickly, saw something warm there, something almost tender, and backed away.

"Lucky me," I retorted too quickly. "Smart me," then added, "I'm going to find Crea. I've left her on her own too long."

Drew put a hand on my forearm.

"Crea's all grown up, Johanna. She'll be fine. You're running away from me, which isn't like you. Where's your about-face and forceful stare?" I liked the feel of his hand on my arm and did not resist when he pulled me closer. "For a strong-minded woman who I've come to believe is fearless, your face told me you wished yourself anywhere but with me just now. Believe me, Johanna, I have no intention of harming you." He spoke softly, his lips brushing mine but not quite kissing me.

"What then?" I murmured. That close he had a wonderful fragrance about him, something light and spicy that mixed with the clean smell of the air and water. I imagined he would taste even better.

He gave a low laugh, rested a hand on the back of my head and briefly wove his fingers into my fly-away hair before kissing me lightly on the lips.

"Only this."

Masking my disappointment as he stepped away, I commented, "What a gentleman you are!"

"Despite public opinion, you mean?"

"I'm afraid so. But feel free to call on me any time to defend you and speak about your good behavior."

"Would you do that?"

Something in his tone made me answer more seriously than I intended. "Yes, Drew, I would. I've said some uncharitable things to you in the past, but I'm beginning to realize that in some respects I wronged you. I listened to rumors and made assumptions based on appearances, a bad habit I'd criticize in anyone else but one I practiced with impunity. You've done a great deal of good in a short amount of time, and you should be commended for that." My words brought a scowl.

"Don't compliment me, Johanna. It's not what I'm used to hearing from you and it makes me uneasy. You don't know my motives."

"Motives don't concern me any more than intentions. They're always so murky and confused, and I'm never smart enough to figure them out. I prefer to look at actions and results, both obvious to the naked eye and more easily interpreted."

"Sometimes you amaze me."

"In a good way?" I questioned, laughing. Drew took my arm and began to walk with me back toward the side deck where Crea dozed.

"Most of the time," he answered, and his wary tone made me laugh again.

When we docked late in the afternoon, Drew suggested we stop for refreshments at the clubhouse.

"The club has a tolerable restaurant, and I can't be the only one who's famished. I can see Johanna's willing, but what about you, Crea?" Crea sent me a questioning look.

"Grandmother's in good hands," I told her, reading her concern correctly. "May was thrilled to be in charge. Ever since we got the invalid chair, Grandmother's been hoping to get downstairs and sit at the table, and May said she and Levi would arrange that this evening. We can afford another hour."

But we didn't stay an hour. Once inside the clubhouse, Drew left to arrange a table, and my attention was drawn to a group of people seated casually at tables along the wall of windows that overlooked the lake. They were a well-dressed group, obviously wealthy and comfortable in the club's exclusive environment, laughing and calling to each other table to table.

One man among them stood and raised a glass, saying in a forceful voice that held a touch of east coast accent, "To Lydia and twenty-five more years of happiness." As glasses clinked and voices called congratulations, I heard Crea give a sudden, deep gasp, and I turned to see her reach out a hand to the wall to keep herself from falling. Every last bit of color had drained from her face, even from her lips, so that she looked bloodless.

Thinking she was about to faint, I said her name and reached out to take her free hand.

"Are you ill?" I asked urgently. At her nod I put an arm around her waist and pulled her uncooperative body along to a nearby chair. She seemed so completely listless and unable to help herself that I became alarmed. "I'm calling for a doctor," I said, rising from where I crouched next to her, but at that she clutched my hand and shook her head in disagreement.

"No, don't. Don't. I felt suddenly light-headed is all. Too much sun, perhaps. I'm sorry to spoil the day, Johanna, but I'd like to go home."

"You might be light-headed from hunger, Crea. Why don't we stay and have some supper first?" Behind us the group of celebrating people gave a collective laugh, reacting to someone's humorous remark, and Crea's grip tightened.

"No. Please. I'd like to go home." I stood and looked over my shoulder at the group by the windows, suspicious now of a connection between them and Crea's sudden collapse. It was obvious to me she'd had a shock that was somehow related to them. After a few minutes Drew found us and I pulled him aside.

"Something's happened to Crea," I told him tersely. "I don't know what, but we need to go home. I'm sorry."

"Is she ill?"

"I think it's something else, some kind of shock, but it's made her ill. We should go."

Drew didn't waste time in questions or comments, one of the things I'd grown to appreciate about him, but went to fetch the car. On the ride home I sat with Crea in the back while Drew drove.

"Are you feeling better now?" I asked in a low voice.

Her color was more normal and her voice stronger. "Yes. I'm sorry to have acted so foolishly, Johanna. I don't know what came over me. I spoiled the whole day."

"No, you didn't. We had a lovely day on the water. Supper was unplanned and unnecessary, anyway. Can you tell me what happened?"

"I don't know," she answered, but she looked away when she spoke and didn't meet my gaze.

"I think you do know, but if you don't choose to tell me, I understand. You have a right to your secrets and private thoughts and I don't have the right to pry only—you know you can trust me, don't you, Crea?" Her answer was not entirely satisfactory, but I had to be satisfied with it.

"If I were going to trust someone, Johanna, it would be you."

Crea, no longer wan, said a polite thank you and good-bye to Drew when we reached home, then waved me away when I attempted to take her arm and help her up the walk to the house.

"I'm much better now, Johanna, thank you. You don't have to baby me." Except for an unnaturally bright pink spot on each cheek, she looked herself again. I watched her climb the porch steps.

"Now what was that all about?" I asked rhetorically. "I hate it that something—or someone—has the power to shake her confidence like that. Did you know those people in the clubhouse?"

"Not personally. I'm sure I've seen a few of them around town, but in general we didn't move in the same circles."

"Didn't?"

"Along with becoming rich, I've also become respectable, which means my circle of proper acquaintances has grown. People once offended by my profligate ways are now eager to be my best friends." He sounded scornful and cynical.

"Maybe it's not just the money. Maybe you're a more likable

man than the Drew Gallagher of a year ago. Maybe once you stepped away from Douglas's shadow and your parents' unfortunate legacy, people discovered you were really quite a nice person."

"That's the second compliment you've paid me this afternoon, Johanna. What exactly do you want?"

"Your unwarranted suspicions hurt my feelings."

"Ha! I know your methods by now, Johanna, and how your mind works. I also know I haven't the ability to hurt your feelings, even if I wanted to. Which, trust me, I don't." Drew paused to examine me with an objective eye, making me feel that I was a rare specimen he'd just discovered under a microscope, before paying me one of the finest compliments I'd ever received. "In fact, you are the one and only person whose feelings I consider more important than my own. I don't know how that happened, and the fact that it did is probably something you don't realize and can't truly appreciate." He put his hat on at a suitably rakish angle and added, "I hope your friend, Miss O'Rourke, is feeling better. I'm sure you'll let me know if there's anything I can do to be of assistance."

I recovered from the slightly breathless feeling his casual comments caused and nodded thoughtfully. "Since you purport to know how my mind works, you know I'm not shy about asking for help, but I don't believe Crea's problem is physical. I think it's something else." I gave myself a mental shake before saying goodbye. "I loved the excursion out on the lake, Drew. Thank you. It was a perfect afternoon."

That night, lying in bed with the windows open to cool my hot room, I recalled the lazy sway of the boat and the cooling breeze off the lake, the enticing smell of Drew Gallagher and the feel of his breath against my cheek. Perfect indeed.

Sweltering August finally passed. The Anchorage filled and emptied and filled again. The typewriting and language classes

I taught began to include women from the neighborhood who were not Anchorage inhabitants but ambitious women looking to improve their skills and thus improve their futures. We bulged at the seams but didn't turn anyone away.

At home Crea slipped back into her role of quiet companion and never mentioned the unexplained shock she had received. I speculated and worried but didn't question her. If Crea decided to make her past my business, I would listen, but the choice was not mine.

Grandmother improved remarkably, able to speak intelligible sentences and squeeze her right hand enough to grasp a pen. She still needed help forming the letters on paper, but we were all pleased and excited at her progress. Levi would carry her downstairs to the waiting wheeled chair where she sat contentedly enjoying the view from the front porch, listening to Crea read aloud, and sipping tea with her left hand in a dignified awkwardness that caused me to feel an odd mix of admiration and tenderness whenever I saw her lift the cup with a trembling hand to her lips. If she happened to spill, we pretended it didn't happen and continued whatever we were doing without interruption. Because she and I were not sentimental with each other before her stroke, I was not going to become so now, but I admit there were times I could easily have said something emotional to her, something to convey my pride and deep affection.

One evening, meeting my look, Grandmother gave her crooked smile and said clearly, "We are not a family that clings and cries, Johanna," so despite my resolve, something of what I felt must have shown on my face.

Jennie visited regularly; Peter, more regularly. When I complimented his faithfulness and commented on the frequency of his attention, he muttered something about going back to school. He seemed embarrassed by my words because he looked away quickly, so I changed the subject by asking about Jennie.

"Jennie's gone for the week with the Milford family to Lake Geneva."

"It must be serious then if your mother allowed such an extended trip and didn't insist on accompanying her."

"Mother chooses to believe it's serious, but Carl and Jennie are two of a kind in a lot of ways, both of them risk-takers and hard to read. Sometimes I get the feeling that Jennie's indulging in a mischievous and not very kind game at Mother's expense. I could be wrong, though. Jennie doesn't talk to me about how she really feels." Peter's fair, open face looked sincerely worried. "Could you talk to her, Johanna? Jennie respects you. Maybe she'll listen."

"Talk to her about what?"

Peter flushed. "Her behavior when she's with Carl, I suppose. The dangers of going too far. The realities of life. You know. Women talk."

"I'm not her mother, Peter."

"Mother would never believe anything about Jennie that isn't virginal and above reproach. I don't believe she's physically or emotionally able to have the kind of conversation that Jennie needs, and Father would simply turn beet red, stutter something incomprehensible, and kiss her on the cheek. Jennie's his little darling and remains perpetually five years old in his eyes. I've tried on more than one occasion to tell Jennie to slow down and be careful, but she doesn't listen to me. Well, she doesn't listen to anyone any more. There's something wild about her I don't understand."

"You sound worried."

"I am worried, Johanna, but helpless, especially now that I'll be back in school within the month. Could you—?"

"I'll talk to her, but I can't make any promises, Peter. Jennie's of age now and she's headstrong. Some people must learn their lessons the hard way: through experience and heartache."

"I know. That's what I'm afraid of." Peter's tangible concern spilled over to me. I heard something even stronger than concern in his voice, heard fear, and determined to spend time with Jennie as soon as she was back in town.

I didn't see Drew Gallagher for the rest of the month once we returned from the boat outing. I was busy at home and at the Anchorage and didn't have time for a visit to Cox's, and while I considered inventing a reason to communicate with him, I resisted the temptation. My instinct said that resisting temptation around Drew Gallagher was probably wise. He had a way of bringing out an outrageous side of me that I found fun and liberating. If I weren't careful, Jennie would have to have a talk with me about my behavior.

Allen Goldwyn stopped by the house one week to the day after my conversation with Peter. Allen's soberly handsome face was welcome but only as a friend. Whatever speculative attraction he once held for me had disappeared in the past few months. Looking at him standing in the doorway, I realized I liked Allen platonically and was content that it would always be so. I admitted to myself that the change of feeling was another result of spending time in Drew Gallagher's company and had a moment of worry that I would someday regret the change. Even worse, I feared that I'd led Allen to believe something that would never be true. His calm demeanor and typical respectful greeting comforted me, however, and I hoped we could remain good friends. Taking his hand, I saw my platonic feeling reciprocated in his eyes when he greeted me and felt relieved. No passion on either side, and that was good thing.

"You look thinner," I remarked critically. "Are you working too hard?" He sat down across from me and shook his head.

"No, that's not possible. It's just the heat. I came by to see how Mrs. McIntyre is doing."

I shared Grandmother's progress, then volunteered, "I saw the windows you designed for the Cox building, Allen. They're ingenious." He looked pleased with the compliment.

"Mr. Gallagher gave me free rein to experiment, so I had the opportunity to try out one of my theories about air currents. The windows turned out even better than I expected. I've had three other clients ask for the same design. In fact, people have begun to call them Goldwyns. I never thought my first claim to fame would be windows, but I'm not complaining."

"Congratulations. You've studied hard and worked even harder and you deserve the accolades." He looked pleased, but tired, too, or perhaps troubled about something. I reached across to him and placed my hand over his. "Is everything all right, Allen? You seem bothered by something." Allen gave my hand a squeeze and stood.

"You're a good friend to care, Johanna, but I'm fine." We walked into the hallway and just as I reached for the front door handle, someone lifted the knocker on the other side. Jennie greeted me when I opened the door, her face flushed and pretty, her hair sun-lightened to gold. If appearance was any measure, the week at Lake Geneva must have agreed with her. She bloomed with color and her eyes sparkled.

Jennie stepped inside, saying, "Hello, Johanna. Is this an inconvenient time? I just got back in town, dropped off my bags at home, and told Papa I was borrowing Donaldson to come and see Grandmother." She greeted Allen. "Hello, Mr. Goldwyn. I haven't seen you in a while. I hope you're well."

Allen, seemingly unappreciative of the energy and attraction that radiated from Jennie the same way heat streamed from the sun, answered in his usual serious manner. "Hello, Miss McIntyre. I'm very well, thank you. Did you say you've been out of town?"

"I spent last week on the shores of Lake Geneva being waited on hand and foot in the largest house I've ever seen. I could grow quite accustomed to the trappings of wealth in no time. And it's no use frowning at me in disapproval, Johanna. I don't have your hair-shirt inclinations. I like luxury." She came in farther. "Is Grandmother resting or may I say hello?"

"She's upstairs doing her exercises with Crea and will probably welcome the interruption."

Jennie, one foot on the bottom step, turned to say, "Goodby, Mr. Goldwyn. If I interrupted your visit with Johanna, please forgive me. I could have waited and made the visit later, but I'm afraid I'm not very patient or circumspect when it comes to seeing the people I care about." She flashed a brilliant smile and hurried up the steps.

Allen left immediately after Jennie's sudden arrival, wishing me good evening with bland inflection. I watched him for a minute before closing the front door and thought that despite his words to the contrary, something did indeed trouble him. Perhaps he would have shared more information if Jennie hadn't come bursting in.

In a short time Jennie reappeared in the front room where I was reading.

"What a change in a week, Johanna!" she exclaimed. "She sits up without any assistance, and I could understand every word she said. I'm so pleased!"

"Yes, Grandmother's made wonderful progress the last few weeks, all due to Crea's good work." I motioned to the chair across from me. "Can you stay a while, Jennie, and tell me about your week? You sound like you were spoiled from the beginning, which sounds wonderfully decadent."

Jennie didn't sit down but moved from chair to table to sofa to bureau, touching the displayed photographs lightly and running a hand over the upholstery. The way she drifted around the room reminded me of a lovely butterfly flitting from flower to flower.

"You'd have felt guilty the moment you crossed the threshold, Johanna, and been in the kitchen organizing the servants into a labor union after the first meal. Eight courses and a fresh set of china for each sitting. I must say, though, that I adjusted to the extravagance quickly and easily. I suppose that makes me a weak, bad person but there you have it."

Without responding to her words, I asked, "How did you get along with the Milfords of Boston?"

"They were charmed, of course. I made it my business to be sure they thought I had dropped down from heaven, intelligent but not too, innocent, thoughtful, and suitably appreciative of the honor implied by the invitation."

"You scare me sometimes, Jennie. Is everyone like clay in your hands?"

"Mr. and Mrs. Milford want the perfect wife for Carl, and I was only granting them their wish. I was doing them a favor, Johanna."

"So there's to be a wedding?"

"Mother would like to think so." Her answer seemed purposefully ambiguous.

"Your mother isn't marrying Carl Milford," I retorted sharply, "you are. Is a wedding what you want?" Jennie gave a harsh laugh that didn't sound like her at all.

"Oh yes, Johanna. It's what I want more than anything."

I doubted her sincerity and was troubled by the tone of her words.

"Jennie, why don't we meet for lunch and go shopping one day next week? I can get away, and I'd like to talk to you further. Now isn't the time because if I know your mother, she's hovering by your front door as we speak, eagerly waiting to hear all about your trip and it's unkind to keep her in suspense."

Jennie hesitated, then nodded. "All right, but I warn you, don't try to give me advice, Johanna. I won't listen to it, not even from you. I'm not sixteen and a schoolgirl any more."

"I can see that, and I wouldn't dare attempt to give you advice. I don't have any answers to life's questions. I'm simply in the mood for cream cakes and a new dress, and who better than you to share the indulgence?"

Jennie smiled at that, but I don't think she believed me, and without a word adjusted her hat and pulled on her gloves. I waved goodbye from the porch as the automobile pulled away and saw her give a quick, almost grudging, wave in return. Really, I thought with a sigh, life was getting very complicated—with Crea and Jennie and Allen all acting in ways that were out of character and bordering on the mysterious. Not even Peter was his usual frank and open self. In earlier times I would have talked it all over with Grandmother and come away with a clearer understanding of the situation. Now I couldn't burden her with any of it and must try to muddle through the mystery of human behavior on my own.

Oh, thou child of many prayers!
Life hath quicksands, - Life hath snares!
Care and age come unawares!

Chapter Ten

J ennie and I met the following week in the dining room of
the downtown Marshall Field's store. She looked in high
color, dressed in a suit the color of buttercream that showed
her slender neck to advantage and emphasized the strands of
pale sun gold in her hair. Little gold hoops at her ears caught
the light.

"How pretty you look!" I told her spontaneously. "As warm
as sunlight. I've always envied your sense of style."

Jennie observed me objectively. "You don't have to envy
that quality any more, Johanna. I don't know how or when the
metamorphosis occurred, but you've come into your own this
summer. You don't realize how many men turn around and
give you surreptitious second glances. It's not just your choice
of color, though I'm relieved you've abandoned those pallid
pastels. It's something else. You aren't in love, are you?"

Startled, I answered, "I don't think so. If I were, I'm fairly
certain I'd know it."

"Don't be so sure. Sometimes love can creep up on a person without warning or invitation."

"Is that how it happened with you?"

"Oh very good, Johanna. Better than Mother, and she's
mastered the leading question."

I had to laugh at her teasing tone. "I'm sorry. That was too

obvious and not up to my usual standard of tactful prying."
I picked up the menu. "Let's have lunch and you can choose
what you want to tell me about your stay in Lake Geneva. I
promise no sneaky questions."

As we ate, Jennie described the house, the lake, and the
family with an amused and uncharitable clarity that caused me
to choke on giggles more than once.

"Please tell me you're making these details up for effect, Jennie. I can't imagine anyone is really that pompous or
affected."

Jennie drew herself up in her chair and pursed her mouth
before she mimicked, "The Milford name has been known in
Boston for two hundred years, and no breath of scandal has
ever tarnished its shining respectability."

"Jennie, I refuse to believe that anyone said those words
with a straight face."

"True, though. Carl would have you think otherwise, but
he's as much a Milford as anyone else in the family. He glared at
me when I tried to point out that it was 1912 and if his family
wanted to live in the past, perhaps they could at least move into
the nineteenth century. Being only one century behind would
show some progress, anyway."

"Carl certainly gives the impression of a more progressive
man. I'd have thought you and he were well matched."

"Mm-mm, he's funny that way. He likes to give the impression of being a man-about-town and he definitely likes a
challenge, but he's still a Milford. His wife must be above reproach, chaste, well-mannered, and preferably beautiful. I once
asked him if it would matter if his wife was as stupid as a stick
and he told me—very seriously—that intelligence in women
was not held in high regard in his family."

"I hope Mrs. Milford wasn't present for that conversation,
poor woman." I gave Jennie an assessing glance. "Are you

making all this up?" I wouldn't put it past her to quote fictional comments she knew would raise my temper. With her sense of mischief, she would enjoy my reaction.

"Unfortunately, no." No mischief in her tone, only something serious and sad so that I reached across the table to place my hand over hers.

"That doesn't sound like the man, the family, or the place for you then."

She carefully pulled her hand away from mine and without looking at me responded, "Mother has her heart set on it."

"For heaven's sake, Jennie, regardless of your mother's aspirations, I know she doesn't want you to marry unhappily. It's not like you to act the martyr. You're young. You have plenty of time to hold out for someone you truly love."

"Love does not come into the picture, Johanna, not for Mother, anyway. You don't know what it's been like growing up in my house."

"What do you mean?"

"Mother married Father for his name and for his finances. I believe she loved someone else, but that didn't matter once she met Father. Ever since I was a little girl, she's drilled it into me that I have the same obligation to marry well."

"Jennie, Uncle Hal loves your mother."

"Yes, he does. Isn't that sad? I think he knew from the beginning that she didn't love him in return, but he was willing to take the chance that someday she might. When you talk about your life in China, your mother singing for happiness, and the way your father loved her, I'm consumed by envy. It's never been happy in our house ever, not like that, just year after year of obligation and guilt. Peter can escape to school but I'm not allowed. I'm trapped and there's only one way out." For a moment I was silent in the face of this bleak revelation.

Finally I said gently, "Your mother loves you, Jennie, and

she loves Peter. She wants what's best for you both. That's worth something."

"You don't understand her kind of love, how it binds and suffocates and—and compels obedience. How it tires you out." She was so impassioned that she stumbled over her words. "Love shouldn't be like that, Johanna, so selfish and enslaving. I've lived with it for nineteen years and I'm tired of it. I'm going to give her what she wants so I can get away."

"Jennie, if you don't love Carl Milford—" My cousin stood abruptly.

"I don't want to talk about this any more, Johanna. Are you serious about buying a new dress?" Just like that Jennie shut off the conversation. She looked at me steadily, daring me to pursue a topic she had obviously ended.

I stood, as well. If she was done with the conversation, I must be, too, at least for the time being.

"Absolutely. Something glamorous and completely inappropriate, and if I never have a place to wear it, that's all right, too."

"How unlike your frugal good sense, Johanna. Are you sure you're not in love?"

I remembered the delicious feeling of having Drew Gallagher's whispered voice against my lips, the anticipation of the warmth of his arms and his mouth. Not love exactly, I thought, but something related perhaps.

Jennie, watching my face, gave an unladylike chortle. "Oh my, oh my, Johanna. I believe you're blushing."

"I am not," I snapped, but knew from the warmth in my cheeks that I probably showed some color.

"Is it your Mr. Goldwyn? He's a very nice man and seems to spend a lot of time in your company."

"No, Jennie," I replied firmly. "If I were in love, which I'm not, it would not be with Allen. He's a good friend but that's all."

"Then—?"

This time it was my turn to squelch the conversation. "I don't want to talk about this any more, Jennie." She caught the mimicked words and grinned as I continued, "Now, are you willing to help me spend an exorbitant amount of money on a completely unnecessary dress or aren't you?"

We found the perfect dress I didn't need at a small, elegant store well off the main shopping thoroughfares of Chicago. Jennie knew of the shop and led me there after several futile searches in the large, expensive retail establishments for which Chicago was known. The woman who met us at the door recognized Jennie and welcomed her with the warmth of an old friend.

"No, Claudette, nothing for me this time, can you believe it? We're shopping for my cousin."

Claudette stepped back and looked me over carefully from head to toe, her eyes moving so methodically she might have been following an elevator up and down my body. "I have one or two gowns that might do. What is the occasion?" Claudette spoke with an unnatural French accent that sounded artificial and slightly pretentious and which I found difficult to take seriously.

She probably came from no farther away than the lower east side, I thought unkindly, but I answered politely, "There isn't one."

"Yet," supplied Jennie. "Johanna just wants to be prepared when her Prince Charming appears to sweep her off to the ball."

Claudette gave a nicely human smile at that teasing remark and I immediately liked her more. After she brought out the amber gown, my esteem grew to enormous proportions. Claudette may never have been closer to France than the local can-can review at the corner theater, but she had an eye for fashion and a talent for design.

"This one, I think," Claudette said. She carried a gown in a beautiful shade of amber over her arm, its rich brown silk georgette crepe threaded through with gold. While Claudette helped me dress in the fitting room, Jennie fidgeted outside the door impatiently and told me peremptorily to stop fussing.

"I want to see," she complained loudly and then when I stepped out so she could see, was properly silenced. "Amazing, really," Jennie said finally. "It's made just for you, Johanna. The color couldn't be more exactly the color of your eyes."

I turned to face the full-length mirror. "You don't think it's just a little too—you know—revealing? I feel like I'm out in public in my chemise."

"The style is very progressive," Claudette agreed. "I've seen it in the most recent fashion plates from Paris, very simple, clinging, and elegant. A man named Paul Poiret is all the rage, and you are exactly the kind of woman to do his designs justice. Layers of lace and modest high-necked frocks do not show your figure to advantage."

"Claudette is always right. Really, Johanna, you have a wonderful figure. For a small woman, I would even call it voluptuous. Why do you hide your gifts under a bushel?"

The soft, simple neckline draped low, showing more skin than was really proper and a swell of bosom that seemed to me quite risqué. The dress itself fell gracefully straight from a slight gathering of fabric under the breasts, no sash and no waist, every curve of my figure displayed clearly under the amber silk. Long full sleeves narrowed dramatically at the wrist, held in place by a cuff of fabric embroidered with the same gold that sparkled through the whole dress. Delicate gold embroidery outlined the neckline, as well, providing an illusion of jewelry, and as a final proof of the gown's revolutionary fashion, vertical slits graced each side of the hem and revealed close-fitting, flounced trousers beneath. The dress's exotic look was completely at odds with the sweet, high-necked, pastel innocence currently so popular in fashion and society.

"Do you honestly think I can wear this in public? People will think I escaped from a harem. I'll be arrested."

Jennie choked back a laugh. "You're afraid, aren't you?"

"Don't be silly. What's there to be afraid of? A dress?"

"Not the dress, Johanna, but how the dress makes you look. You're afraid of looking like a woman, having the curves women have, being looked at by men who will know without any doubt that you have all of a woman's parts and will enjoy speculating about what they'd like to do with them. How interesting! I never realized that about you before."

"I am not afraid," I repeated, but Jennie was more right than I wanted to admit. Despite progress, women were still patronized, repressed, mocked, undervalued, and abused and for many years I'd worked hard to avoid those offenses. Perhaps that's why this flowing, elegant dress made me feel exposed and vulnerable. "Anyway, I'll wear a corset underneath."

"Dare you not to." Jennie's eyes gleamed, enjoying herself.

With as much haughtiness as I could muster, I told Claudette, "I'll take it."

"If you'd rather look at something else—"

"No. I have to take this one or my dear cousin Jennie will never let me forget it." I smiled to soften the words. "I like the gown very, very much, Claudette." To Jennie I added, "It's safe enough to take your dare because I haven't any place to wear it."

Walking out of the little shop, Jennie stopped long enough to say, "I'm proud of you, Johanna. There's nothing wrong with looking like a woman, and you might find that you enjoy the attention."

"Being a woman is more than appearance and clothes, Jen.

I've known women I consider truly remarkable, despite the fact they were wearing second-hand clothes and their hair had been cut with a kitchen knife. Their worth was determined by more than their outward appearance."

Jennie held up a hand. "Don't start one of your women's sermons, Johanna. You'll never convince me that your remarkable women wouldn't love a new dress and a jar of face cream as much as anyone else. You're so caught up in causes that you forget the simple basics. Women are all alike under the skin."

"How can you say that?" I demanded, and we bandied the issue back and forth until Jennie found a cab home and I headed for the train station.

When the gown was delivered the next day, I looked it over one more time, appreciating even more its drape and color, and then put the garment in the back of my closet, where I was sure it would stay for a very long time.

Peter stopped by in September to say his good-byes before heading off for his final year at the university.

"I'll still have two years of law school and the bar exam, but at least I'll have finished my undergraduate work. I wish I could hurry the process along."

"Don't wish your life away," I responded. "You're still young. Will we see McIntyre and McIntyre on the door someday?"

"Probably not. Father's corporate law holds no appeal. I'm more interested in criminal law."

"Prosecution or defense?"

"Oh, defense. I like to be needed." We walked up the stairs together toward Grandmother's room where we stopped at her door.

"Crea's been working on getting Grandmother out of that invalid chair, Peter. She's so wonderfully patient with her and so encouraging! Don't be surprised if Grandmother is walking with a cane the next time you're home." I knocked on the door and poked my head in the room to see Crea at the foot of the bed lifting one of Grandmother's legs. "Peter's here to say goodbye," I said, then added to Peter, "Just go in. I'm going to talk to Mayville about menus, so pop into the kitchen before you leave and say a proper goodbye to both of us there." I heard Peter call a cheerful hello before he closed the bedroom door behind him and I went in search of May.

After a cup of tea followed by a discussion with May about a quiet celebration for Grandmother's birthday, I looked at the large kitchen clock in surprise.

"Look how late it is! I wonder where Peter got to. I hope he didn't leave without saying good-bye." I left the kitchen and came toward the central staircase from the back hallway and so was unable to be seen by Crea and Peter, who stood at the foot of the stairs in muted, serious discussion. They were so intent on each other, I could have ridden a bicycle down the hallway and they wouldn't have noticed me.

"Stop, Peter. You're speaking foolishly and I won't hear another word." Crea stood stiffly, hands clenched into fists at her sides and cheeks scarlet. From my side view, the light coming in from the hall window seemed to illuminate her face and emphasize the glitter of unshed tears in her eyes. Peter reached out both hands to her shoulders.

"My love," he began, and at the tenderness in his tone, Crea gave a little gasp, whether of pain or longing I couldn't tell, and spoke sternly, her voice breaking only at the end.

"You mustn't talk to me like this. It isn't right. Please, Peter."

"What isn't right is your stubborn refusal to admit that we have—"

At that point I decided I had already overheard too much and could either retreat or move forward. Making a quick decision, I cleared my throat loudly before stepping around the corner of the stairs where Peter still stood with his hands firmly on Crea's shoulders. Both of them looked at me in surprise, but it was Crea who jumped back from Peter, forcing herself away from his touch.

"I'm sorry. Am I interrupting?" I asked mildly. Crea's face went pale, then fired to a wave of crimson.

"Johanna, I—" she began, but her voice finally broke completely and she couldn't say another word. Instead, she turned and rushed upstairs.

Peter's unwavering gaze followed Crea as she made her hasty departure, and I recognized the look on his face: a man in love, completely smitten, head-over-heels, and lost completely. I felt a quick rush of sympathy and understanding.

When it was clear Crea wasn't going to reappear and fling herself into his arms, Peter turned to me and said simply, "I love everything about Crea O'Rourke. Everything."

"I can see that," I said and took his arm. "Come and sit down and tell me about it."

"There's not much to tell. I appreciated how kind she was to Grandmother first and told her so and we started talking and one thing led to another—" Peter met my inquiring look with defiance. "We haven't done one thing to be ashamed of. After the first time I told her how I felt, she's tried to keep her distance, but I don't think I'm wrong. I think she cares, too, at least a little bit. I kissed her once and there was definitely something there before she got all icy and threatened to slap my face."

"Peter, I—"

"If you're going to tell me she's not my type, Johanna, that it wouldn't work, that we're from two different worlds, don't bother. Crea's told me all that before, and a lot more about her being poor and uneducated and having a past."

"I can't deny that's true, but I wasn't going to say anything like that."

"It's the twentieth century," Peter continued, ignoring my interjection. "We don't have a caste system here. If you find someone who's kind and smart and beautiful and brave, what do those other things matter? I love her, Johanna. What should I do?" His last words held such pathos I could hardly restrain from putting my arms around him, and when he turned his face to me, that open, honest, fair face, the urge grew even stronger. But Peter wasn't a boy. He was all grown up, and this was a situation to discuss as adults.

I told him gently, "You have to respect Crea's wishes."

"But—"

"There's no *but* about it, Peter. It was apparent to me that while Crea may have feelings for you, your behavior just now distressed her deeply."

"I didn't mean to trouble her."

"I know that, but nevertheless you did. I could see it in her face. You have to respect her wishes, Peter, and leave her alone." Then I added, smiling, "At least until she and I have a chance to talk."

His face brightened with hope. "Will you, Johanna?"

"Sometime in the next few days I'll try to discuss this with her, but it's her choice and I won't force the conversation." I stood. "And you must go off to school exactly as planned."

"I know." He looked as if I'd told him he had to shoot the family dog.

"Peter, there's adequate mail service from the east coast. Sending Crea a friendly letter once in a while can't hurt. You know you have to finish school so you have time. There's no need to rush anything right now. Be patient with her."

"But what if I lose her? What if I go away and she finds someone else or disappears completely?"

I regretted the cliché of my response but told him, "Then it wasn't meant to be, Peter, but I think those alternatives are very unlikely. Keep in touch with Crea on a regular but friendly basis and plan your next approach more strategically."

"I didn't know it would feel like this," he admitted shyly as we walked to the front door. "I thought, well, I guess I thought someday I'd meet some respectable girl and marry her and that would be that. I've never been very interested in the kind of girls the fellows at school bring around, and it didn't faze me at all when the only other girl I ever felt anything for took up with someone else. But then I walked into Grandmother's room and Crea was reading out loud, her Irish voice as musical as a song, all that red hair and skin like cream"—a momentary pause for recollection—"and I was lost." His voice held the unlikely combination of anguish and bliss.

I stretched to kiss him on the cheek. "Poor boy. It happens like that sometimes, I'm told. I wish I could snap my fingers and make things right, but I can't. You need to get on with your education and your life, Peter."

He nodded, then added in a low voice on his way out the door, "But I don't think it will be much of a life without her, Johanna."

Well, I thought to myself after he left, how had I missed that, in my own house and right under my nose? No wonder Peter was underfoot the last few weeks. And how painful for Crea, especially if she reciprocated Peter's feelings even a little bit. With her pride and the mysteries of her past, I could see that she would feel Peter was above and beyond her, despite the priceless qualities Peter had listed. I sighed. Who'd have imagined life would get even more complicated?

That afternoon and evening, Crea's behavior showed nothing out of the ordinary. If I hadn't been an eye witness, I'd never have believed that only a few hours before she had swept up the stairs with a sob in her voice, that her hands had trembled on the banister. We talked casually in Grandmother's room, teasing Grandmother about another birthday and discussing her upcoming birthday party. Grandmother noticed that Crea was more subdued, gave me a questioning look, and I quickly shook my head, mouthing the word *later* when Crea's back was turned. While Crea ate a solitary late supper in the kitchen, I kept Grandmother company and filled her in on the basic details of the drama I'd seen unfold earlier.

"I've been thinking about the situation for the past few hours," I told her, "and I can see why Peter and Crea might be attracted to each other. Despite their differences, they're both steady, kind, even-tempered, and faithful. I don't know, though, if Crea has any strong feelings for Peter."

Grandmother, sitting in her chair by the window and eating slowly from her supper tray, said, "Of course, she does." Her physical improvement was especially noticeable in her speech, which, while slurred and soft, was now understandable.

"How do you know?" She shook her head, her expression familiar from previous occasions when she had considered me dense as a post.

"I pay attention, Johanna. I haven't had much to do lately other than observe the people around me, you know." I grinned at her, glad to recognize that tone of dry brusqueness, however weakened the volume.

"Are you implying I don't pay attention?"

"You're too busy saving the world to see what's going on in your own house, my dear." But she gave me a crooked smile when she spoke and wasn't chiding.

"I suppose I am." After a pause, I added, "So what do you think about Peter and Crea? What should I do?"

"There's nothing you can do except be a friend to both of them. I've become very fond of Crea and, of course, Peter—" Her voice trailed off.

"I know Peter's the favorite, so don't worry you'll hurt my

feelings," my remark only half-teasing.

Grandmother didn't protest my statement, only said thoughtfully, "Sometimes relationships cannot be fixed, Johanna. Sometimes, no matter how much you wish it otherwise, they're never able to be made right."

"You mean Peter and Crea?" She didn't answer but held out an imperious hand.

"I'm tired. Will you help me to bed, please? And then return this tray and tell Mayville she outdid herself with supper this evening."

I spent some time with May and Levi in the kitchen and then went upstairs to bed, the house and the street outside still and dim. September now and the light fading earlier, a reminder of the short days and crisp air of autumn that were right around the seasonal corner. How quickly the summer had sped! Five months ago to the day I had stood on the tilting deck of a sinking ocean liner and now, with time already dimming the sharp edges of that memory, I puzzled through a different, less dramatic dilemma—what to do about Peter, who was in love, and Jennie, who wasn't. And to be honest, struggling with my own feelings, too, about Drew Gallagher, the kind of slippery man I should distrust and Allen Goldwyn, whose sterling qualities should have appealed to me but didn't. All contrary. At the risk of trivializing a terrible tragedy, I thought that true life-and-death situations possessed their own kind of simplicity and a certain ease of solution that eluded emotional affairs completely. I was at my best in the former circumstance but at a loss more often than not when it came to the baffling emotional depths of the human heart.

Unable to sleep, I propped my back against my bed's headboard and settled in with a book but was startled soon after by a knock on my door. I knew immediately who it was and called, "Come in, Crea." She came a few steps into the room and stopped, face pale, mouth resolutely grim.

"I want to explain," Crea announced.

"All right but sit down first, or I'll get a cramp in my neck from looking up at you." I motioned toward the foot of my bed and said again, "Sit down, Crea." She sat gingerly, hands in her lap and eyes on my face.

Finally she spoke, all in such a rush that I guessed she had prepared and practiced in advance what she was going to say. "You must think I've betrayed you, sneaking around in your house behind your back while you trusted me, but it wasn't like that, Johanna. I swear it. As soon as I realized Peter was—was interested in me, I tried to avoid him. I never encouraged him. After all you've done for me, I'd never act in a way that would upset you."

"Why do you think that would upset me?" My question clearly took her aback.

"Because he's your cousin and I'm from the Anchorage."

"Those are both true statements, but I repeat, why would that upset me?"

"Johanna, don't talk to me like I'm ten years old. You know exactly what I mean. Peter is educated and handsome and I'm a servant in your house." I winced at the words.

"You're not a servant."

"Of course, I am," she shot back. "What else would you call me?"

"You're an employee, Crea, not a servant, free to come and go as you please, stay or leave as you choose. And I thought we were friends, besides."

She flushed. "How can we be friends? Look at you, an educated, wealthy, world-traveler. Then look at me." At that I shut my book with a pop.

"Crea, let's agree to forego the melodrama. You're an intelligent woman who must certainly realize that real friendship is not predicated on bank accounts or train schedules. As for love—" I sighed. "My cousin Peter thinks you are a supernatural mix of angel and goddess. He's so smitten with everything about you, he can't think straight, and what's wrong with that?" I paused, then added, "Are you telling me he was bothering you with his attentions? Because if that's how it was—"

"No, of course not! How could you think such a thing? You know Peter would never act that way. He's too much of a gentleman." Her vigorous defense of my cousin made me smile.

"I see his affection isn't entirely one-sided." Crea didn't smile in return.

"What does it matter? Spout as much fancy talk as you like, Johanna, you can't change the differences between Peter McIntyre and Crea O'Rourke. His mother would slit my throat before she'd allow us to be together, and you know it. Shall I count my offenses?" She held up a hand and ticked them off on her fingers. "I'm Irish, I'm Catholic, I'm the bastard daughter of a house servant with no formal education, no family, and no fortune. How do you think I'll stack up against your aunt's plans for her only son, young rising star lawyer and bearer of the family name?"

"I think we should work through one issue at a time. I know Aunt Kitty is difficult, and I know she would not approve of you. At first, anyway. But if you're my friend and if Peter loves you, she might come around. We don't know otherwise."

"Do you think Peter does love me, Johanna?" Crea latched onto the one part of my little speech that caught her attention and her heart.

"Yes, I think he does." Her reaction was to get up and pace to the door, turn around and come back and stare at me.

"I wish I could change the past. I wish I could be someone different, someone who deserved to be loved." The anguish in her tone caught me unawares.

"No one can change the past, but because we spend our lives in the future, it seems to me that's where we should concentrate our energies." I got up, too, threw on my robe, led her to the stuffed chair at one end of my bedroom, and pushed her into it. I dropped inelegantly onto the ottoman at her feet. "I don't know what's tormenting you, Crea, but let it lie. Whatever it is, it's over and past. No one needs to know."

"*I* know," Crea cried. "Oh, Johanna, you don't understand." She began to weep, trying in vain to wipe away the stream of tears with the palms of both hands. Wordlessly, I rose to dig out a handkerchief from a bureau drawer and hand it to her. She stopped crying after a while and leaned her head back against the chair, eyes closed and clutching the soaked square of cloth. "What a mess I've made of things!" she said finally. "What a terrible mess!" When I didn't respond, she opened her eyes. "I've lived with a man without being his wife. The man was married and I knew it from the start. I had his child. How do you think that will go over with the McIntyres?"

In my line of work, I was used to hearing unbearable stories, so I was able to say with admirable equanimity, "I don't know," displaying no shock or disappointment or surprise when in fact I experienced all three.

"Well, I know. Peter will be disgusted and his parents horrified. It is, after all, a disgusting and horrible story."

"Crea, stop doing this to yourself." The self-loathing in her tone was painful to hear. "You must have been very young."

"I was, but why does that matter? I took the easy way out."

"And paid dearly for it."

"Yes, Johanna, I paid very, very dearly for it, but nothing more than I deserved."

"Does it have something to do with the man we heard

talking at the party at the Yacht Club? The man whose voice almost made you faint?"

"Of everyone in the world, I didn't expect to see him there and I was afraid he would see me—or his wife would. It just hit me so hard to hear his voice."

I remained quiet, thinking she wanted to continue but didn't know how to start the story, and waited for her to speak in her own time and in her own way.

In a low voice Crea finally began, "My mother conceived me on the trip to America on board ship. Can you imagine? I try to picture how and where they found the privacy, and I just can't. She said my father was a sailor—and Irish, which in her mind seemed to make her condition more acceptable. She told me they planned to marry, but I don't think that's so. My mother was a young and wild girl, off to America on her own, despite her da's wishes, and I think she reveled in her newfound freedom. She didn't have an ounce of fear in her. After I was born, she took to the streets for a living, but she was a bright woman and knew there was no future there, so when I turned five, she found work in the large house of a prominent Chicago family. How that happened, I don't know and she never said, but she worked in the laundry and the kitchen and lived there with me for almost eight years. You'd recognize the family name, but that part isn't important. I told you before that I was twelve when my mother died and at my wit's end with grief and fear. I didn't know what to do. I had no family but her, no education, and only the most common of household skills. One day not long after my mother died, he came downstairs and said he talked to his wife and they both wanted me to stay on—if I was willing—and work for them the same as my mother had. It was a blessing dropped from heaven, I thought. I could stay where I was wanted and where I felt comfortable and safe."

I pulled up my knees and wrapped my arms around

them, my attention fixed on Crea's green eyes and the delicate shadows of memory that colored her complexion as she spoke. She must have been a lovely child.

"But it wasn't much of a blessing after all, was it?" I asked.

"It isn't what you think, Johanna. I wasn't taken advantage of or brutalized or coerced. He was never unkind or even un-truthful. In fact, sometimes he was quite tender with me. It was something I could do for him, a way to thank him for letting me stay on and for giving me a home. I could make him happy. He was always so grateful to me afterwards and that made me feel important and powerful in a way. I knew he had a wife, but he said he had the ability to love two women, and I thought, why wouldn't that be all right? I wasn't taking him away from her. He came to me, but he always went back upstairs."

"How old were you, Crea, when it started?"

"He found me crying on my thirteenth birthday, miss-ing my mother and scared of the future. It started then. For comfort."

My face must have reflected my anger because she said quickly, "He never forced himself on me or threatened me. He was never anything but kind to me."

"You were thirteen and he was a grown man." I remem-bered the words "to Lydia" I had overheard at the Yacht Club. "Didn't he have children older than you?"

Crea flushed. "Two daughters older."

"And he still had the conscience to sleep with the thirteen-year-old orphan who worked in his kitchen? His conduct was indefensible, Crea. You were a child with no family and no one to counsel or protect you, and he took advantage of your situation."

"Sometimes, Johanna, you wear blinders. You want to make all women victims, but sometimes women deserve exactly what they get. Sometimes they make bad choices or they disobey the rules on purpose, and what happens to them is what they deserve."

"If you were a woman at the time, I might agree with you, but you weren't a woman at thirteen, just a lonely, grieving girl."

"I was raised a good Catholic girl, though, and I knew it was wrong. I just didn't care. I loved being important to someone and having him pay attention to me and bring me presents. I'd still be there today because it was safe and easy, only I got pregnant."

At first I didn't know what to say at that, but as the silence lengthened I asked, "Is that what brought you to the Anchorage?"

Crea nodded. "I never thought it could happen to me, never considered the possibility. I guess I thought I was too young or he was too old. I really can't remember what I thought. I didn't even know what was wrong with me at first, but when I told one of the day girls about being so sick in the morning, she asked me a few questions and then said, 'You're having a baby, you simpleton, and don't tell me the fairies brought it. You've been doing what you shouldn't have.' I remember how those words stuck in my head—*doing what you shouldn't have*—and I knew she was right. Everything changed then."

"I imagine it did. How exactly?"

"After I thought about it and got used to the idea, I was happy. I'll have a babe, someone of my own to love and it'll make him happy, too, I thought. He'll take care of us and we'll be our own little family. I was nearly sixteen then and I had all these dreamy pictures of what it would be like."

"Let me guess. The baby's father didn't share your dreams." I could tell by Crea's expression that she still couldn't believe what had happened, that the memory still surprised and hurt.

"He said, 'Get rid of it,' just like that. 'I can arrange for you to get rid of it,' he said. Then he reached into his pocket and tried to give me money. He was angry—but frightened, too, I could tell."

"I imagine he was," I commented. "A man like that would have a lot to lose."

"I didn't understand what he meant, and he explained that he knew someone who could get rid of the baby before it was born. He said I'd hardly feel anything and then we could continue just as we were. 'You don't need a baby to be happy,' he told me. 'Aren't we happy just like we are?' But the more he talked, the more I knew I wanted that baby. I wanted a daughter and I'd name her after my mother and we'd be a real family. I'd take care of her and she'd love me. I wanted that baby and no matter how he talked to me or tried to bribe me, I wouldn't give in." Crea curled herself into as small a ball as she could manage, feet pulled up into the chair and arms hugging herself. My heart went out to her.

"You don't have to tell me any more, Crea. It's past now and I don't need to know the details. They won't make me like or admire you less."

"The only other person I ever told this to was Matron, and I didn't go into all the details even with her. I'll feel better if you know, Johanna, and I don't mind talking to you. You never let anything you hear affect how you treat people. You never scold or judge. At first I kept waiting for you to act all high and mighty like some of the other women who came to the Anchorage, but you never did. That's why we all took to you so fast. You make it easy for people to talk to you."

"Thank you," I said, touched, then in a brisker tone went on, "If you're eighteen now, you must have been at the Anchorage at least two years."

"I came to the Anchorage purely by accident. When I

packed up the few things I owned and left the house, I didn't know where to go or what to do. I knew I had to find work so I went downtown to ask at all the department stores, and when I was coming out of Scott's, I slipped and fell on a patch of ice. I panicked and thought I'd hurt the baby. Of all people, it was Matron who helped me up and listened to my fears and took me straight to the Anchorage with her. Matron says it was the hand of God, but I don't know if I believe that. There's so much suffering and grief in the world, Johanna. It's hard for me to believe in the hand of God at all."

"I don't think we should blame God for the world's suffering and grief when ninety-nine percent of it is caused by humans."

"That's exactly what Matron told me," Crea said with a wisp of a smile. "You two are cut from the same cloth."

"I'll take that as a compliment. Hilda Cartwright is a strong woman who doesn't let false sentiment get in the way of her duty to the women and babies in her care." I remembered Flora's baby placed into the hands of new parents before Flora was even buried. "What happened to your baby, Crea? Did you give it up?"

"Oh, no! Oh, no, Johanna! I'd never have done that. No. I carried her to term and she was a beautiful daughter, perfect in every way, except she was stillborn."

"I am so sorry, Crea." My heart lurched with shock and sadness, and I leaned forward to put my hand on her arm. "I am so very sorry."

"I knew something was wrong, poor wee girl. I could tell. She stopped moving. For a long time I thought she died as a punishment for my sins."

"But you know better now, I hope," I responded sharply.

"It took a while, but yes, I know that babies born to perfectly respectable married women can be stillborn, too, that it's just something that happens. But I didn't understand it at first and I blamed myself. That's why Matron let me stay on for all that time at the Anchorage—because I wasn't strong enough to understand and accept that. I think she was afraid of what I'd do if she turned me loose. Then after a while, after I began to see things differently, I was able to be a help to her and to the Anchorage. I could help with the women who came and I could help with the babies. I suppose I'd still be there except you came along and blew through the place like a tornado and forced me to look at life differently."

"Good. That's my goal in life: make people see things differently, just like putting on a new pair of glasses." Crea gave a weak laugh.

"I have never met a woman like you, Johanna, who's most satisfied when she's making people uncomfortable."

"But it's always for people's own good," I protested, my feelings a tiny bit hurt.

"Yes," she agreed, "it always is, but so is castor oil and pulling a tooth so you shouldn't be surprised when you meet with resistance or resentment."

"I know. Always being right is one of my greatest flaws." Crea laughed again, this time sounding more like herself, and we sat quietly for a while. She looked exhausted. Reliving the sad story seemed to have sapped her of all energy.

"I'm glad I told you, Johanna. I wanted you to understand why there could never be anything between Peter and me. I'm not the woman he thinks I am, and I couldn't bear to see the look on his face if he knew who and what I really am. Do you understand now?"

I stood and stretched. "I understand that it's late and we're both tired."

"Johanna—"

"Crea, you're not a thirteen-year-old girl any more. You've

grown and changed. Peter loves the woman you are now, not the child you were. I have no idea how your story will end, but you should give Peter a chance. He has a generous heart and he's quite capable of listening and understanding. I think you underestimate him." She started to speak again, but I continued inexorably. "I know it's not my business. It's yours and Peter's. All I ask is that you be kind to him. My cousin Peter is the best person in the family."

Crea rose and with a hand on the doorknob, turned to say softly, "Second best person, I think. Good night, Johanna."

Maiden, that read'st this simple rhyme,
Enjoy thy youth, it will not stay;
Enjoy the fragrance of thy prime,
For oh, it is not always May!
Enjoy the Spring of Love and Youth,
To some good angel leave the rest;
For Time will teach thee soon the truth,
There are no birds in last year's nest!

Chapter Eleven

C rea's story stayed with me much longer than I expected
and as often happened—because of the intensity of the
story, I imagine—Crea materialized in my dreams. When she
was not being chased by an ominous faceless figure who meant
her harm, she wandered aimlessly through the city streets in
the dead of winter searching pitifully for something important, yet she could not articulate what that something was. Regardless of the dream's form, my odd role in it was to follow
after Crea—*skulk* would be more accurate—and try to warn
her of impending danger. "Don't go there!" I would call to
her in the dream, certain that something horrific waited in the
shadow, but no matter how often and how loudly I called, Crea
could never hear me and would disappear completely into the
darkness, leaving me angry, fearful, and helpless. The images
had the same nightmarish quality of my *Titanic* and my Cox
dreams, and I was annoyed that no sooner had one troubling
dream faded than another one took its place.

Plans for Grandmother's late October birthday continued

uninterrupted, Aunt Kitty doing her best to take over all the planning but meeting her match in Mayville's truculent devotion to Grandmother. I stayed out of as many of the discussions as I could. Having either of those two women angry with me was a prospect that bred its own nightmares. Both understood that Grandmother was not quite ready for a dance band and so her party must be small and quiet. About menus, decorations, location, gifts, and guest list, however, there was less accord. Privately, I thought May had the upper hand because regardless of Aunt Kitty's stated preferences, the refreshments must still come out of May's kitchen. Nevertheless, I conveniently drifted out of the vicinity whenever the conversation turned to the party.

Autumn seemed to come to Chicago literally overnight that year. I awoke on the first of October to a vigorous, cold breeze rattling the window. As I walked to the train station, I saw only bare trees. Sometime during the night the wind had shaken all the leaves loose and scattered them into messy piles in the streets and along the walks.

"Summer's gone, for sure," I commented to Eulalie when I arrived at the Anchorage.

"Yes. Get ready to be busy."

"Busier than summer?"

"My, yes. Winter's rough here, and we always have a steady stream of women looking for shelter. Matron finds needy girls on every corner during the winter and she brings each one of them home with her." Pride, not complaint, colored Eulalie's tone. I thought of Crea, fifteen and pregnant and falling on a patch of ice at Hilda Cartwright's feet. The hand of God, for sure, no matter what Crea believed.

At the end of the day, as I bundled up for the trip home, Drew Gallagher appeared without warning at the front door of the Anchorage. I didn't particularly like the way my heart fluttered at the sight of him and must have scowled because he stepped inside and commented, "Ah, glad to see me as usual, Miss Swan."

"I am glad to see you," I protested, ending with a feeble "of course" that made him laugh.

"I don't know what else I can do to get into your good graces. I've applauded women's suffrage and built factories for you and still you scowl when you see me."

"You applauded women's suffrage before you ever met me," I retorted, "and this is the first I've heard that Cox's had anything to do with a desire for my good opinion. I don't notice you offering to share the profits with me."

"You told me you already had your fortune. I didn't want you to think I wasn't paying attention." He eyed my scarf and the cloche hat I was in the process of donning. "I'm glad I caught you. I wanted to give you a ride home. You were on your way home, weren't you?"

"Yes, and why?"

"I know this reverses the natural order of things but I have a favor to ask of you." I wouldn't have been able to tell from his tone but from the slightly self-conscious expression on his face, I thought he might be telling the truth.

"All right. No one can accuse me of being unfair, and after all you've done I suppose it is time for me to reciprocate in some fashion." Drew held open the front door for me and I preceded him down the porch steps and onto the walk.

"How you flatter me, Johanna. Your tone held the definite ring of martyrdom."

I chuckled at his dry comment and waited for him to crank the car and get into the driver's seat before asking, "Why do you keep Fritz around if you always do the driving? Or have you let him go?"

"And risk the wrath of Yvesta? Not on your life. I told you

I like to drive and for a reason that as yet remains a mystery, I especially like to drive you around. Obviously, it isn't your heartfelt gratitude that motivates me, so I must have an unrecognized need to be humiliated." The automobile, sleek and roomy enough for seven people, pulled smoothly away from the curb with just the two of us side by side in the front. "How is your grandmother's health progressing, Johanna?"

I sat contentedly, mesmerized by the sight of his hands on the wheel, very nice hands, broad in the palm with long, tapering fingers and unexpectedly sun-browned. Perhaps he spent more time than he cared to admit cruising on the *San Francisco*. I pulled myself back to the moment.

"She's coming along very well. Between Crea's patience and my bullying, Grandmother can now walk a few steps with a cane and speak more intelligibly. Her right side is still very weak and she tires easily, but I hope a few more months will see her back to her old self with only a few residual effects of the stroke. Her birthday is this month and she's actually looking forward to the little party we have planned, so I know she must be feeling better."

"The party isn't scheduled for October nineteenth, is it?"

"No, the weekend after. Why? Does that have something to do with the favor you want to ask?"

"It has everything to do with it, but let's make small talk until we get to Hill Street so I can concentrate on the drive." Which we did, chatting easily about progress at Cox's and the imminent sale of the *San Francisco,* the latter topic causing a slight sigh from me, which Drew noticed.

"I can't believe I'm saying this," I admitted, "but what a shame to give up that glorious boat. I know it's showy and pretentious, but the *San Francisco* certainly had an effect and left an impression. I hope you found it a good home."

"I did. One of Douglas's business acquaintances who long

coveted the vessel snatched at the offer immediately. If everything goes through, the *San Francisco* moves into new hands November first. I didn't know you possessed such a fondness for boating, Johanna. Have you ever been on a sailboat?"

"No. I'm not sure there's enough boat between me and the water. Do you sail?"

"In my disreputable younger days at several eastern schools, I spent more time on the ocean than I did in class. There's something about the challenge of a single sail against the elements that I enjoyed. You should try it sometime. You have the kind of temperament that would enjoy the contest."

"I think I've had enough of the ocean for a while," I said quietly.

He was immediately sympathetic. "Sorry. Does it still bother you? Are you still having those *Titanic* dreams?" I liked his quickness to understand.

"Sometimes. And no, I've moved on in my dreams to another dramatic highpoint in my life."

"You certainly have your share."

"None of them on purpose." We pulled up to the curb in front of my house and I turned to face him. "At last. Curiosity is going to kill me. Come inside so you can tell me what's so special about October nineteenth."

Mayville met us as we stepped inside. "Just so you know, Johanna, Jennie's upstairs with Mrs. McIntyre. Her father said he'd be back to get her as soon as he finished some business." May gave Drew a speculative look. "Shall I set an extra place for supper for your friend?"

Drew answered quickly, "No, thank you. I can't stay," and I knew a fleeting disappointment. A meal with Drew always promised complimentary attention and intelligent conversation and I would have enjoyed both. If I didn't take my evening meal upstairs with Grandmother, I ate either in solitude or informally at the kitchen table with Crea. His company would have been a rare treat.

We shed coats and hats and went into the front room, where I sat down with my hands in my lap. "Enough suspense. I think you're enjoying this too much. What can I do for you, Drew?"

Instead of sitting, Drew stood with his hands in his pockets and gave me a quick, self-conscious smile that was quite endearing. I hoped my appreciation didn't show on my face. He sounded embarrassed as he confessed, "As incredible as it seems, the city of Chicago wants to give me an award."

"What kind of an award?"

"I know you'll think this completely inappropriate, but I believe the Mayor and a consortium of high-level Chicago businessmen want to give me an award for being a good citizen of the city and for promoting the common good through business."

After a thoughtful moment, I asked in awe, "Drew, are you getting the Starr Award?" He looked embarrassed.

"Yes, I am. You know of it, then?"

"Only because my Uncle Hal has spoken of it on several occasions. He's often said it's the only time in the year when the political and the business arenas intersect without rancor or graft. Why would I think such an achievement is inappropriate for you? Congratulations, Drew."

"It's not me, of course, Johanna, it's Cox's. Many of the men in the voting group knew Douglas, but they never heard of me until they began to hear whispers of Cox's success. You haven't visited Cox's over the past few weeks, but if you had, you'd see one touring group after another. Everyone's fascinated by the idea of housing and employing workers in the same building. At first there was a great deal of skepticism about the need to provide childcare, but I gave the visitors free rein to talk to anyone they wanted, and that was the one benefit every worker couldn't say enough about. Productivity is up because no one wants to risk losing her spot, and there's a line of qualified applicants just waiting to work at Cox's. The place was a hit with every Chicago capitalist who visited and that's why I'm getting the Starr Award." At the end of his little speech, he sat down across from me.

"It's a huge honor, Drew. I'm pleased for you. You deserve it."

"No, I don't think I do. I'm not sure I didn't start the Cox experiment because you annoyed me and because I wanted to prove to you that I wasn't the complete insensitive, self-serving oaf you thought me. Don't argue, Johanna, because you know you did. I'm not sure your opinion's changed much either, despite my altruistic behavior, but that's beside the point."

"I don't see what difference it makes why you opened Cox's. You spent your own money and your own time and risked your own capital and reputation. You should be recognized for it." As an afterthought I added, "Insensitive, self-serving oaf or not," which made him smile.

"Thank you, I think."

"I still don't understand the connection with October nineteenth, though."

"That's the night of the awards banquet. Quite a production, I'm told. Held in the ballroom at the Auditorium Building and very black tie. Everyone who's anyone in Chicago attends. I can't say it sounds like the kind of affair I'd ordinarily attend, but it seems churlish to refuse, especially for the guest of honor."

"Of course, you should go, Drew. Your appearance will help your business reputation and perhaps motivate others to follow in your footsteps."

"Will you come with me?" He asked the question abruptly.

I was speechless for a moment and then responded just as abruptly, "Why are you asking me? I won't know a soul and I won't add any glamour to the occasion. Wouldn't you be more comfortable with the beautiful Viola?"

"More comfortable?" He gave the words some thought. "Yes, that's true, I would, because when you're not annoying me, you're often making me uncomfortable, but that's not the point. The point is that if you hadn't prodded me into good works, the Cox experiment wouldn't have happened. It seems only fitting that you should be there to bask in the glory, if only from the sidelines."

I might have wished for a more complimentary invitation, something that included the color of my eyes or the pleasure he found in my company, but I supposed I should be content with being considered an annoying and prodding female. I looked up to find his gaze on me, a surprisingly anxious expression in his eyes and some other, more enigmatic emotion as well.

"I'd be honored to go with you, Drew," I responded formally. "It was thoughtful of you to include me." Then I spoiled the effect by asking, "I don't suppose there's a dance band on the program."

"No. It sounds like a very staid and formal dinner with too many speeches, but we could find a club afterwards if you'd like. Someplace off the beaten path."

"I would like. It sounds like fun and I'll trust your judgment."

"Good. Good."

The silence that followed was awkward. Drew seemed at a loss for words, a situation so rare that I think we were both surprised by it. Then as we both stood and moved toward each other, Jennie appeared in the doorway. I was relieved to see her and simultaneously mentally cursed the interruption. When I introduced Jennie to Drew, I watched his reaction surreptitiously. Jennie was in beautiful form that afternoon, dressed in a pale blue wool suit and a particularly charming hat, the kind that would have looked absolutely ridiculous on me but that suited her perfectly.

I felt an unworthy satisfaction when Drew gave Jennie only a cursory look and polite greeting before turning back to me to say, "I'm keeping you from supper, Johanna. Will seven o'clock suit?"

After he left, Jennie looked at me mischievously. "What a woman of secrets you are, Johanna! How did you ever meet the innovative and progressive Mr. Gallagher?"

"I met him through his brother," I said tersely, not in the mood for Jennie's teasing, at least not about Drew Gallagher. "How do you know he's innovative and progressive?" At her nonchalant shrug and amused eyes, I changed the subject. "You're looking quite stylish, Jen. Have you been out and about?"

"Both out and about. I came by to show Grandmother my new jewelry." Jennie stretched out her left hand so I could clearly see the large sparkle of diamond on her ring finger.

"Are congratulations in order for you and Carl Milford, then?" I asked carefully.

"How could I possible refuse so attractive an offer?" I thought I detected a touch of self-mockery in her tone, but that may have been my imagination. Jennie seemed truly pleased with the ring, turning it this way and that so the stone caught the late afternoon light through the windows. "Five carats, Johanna. Can you imagine how much this ring cost?"

"The cost to you will be even higher, Jennie, if you're not sure about this match."

"Mother's beside herself with joy."

"That's hardly a response to my comment but never mind. I can see you're not in the mood for serious talk. Have you set a date for the wedding?"

"No. Carl's parents have to check their social calendar first." The words were innocent, but this time Jennie's muted mockery was easier to detect and harder to ignore.

"Jennie, for goodness sake—"

"Don't lecture, Johanna. It's never becoming in you." We had moved into the front hallway and she turned to peer through the long, narrow window beside the front door. "Father's here and I need to go. He's leaving for a lengthy stay on the east coast tomorrow and can't come in. I have a feeling he'll be checking out his future in-laws while he's there. He told me to give Grandmother his love, which, of course, I did."

"Was she pleased about your news?" Jennie made a face.

"She's like you. Too perceptive for her own good." With a laugh she added, "I liked your Mr. Gallagher. Too bad I didn't see him first or I might not be walking down the aisle with Carl Milford." She examined my face. "I meant it as a joke, Johanna. Don't give me that look." Then she was out and down the steps to her father's waiting motorcar.

Grandmother seemed tired that evening, so supper was an uneasy meal that I shared with her in her room, both of us speaking casually about Jennie's engagement and both uncomfortable with the news. I couldn't tell why Grandmother was concerned because she was deliberately noncommittal, but I knew from her tone that she had misgivings about the match.

"I'm going with Drew Gallagher to the Auditorium Building to watch him receive the Starr Award," I volunteered. "The city wants to commend him for the Cox Experiment."

"Is this the brother of the Mr. Gallagher on board the *Titanic*?" Grandmother spoke slowly and still slurred her words at the end of the day when she was tired, but I was able to understand her easily.

"Yes."

"Have I met him?"

"No."

"I would like to."

"He'll be here two weeks from Saturday. I could bring him upstairs to meet you then if you'd like."

"Yes, I would. I've attended that presentation in previous years, Johanna, and it's quite grand. What will you wear?" Until her question I hadn't given that issue a thought, but as she spoke I had the clear picture of a straight, elegant gown of amber silk threaded through with gold. Grandmother smiled. "No, don't tell me, Johanna. Just show me that evening."

"You might be shocked. It's not Jennie's dress."

"How fortuitous then since you're not Jennie. Don't forget your mother's diamonds." I remembered how the diamond had sparkled on Jennie's finger. My mother's diamond earrings weren't five carats, but they were faceted beautifully and caught the light in a dangle that sparkled as brilliantly as Jennie's engagement ring. The earrings would be the only jewelry I would need.

"I won't. They'll be perfect." Impulsively I leaned down to kiss her on the cheek. "Good night, Grandmother." I almost told her I loved her, but she was not one to welcome sentiment, and I didn't want to embarrass her or myself. She reached out and briefly took my hand in hers.

"Good night, Johanna. You look very much like your mother tonight."

"Truly?" I was surprised and pleased by the comparison.

"Yes." Grandmother's eyes held a definite twinkle. "I remember that same look on Nettie's face the night she came home and announced she had met a man named David Swan."

"Drew felt obligated to ask me," I protested, "because of our mutual connection with Cox's. I wouldn't read anything into the invitation."

Grandmother did not have time to respond to my words because Crea knocked on the door and stepped inside, saying with a smile, "I think it's time for your exercises, Mrs. McIntyre, and then I can help you get ready for bed unless you'd prefer Johanna's help tonight."

"No, Crea," my grandmother replied. "Johanna is too busy being evasive."

Crea looked at me curiously. "That doesn't sound like the Johanna I know, the woman who's usually blunt and practical to a fault."

"She's only efficient with other people's lives." Turning to me, Grandmother added, "Good night, Johanna," and I realized I was dismissed for the night.

Before I went to bed, I took out the amber dress and held it up against me as I stood in front of the full-length mirror in my room. The garment was beautiful even on the hanger, nothing corseted or cinched anywhere, the fabric flowing and shimmering with its low, elegant drape of neckline and those unusual sleeves that flowed seductively before being caught tightly at the wrist by golden cuffs. Very far removed from the tailored, corseted dresses of current style. No rustling satin, no scalloped lace or heavy rows of seed pearls, nothing pastel or traditionally feminine to be found. Nothing of Jennie there but perfect for me somehow as Claudette had predicted. I thought my words to Grandmother were at least partially true: Drew had invited me for the evening because he thought such a gesture fair. I refused to speculate on any additional reason for the invitation. Whether there was more to it or not, I was excited to be going and intended to enjoy myself every minute of the evening.

By mid-October, Hill Street turned to a blaze of gold and crimson. The oaks and elms that lined the street were resplendent, the colors as vivid and glorious as I could ever remember.

"All that color means a hard winter," predicted May ominously, thinking of the winter winds off the lake and Chicago's January bite of ice and snow. Before the next spring, though, I would recall May's comment with grieving irony, her prophecy more accurate than either of us could have imagined.

October nineteenth turned into the quintessential autumn evening. The cool, azure afternoon sky became cold and black and crystal-clear, overflowing with stars and a brittle, white sliver of moon. I had not heard one word from Drew until the day before when I received a brief, hand-written note, reminding me of the date and time, concluding with a casual, *I'm looking forward to the evening, Johanna,* tacked on almost as an afterthought. I accepted the fact that I was looking forward to the occasion more than he and decided not to let the knowledge bother me. Since Grandmother's stroke my life had included little outside of home and the Anchorage. I hadn't attended one social occasion and I spent my personal time either with the family or with May and Crea. Allen Goldwyn seemed to have dropped off the face of the earth. Once in a while I thought guiltily that I should send him a friendly note just to see how he was, but the moment invariably passed without my taking any action. Considering the humdrum routine I'd fallen into, it was perfectly natural that I would be excited about attending a gala affair with an attractive man. Any attractive man would have done just as well, I told myself, but why shouldn't I look forward to being with Drew Gallagher? The evening's main guest of honor, after all, so perhaps some of his sudden splendor would rub off on me.

Crea knocked on my door just in time to help me with the small, gold-flecked buttons that ran down the back of my dress. I turned my back to her as she entered my bedroom, saying, "Good timing, Crea. Will you help me with these buttons? Why do they have to be so blasted small anyway?" I waited for her to begin and when nothing happened, turned around to see her still standing in the bedroom doorway. "What?" I demanded, trying to decipher the look on her face.

"Johanna, you look—" Crea began and then stopped, searching for the right word.

"Is the dress wrong?" I asked, suddenly anxious. "I don't have to wear this dress, you know. I have others that would do just as well and would be much less noticeable. Just tell me. I promise I won't be offended." At her continued silence, I added, "That does it. Never mind about the buttons. Help me get into something else. Drew will be here—"

"You look extraordinary," Crea finished. "Simply extraordinary."

"Not beautiful?" In my simplistic way, I would have been content with pretty and was not above seeking out the compliments I preferred.

"Better than beautiful," Crea stated firmly, coming farther into the room and smiling at my expression. "Johanna, there's nothing traditional or ordinary about you. In that dress, you look—" Another pause, then, "Glamorous is all I can think of. Absolutely glamorous. You'll take people's breath away. I guarantee it."

"A hard fall off a ladder does the same thing," I commented dryly, turning around once more. "Now will you please finish these buttons for me?" Crea laughed and came forward to make quick work of the buttons.

"You're always so businesslike, I never suspected this side of you." She turned me around by the shoulders. "With your hair all soft and curly and the way that gown turns your skin golden, you look like a different woman from the one who stood in the doorway and dared Yvesta's husband to take a swing at her." The downstairs bell rang just as I turned to view myself in the mirror, and I met Crea's gaze there.

"Oh, dear," was all I said in a little voice, suddenly uncertain and bashful and twelve again. Crea gave me hard hug.

"You look splendid, Johanna. Mr. Gallagher won't be able to take his eyes off you and isn't that what you intended, after all?"

As she headed out the bedroom door and down the stairs, I started to call a protest and then stopped to turn back to the mirror and give myself a rueful smile. "Oh, yes," I agreed softly. "That is exactly my intention." My mother's diamond earrings twinkled agreement.

I threw my evening cape over my shoulders and went downstairs. The butterflies that fluttered somewhere in the pit of my stomach disappeared entirely when Drew turned from speaking to Crea to say pleasantly "Hello, Johanna." He looked very handsome, dressed formally in a black dress suit with black silk lapels and a very fashionable waistcoat that showed a slight flicker of silver when he moved. The gold of his hair and the silver sheen of his vest would show to advantage under the Auditorium's renowned gold stencils and myriad of electric lights. Crea murmured something and slipped away quietly.

After I gave Drew a quick greeting, I asked, "I know this may seem foolish to you, but would you mind very much meeting my grandmother? We've been talking about the Starr Ceremony all week. She and my grandfather attended the very first award banquet a number of years ago, and she said she'd be honored to meet you." Of course, she hadn't said that or anything like that, but I'd practiced making something up and thought what I invented sounded plausible.

"Naturally you set her straight about my character first thing." Drew gave me a grin. "Never mind, Johanna, and I doubt your grandmother said anything of the sort. She's probably much more concerned about the kind of man you'll be spending the evening with, and I can't say I blame her. If I were your grandmother, I'd forbid you to be alone with me, just on general principles."

"If you were my grandmother, you couldn't be the recipient of the Starr Award because you're female, so we'd have no reason to spend the evening together. The issue would be entirely moot." I led him toward the front room. "She's sitting up in her chair and has been waiting to meet you for the better part of an hour. I hope you appreciate the effort."

"I'll try to be on good behavior and not say anything to upset her." I knew from his meek tone that he was laughing at me.

"Believe me, Gertrude McIntyre is completely unflappable. You could cross your eyes, mispronounce words, and eat peas with a knife and it wouldn't faze her good manners one little bit."

"Even if I did all three at once?" Drew whispered from behind me, and I had to swallow a laugh.

"Even then," I retorted in an equally low voice and then raised it for introductions. The part about Grandmother waiting for a while had been true enough. She'd dressed for the occasion and now sat on the edge of the parlor loveseat, straight-backed and regal, with both hands resting on the head of the cane she held before her.

"Mrs. McIntyre, I was sorry to hear of your illness, but I admit that if I didn't know of it, I would never guess you had been incapacitated. You look very fine this evening."

Grandmother's words were slow and measured so she was sure she would be understood without excessive effort or ambiguity. "I feel very fine, Mr. Gallagher. Thank you for your kind words and thank you for the flowers you sent as well. They were beautiful and stayed fresh for an uncommonly long time. Johanna must have shared my particular fondness for yellow roses with you." I didn't know Drew had sent anything to

Grandmother, let alone her favorite yellow roses, but I wasn't about to admit such a lack of knowledge and only smiled agreeably as they both turned to look at me. At that moment, I had an odd, fleeting sensation that Grandmother and Drew were in some way aligned together against me, an impression that continued for a few more minutes as they conversed easily, two old friends chatting and my presence completely superfluous.

Finally Grandmother said, "You'll be late, Mr. Gallagher, if you don't leave now, and it's never good form to be late to your own party. I've enjoyed meeting you. Congratulations on the Starr Award. The recipients comprise a rare and prestigious group of men."

"Exactly the problem, Mrs. McIntyre. Johanna is outraged that no women have been included in that group, and I believe she would like me to sit out the banquet in protest of its exclusivity."

"Johanna," commented my grandmother, "finds comfort in protest. Now go along and enjoy your evening."

"I'll try to return your granddaughter at a reasonable hour."

"Johanna is quite grown up, Mr. Gallagher. I long ago gave up trying to set limits for her."

"Johanna also has the power of speech and rational thought," I interjected, irritated at being talked about in the third person as if I were invisible or absent. I leaned down to kiss my grandmother on the cheek. "Good night and don't wait up for me."

"I gave that up long ago as well," Grandmother responded, but her eyes twinkled so I knew she was enjoying herself.

Settled into the motorcar with Drew in the driver's seat, I commented, "I didn't know you sent flowers to Grandmother."

Drew turned to give me a quick, smiling glance. "I suspect

there are a great many things you don't know about me, Johanna."

I sat back and made a pretense of smoothing the folds of my cape. "They say ignorance is bliss," I replied calmly and heard him chuckle as the auto pulled away. "Do you have a speech prepared for this evening, Drew?"

"Not exactly."

"What does that mean?"

"It means I'm not used to this type of situation and I haven't made up my mind what to say or if I'll say anything at all." His tone, gruff and defensive, sounded unlike him.

"Are you nervous about accepting the award?" When he didn't answer, I exclaimed, "You are, aren't you? I didn't believe there was anything that could unsettle you!"

"I am not nervous and I am definitely not unsettled." His reply came out somewhere between a snap and a bark.

"Of course, you're not. My mistake." Then after a pause, I said, "But if you were either nervous or unsettled, it would be a perfectly understandable state of mind. I know if I had to get up in front of the elite of Chicago, I'd be petrified even if all I had to do was recite my name."

"That's very kind of you, Johanna," Drew's voice was back to normal, "but you and I both know that nothing petrifies you, and if given the opportunity, you'd love to give Chicago's capitalists a piece of your mind about their collective lack of social conscience. The truth is I'm not looking forward to the evening. I feel as though I'm receiving this award under false pretenses, that I'm an imposter pretending to be a solid citizen. Douglas would have loved the honor, but it's not a role with which I'm very comfortable."

"Douglas would never have had the creativity or compassion to have earned it."

"Johanna, what image of me are you creating? Don't turn

me into a do-gooder out to save the world. That's not who I am."

"So you say. You act like I accused you of some particularly horrible character flaw. There's nothing wrong with being a good person." I paused before concluding, "Even if it is infrequent and half-hearted."

He laughed. "What a comfort you are to have around! Did I mention that Cox's is officially running in the black now?" and we were off on another topic of conversation.

As we chatted, I was conscious of a queer but deep compassion for this man who was made uncomfortable by his own good qualities. Once or twice before I had experienced this same feeling when in his company, a feeling that made me want to comfort and protect him, to place myself as shield between him and the world. And that was inexplicable because if ever there was a man who would not welcome and did not need such defensive attention, it was Drew Gallagher.

The Auditorium Building, built two decades earlier in a severe, rectangular Romanesque style that belied its gorgeous interior, housed a huge hotel, an office tower, and the lavish Auditorium Theater, home of the Chicago Symphony Orchestra. Over time it had become a prestigious and exclusive Chicago landmark. When Drew and I entered the lobby, I looked around in awe as speechless as I am capable of being.

Lowering my voice, I said, "Grandfather brought me here for an afternoon visit years ago, before the electric lights were installed, but I don't remember the onyx walls or that grand staircase. How odd that I could forget such extraordinary beauty."

Drew was in the process of lifting my cape from my shoulders to hand to the woman in charge of the lobby's cloak room, but as I finished my comments about the Auditorium and turned back to face him, he became suddenly still, holding my cape in both hands and staring at me, clearly taken aback. In my admiration for the sumptuous building, I had forgotten that I'd worn the cape from his arrival at Hill Street and Drew hadn't had a chance to see my dress. He certainly saw it now. With no apparent shame and as far as I could tell with no deliberate intention to discomfit me, he looked me up and down, lingering on several locations I suppose should have made me blush but didn't. Finally his gaze came to rest on my face.

For a moment I was self-conscious and then, seeing a look in his eyes that was extremely flattering, I said, "You recommended dramatic and I took your advice to heart." He cleared his throat before he spoke.

"The one and only time then that you have ever listened to me or respected my opinion."

"That is simply not true." I suppose I had hoped for a more definitive reaction—an enraptured exclamation at my beauty would have been satisfactory—and the absence of any such gratifying response explained the touch of curtness in my voice.

Drew finally handed my cape to the waiting woman, then came to stand before me, looking down at me with a guarded, quizzical expression I could not decipher. "It is gospel truth and you know it, but I don't care. If anything I said is responsible for you looking like that, I can't begin to tell you how satisfied I am that you chose to listen." He lifted my chin with his index finger, and I had the very real feeling that he might kiss me. Instead he said quietly, "You look spectacular, Johanna. I don't think you understand how very attractive all your attributes are to a man."

Then the moment passed, and he tucked my hand under his arm. We walked through the lobby together, speaking in a desultory manner with each other and stopping every few steps for conversation and introductions to people we met along the way. I recall a few comments directed to me that recollected my grandfather and I know several people congratulated Drew but by and large, I have few memories of any of those early conversations. Because I had been taught well, I went through the motions of courteous smiles and social greetings, but inside I was remembering Drew's frankly admiring stare and the low, intimate sound of his voice as he complimented me. The Auditorium's lights turned the gold that flecked through the amber silk of my dress into tiny, muted sparks. How propitious, I thought, because for a moment sparks of another sort had flown between Drew Gallagher and me. Even if it were a game he was playing, I believed that for all his practice and experience, I had held the better hand for a little while.

The awards banquet was scheduled for the hotel's dining room on the tenth floor. As guests of honor, Drew and I were seated at a large table with a glorious view of the lake through the wall of windows on the opposite side of the room. The reflection of the moon gleamed off the dark water and stars were everywhere, so many that it seemed there were more stars than sky.

We sat side by side and as the dining room filled up with crowds of darkly tailored men and women in resplendent gowns, all of them facing Drew and me as we sat at the head table, I whispered, "Are you all right? No jitters?"

He turned and brought his mouth close to my ear. "Not a one, Johanna. You?"

"Me?" I was surprised and turned quickly to face him so that his face and his mouth were very close. He didn't move away and I resisted the impulse to pull back. Instead, I murmured, "I am strictly ornamental, Drew, here because you felt compelled to ask me along for a reason that still escapes me. You're the one with the obligation." He smelled wonderful, the same fresh, slightly spicy fragrance I remembered from our time on board the *San Francisco.*

"Do you really not know why I asked you to come with me, Johanna?" Drew asked but before I had a chance to respond, Mayor Harrison came up behind us and clamped a hand on Drew's shoulder. I pulled away quickly from the unsettling proximity, my abrupt movement making Drew smile with what I considered an unseemly smugness before he turned slowly toward the mayor.

"Well, Gallagher," Mayor Harrison spoke with the common bonhomie of politicians, "this is a night for you to remember."

"Yes, Mayor, I admit it is," but something about Drew's tone made me think that he was not speaking entirely of the Starr Award.

After the dinner several prominent businessmen received recognition for one thing or another and all of them made brief speeches celebrating Chicago's past and its burgeoning business future. Listening to the last man, whose name was synonymous with the meat-packing business, became almost unbearable for me. I knew for a fact that he treated his workers abominably, paid unlivable wages, and refused to correct the dangerous working conditions of his plants because—as he had once been reliably quoted—"the Irish and the Germans are a dime a dozen off the boat." I must have made some kind of unconscious movement at an especially outrageous self-congratulation because Drew casually placed his hand over mine as it lay on the table.

When I looked at him quickly, he said in a voice only I could hear, "I thought you were reaching for a knife." His comment made me laugh out loud and when I tried to cover my inappropriate giggle with a cough, he handed me a glass of water and murmured solicitously, "Will you be all right, Johanna?"

"I'm fine. It's only—"

"I understand exactly," Drew said, and I knew that somehow he did understand, had read my thoughts, and felt the same reaction. For the first time I understood what he meant when he said he felt like an imposter, a man who didn't belong here, and I sympathized. The speeches of Chicago's industrial elite generated that same feeling in me, a feeling that made me think I must live on a different planet and speak a different language from everyone else in that grand, vaulted room.

The mayor concluded with a speech that would have been twice as effective if it had been half as long and then introduced Drew as the "brilliant creator of a new idea for industrial employment, sure to reduce the threat of labor unions and foster a more tractable and obedient workforce." The man managed to turn the reality of the Cox Experiment—what I knew to be an exciting, mutually beneficial arrangement to better the life of poor working women—into a cleverly disguised opiate to pacify workers so they wouldn't get in the way of profits. Drew, his hand still resting comfortably on mine, gave it a brief squeeze and stood to take his place at the podium.

From where I sat, I could watch his profile as he spoke, a very nice profile now that I had the chance to study it, straight nose, strong chin, a well-defined brow, and blonde hair that brushed the top of his collar in back, just long enough to give him the air of a semirespectable pirate. Not quite the current fashion but dashing and undeniably attractive. Drew might pride himself on his dissipation, but he looked trim and muscled and one would have thought from the clarity of his eyes and smile that he had no acquaintance with vice whatsoever. Contemplating Drew's appearance made me miss the mayor's words as he handed Drew the Starr Award, a small, plain wooden plaque with a modest appearance that contradicted its prestige. After the polite applause ceased, the audience waited for Drew's words. Truth to tell, so did I because I was suddenly and unaccountably nervous on his behalf. By contrast he looked very comfortable as he stood smiling out at the guests and holding up the award in both hands, giving the impression that he wanted to share it with everyone present. Drew's speaking baritone, despite the tables crowded with people and the dining room's high ceilings, carried out and over the crowd.

"Last October, if anyone would have suggested that I would stand in front of you this evening to receive one of the highest honors of the community from the hand of the mayor himself, I would have laughed at the idea. My brother Douglas was the financial genius, a man who went to work faithfully every day and used his business acumen to increase the size of his company's coffers. My purpose however—as many of you may know from firsthand experience—was to fritter away the family fortune just as quickly as Douglas increased it." A small swell of laughter greeted that remark, indicating that at least a few listeners understood Drew's oblique observation.

"But last spring two events occurred that for better or worse changed the direction of my life, and both incidents are directly responsible for my receiving this award. First, as many of you know, my brother died in the *Titanic* disaster," Drew's mention of the catastrophe, still fresh in people's minds, caused the room to grow still, "and because of that sad and terrible calamity, I became wealthy literally overnight. But it isn't Douglas's death, as tragic and shocking as it was, that is the primary reason I stand before you this evening. In fact, if what followed my brother's death hadn't occurred, I have no doubt I would still be happily spending my prodigal way through Douglas's hard-earned prosperity."

From my seat, I could observe the room and it was obvious that Drew's remarks with their touch of pathos and air of mystery had commanded everyone's attention. Even the well-dressed waiters who stood against the back wall listened carefully.

"One day in early May I met a young woman named Johanna Swan," Drew went on, "and I stand here today, award in hand, because of her." His effortless words took me completely by surprise, but besides one quick, reflexive intake of breath, I continued to smile faintly and keep my attention on Drew, acting—at least on the outside—with an aplomb that suggested I had expected the allusion. Several heads turned to seek me out at the table, apparently saw nothing out of the ordinary, and returned to Drew.

"Miss Swan comes from a fine Chicago family known to many of you, but that's not what this is about. Instead, this is about Miss Swan's remarkable vision of the future, a vision that somehow made the Cox experiment seem a reasonable and natural undertaking. Miss Swan sees a world where women have both a voice and a vote in their own political future. She envisions a time when all laborers earn a fair wage and work in environments that do not threaten life and limb. She sees a world that offers healthcare to the poor and fresh air and water and enough to eat to all children. Miss Swan sees—no, she demands—a world free from fear and poverty and it is her world that I came to see, too. I take some small credit for being the brain and the bank of the Cox Experiment, but Miss Swan is its heart and as such, it is she who truly deserves this award. I thank you and accept it on her behalf."

I knew Drew's remarks were not what that group of capitalists and captains of industry expected or even wanted to hear. The room was populated with some I knew to be fiercely and publicly antisuffrage, some who sent the disgusting offal of their packing plants into the Chicago River without apology, some who heartlessly abandoned any worker who had the effrontery to be injured on the job. No doubt Drew's comments had pricked more than one conscience, which would account for the awkward quiet moment before polite applause began, an applause that was tepid and half-hearted. Appreciate the award tonight, my dear, I thought, my eyes fixed on Drew's profile with an expression calculated to hide my feelings, because it is probably the last compliment you are ever going to receive from this gathering. Drew turned and gave me a quick grin, that wonderfully boyish, slightly crooked grin against which I had no defenses and at that precise moment, for better or for worse and entirely against my better judgment, I realized that I was hopelessly, annoyingly, gloriously in love with him and that I would never love any other man for all my life.

What I always imagined would make me deliriously happy had the perverse effect of making me cranky and fidgety instead. How dangerous would it be to let on to Drew Gallagher that he had wormed his way into the core of my being and was now settled there for life? Did he have feelings for me other than his professed admiration for my social ideals and my attributes displayed by a low-cut gown? I did not consider either of us a particularly trusting or trustworthy individual. How our relationship would end or even if there would be a relationship of any substance remained to be seen. I knew only that I must be absolutely sure of a reciprocal regard before I ever let down my defenses and shared my true feelings with him, and I wasn't sure that such certainty was possible. Whether that was my character flaw or his I couldn't decide. Possibly both.

By then the crowd was on its feet and milling about, and Drew was interrupted twice on his way back to his seat by someone wishing to comment on his words. Even as he arrived next to me, a woman came up on my other side and introduced herself as Lydia Pruitt. She was a stout woman in her forties with soft graying hair and a gentle face. I stood as she spoke.

"Miss Swan, please extend my regards to your grandmother. She was very kind to me years ago when I was a new wife, fresh on the Chicago scene and unsure of the intricacies of social conversation and behavior. I also met your mother once. Such a lovely girl, kind, too, and very spirited. How proud she would have been to hear Mr. Gallagher's tribute to you!"

I liked this woman, not just because she paid compliments to my family but because she was obviously sincere and considerate enough to seek me out for conversation. When I began to thank her, Mrs. Pruitt looked out into the milling crowd and added, "There's my husband. Excuse me while I get his attention. He knew your grandfather and I believe patronizes your uncle's law firm. I know he'll want to extend his regards."

As she disappeared, I turned to say something to Drew about his speech, only to see that he was monopolized by a prestigious banker intent on presenting a business opportunity he thought Drew would be interested in. Somehow sensing my attention, Drew put a hand under my elbow and while still speaking to the man, disengaged himself from the conversation and maneuvered us both slowly away. The banker faded into another group. I turned to Drew once more but before I could say anything, Lydia Pruitt returned with her husband in tow.

"Miss Swan, please forgive the delay. The crowd has suddenly become very lively, and it was a challenge to get back to you. This is my husband, Ransom Pruitt." Pruitt was a pleasant-faced man of medium height with salt-and-pepper hair and a distinguished mustache. I put out my hand to him. "How do you do, Mr. Pruitt? Have you met Drew Gallagher?"

The two men shook hands as well and Mr. Pruitt said, "I had some business dealings with your brother, Gallagher. I was sorry to hear of his death." Drew made a polite response that I did not catch because the sound of Pruitt's voice diverted me. I had heard it before and fairly recently but could not recall when or where. We chatted a while about the need for business men to take responsibility for their employees, and Pruitt asked my opinion about the likelihood of national suffrage for women. That topic needed more time and attention than was possible that evening, so I made a diplomatic response, something bland that did not wholly betray my passionate commitment to women having the vote but still resolutely hopeful. Lydia Pruitt looked more skeptical about the prospect than her husband, who raised the glass of whiskey he held and said firmly, "I have two college-educated daughters, who would like nothing more than to take their place at the ballot box. To women and the vote. A prospect long overdue."

At the sound of his carrying voice, I suddenly recalled an afternoon at the Chicago Yacht Club and a man with a raised glass toasting his wife Lydia of twenty-five years. I knew I should continue without displaying any shock from the memory, but I couldn't. All I could see was Crea, weary and despairing and wishing, wishing with all her heart, that she could start again, regain what she had lost and love Peter openly, be the girl she'd been before this man stole all that away from her. I was overcome with such fury and outrage that I could not speak.

My expression must have paled because Lydia Pruitt asked considerately, "Miss Swan, are you unwell? You've gone very white. It's the press of the crowd, I imagine, and not very good ventilation besides."

I gouged my fingers into Drew's arm and managed to say, "Yes, I'm sure that's it. Please excuse me. I believe I'll just step out into the hallway."

Drew followed a step behind as I pushed through the people, out of the dining room, and into the broad, paneled hallway. He said my name—concerned and puzzled, I thought—and I answered, "I'm fine. I'm just going to take a brisk walk to the end of the hallway and back and then perhaps we could leave." In a lower voice I muttered, "Before I spoil your evening by murdering one of the guests." Giving the impression that such a threat was commonplace to a man of his experience, Drew took out his cigarette case.

"Fine with me. I'll step out to the balcony and meet you back here in a few minutes. You do look murderous. You don't have a weapon hidden on you, do you?" He gave me a long, leisurely look and answered his own question with a provocative smile. "No, I'm sure not. There would be absolutely no way you could disguise its presence under that gown." I resisted the impulse to stick out my tongue at him.

"If you're not careful," I glowered, "you'll be the first victim and have no one to blame but yourself. Don't let all this attention go to your head; you're still mortal. Give me ten minutes." I turned my back to him and walked to the ladies' lounge, strode through it, looked into the full-length mirror on my way past at a black-haired stranger in an amber dress, exited the door on the other side, and entered an empty, darker hallway.

I was angry about everything: about the frustrating contrariness of Crea longing for an education and Ransom Pruitt having two college-educated daughters, about lost childhood and the abuse of power and the vulnerability of wives, about the unfairness of life and the unexpectedness of love, about caring for Drew Gallagher, whose capacity for faithful and reciprocal affection was undefined and untried. I feared I had set myself up for heartache, a woman rejected entirely or another Lydia Pruitt. Something somewhere should make sense but at that moment nothing did. Nothing at all.

Drew waited patiently exactly where he said he would be, leaning against the hallway wall with both hands thrust into his pockets in the timeless pose of man waiting for woman. He straightened when he saw me.

"Better now?"

"Yes. I'm sorry. Do you want to go back in?" I motioned

with my head toward the dining room, still abuzz with conversation.

Drew responded with a mock shudder. "Not unless you tell me I have to."

"I don't want to cut short your moment of glory."

"Fame is fleeting and I'm already a has-been. Is the night still young for you or would you like me to take you home?"

I eyed him thoughtfully. "That depends on where we're going."

"I was planning Creole jazz at the Pekin Café."

"If you guarantee dancing, I am with you until the early hours," I responded promptly. "Will you care if I step on your toes?" With a gesture that seemed natural and unconscious, Drew took my hand and we turned to walk down the hallway.

"I'm not worried. I don't think there's a dance step you can't pick up in a minute, but if I'm wrong, you have advanced permission to step on any part of me you want."

Downstairs in the lobby Drew retrieved my cloak and settled it on my shoulders before we went out into the crisp, cold night. Walking toward the automobile, Drew asked casually, "So, what was it about Ransom Pruitt that made you want to help him along to an early and painful death?"

"It might have been the ventilation, you know."

"Johanna, Johanna, you forget who you're talking to." When I remained silent, Drew went on, "Sorry. I didn't mean to pry. You can tell me it's none of my business if you want. You should know by now I don't have a sensitive bone in my body."

I slid into the passenger side and waited for Drew to crank the engine and get in before I spoke. I wanted to unburden myself by telling him Crea's whole sordid story, let him apply his typical light touch to it, and erase the residual feelings of anger and frustration that remained from meeting the Pruitts.

Yet I couldn't, not if I wanted to respect Crea's confidence and protect her privacy, an essential rule I'd been taught by Sally Gray at Bryn Mawr College. Miss Gray had drilled into the class that the people we serve must be protected at all costs from additional victimization. "As sacrosanct as the priest's confessional," Miss Gray had lectured. "Never share another's personal details without permission."

"Five years ago Ransom Pruitt did something unconscionable to a friend of mine, who was young enough to be his daughter. She'll never be the same, and he'll never be held accountable for his indefensible conduct."

Drew accelerated the motorcar away from the curb before he responded. "Since you know the story, why don't you force accountability? Doesn't the knowledge you have give you the upper hand to take whatever vengeance you like?"

"What purpose would that serve? A public declaration would wound his wife and shame his daughters, and nothing can replace my friend's lost childhood. The fact that others besides Ransom Pruitt would bear the burden of his misconduct infuriates me. How could he take advantage of someone he should have protected? Why would it even cross his mind to act in such a deplorable way?"

I hardly recognized my voice and Drew, too, must have heard something out of the ordinary because he turned his head to give me a quick glance before turning his attention back to the road. I watched him as he considered my question, his eyes gazing ahead but brows furrowed. Poor man, I thought with rueful tenderness. It's not enough that I drag you into a moral rectitude for which you feel no natural affinity—now I demand answers to questions about human behavior that philosophers have wrestled with for centuries.

"Never mind, Drew," I told him quickly. "I know life isn't fair and I know there aren't answers for everything. Forget I even mentioned the matter. It's just difficult when the person hurting is someone you care about."

"I know. It's a good thing you don't expect any answers from me, Johanna, because all I know for sure is that a man's behavior is influenced more by a need for power than by a need for women. Power breeds entitlement. I'd guess that was the case with Pruitt."

"Does entitlement erode conscience then?"

"Not necessarily. You're assuming that Ransom Pruitt doesn't wake in the middle of the night horrified by what he's done and at the mercy of all sorts of demons." I remembered Drew's comment from our first meeting about his brother's demons and how those same demons haunted all the Gallagher men.

"Does it really happen, Drew, that remorse haunts a man and keeps him up at night? Somehow I can't quite believe it."

"Believe it. Do you think you're the only one who has bad dreams, Johanna? Do you think only women feel regret and wish they could undo the past?" I wanted very much to ask what, if anything, haunted Drew Gallagher, wanted to ask him about his own regret, but something held me back.

Instead I responded lightly, "I don't know, Drew, and I'm sorry I forced this serious conversation on you." I made a point of looking out at the street. "Where are we, anyway?"

"We're on State Street, coming up on the Pekin Café." We pulled up in front of a two-story brick building with lights that shone out of every window on the façade of both stories. After the automobile stopped, he turned to me to ask, "Can you leave everything behind, Johanna, and just enjoy yourself? Could you set that load of responsibility down and not try to save the world for a little while?" He didn't ask unkindly and I wasn't offended.

"Absolutely. Have I mentioned that I love to dance?"

He grinned, reached to flick my cheek with a forefinger, and answered, "I seem to recall the subject coming up on at least one other occasion. How are your shoes?"

"Tapping already. What are we waiting for?" I was out of the auto before he was, determined to do exactly as he suggested: enjoy the evening, the music, the dance, and the man.

Later, well into the early morning hours, we sat at one of the little tables at the edge of the dance floor, sipping on drinks in a smoke-filled room and listening to the best New Orleans jazz in the city. I had slipped out of my shoes and sat with one foot tucked under me and both elbows resting on the table examining Drew, who for the first time that evening appeared winded.

"Ha! And you thought I couldn't keep up. Next time watch out what you say or I may have to make you eat your words again."

"I never said you couldn't keep up."

"You implied it and that's the same thing. 'Should we sit this one out, Johanna?'" I mimicked. "'You're looking a little tired.'" I raised my glass triumphantly. "Ask anyone. At this moment I am not the one who's looking tired."

Drew had slipped off his jacket and pulled off his tie and now sat with slightly tousled hair and his shirt open at the neck as disheveled as I had ever seen him. He looked younger by five years and very attractive. At that moment some part of me was reacting to his appearance in a very primitive way. I blamed the champagne.

"All right, I admit it. I underestimated you. You are the daughter of Presbyterian missionaries, after all. How was I supposed to know you'd be so practiced at dancing? I didn't think it was allowed."

"King David danced before the ark," I pointed out, "so we have precedent."

Drew didn't answer at first, just sprawled back in his chair, legs out and one arm extended on the table, his hand playing with a small glass of whiskey.

Finally he said, "I'm afraid my Old Testament history isn't what it used to be." He smiled as I stifled a broad, inelegant yawn with the palm of my hand. "Come along, Johanna. It's after three and time to go home. Your poor grandmother will be beside herself."

"She'll be soundly asleep and completely oblivious to my coming and going as she has been for the last five years, but I think you're probably right. It is time to go home." Neither of us made any effort to move, however, both of us pleasurably tired and on my part, content to sit across from Drew Gallagher for as many sunrises as I could get away with.

The band started up again, something slow and rhythmic with a mournful saxophone and poignant chords on the piano that begged for attention. Drew stood and held out a hand.

"Since you insist, one more and then we're leaving." I slipped my shoes back on and stood, too.

"I don't remember insisting. Did I?" We stepped out on the dance floor that was still crowded despite the hour, and I moved into Drew's arms.

"Those amber eyes of yours did. They don't keep many secrets, you know."

"Think not?" I was very comfortable in his arms. The top of my head reached his chin in a perfect fit and I was winding down enough to lean against his chest and let him lead without protest.

"I know not." After a pause, Drew said, "Johanna, may I ask you something rather intimate?" Curious about his sober tone, I pulled away to look up into his face.

"Yes?" I could feel my heartbeat speed up at the look in his eyes.

In all seriousness he asked, "Are you wearing anything at all under that gown?" I gave his shoulder a smack with the flat of my hand and scowled at his grin.

"What kind of a question is that? Your Viola might find it titillating repartee, but I don't. Are you ever serious?"

"I'm serious right now. Are you?"

"If it's any business of yours, which it isn't, I'm wearing only the minimal essentials, and it's all my cousin Jennie's fault. She dared me to fly in the face of proper fashion." He pulled me closer so I couldn't see his face, but I could hear a smile in his voice.

"Bless your cousin Jennie," was all he said, and we danced the last dance without further conversation.

On the drive home I yawned again and, resisting the impulse to lean my head against Drew's shoulder for a short snooze, asked, "You realize that you're never going to receive another award from the Chicago business community, don't you? You fell from grace somewhere between women's suffrage and labor unions."

"Did I? Dear me. Well, I imagine I can blunder my way through life without public approval for the next thirty years. I survived the first thirty without it just fine." He seemed completely unconcerned.

"I should have told you sooner that I appreciated your kind words." My comment came out halting and somehow churlish, and I tried again for a more gracious touch. "I was proud of you, Drew," then added, "For what it's worth to you, and I don't imagine that's very much."

"You imagine wrong, then."

He didn't say any more, but I was content enough with that brief remark to lay my head back against the seat and close my eyes. I knew Drew Gallagher didn't love me—not yet, anyway, and maybe not ever—but his quick, forceful response pleased me and made me smile. Some emotion had colored his voice even if I wasn't smart enough at the moment to know exactly what it was I heard. Maybe only whiskey and smoke and the end of a long day. Maybe something more. But I loved a challenge and thought that in the long run the score for this night would go on my side of the card.

I slept without meaning to and awoke as the auto pulled to the curb in front of my house on Hill Street, my head against Drew's shoulder despite all my good intentions. Straightening and giving a little stretch, I told him, "See? The house is dark. I told you no one would wait up. The day after my eighteenth birthday I told Grandmother I was all grown up and could take care of myself, and she was to stop worrying about me."

"Did she?" Drew half turned in his seat to face me.

"With her it's hard to tell, but I don't think so. She lost my mother twice, first when my parents left for China and then when they were killed, and I don't think she ever completely recovered from that grief. My father's family lives in Kansas, but every time I mention going to visit them, Grandmother gets all cool and distant, perhaps fearing I'll go away and not come back, just like my mother. I don't have the heart to hurt her."

"No, I don't imagine you do." Then without warning, Drew leaned toward me and kissed me on the mouth, a hard kiss but not lengthy and not intrusive. I wouldn't have minded if the kiss had been more of both but wasn't in a position just then to suggest that. I wasn't thinking as clearly as I usually did and blamed the champagne again.

Catching my breath, I asked, "What was that for?"

He gave a bark of laughter without much humor in it and pushed open his door. "No reason. Just because I thought the situation called for it." He closed his door more forcefully than was necessary and came around to my side to take my hand and help me step out, all without a smile and without a word. I had no idea what caused his mood change.

"Are you angry about something?" I asked meekly. "I know I fell asleep while you were driving. Was I awful? Did I snore?" He peered at my face in the faded light of the early morning moon and saw something there that made his mouth twitch with a smile.

"Yes," he told me, "you did and it was awful. I didn't think a woman could snore with such force and volume."

"Well, if anyone has the necessary extensive knowledge of women to make such a comparative statement, it would be you."

At my remark, he said my name with a rough laugh and pulled me into his arms and into a kiss that satisfied all my criteria, lengthy and intrusive, not to mention practiced and pleasurable. He tasted like smoke and whiskey—as delicious as I had expected.

With his cheek against my hair, Drew said, "You don't kiss like a missionary's daughter."

"How many missionary's daughters have you kissed then?" I asked into his shoulder. As cold as the night was, I believe I could have stood there, warmed and comfortable in his arms well into the next day.

"You're my first."

"Then you're obviously working under a preconceived convention," I pointed out. With a force of will, I pulled free from his embrace. "Be careful with assumptions, Drew. They can get you into trouble. Now I should go in." He walked with me up to the porch where we both stopped at the bottom of the steps. It seemed neither of us wanted the evening to end.

Looking up at the starry sky, faint flecks of dawn beginning to show to the east, Drew quoted softly, "'The white drift of worlds o'er chasms of sable, / The star-dust, that is whirled aloft and flies / From the invisible chariot-wheels of God.'"

"Lovely. I didn't imagine you were a man to read poetry."

If there had been more early morning light in the sky, I would have been better able to read the slight coloring of his cheeks. As it was, what might have been a rare, self-conscious flush on his part could just as easily have been the effect of a moon shadow.

"For some reason I have a fondness for Longfellow."

"I'm surprised. Longfellow's writing is graceful and sometimes sweet, but I would have thought him too religious and too common for you—with themes of lost love, death, and darkness you'd find relentlessly dismal."

"Do you think I'm too shallow to appreciate profoundly human themes?"

"Not shallow, no, but you purposefully cultivate such a sophisticated facade, I would have thought anything shadowed or tinged with melancholy would clash with the image you work so hard to perpetuate. Who would believe that Drew Gallagher, bon vivant and man about town, spent his leisure time reading 'The Children's Hour'?" I mocked him but gently, gently. The evening was still mine.

He answered in a tight voice that indicated he didn't find me amusing. "Don't take up a career in diplomacy, Johanna. You haven't the tact for it."

"I know. You're not the first person to point out that fact. It's a great character flaw for which I have no excuse." He laughed once more, the familiar laugh he used to camouflage his feelings, sardonic, with no true emotion in the sound.

"Good night, Johanna, although more accurately it should be good morning now."

"I suppose it is morning, but I much prefer the 'melting tenderness of night.'" At Drew's quick, searching look, I smiled. "Longfellow, too. 'It Is Not Always May.'"

"I recognized it. 'There are no birds in last year's nest!'"

"Yes," I said, "exactly. The past can't be relived, can it? It's always irrevocably gone. Good night, Drew. I had a splendid time. Thank you for everything."

I went up the porch steps and into the house without a backward glance. Once inside, I leaned with my back against the closed front door and stood there mute for several minutes, shaken and exhilarated by the emotions I felt, all of them new to me and not completely welcome. Finally, I went up the dark, still stairs and undressed, draped the amber gown lovingly over a chair, and fell deeply asleep before I had the chance to waste any more time in useless introspection.

Therefore I hope, as no unwelcome guest,
At your warm fireside, when the lamps are lighted,
To have my place reserved among the rest,
Nor stand as one unsought and uninvited!

Chapter Twelve

The following week sped by without a word from Drew, which shouldn't have surprised or bothered me but did both. I suppose I thought that somehow he must have shared my emotional epiphany, despite the fact that he'd offered no evidence on which to base such an assumption. For Drew Gallagher passionate kisses must have been as common as wind off the lake and held as much meaning. Realistically, I understood that the late night, the time spent in proximity dancing, and the freely flowing alcohol encouraged intimacies. An ordinary night on the town for Drew and nothing to think twice about. I was annoyed that I should be the only one who came away from the evening changed, dreaming of a man who probably hadn't given me a thought once he pulled away from the curb. The whole situation was straight out of a romance novel, and its commonness was another sore spot. I felt more unsettled than passionate and was determined not to allow love— especially an unreciprocated love—to get in the way of my life and plans. Not for me the pining heart and melancholy expression. Drew Gallagher needed to be pushed into some far corner of my heart, where he could reside in relative obscurity while I decided what to do about the situation.

One evening Crea and I joined Grandmother for supper in

the dining room. Grandmother could now sit and eat downstairs, comfortably pulled up to the table in her wheeled chair, and we discussed the birthday party planned for the following Sunday afternoon.

"It's just a small group," I explained to Grandmother. "Uncle Hal and Aunt Kitty, Jennie, Cousin Roslyn and Cousin Thaddeus, your friend Mrs. Florence from church, Reverend Briscoe and his wife, and I've asked Allen Goldwyn despite Aunt Kitty's protests. Peter's home and I think he's bringing Carl Milford. Counting me, that makes twelve guests."

"Thirteen," replied Grandmother.

"You don't count as a guest."

"I know that, Johanna. I'm the guest of honor, or so people have been telling me for the past month. However, I wasn't thinking of myself. I invited Mr. Gallagher."

"You what?"

She fixed me with an innocent eye. "I invited your friend Mr. Gallagher and he accepted."

"You've met him once. You don't even know him." From the corner of my eye, I noticed a quick smile on Crea's face before she picked up her fork and continued with her meal, careful not to look in my direction.

"It's my party, Johanna, and I'll invite whomever I choose. I liked Mr. Gallagher. He reminded me of Richard."

"Of Grandfather?! That's ridiculous. He's nothing like Grandfather." Grandmother gave me a cool stare.

"Mr. Gallagher is a good example for you to emulate, Johanna. I'm sure his tone would remain respectful even if he disagreed with me. One anticipates impeccable manners from the most recent recipient of the Starr Award, and I can only hope he'll be a good influence on you." I opened my mouth for a sharp retort but closed it without voicing the comment I was thinking.

Instead, I replied calmly, "You're right. It is your party. Invite anyone you like. Are there any other unexpected guests I should know about?"

"No."

"Fine. It's thirteen then, fourteen counting you and fifteen with Crea." That brought Crea's head up with a jerk.

"Oh, I'm not attending, Johanna."

"Why not? For the past months you've been closer to Grandmother than anyone else, closer than her own family."

"I have other plans."

"Such as?"

"Johanna, I can only hope Mr. Gallagher's influence on your behavior takes effect soon," Grandmother interjected. "Crea knows she is welcome to attend the party, but if she says she has other plans, why is it your business to know what they are?"

She won't come because Peter will be there, I wanted to say, and then, reading Grandmother's glance, realized she knew it, too. A week ago I would have insisted on a meeting between Peter and Crea regardless of its effect on them or on any of the other people present. After Saturday night, however, I saw things differently, realized how vulnerable love made a person, how painful it would be for Crea to see Peter in a family setting, how difficult for them both to be close and yet unable to speak freely. This uninvited stir of feeling in my own heart gave me a curious empathy for lovers everywhere.

"I'm sorry, Crea" I said, looking at her directly. "Of course, you have a life apart from Hill Street. Grandmother's right. Your plans are none of my business. I only wanted you to know that you were welcome at any party or gathering we have. Please forgive me."

"I know, Johanna. Thank you. There's nothing to forgive." After Crea's quiet response, she finished her meal quickly and excused herself.

"I didn't mean to distress her," I confessed after she left. "I didn't consider the situation from Crea's perspective."

Not arguing with my confession, Grandmother said only, "No, you didn't, but you're getting better at thinking before you speak, Johanna." I recalled my Saturday night meeting with Ransom Pruitt.

"I try, but I admit I'm much more comfortable with saying exactly what's on my mind."

"Discretion is a learned skill."

"It seems dishonest somehow."

"Not dishonest," countered Grandmother before returning to her supper, "but smart and kind."

Later that evening I went to Crea's room. "Crea, you do believe I didn't mean to invade or question your privacy, don't you?"

She was tucked into a chair with an open book on her lap, one of several books an acquaintance of mine at the Chicago Teachers College recommended Crea complete before entering college in the spring. She raised her head as I entered and smiled. With the light spilling across her hair and face, she looked especially young and lovely.

"Yes, Johanna. It's just that—" I held up a hand.

"You don't have to say any more. I can be thick-headed sometimes, but I understand how difficult it would be for you. Peter would monopolize you if he could, regardless of who's present, and I know you'd be uncomfortable with that. Only, you won't snub him, will you, or be unkind to him?" Her green eyes flashed.

"I would never be purposefully unkind to him."

"Purposefully?"

"I may have to act a certain way for his own good, but I would never willingly hurt him. He says he understands that but—" She stopped abruptly.

"So you've heard from him?"

Crea colored slightly at my question and hastened to reply, "Yes. Perfectly innocent letters that talk about school and classes and the weather. Nothing his mother couldn't read. And I never respond."

"That seems rude, but of course, if you feel you must be discourteous to one of the nicest men in the entire world, who am I to judge?" Crea glared at first but followed that with a look I could only describe as sly.

"It seems to me, Johanna, that you should control your own heart before you worry about everyone else."

"I have no idea what you're talking about."

"Your face turned the color of paper when Mrs. McIntyre mentioned Drew Gallagher. Not that I needed such a reaction to tell me something's going on there."

"Nothing's going on there, as you put it. You're just trying to distract me from talking about Peter."

"What time did you wander in the other night? Four in the morning or was it five? What other man could hold your interest that long? Don't bother spinning a tale for me, Johanna. You're in danger of succumbing to a man, just like the rest of us common women. Look at you now. Your cheeks are as pink as cotton candy." Then she softened. "He's no one I would have picked for you. I don't think he's good enough, and I'm not quite sure he's trustworthy. You will be careful, won't you? My mother used to say men like that carry heartache in their back pocket."

"Regardless of how I feel about him, I owe Drew Gallagher something for what he's done for so many of our friends at the Anchorage."

"He might ask for something you'll regret giving."

"He might, but I doubt it. We have an understanding of sorts."

"So you say."

"I admit my experience and knowledge are limited, Crea. Anyway, I'm all grown up and he's not one to hide his intentions, so neither of us can make a claim to innocence, whatever happens."

"I worry about you."

I smiled. "You don't have to, but thank you. That's the kindest thing you could have said. You should be spending your time thinking about my cousin Peter's grand passion for you, though, and not dwelling on the little dramas in my life."

She gave a diffident shrug and responded only with "Goodnight, Johanna."

Despite my bravado before Crea, the experience of being in love was new to me and not agreeable. Where before I had contemplated Grandmother's birthday party with pleasant and comfortable anticipation, I now felt the uneasy flutter of butterflies in my stomach just because—I hated admitting it though I knew it to be true—Drew was coming. I had not given my own appearance much thought before because a family birthday party was hardly high society, but now I was suddenly preoccupied with what I should wear and how I should arrange my hair. The realization that simply contemplating one man's presence could throw me into fluttering disarray put me out of temper.

Saturday was sunny and unseasonably warm, Indian summer, a final, teasing, slightly cruel good-bye to the season just past. Grandmother was in good spirits, looking as well as she'd looked in months, even before her stroke. Her hair was a soft, attractive halo of white and her eyes sparkled. I thought affectionately that although she was a brave woman with no tolerance for complaining, the past months had been difficult for her, had compromised her independence and her dignity. Now she contemplated company and a modest celebration with a delight out of proportion to the festivity. Stopping by her chair, I leaned down to give her a light kiss on the cheek.

"You're looking very pretty in that green stripe, Grandmother. I don't recall seeing it before."

"You're not the only person in the house who enjoys a new frock now and then, Johanna," she retorted, but she smiled when she spoke and patted my hand. "I might say the same thing about your ivory shirtwaist. Isn't the skirt new, too?" I looked down at myself critically.

"Yes. I saw it when I was out with Jennie recently, and she coaxed me into buying it. She's very good at spending other people's money. I think it would look better on a woman of more height, but I can't do much about that, can I?"

She didn't answer directly, but after giving me an objective review, pronounced, "Jennie was right. The style is becoming to your small waist and those long narrow pleats give the illusion of added height. Stick to your specialty of social reform, Johanna, and trust your cousin when it comes to fashion." The front bell rang and I heard Uncle Hal at the door, so I could only grin a response. I was pleased to have Grandmother back, sharp tongue and all.

Allen Goldwyn arrived on the heels of Aunt Kitty and Uncle Hal, Peter, Jennie and Carl Milford. I met Allen at the door and was surprised by the change in him, his face thinner and his manner restless. I'd never seen him unsettled before.

"I won't stay very long, Johanna," Allen told me after he made polite conversation all around and moved over to my side, "but I haven't seen much of you and wondered why. You must be busy at the Anchorage."

"The Anchorage and Grandmother do keep me busy. What about you? You're too thin, Allen, which makes me think you're working harder than I am. Doesn't the firm give you time to eat?"

KAREN J. HASLEY

"I'm engaged in a number of projects," he responded evasively. "Now excuse me while I greet your grandmother. She looks and sounds remarkably well."

"To Crea's credit." When I said those words, I saw Peter turn toward me briefly. How easily one heard the name of one's beloved, I thought. Of all the conversation in the room, Peter had caught Crea's name. I wasn't surprised when my cousin drifted over to my side later.

"I thought she might be here," Peter said without explanation.

I shook my head. "No. I told her she was invited and welcome, but you understand why she wouldn't come, don't you? How's the letter writing campaign coming along?"

"She never responds."

"I'm working on that. I know she reads and rereads every letter, so I think you're making some headway."

"It's been hard." His usually pleasant face was grim. "Do you think there's any hope for me?"

"As much hope as you have patience. She's upstairs in her room. Why don't you slip upstairs to say hello? We're still missing several guests and your mother is busy trying to boss May around in the kitchen, which should keep her occupied for a while yet." A too shrill laugh drew my attention to Jennie. "What do you think about your sister's engagement, Peter?"

"I don't know what to think. She and Carl both seem to treat the relationship like a business arrangement."

"Jennie doesn't seem happy."

"Happiness seems elusive all the way around lately." Then on a more hopeful note Peter added, "I think I will just pop upstairs and say hello. The worst she can do is slam her door in my face."

Sometime during that conversation with Peter, Drew arrived, and for all my theorizing about being instantly aware of the beloved's presence, I missed his entrance entirely. I watched Peter disappear from the parlor and when I turned back, Drew was bending over Grandmother's hand and extending a wrapped package to her. She took the box, as animated as a girl, and patted the seat next to her as an invitation for him to sit down. The two looked thick as thieves and the sight made me unaccountably wary. Practically speaking, there was no reason to suspect they were discussing me, but they had an air of collusion about them that seemed suspicious. I paused for a few innocuous words with Cousin Thaddeus before drifting over to where Drew sat with Grandmother. He stood when he saw me.

"Hello, Johanna."

Grandmother looked up at me. "We were just sharing our mutual fondness for good cognac, Johanna. Your grandfather favored it as you recall." Reminding me about the fiction that Drew resembled Grandfather, was she? What a rascal!

In response I said, in as quelling a voice as I could muster, "No, I seem to have forgotten that detail," and then to Drew added, "Hello, Drew. How kind of you to join our little gathering!"

"Not as kind as the invitation," he responded with a quick smile down at Grandmother—Drew Gallagher at his most appealing.

I had to admit that even without my inordinate bias the man was very handsome and at that moment unbelievably charming. Charming when he wanted to be, of course, and depending on how much mischief he planned to promulgate. I would have said something to that effect except Grandmother spoke first.

"Go make introductions on my behalf, Johanna. I can't expect Mr. Gallagher to follow me as I shuffle him around to all the guests."

"I have all the patience in the world, Mrs. McIntyre."

"Yes, I do think you're a patient man," she responded thoughtfully, "but I still won't ask that of you. Johanna can do the honors."

Walking away with him, I commented, "Grandmother has become your biggest fan. I thought she'd be immune to your charm at her age but apparently not."

"Age is no barrier to the enjoyment of good conversation and honest compliments, Johanna. Where did you ever get the idea it was?"

Instead of answering I stopped in front of Uncle Hal, introduced Drew, and left the two men together, hearing Uncle Hal congratulate Drew on the Starr Award as I walked away. Reverend Briscoe and his wife arrived next and by the time I returned from welcoming them and moving them to Grandmother's side, Drew stood deep in discussion with Jennie. Carl Milford had shifted his attention to Aunt Kitty, who'd rejoined us from the kitchen, Allen spoke with Mrs. Florence, and Uncle Hal listened politely to one of Cousin Roslyn's interminable cat stories. Like a game of musical chairs, all the guests seemed to have shifted places and partners. With a private pang I watched Drew nod and smile easily to Jennie. She placed a hand on his arm and gave him a warm look in response before she walked over to where I stood.

"I like your Mr. Gallagher, Johanna, but I must say I was surprised to see him here. Why would he be invited to our little gathering of family and friends, I wonder?" I found her teasing tone abrasively arch.

"Grandmother has taken a shine to him. She's the one who extended the invitation, not me."

"I don't know if I believe that. When he thinks no one's watching, his eyes follow you around the room. Quite smitten, I'd say." I was not entertained.

Echoing Crea's earlier sentiments, I told Jennie, "You should concentrate on your own love life, Jennie. I'm sure that would be enough to keep you occupied so you wouldn't have to waste your time considering things that are none of your business."

Unaffected, Jennie answered, "Ouch! I must have hit a nerve. Who would have guessed our free-thinking, independent Johanna would be attracted to a man like Drew Gallagher? I always pictured your great passion as a bearded socialist, the two of you carrying a banner down the street at the front of a labor rally or at best an intellectual professor who would spend his private moments whispering famous dates of history into your ear. Instead, you bring home a connoisseur of women, a man who undoubtedly knows exactly what to say and what to do to make a woman feel very satisfied."

She bordered on offensive and I began warningly, "Jennie—"

"There's no use looking at me like that, Johanna. I know something's going on between the two of you and if you don't share details, I'll be forced to imagine all sorts of salacious activities."

"Imagine all you like. I'm going to check on May in the kitchen. Maybe by the time I'm back you'll have dispensed with that unattractive teasing tone. I recall your parents thought it adorable when you were younger, but I found it grating even then."

When I returned from the kitchen, the room of guests had shifted yet again. Jennie, Carl, and Allen conversed together, and Aunt Kitty stood with the cousins, Uncle Hal with the Reverend and his wife, Drew beside Grandmother. No sign of Peter, so Crea must not have slammed the door after all.

Drew separated himself from Grandmother and came over to me. "This is an interesting group of guests, Johanna. Eclectic."

"A very charitable comment," I replied, smiling. "The cousins have been called many things but eclectic is not one of them. Thaddeus is a fanatic about flower gardens and Roslyn about cats. Allen looks unwell and Jennie is acting out of an unpleasant mix of mischief and malice. My aunt is up in arms and trying not to show it because Mayville had the nerve to change a menu item without asking her permission first. Uncle Hal, the family's secret agnostic, has been trapped in conversation with the Briscoes for the last fifteen minutes, and my cousin's fiancé, whom I'm trying very hard but unsuccessfully to like, treats Grandmother as if she were deaf, dumb, blind, and mentally impaired. I'd wager she's sharper than Carl in almost every area, but he's not bright enough to realize that."

"You've left me out of the summary."

"Oh, everyone's busy speculating about why you're here and if you're my beau."

"They can't know you very well to imagine you would bring someone with no social worth or purpose into the family."

"You won the Starr Award. They might think that's made me starry-eyed."

He laughed at the play on words and asked, "Are you starry-eyed? I hadn't noticed." I glimpsed Peter slip quietly into the room.

"No, I'm not, but my cousin Peter is." Drew followed my gaze.

"He does have a noticeable flush on his face."

"Poor Peter."

"Why 'poor Peter'?"

For answer I said, "Isn't life funny sometimes? All Peter wants is to spend time with the woman he loves, but he can't because my aunt would forbid it and absolutely refuse approval of the woman. Jennie, on the other hand, has her mother's total endorsement of her husband-to-be and could spend all the time she wants with Carl, only Jennie doesn't want to. She's marrying for practical reasons, you see, none of which is affection."

"That explains it, then."

"Explains what?"

"Jennie's flirting with me," Drew answered carefully. "I wondered why she should hint that she was impressed by my motorcar, ask if it really rode as smoothly as it appeared, and then give me an unmistakable look of invitation."

I had the instant desire to smack Jennie silly but instead replied, "Jennie is and always has been a beauty and cannot resist the challenge of a handsome man, but lately she usually waits until her mother is close enough to overhear her inappropriate remarks."

"You mean she wasn't bowled over by me?" I turned to view him dispassionately.

"She may have been, I suppose—you do look very cosmopolitan today—but don't worry. Even if it was only Jennie being Jennie for contrary reasons, Grandmother is quite taken with you, so you've made at least one true conquest in the family."

"But not the conquest I want, Johanna." I looked at Drew quickly to see if he was still teasing. He gave me a serious look with a slight smile as follow-up, and I tried to gauge his intent. Teasing but not entirely, I decided and felt heartened.

Aunt Kitty took over, ushering everyone into the dining room where May had set a pretty buffet, bowls of fall chrysanthemums interspersed with mounds of small sandwiches, a spinach bisque, and a beautiful, multilayered cake as focal point. I could tell Grandmother was pleased and could have hugged May for braving Aunt Kitty's disapproval—in her opinion sandwiches and chrysanthemums were entirely too casual for the occasion—and adding such lovely details to the table.

Finding a seat next to Allen, I asked, "Are you in the middle of any exciting building projects? Every time I take the train, I seem to see a new skyscraper on the horizon."

"I'm not involved in skyscrapers, Johanna. I prefer the less contemporary. I am working on a renovation of St. Michael's Cathedral, though. Have you ever seen the stained glass there? I'm going to keep the windows exactly as they are except use less ornate trim so the colors show to greater advantage. There's a splendid blue in the leaded glass I've never seen anywhere else, so I'm edging the windows with a narrow band of muted orange. You should see what the contrast does." I was pleased to hear Allen excited about his work and see the sparkle in his eyes as he spoke.

Putting my hand over his, I said, "This is the Allen I've missed seeing for a while. I wish I could be sure you'd tell me if something was wrong."

He pressed my hand gently in return. "Nothing's wrong, Johanna, except for the general vagaries of life that have no resolution. Now tell me about your Mr. Gallagher."

"Not mine," I corrected. "I met his brother on the *Titanic* and when I got home, I made it a point to look Drew up. The tragedy brought us together. Grandmother is his devotee, not me. She says he reminds her of Grandfather." Allen's gaze never left my face as I spoke.

"I've known you a few years, Johanna, and there's something about you at the moment that doesn't ring quite true. But before you glare at me and tell me to mind my own business, I'll change the topic to the Anchorage. How are you managing there?" We talked comfortably until it was time to sing a happy birthday to Grandmother and watch her open her presents. By the time she finished, she looked pale and her hands trembled slightly, an indication she'd grown fatigued, so I shooed people out without compunction.

"That was a lovely gift you brought Grandmother," I said to Drew as I walked with him to the front door. "She recognized the plaid immediately."

"I'm glad she liked it. The McIntyre plaid is distinctive and with winter coming, I thought the shawl might have some practical worth. I do have my thoughtful moments, Johanna." There was no mistaking the irritation in his voice.

"I complimented you, Drew. There's no reason to snap at me."

"I wasn't snapping. I was stating facts."

"Of course, you were. In a tone that sounded like you were chastising an especially annoying child."

"I would never dare correct you. That would imply you were wrong, and if I know anything about Johanna Swan, it's that she's never wrong."

His words surprised and his tone hurt so I snapped back, "If I knew what I did to deserve your bad temper, I'd feel better. You have the rare ability to spoil a perfectly nice afternoon."

He stopped buttoning his topcoat and replied frankly, in the way I found so endearing, "I do, don't I? I've only just discovered that 'rare ability' since I met you. You're right. I was bad-tempered and I'm sorry. Will you forgive me?" When he gave that special smile of his, the appealing one without artifice or motive, I would have forgiven him mass murder.

"Yes. I've often felt the same way after being trapped in a room with very correct people for an extended period of time."

"I like some of your family."

"Not all?"

"Not all," he replied firmly but would not give details. "I like your friend Goldwyn, too, but not as much as you apparently do."

"What does that mean?"

Drew adjusted his hat to a fashionable angle without having to look in the hall mirror. Certainly a man of many talents.

"It doesn't mean anything. I was just—"

"I know. Just stating a fact."

"Exactly. Extend my regards to your grandmother, Johanna. You rushed us out of there so fast I didn't say a proper good-bye."

Later, thinking through Drew's departing comments, I had the sudden idea that he might have seen me place my hand over Allen's and had read into the gesture some emotion on my part. He might be jealous, I speculated, but eventually dismissed the notion despite the hopeful lift to my spirits the idea offered. How low I've fallen, I told myself with disgust, shamelessly searching through actions and imagining motives, looking for the slightest hint that Drew Gallagher viewed me as more than a social reformer or business partner. I wanted to be something to him other than a conscience, but I didn't know how to get to that place in his life.

Filled is Life's goblet to the brim;
And though my eyes with tears are dim,
I see its sparkling bubbles swim,
And chant a melancholy hymn
With solemn voice and slow.
This goblet wrought with curious art,
Is filled with waters, that upstart,
When the deep fountains of the heart,
By strong convulsions rent apart,
Are running all to waste.

Chapter Thirteen

Never having been in love before, I found the experience revealing, and when I was able to work up the necessary detachment, even interesting. Eventually I grew tired of thinking about Drew first thing when I awoke, reliving moments together, and remembering the nuances of his words and was both relieved and unsurprised to discover that being the mopey heroine of a Gothic romance was not for me. I definitely felt more edgy than usual, however, and to combat restlessness I rose earlier, took more frequent walks in the brisk autumn air, and spent longer days working at the Anchorage. My emotions were not going to hold either my will or my energy captive.

Election Day came early in November, another reason besides my personal emotions to make me feel powerless and frustrated. As an intelligent and informed Progressive, I would have voted for my candidate but, of course, was not allowed to vote and could only watch in disappointment as Mr. Wilson took his place as the twenty-eighth president of the United States. Theodore Roosevelt's support for women's suffrage and his impassioned defense of working people had impressed and inspired me, and I remained bad-tempered about his defeat for a good two weeks following the election.

One afternoon May lost all patience with my short temper and told me to find something worthwhile with which to occupy my mind. That's when I had the idea of taking Thanksgiving to Cox's.

"A Thanksgiving meal for a factory of people?!" exclaimed May. "Johanna, you have your share of outlandish ideas, but this one takes the cake. I'm only one woman, and I've only got one kitchen. Besides, we've got our own Thanksgiving to think about."

"No, we don't. Aunt Kitty has invited Grandmother and me to their house this year, but I just can't make myself be thankful for Aunt Kitty. Cox's will be a noble reason for refusing the proximity of family. I'll help, May, if you think you can't do it."

"You in the kitchen, Johanna?! Heaven, spare me. And I didn't say I couldn't do it." I could tell her culinary pride was engaged. "Let me think about it."

I sent a note to Mrs. McElhanie to get a count of residents and families and went in search of Crea to see if she had plans for the holiday.

"I've been invited to the Anchorage, Johanna. I'm sorry. I can cancel."

"Don't be silly. I forgot about the dinner they had planned. You'll enjoy yourself, see old friends, spend time with Hilda and Eulalie. They always ask about you."

"But you can't make a dinner for fifty people all by yourself."

"All I have to do is transport the food, Crea. How hard is

that? Levi can drive everything over and help me set it up on the first floor of Cox's. I'll be fine." The more I thought about it, the more I looked forward to the prospect, and Crea's suggestion that I couldn't do it alone made the idea even more inviting.

The Saturday before Thanksgiving, Fritz delivered a note from Drew to the front door. For the past four weeks I had pushed Drew Gallagher to a far corner of my mind and heart, where he was hardly allowed to make his presence known, but at the sight of his auto at the curb and his distinctive handwriting on the envelope, all my hard work of the past month was ruined. My heartbeat slowed as I took the note from Fritz, however, and tried not to let my disappointment at Drew's absence show.

"He said I'm to wait for an answer, Miss Swan."

I read Drew's abrupt message: *You could have told me about your Thanksgiving plans. What do you need? I think pies. How many and what kind? Anything else? Cox's is my company, after all, Johanna. Drew.*

I scribbled an answer on the back: *Nothing in particular. A dozen. Ask Yvesta. Yes. Potatoes but don't make Yvesta do all the work. Sorry. I didn't think you'd notice or care. I hope you're not making your employees work that day. Johanna.* Hardly the stuff of love notes but hearing from him made me inordinately happy, regardless of the content of the message.

On the last Wednesday of November, May grudgingly conceded that I had been a greater help than hindrance, a remark I never thought to hear her say. I knew more than I really wanted to know about turkey and the inner workings of stuffing and gravy. Because I'd eaten my share of Thanksgiving feasts without a thought to the work involved in their preparation, I felt properly humbled. Fortunately, nothing fazed May, not even my amateur presence underfoot in the kitchen, so the feast was ready as promised. Thanksgiving morning Levi, May, and I wrapped all the pots and dishes in layers of newspaper and loaded them into the back of the automobile.

When I bemoaned the fact that everything would be cool by the time we arrived at Cox's, May asked practically, "Didn't Mr. Gallagher put kitchens into any of those apartments he built?" At my nod, she added, "Then you can have folks heat things up on that end if need be."

"I never thought of that." Sometimes with May I felt twenty-three going on ten.

"For a smart woman, Johanna, you don't always think," she replied, and I couldn't argue the point.

Betsy and Etta waited at Cox's side door, and I hardly had half a sentence out about warming up some of the dishes when the two young women took over. Before I knew it, Betsy had rounded up several women from the apartments to handle that issue and to set up serving tables on the first floor. We moved sewing machines out of the way and several women lugged down small kitchen tables from their apartments. Children watched wide-eyed and quiet from the sidelines. Within an hour of my arrival, the pans of meat and vegetables were laid out and the enticing smells of May's cooking filled the corners of the first floor. I didn't know when to expect Drew's contribution but trusted Fritz would deliver them in time. Whether Drew himself would come for the occasion remained to be seen, but truthfully, once the tables were up and the food ready, I didn't have time to give him much thought. Hungry people milled about the first floor ready to eat, the tables decorated with the women's own tablecloths and dishes from upstairs.

"I suppose we should start with a blessing," I called out into the room and was greeted by a quick silence. I repeated the one I'd learned as a child, and when everyone gathered with plates in hand, I said to Betsy, "You scoot now. Go find

Etta and the babies and get in line. I can keep things moving without you." She viewed me with enough skepticism to make me say, "I'll be fine without you, Betsy. I can lift a spoon or stir a pan as well as anyone else. I'm not completely helpless in the kitchen, you know."

"Close enough to helpless to make us all nervous, though," commented Drew. I turned toward him, my heart lightening at the sight of his grin and those laughing eyes.

"You should talk," I retorted. "I bet if we held a kitchen contest, I'd win." Behind him, Fritz bore boxes of what must have been pies because a heavenly smell of autumn spices emanated from the crates. Drew took off his topcoat and suit coat then pulled off his tie.

"I won't argue, but the outcome would be closer than you think."

"Drew, what are you doing?"

"Rolling up my sleeves."

"I can see that. Why?"

"I'm here to help, Miss Swan. This may be the only time you'll ever hear these words from my lips but put me to work." He was so engaging, hair casual, shirt open at the neck and the sleeves rolled up inelegantly to his elbows that I felt an attraction to him so strong and intense I turned away, ostensibly looking for something. Grabbing an apron, I turned back and tossed it to him.

"I treasure the moment," I said, smiling in response, "so put this on. Did you bring potatoes?"

"When do I ever not follow your orders to the letter? Fritz just set them down at the end of the table." The line of women and children began to move toward the serving table, ready to start.

All I had time to say in response was "Good. Make yourself useful then," before I hurried away to keep a watchful eye on all the serving dishes. For the next hour I caught Drew only occasionally out of the corner of my eye. Of course, he was comfortable with a room full of women, cordial with them, joking but not disrespectful or condescending, charming enough to cause several of them to look back at him speculatively, a man obviously in his element. I might wish it weren't so, but he had an unaffected and open ease with women that was impossible to miss. He'd learned that behavior through the years, I suppose, and now it came as naturally as inhaling. Wasn't I living proof of its effectiveness?

Once everyone had been served and the room filled with the subdued murmur of dinner conversation and the intermittent clinking of utensils, Drew drifted over in my direction to ask, "Are you assigning me pie duty?"

"Only pie cutting duty. I think this crowd is capable of serving their own dessert. Aren't you hungry?"

"By the look in your eyes, I'd guess I'm not as hungry as you are. Why don't you find a plate and get started? I'll cut a few pies and join you in a minute." It didn't take much to persuade me to follow his suggestion. I was suddenly ravenous, overwhelmed by the smells all around me, and I piled as much as I could on a plate, pulling a rickety chair before me to use as a small table. Tucking a napkin under my chin, I waited for Drew to join me. When he walked over with his own filled plate, something about me made him laugh out loud.

"What?" I asked. Shaking his head, he did the same as I, and set his plate onto a second chair.

"I wish you would have dared to tuck your napkin under your chin at the Auditorium the other evening. That would have caused more of an enjoyable stir than my few remarks."

"What would I have tucked it into?" I asked practically. "You'll recall I was wearing a considerably different neckline that night."

"Oh, yes, I definitely recall." Something gleamed from his eyes for a moment, salacious or admiring or a combination of the two, and then he waved his fork at me. "Why aren't you eating?"

"I was waiting for you." I tried to invest my words with dignity. "You remember good manners, I'm sure."

"Johanna, that's very courteous of you, but," he speared a piece of turkey and stuffed it into his mouth, "no one asked you to wait for me." With his mouth full, his last few words were hard to understand, but I caught the gist of them without much effort and followed his example. We must have looked like competitors in a gastronomic contest, hunched over our makeshift tables and forking in our food.

Later, after the sounds of focused eating were replaced by a contented murmur of conversation, both Betsy and Etta took over the clean up of the room. Children giggled and played games as their mothers returned sewing machines to their rightful places and carried off tables and chairs. I shared in the general feeling of well-fed contentment, perfectly satisfied to have no role in the bustle of activity. Betsy stopped by to say thank you on everyone's behalf, spoiling the moment by telling me I had gravy on my cheek.

I replied with a dignified thank you, but after she left I asked Drew accusingly, "Were you just going to let me walk around with dinner on my face and not tell me?"

"In general I make it a practice never to point out to a woman any flaw in her appearance. No matter how kindly intended, such a gesture is never well received."

"Ha! At our first meeting you told me I wasn't pretty."

"Not our *first* meeting, surely?" He was teasing, sprawled out in the chair with both hands clasped across his stomach.

"You said I shouldn't wear hats because I wasn't pretty enough for them."

"That is not what I said."

"That's how I remember it."

"I know you well enough to realize that you remember only what you choose to remember. What I said was that you shouldn't wear those monstrous chapeaus that are so stylish right now because they don't become you. I recall telling you your face was remarkable and it is. There's always an abundance of pretty women, Johanna, and in ten years their looks will have faded or disappeared completely. In ten years you will be magnificent."

I looked at him closely to be sure he wasn't still teasing before I said, too stiffly, "Thank you," then "Are you being nice to me for a reason?"

"Of course. I learned that trait from you and it seems to work pretty well."

"So what do you want?"

He took time to answer, meeting my look with a slight smile before he stood to tuck in his shirt and reach for his jacket that hung over the back of a chair. Finally he said, "I want to kiss you again, right at this moment, gravy and all. What are my chances?"

I considered the question and briefly toyed with the idea of full cooperation before common sense kicked in. "Slim," I answered regretfully. "Very slim."

Drew gave a good-natured shrug. "I thought that might be the case."

"Slim right at this moment at least," I amended and stood, too. "But I believe that persistence is everything, Drew." I smiled sweetly and directly at him.

"I've noticed that trait in you," he replied mildly, refusing to react to my teasing. Drew took both our chairs and replaced them in their original positions, then stepped out the back door to return with Fritz. The previous topic of conversation apparently dismissed, he asked, "How are you getting home?"

"Levi will be here anytime now. And thank you for your generosity today, regardless of your reasons. It was a real treat for all your employees and who knows, you may even win another award for it." I meant it as a joke but he didn't smile in return. I thought he might be uncomfortable with the sentiment or was just bored. "Why don't you go home, Drew? You don't have to stay here any longer on my account. I'm fine without you."

"Unfortunately, truer words were never spoken, Johanna. You owe me, though, and I won't forget." He threw his topcoat over his arm and left me standing in the large first floor room, now returned to the look of a factory despite the last, lingering smells of the Thanksgiving meal. All the light seemed to disappear from the room with Drew's exit, and I had to stop myself from calling him back. Of course, that would never do, not yet anyway. Too much was still unsaid. What did I see in his eyes when he looked at me? Admiration or something even deeper? The gleam of challenge based on his male need for conquest? I was determined to find out but on my own schedule and in my own way.

December rolled in with bitterly cold temperatures and a frigid wind off the lake that forced several women to the Anchorage for shelter. As Hilda predicted, space became the most valuable commodity we had to offer, any kind of space that provided warmth and protection from winter's first full-force attack. We put up cots in the hallways and in the classrooms.

Despite all the pitiful stories and sad situations, I was unable to stir up my usual feelings of outrage and anger. Instead, I went about humming Christmas carols under my breath. The phenomenon carried over to home, where Crea gave me a knowing, devious look whenever she caught me humming a subdued chorus of "Joy to the World." I knew the world was full of needy people and injustice and corruption abounded, but I couldn't help myself. I was simply happy and unable to work up righteous wrath about anything.

Crea appeared happier, too. Letters appeared for her at least once a week. She would stuff them into her pockets with a fake frown, pretending they were a nuisance more than anything else, but I was never fooled. On one occasion I posted a return letter for her.

"Peter asked for some ideas about Christmas presents for Mrs. McIntyre," she explained quickly as she handed me the envelope. "I thought it would be rude not to answer."

"Crea, you don't have to explain anything to me. You may send letters to every member of my family for all I care. When is he coming home, by the way?"

Without having to ask whom I meant, Crea answered happily, "He's catching the train December thirteenth," her face lighting up with anticipation. Then, perhaps thinking she had given too much away, she added, "As I recall, anyway," and disappeared quickly into her room.

Jennie visited early in December to spend time with Grandmother and then joined me for a snack in the warm kitchen.

"Have you been under the weather, Jen? You look pale."

"A touch of a cold, I think. My stomach's unsettled and my head thumps for no reason. Yesterday Mother kept me in bed wrapped in layers of wool and drinking enough tea to float an armada. I feel a little better now." She didn't look better to my eye, her complexion wan and her eyes holding less sparkle than usual.

"Have you seen a doctor?"

"Now you sound like Mother. I don't need a doctor." Changing the subject, Jennie said, "Your friend Allen Goldwyn's name was in the paper this week. Did you see it?"

"No. For what?"

"Apparently he's involved in the restoration of St. Michael's. The paper gave him credit for restoring the cathedral to its former beauty, especially the windows and their setting. The article said the refurbished church will be rededicated Sunday morning. I thought you'd know all that. Aren't you and Mr. Goldwyn friends any more?"

"Of course, we are but he has a job and I do, too. We're both busy."

Looking at me over her teacup, Jennie remarked, "Really, Johanna, you're learning to be very slippery and more like me every day. I'm proud of you. It's obvious to me and anyone else with an ounce of perception that Mr. Goldwyn, poor man, has been replaced in your affections. If I promise not to tell a soul, will you tell me more about Drew Gallagher?" I didn't like my cousin's admiring tone when she said Drew's name, in fact, felt an unbecoming twinge of jealousy and suspicion at her words. My reply came out too sharp for the occasion.

"There's nothing to tell, Jennie. Why don't you concentrate on the mistake your marriage could turn out to be?" I wished I hadn't made the unkind, unwarranted comment as soon as the words were out of my mouth.

"I wasn't trying to be nosy, Johanna." Jennie spoke with a dignity that made me even more ashamed. "You've always been more like a sister than a cousin to me, and I really do wish you a happy life. I'm good with confidences, too. You'd be surprised." She stood to go.

"I'm sorry, Jen, for being rude and bad-tempered. I've been on my own a long time and sharing private thoughts isn't easy for me. Forgive me?" She smiled.

"Sure. You may be older, but sometimes I feel like I'm way past you in experience. I understand more than you give me credit for." She gave a quick look at the old kitchen wall clock. "Now I'm late. Mother's picking me up so I can be fitted for my wedding dress."

"You didn't tell me you set a date!"

"I had nothing to do with it. The Milfords have decided they can fit the occasion into their schedule the Saturday after Easter, March twenty-ninth. So who am I to argue?"

"It's your and Carl's wedding, Jennie. If you're not happy with the date, pick another. Surely Carl will support you."

"Carl is a Milford and as much under the control of his parents as I am of mine. Anyway, the date is all right. If anything, I wish it was sooner."

Her comment surprised me. "Why?"

She was fastening the buttons of her coat so her head was down and I couldn't see her expression when she answered, "Less time for something to happen that would ruin my chance to get away from my mother. That's what I worry about." She lifted her head and gave a laugh that was intended to give the impression she was making a joke. After she left, though, I remembered the look in her eyes and knew she hadn't been joking. Jennie was unhappy and close to desperate. I wished I knew what to do for her but couldn't think of anything that would be helpful. Christmas Eve, when the family was together, I'd talk to Peter. Maybe he'd have an idea.

I found the newspaper article Jennie mentioned and decided to attend the Sunday morning dedication at St. Michael's. It was true that the bond of friendship Allen and I shared was not as close as it had once been, but I was still fond of him and truly admired his talent. My attending the ceremony would give me the chance to affirm my regard for him. Besides, I was curious about the windows.

"I'll take the trolley home," I told Levi when he let me off at the curb in front of the beautiful, old church, one of the few buildings that escaped the ravages of the great Chicago fire forty years before. Time and weather had darkened the exterior, but inside light poured into the sanctuary through the most gorgeous stained glass windows I'd ever seen. Coming in through the narthex, nothing prepared me for the startling effect of the windows' vivid colors, a bright yellow that made the streaming sunlight almost unbearably bright, rich purple and scarlet, and especially a vivid turquoise blue that dominated each pane. All the walls and windows were refurbished, years of city grime scraped away and the muted orange color, which I had thought a curious choice when Allen first mentioned it, was exactly right as trim for doors and windows. He'd painted the walls a delicate, paler orange. The result was perfection. I sat in a pew along a side aisle and gawked at every corner as openly as a newcomer fresh off the farm. What was originally a beautiful interior was now something extraordinary, a landmark of renown to honor both the Creator and the city of Chicago and all due to Allen's unerring, creative eye for form and beauty.

Although the service hadn't yet begun, from the loft at the rear of the cathedral the organist played one of Bach's concertos on a large pipe organ. For just a moment, I felt overwhelmed with beauty, surrounded by color and music that set my heart at rest for the first time in a long while.

The pew squeaked as someone sat down next to me and whispered, "Are you asleep?"

My eyes flew open. "Of course not," I snapped. "I was meditating."

"You know how I hate arguing with you," Drew said, "but it really looked a lot more like sleeping than meditating." I ignored the remark.

"What are you doing here?"

"You mean here specifically, or more generally, what am I

doing in church?" The Bach concerto ended with a flourish of bass pedal.

"Either one."

"I came to see your Mr. Goldwyn's masterpiece." Drew, holding his hat in his lap, looked around the cathedral. "The paper didn't do the finished product justice. It's glorious."

"It is, isn't it?" I agreed warmly. "All Allen's ever wanted to do is create and construct, and he's always had an eye for beauty, both in color and in form. Having the opportunity to work here must have been an answer to prayer." Drew started to speak exactly when the organ started up again and I shushed him. "Could we just look and listen, please?" I asked, and he promptly crossed his legs and leaned back against the pew without another word.

After the service ended and people began to rise and leave, Drew and I continued to sit comfortably side by side.

"Is it all right if I talk now?" he finally inquired humbly.

"You have never needed my permission to talk, and I can't imagine you're going to start now." But I spoke lightly, to tease. His presence was an agreeable surprise, and I was happy simply to sit beside him, an unexpected and unplanned pleasure that warmed my words. "What a lovely morning it was! There was something for practically all the senses." I stood and he did, too, ever the gentleman. Through the crowd of people, I saw someone move quickly out the side door, a certain motion of the head and a streak of gold that looked familiar. "Is that Jennie?"

Drew turned, taller than I and more able to see over the heads of the people exiting. "Where?"

I hesitated. "Never mind. It must have been a trick of light. Jennie would have told me if she planned on being here today."

We walked outside where the December wind greeted us

with a gust so cold and forceful that I lost my balance for a moment and fell back against Drew. He steadied me but then kept his hand on my arm.

"Was Mr. Goldwyn in the crowd, Johanna? I didn't see him."

"No, I didn't either, but he may have been. The sanctuary was packed."

Drew offered obligingly, "I'll wait with you until your driver comes."

"Oh, I'm taking the trolley home," I said and heard him make a sound that communicated both disgust and admiration.

"You really push good sense to the limits sometimes. I'll take you home and don't argue with me about it. It's freezing out here. By the time the trolley arrives, you'll be as stiff as Lot's wife."

"I never look back, so your comparison is flawed," I pointed out but picked up speed to keep pace with his longer strides, not about to argue. Besides the extended enjoyment of his company, the wind seemed to have grown colder with the day, and I'd already regretted I hadn't asked Levi to come back for me. I continued to shiver once we were in the automobile, even after Drew draped his wool topcoat over my shoulders.

"I hate this damp cold," I admitted, "and it gets worse every winter."

"Then you should spend the winter in Italy or the south of France, Johanna. There's no sin in spending some of your fortune on yourself. You don't do it all that much as far as I can tell. Why not spend a few weeks where the sun soaks into your bones, where the lush fragrance of lemons is everywhere, and colorful flowers cascade down terraced gardens?"

"You make it sound irresistible."

"A villa overlooking the Mediterranean is more than irresistible."

I pulled Drew's coat more tightly around my shoulders. "Maybe I'll take your recommendation but only to celebrate my first vote in a presidential election."

"Aren't you afraid you'll be too old to enjoy the trip?"

"Not at all. I predict women will be voting within the decade."

"I hope you're right."

Once in front of my house, Drew came around to walk with me up to the front door. "I'll see you in a couple of weeks" he remarked casually. When I looked a question at him, he said, "Christmas Eve," apparently assuming I knew what he was talking about. Another look at the blank expression on my face made him laugh. "Your grandmother invited me to stop by anytime that evening. I told her I wouldn't think of intruding on your family's holiday, but she insisted. Didn't she tell you?"

"No."

Just like her to spring it on me at the last minute again, I thought, but I couldn't work up any pique. Having Drew around for any length of time would be welcome, both for his own company and as a respite from the emotions that seemed to swirl around the members of my family. Drew would be an impartial antidote to Peter's unhappiness, Jennie's reckless rebellion, Aunt Kitty's gloating over the wedding, Uncle Hal's ineffectual attempts to restrain both wife and daughter, and Grandmother's frail health, a reminder of her mortality that caused a pang in my heart every time I saw her.

"But you don't know what you're letting yourself in for with my family," I went on. "Surely you can think of other, more attractive plans for Christmas Eve."

"Last year Fritz and I celebrated by sharing a bottle of whiskey."

"On Christmas Eve?"

"Neither of us had family around and it seemed like a good idea at the time. In retrospect, however, I admit that a hangover on Christmas morning is in poor taste." I felt a quick compassion for him but was careful not to show it.

"I'll see if we can spike the Christmas punch if you'd like. I'm afraid you may find the festivities tedious, Drew, so consider yourself warned." I hesitated before adding spontaneously, "But I'm glad you're coming." For no reason and completely unexpected by both of us, I stood on tiptoe and kissed him lightly on the cheek. "No one should be alone on Christmas Eve." Whatever he expected, it wasn't that casually affectionate kiss and some emotion changed his face, removed the slight smile that had been there and darkened his eyes.

"Johanna," he began, but I didn't wait to hear more. Instead, I said a quick thank you for the ride and hurried inside. I considered inviting him in but decided I'd thrown us both off guard enough already. I wanted to spend more time with Drew but perversely felt an odd relief once I was away from him. If what I felt was truly love, it was nothing like its description in popular novels. I was restless when I was away from him and even more restless when I was with him. How peculiar, I thought, and wondered if my reaction was the rule or the exception.

At supper that evening I said curtly, "It would be nice to know what's going on in this house, Grandmother. I found out from Drew Gallagher that you invited him to join the family for Christmas Eve. Don't you think that's something you should have asked me about first?"

Without blinking, Grandmother responded, "Why?" and waited attentively for my answer.

"Well, because he's my friend." A lame answer that Grandmother did not leave unchallenged.

"I had no idea he was permitted only one friend in the family."

"You know what I mean."

"Johanna, contrary to your youthful opinions, the planet does not revolve around you. The fact is that I found Mr. Gallagher to be amusing, attentive, courteous, and intelligent, and enjoyed his company. I didn't realize I had to ask your permission to invite people into my own home."

Grandmother's pretense at rational thought did not fool me. I knew her too well. For some reason she wanted Drew Gallagher in closer proximity, and if I wasn't sure I had kept my emotions to myself, I might have suspected her of matchmaking. That motivation didn't make sense, though. She didn't take the same interest or practice a similar subterfuge with Allen Goldwyn even though she could have reasonably suspected I had an amorous interest in him. Perhaps she really did like Drew for his own sake. Why that didn't ring true I couldn't explain. She seemed to find his presence stimulating and as Drew had remarked the afternoon of her birthday party, there was no reason that advancing years should keep a person from enjoying the company of the opposite sex. Still, the fact that I was certain Grandmother had purposefully invited Drew to draw out a reaction from me annoyed me as did the quickly suppressed grin on Crea's face during the conversation. It seemed I now shared a house with the entire Machiavelli family.

The holidays brought the Anchorage an influx of donations from generous patrons, and combined with my own contributions, we were able to decorate, provide gifts, and plan for a large holiday dinner. I sent special presents to Henrietta and Betsy and their children, to Mrs. McElhanie and all the alumnae of the Anchorage who worked at Cox's. It only took me one Saturday to complete all my Christmas shopping, starting out early and plundering my way through the stores along Michigan Avenue. One of the few, true, and uncomplicated benefits of having comfortable wealth is the ability to buy presents for the people one cares about. My purchases were delivered to the front door over the next few days and I hurried them all off to my room where I spent several evenings unsuccessfully trying to wrap each item in a way to do it justice.

For all the emotions swirling around the family that year, I remember those early weeks of December 1912 as a time of innocence and personal happiness. I thought that Jennie would either come to her senses and cancel the wedding or marry and discover that she enjoyed being Mrs. Carl Milford. I believed that with patience and love, Peter could convince his mother to dance at his wedding because eventually Aunt Kitty would recognize Crea's true worth in my friend's kindness, industry, intelligence, and beauty. And I suppose—though it's hard to remember exactly what was going through my mind at any given moment—I believed that something would happen that would assure me of Drew Gallagher's undying and reciprocal affection for me and we would live together happily ever after. A time of innocence indeed.

Snow refused to cooperate with Christmas. No picturesque snowfall softened Chicago's dark streets and dirty smoke stacks. No flakes floated out of a midnight blue sky to frost the rooftops. Besides the aesthetic, snow would also have been welcome because its insulating presence would offer relief from subfreezing temperatures, but no such relief came that December. Frigid air and wind so sharp with cold that it cut deeply into the bone arrived early in the month and continued daily through the holiday. Coal became a black-market commodity among the poor, and newspapers reported people freezing to death in alleys and unheated apartments. Christmas Eve morning dawned as the coldest day of the month.

Despite May's protests, by mid-afternoon I insisted that she and Levi spend the evening with their sons' families.

"You've done all the work," I told May, taking in the sights and smells of the warm kitchen. "Crea and I are quite capable of transferring dishes to the buffet table and putting out the silverware. Don't argue with me, Mayville; I haven't the time. I promise we'll leave every dirty dish for you to wash if you're so set on being helpful. Now, go wish Grandmother a merry Christmas before you leave. She has something for you." Grandmother had something for May and Levi every Christmas: a generous gift of cash and a sincere thank you. Truly, I don't know which of those two offerings May most treasured.

"Will you come with us to midnight service, Crea?" I asked as we put the finishing decorative touches on the table.

"No, but thank you for the invitation, Johanna. I'm going to early Mass so I'm not out late in this weather. I'll be home early enough to help you in the kitchen, though, if you need me." Her inadvertent use of the word *home* warmed me. I had grown very fond of Crea over the past weeks and enjoyed her conversation and company. To me she was already a member of the family. She might hesitate to admit it, but I believed she felt the same about Grandmother, May, and me.

"You don't plan to go out by yourself in this weather, do you?"

"St. Mary's is a straight line on the trolley, and I'll be back before it's completely dark."

"But—"

"Johanna, why is it acceptable for you to gallivant all over the city and take the train by yourself at odd hours of the day and night but not acceptable for me to do the same?"

"Because—" I stopped, meeting her laughing glance, and instantly capitulated. "You're right, of course. You're a grown woman with a mind of her own and if you want to walk to Milwaukee this evening, by all means go ahead. I worry because I care about you, but that's no excuse for me telling you what to do. I'm sorry." She patted my arm on her way out of the room.

"You're forgiven. I know that despite the appearance you try so hard to present, your heart rules over your head every time."

As I dressed, I considered Crea's observation and supposed she was right. Drew wasn't the only one who cultivated a façade. Apparently I did, too. Did we do it to protect ourselves and if so, from whom or what? Was everyone guilty of a similar deception, I wondered, and is that why manners and pretense were so important in social interactions? All of us needed a special, inviolate place where we could feel secure and safe, where only the most trusted person was offered admittance. I might love Drew Gallagher but to trust him with my personal vulnerabilities was another thing altogether.

After we dressed for the evening, I helped Grandmother slowly down the stairs, she resting one hand lightly on the banister and the other more heavily on my arm.

"You're looking very festive this evening, Grandmother."

She wore Drew's birthday gift in its colorful McIntyre plaid of red, green, and black over a black dress with a high lace collar. Her silver white hair was wrapped at the back of her neck and fastened with hairpins tipped in red jewels that glittered in the light. The two spots of color on her cheeks were caused by excitement and took ten years from her face.

"I'm feeling festive, Johanna. We haven't had all the family here for Christmas Eve in several years. When Jennie and Peter were little, it seemed more practical for Harry and Kitty to host the evening, rather than dragging their children out into the cold."

"You didn't have a problem dragging me out into the cold," I pointed out.

"You were never as delicate as Jennie and Peter." She looked over at me with a twinkle in her eyes. "Just ask Kitty." Her off-hand remark made me giggle and I gave her arm a squeeze. The thought that I had almost lost this woman, lost her humor and caustic, good sense, her quiet affection and understanding, constricted my throat and for a moment made me too emotional to speak. The doorknocker sounded as we reached the bottom of the stairs and the brief heart pang I felt disappeared, replaced by a flutter of excitement. Drew perhaps, I thought, but it was Peter arriving early to see whether he could offer some help.

"Johanna," Peter said, turning from hanging up his coat to examine me. "You look wonderful. You should wear that shade of sapphire blue more often. It becomes you."

"Thank you for the compliment, Peter." I saw him take a surreptitious look around and went closer to whisper. "She's at church, but I've taken her up on her offer to help in the kitchen later just to give the two of you a chance for some time together. Take advantage of the opportunity." His face brightened.

"Thanks, Cousin. If I can ever return the favor, don't hesitate to ask." The grin on his face made it clear that he had heard something about my love life and assumed the account was true. Jennie, I supposed and wondered exactly what she'd told Peter. When she was in the right mood, she could make gossip outrageously entertaining and Peter had always been an appreciative audience.

My aunt, uncle, and Jennie arrived not long after Peter, and Drew shortly after them. He hung his coat and hat on the hallway coat tree and turned to follow me into the front parlor.

"A small group," he said and catching something hesitant in his tone, I turned to look at him. A rare circumstance indeed, but I thought he looked uncomfortable.

"Just family."

"And me."

"We're very selective about how we supplement our small family," I answered with a smile, "so consider yourself fortunate that Grandmother believes you worthy of the honor." When he didn't smile in return, I added, "Did you feel obligated to come? It was kind of you to accept Grandmother's invitation and you don't have to stay very long, if that's the case. I can understand that the idea of spending Christmas Eve with this little group is less than a scintillating prospect. Or did you replace other, more enjoyable plans for the evening with this visit?" Drew gave a brief, humorless laugh.

"No matter who's here or what happens, the evening will certainly be an improvement on any memories I have of Christmases past. My father went to work at his bank on Christmas Day, and my abandoned mother would set Douglas and me so far apart at our imported dining table that we'd have to shout to be heard. Recent Christmases are just as blurry. Too many Christmas mornings spent nursing a splitting headache and hazy recollections of bad company from the night before."

Acknowledging his uncharacteristically bitter words, I said, "Before you expect an improvement over those unfortunate memories, let me share with you that a hangover might be preferable to an evening with the McIntyres. I've always tolerated the togetherness for Grandmother's sake, but having been away last Christmas and nearly not making it home this year makes me more appreciative. There is something about being alive that puts one in a more charitable frame of mind." I added, feeling awkward, "But I'm sorry you missed out on Christmas when you were a child. It's one of my favorite family memories from when I was a little girl. In fact, now, so many years later, the memories seem almost too good to be true. I suppose my recollections could be as hazy as yours even if it's for different reasons."

The serious expression disappeared from Drew's face. "When you're kind to me, Johanna, I get nervous."

"It's Christmas," I retorted, "so don't worry that I have an ulterior motive. It's a time of good will to our fellow men, after all."

"And you aren't angling for something?" he asked in a low voice, following me into the parlor. "Then it really is the season of miracles." His comment made me laugh out loud, which Jennie caught as we entered. She gave us both a speculative look before coming over to our side.

"Mr. Gallagher, I believe you are becoming a family fixture." Jennie wore a white wool dress, plain except for a touch of lace at neck and cuff, and tailored to display her perfect, hourglass figure. The only place she showed a spot of color was in her hair, where a sprig of red holly berries curved down to one cheek.

"You look lovely, Miss McIntyre, as I imagine the Snow Queen would look," Drew remarked.

"Looks can be deceiving," Jennie replied lightly. "I'm not nearly as pure of heart as Johanna, for all her gypsy looks."

I shook my head at her but hadn't the heart to scold. It may have been the white of her dress, but she looked pale and drawn to me. Still unwell? I wondered with a niggling worry and requested, "Jennie, steer Drew over to Grandmother, will you, while I check out the kitchen? I sent May away to her family tonight and put myself in charge of the dinner, which is, as you know, a frightening prospect."

Crea was in the kitchen ahead of me, her pink cheeks a sign that she had recently come in from the cold. We worked companionably a while before I casually mentioned, "Peter arrived early tonight to see if I had anything for him to do. We might need him to slice the roast."

"Johanna, don't you dare match make. This is a special

night, and I don't want any scenes."

"All I said was—"

"I know exactly what you said and I know exactly what you meant. Don't act all innocent with me. I know you too well."

"All right, all right. I promise not to practice any subterfuge, but Peter's a grown man and may do what he chooses. I'm not his keeper. Now hand me that tray of glasses. They belong on the sideboard."

Crea glared at me, trying to read something into my purposefully innocent expression before she finally picked up the tray. "I mean it, Johanna."

I smiled a response because she did indeed know me well and wouldn't have believed anything I said on the subject.

The evening, as far as our family evenings went, moved along comfortably. Grandmother patted a place of honor for Drew next to her on the loveseat and seemed sincerely to enjoy his company. I couldn't explain why I still had doubts on the subject. I certainly enjoyed his company and found him incredibly attractive besides, so why shouldn't she? My suspicious nature might attribute other, less obvious motives to the woman, but she gave me no reason to do so. Grandmother enjoyed intelligent repartee with Drew, found his comments amusing, and probably was no more immune to his physical appearance than I was. If he put healthy color in her cheeks and brought a sparkle to her eyes, I should be grateful to him instead of uncharitably wishing he would spend all his time with me.

Despite Jennie's subdued behavior and appearance, her parents clearly enjoyed themselves. Uncle Hal indulged in more sherry than he probably should have, but he became more amiable and sentimental each time he refilled his glass. Aunt Kitty was full of information about the upcoming wedding. I recognized a happiness in her voice I'd never heard before and a certain relief, too. She could finally stop worrying about Jennie once her daughter was in the care of a willing husband who met Aunt Kitty's requirements of a prominent family and suitable wealth. If she noticed that Jennie was quieter than usual and too pale, her comments led me to believe she thought it was wedding jitters.

"Every bride gets nervous," she said kindly, patting Jennie's hand, "but Jennie knows how very fortunate she is."

"I hope Carl realizes his good fortune, too," I interjected, "because Jennie's a jewel. It's not a one-sided arrangement and she doesn't have to be grateful for being the chosen one." As soon as I spoke, I wished I hadn't because Aunt Kitty's good humor disappeared into a frown.

"That's not at all what I meant."

"I know you didn't, Aunt Kitty. I'm sorry. The words didn't come out as I intended. Please forgive me."

My quick apology so took my aunt by surprise that she was momentarily speechless. Then she rallied to say graciously, "Of course, Johanna. You've been with foreigners and out of polite company for nearly two years, and one's social skills can be diminished when they're not practiced regularly."

I swallowed a laugh, turned it into a cough, and when I was sure my voice was steady, replied, "That's true, Aunt. I do seem to have forgotten some of the nuances connected to social success. It's a good thing we're only family tonight."

"And Mr. Gallagher," Aunt Kitty replied, giving Drew what, for her, was a kind and inclusive look. Evidently he was on her short list of approved persons.

"Ah, yes, of course." I knew the exchange had amused him and kept my tone bland. "If anyone understands social nuances, it's Mr. Gallagher." Then, to cover the way my heartbeat sped up when he looked at me in the laughing, intimate way he had, I made a tactical but purely unpremeditated error. "Peter, would you mind bringing in the punchbowl from the kitchen? I'm afraid I'll drop it," sending Peter into the kitchen and into a temptation he could hardly be expected to resist.

Peter did exactly as I asked and continued to help throughout the evening, carrying items back and forth from the kitchen to the dining room without complaint. Caught up in the warmth of the evening, the fire in the hearth, the glow of candles on mantel and table and because of Drew's presence happy in a way that made me forgetful of anyone else, I never gave Peter's eager assistance a thought. Only after we finished eating and sat contentedly around the table did I realize Peter had been gone much longer than it would ordinarily take to carry in the platter of holiday cookies, cakes, and breads that May had spent the last week baking.

The repercussions of Peter's delayed appearance didn't dawn on me until Aunt Kitty rose to her feet with unexpected lightness and with a touch of affectionate impatience said, "What could be taking Peter so long? With his sweet tooth, I wouldn't put it past him to be sampling all the confections first." I moved to rise, too, and she waved a hand at me. "Sit down, Johanna. If you hadn't sent Mayville away this evening, we wouldn't have to wait between courses, but I suppose it was the right thing to do."

Her tone didn't suppose that at all, but with a sinking heart I didn't give a thought to my aunt's talent for damning with faint praise. All I could think was that she mustn't be allowed to enter the kitchen unannounced. I pushed back my chair and went after her but knew as soon as I reached the kitchen door that I was too late. She stood immobile in the doorway and when I went up behind her, I saw what had frozen her to the floor. Peter stood defiantly with both arms around Crea, staring at his mother as Crea tried to push herself out of his embrace. For a moment I was as frozen as Aunt Kitty.

"Mrs. McIntyre, it's not what it appears," Crea began, tears clearly close to the surface, but when she would have backed away from Peter, he took her arm.

"Don't, Crea." No one, not even my aunt in her outraged state, could have mistaken the tenderness in Peter's tone. To his mother, he stated calmly, "It's exactly what it appears, Mother. Exactly. I love Crea, and I've been asking her all evening to allow me to publicly pay my regards to her." When his mother still did not speak, he went on, "I wish you'd try to know and love her as I do, but if that's not possible, it doesn't matter. If she'll have me, I intend to marry Crea O'Rourke someday."

"Oh, I'm sure she'll have you." Aunt Kitty found her voice, so much scorn and loathing in her tone that I saw Crea flinch. "No doubt it's the culmination of all her well-laid plans. Her kind of woman knows what to use to appeal to an uninitiated boy like you."

"Mother, don't say—"

"Really, Peter, young men sow their wild oats but they don't marry them." To Crea, she asked, "How much do you want? I hope you're not foolish enough to believe there will ever be a wedding because I assure you there won't. I guarantee it. Within reason, we'll pay you to go away. I have plans for my son that don't include bringing an Irish whore into the family."

"Aunt Kitty, stop," I said. "You'll be sorry if you go any further."

She turned to me, her face close to mine but still raising her voice so that it must surely be heard in the dining room. "This is your fault. You and your progressive ideas. No one's ever wanted to discipline you or tell you your faults to your face because the fact that your parents were dead afforded you some special privilege. Do you think I don't know what kind of women frequent that place where you work? What good can it possibly serve to bring that kind of woman into our world?

What purpose but to fulfill your selfish and undisciplined sense of superiority?" My aunt was furious, her words brittle and distinct and as slashing in their own way as the knives used to murder my parents.

Uncle Hal, coming up behind me, must have figured out the situation from the motionless tableau of Peter and Crea and from his wife's words carrying into the dining room. "Kitty, enough. You're making a scene." I had never heard him speak to her so sternly.

"*I'm* making a scene? What do you think *that* is?" She flung out a hand toward Crea, who finally broke free from Peter's touch. Without a word or glance our way, Crea headed for the doorway that led through the pantry and to the back stairs.

When Peter started after her, his father said, as sternly as he had spoken to his wife, "Not now, Peter. You have upset your mother and you owe her an apology."

"When she apologizes to Crea or when hell freezes over, whichever comes first," responded my usually even-tempered cousin, who then shouldered his way past us, stomped into the hallway, and eventually exited the house, slamming the front door behind him. At the sound my aunt gave me a look with enough poison in it to kill before straightening her collar with hands that trembled.

"I wish to go home." She lifted her skirts, apparently certain they would be soiled by any contact with me. "Now." Jennie and Drew, who stood behind Uncle Hal, parted for her as the Red Sea must have done for Moses. "Come along, Jennie."

Jennie opened her mouth to argue, met her father's look, and meekly fell in step behind Uncle Hal without a word.

"You may explain to Mother what happened here, Johanna, because I'm damned if I know." That said, Uncle Hal followed Jennie out into the hallway and proceeded to help his wife and his daughter on with their coats, the scene made bizarre by the complete absence of word or sound on anyone's part. After the door closed behind them—no slam this time but only a hushed click of the latch—I looked at Drew standing in the shadows of the hallway. In the silence I heard the rap of Grandmother's cane on the floor as she stepped into the hallway, too, the three of us arranged in an uneven triangle.

"What happened, Johanna?" she asked. I told her in as few words as possible.

"I've never seen Aunt Kitty that beside herself or Peter either. I didn't know what to do." I paused, then added in a rush, "If it was my fault, I'm sorry. I didn't intend or plan such a thing."

"You never do, Johanna, but chaos seems to follow you nevertheless."

"Why is it my fault that my cousin is in love and my aunt hates me?" Grandmother gave me a chiding look, giving the distinct impression that the question was unworthy of me.

"I never said it was your fault. It isn't about fault and it isn't about you." Then in a quiet voice she added, "Poor Kitty."

"Poor Crea, you mean," I retorted. "She was more of a victim than anyone else in that nasty scene. This is 1912, not 1812, Grandmother. We're past the poor scullery maid warming herself over leftover coals and bowing to the master of the house. It's a different world now." Grandmother held up a hand.

"Not really as different a world as you like to think, Johanna, nor ever will be as far as I'm concerned, but never mind. I hope I'm wrong about that." She gave Drew an apologetic smile. "I'm sorry that you were exposed to the dark side of our family, Mr. Gallagher. It's not always so. Sometimes we all manage to coexist quite amicably."

"Don't give it a thought, Mrs. McIntyre. Compared to some scenes I've had the misfortune to witness, this was innocuous. I hardly noticed anything out of order."

"You are a man of true diplomacy. If you ever decide to take up a career in political service, I volunteer to write you an endorsement. Johanna will have to see you out. I am fatigued and ready for bed. Good night." When I went forward to help her up the stairs, she brushed me away. "I may be slower than I used to be, but I am still capable of seeing myself to my own room." She placed a foot on the bottom step and reached to grasp the banister when I heard Crea's soft tread on the stairs.

"Let me help you, Mrs. McIntyre," Crea offered. She looked remarkably composed, her expression suggesting that she was the recipient of vitriol on a regular basis but had grown so accustomed to it that she could afford to be nonchalant. Where she had refused my help, Grandmother smiled, propped her cane against the hall table, and reached out a hand to take Crea's arm.

"Thank you, my dear." Wordlessly I watched the two of them make their slow but steady way up the staircase and then turned to find Drew watching me.

"I feel this was all my fault," I admitted miserably, "but I still don't know what I did that was wrong. Crea's my friend and I like her. I honestly don't understand why her past or her nationality should matter so much. Do you?" When he didn't answer, I sighed. "Poor Drew. Were you anticipating carols at the piano and chestnuts roasting over the hearth fire? We aren't exactly the Cratchets." Drew laughed aloud at that and came closer.

"I'll grant you that." He put a hand under my chin and lifted my face to his. "Johanna," he began when we heard banging from the kitchen. Reluctantly I stepped away.

"May must be home. Wait for a moment before you leave, will you?"

"I didn't plan to leave just yet." My heart lifted at his words.

"Good. There's something I want to show you after I check in with Mayville."

When I returned, Drew had settled comfortably into the chair by the fire, his feet stretched out toward the flames. He looked a question at me as I sank inelegantly into the chair opposite him.

"May doesn't want my help. She said she wasn't surprised tempers flared because my presence in the kitchen is always a recipe for disaster. I offered to help clean up, but she ordered me out of the room."

"A prophet is never respected in her own country," he responded soberly, forcing me to bite my lip to keep from grinning at him. Drew Gallagher had the ability to find the ridiculous in a situation and make me laugh at myself, a gift not to be underestimated in a world of people who took themselves much too seriously.

"Yes, well, I don't feel very respectable right now. Just tired and annoyed."

"Annoyed with—?"

"Myself, I suppose. No, that's not exactly true. Most annoyed with Aunt Kitty and her precious society that demands a certain breeding and behavior and is so unforgiving. And a little annoyed with myself that I wasn't paying attention this evening. If I'd been more alert, I might have been able to head off the whole incident."

"From what little I observed, you would only have postponed the inevitable."

"I suppose, but I hated ruining Grandmother's evening."

"She strikes me as a strong woman. She'll manage."

"I know." We sat in front of the fire quietly until I roused myself and reached for a box on the side table. "Here. I have something for you." With sudden diffidence, I reached to hand him a small wrapped package.

Instead of taking it from me, he only looked at the present, surprise on his face at first and then suddenly no expression at all. I was reminded of our first meeting and the way he had been briefly immobilized by the unexpected sight of his brother's jewelry.

"You don't have to look so suspicious, Drew. I have no ulterior motive. It's Christmas and presents are a tradition. This is only a memento, anyway, hardly anything to speak of." He took the little wrapped package from me, his fingers stroking my palm in the process so that I shivered from the contact. "You're supposed to open it," I instructed and watched as he tore away the paper to reveal the small leather-bound volume beneath.

"Longfellow."

"Yes," I said happily.

I could tell by his expression that he was surprised and pleased and so I was pleased, too. For me that moment crystallized life into something obviously, ridiculously simple. If what I did made Drew Gallagher happy, then I was happy, too. Fatuous and adolescent, perhaps, but true. I felt such a tenderness for him that if I hadn't looked away and muttered inanities, I might have blurted out much deeper feelings that would have surprised and embarrassed us both.

"His sonnets. The man at the bookstore told me it's old and rare, the only published edition of just the poet's sonnets. He said that after publication, Longfellow decided he wanted to include the sonnets in a larger work and tried to recall the earlier small volume but wasn't entirely successful. This was one of a few books that apparently got away. I hope the story is true, but even it it's not, the poetry is valid." I was conscious that I was talking too much and too fast and quieted myself, content to watch Drew's hands caress the little book, touch the leather binding, turn the pages gently, skim his fingertips over the engraved title on the cover.

"This was very thoughtful of you, Johanna."

I didn't know how to respond to his serious tone and feeling a loss for words, said with a flippant tone, "Since I'm so selfish and undisciplined, it's nice to know I may have one redeeming quality."

At my comment, he looked up from the book to state, "Her words hurt."

"Yes." No flippancy now, just acknowledgment.

"They were malicious words intended to hurt. Let them go. They say more about the speaker than they do about you. You have more redeeming qualities than anyone I know, and I have a wide circle of acquaintances." Drew rose suddenly, stepped out into the hallway and returned with something clenched in one hand. Standing next to my chair, he dropped a small box covered in sable brown velvet into my lap. "I've left a small token of regard for your grandmother on the hall table and was going to do the same with this, but you're looking so gloomy, I thought you needed cheering."

"I'm not one to mull and mope so my gloomy moods usually pass quickly." I couldn't take my eyes off the small box that now lay on the rich blue satin of my dress.

"And then reappear in your dreams."

That remark made me look up at him as he stood beside me. "I'm not sure I should ever have shared that personal detail with you."

"You may tell me anything, Johanna. At anytime for any reason. I told you I'm good with shared confidences."

"Yes, I imagine you are." Because you have had too much practice, I thought, especially with women. My tone may have betrayed my thought because he stepped away from my side abruptly and sat down again.

"Your turn to open" was all he said, but for a moment I

thought I had seen a spark of irritation and an inclination to argue in his eyes. The look disappeared as soon as I lifted the cover of the little box.

"They're beautiful, Drew." A pair of earrings lay before me, a diminutive dangle of amber beads on each delicate, flowing gold wire. I wasn't just being polite. The earrings were beautiful, the beads faceted in such a way that when I held the clusters up before me, the gems caught the firelight and reflected a quick sparkle onto the wall. I continued, "But I can't accept them." Despite my words, however, I continued to finger the earrings, the tiny amber beads as liquid and golden as drops of dark honey.

"Why?"

"They're too expensive."

"That's all relative, Johanna, and you know it." He spoke in a dry, practical tone without an ounce of emotion. "Proportionately speaking, your friend Mr. Goldwyn could give you a pair of gloves that would be much more expensive for him than these earrings were for me. Knowing you, I doubt it's the expense that truly bothers you."

"They're too personal," I admitted reluctantly.

"A proper gift is impersonal, then?"

"You know what I mean."

"Yes, I know what you mean." Something changed in his tone that shifted my attention from the earrings to his face. "I bought them because the beads are the exact color of your eyes and the curve of the wire reminds me of the curve of your lips. That is very personal."

"Oh."

"I'm not going to take them back so do what you want with them. Wear them, I hope, but that's up to you." Then because I was still staring at him, he added, "Don't look at me like that, Johanna. How did you put it before? 'I have no ulterior motive. It's Christmas and presents are a tradition.' Just accept graciously as I did. There's something to be said for good manners." I snapped the small box shut and smiled.

"You're right. I love the earrings and, of course, I'll wear them. Thank you." Then, as he had quoted me, I returned the favor. "This was very thoughtful of you, Drew. Now if you'd like, I could bother May for a cup of coffee or I could find the few drops of sherry that Uncle Hal left at the bottom of the decanter."

"No, thank you. It's been an interesting evening, but it's late and I should let you go to bed." We both stood as the hall clock struck midnight.

"*Interesting* is a very charitable word for this evening. Usually we attend the midnight candle service at church on Christmas Eve, but unfortunately tonight that family tradition got lost in the fracas." We walked together to the front door.

"You're going to let the confrontation bother you much more than it should," Drew predicted. "People are people and tonight everyone acted true to type. Nothing that happened was your fault."

"I wonder. As much as I hate to admit it, I think Aunt Kitty may have me pegged pretty accurately. I am undisciplined at times and I'm afraid I do expect special privileges or at least take them for granted. I'm always evaluating my motives, worried that I'm acting self-important or condescending. Grandmother calls it hypocritical elitism." Drew shook his head with a touch of asperity.

"What an idiot you are sometimes, Johanna. You're none of those things and I forbid you to change." He put his hand on the doorknob, then turned back to ask casually, "I'm having friends over on New Year's Eve. Will you come?" When I hesitated, he said quickly, "If you have other plans or would rather not, that's fine."

"No. No, I don't have plans, I mean. I'd like to come. Is it formal?"

"A party at my house? Hardly. It will be a gathering of the peculiar and the eccentric, and their attire will reflect the personality of the group. Wear what you want but you needn't dress up."

"Which am I?" He looked at me without comprehension and I explained, "Peculiar or eccentric, you said. Which am I?"

Drew bent down to kiss me lightly on the lips. "Neither. Both. Good night, Johanna. Sleep dreamlessly." After he left, I took his advice and did just that.

Out of the bosom of the Air,
Out of the cloud-folds of her garments shaken,
Over the woodlands brown and bare,
Over the harvest-fields forsaken,
Silent, and soft, and slow
Descends the snow.

Chapter Fourteen

The days between Christmas and New Year seemed a fairly useless and insignificant time, a quiet interlude between endings and beginnings. The last week of 1912 began with a sense of marking time, Christmas Day subdued after the uproar of Christmas Eve and the next day, Thursday, much the same. I wanted to talk to Crea but felt intrusive. She did not exactly avoid me, but we shared no confidences and I sensed a dignified austerity about her intended to keep me at arm's length. Grandmother rested most of the week and by Friday morning I was restless and impatient for something with no clear idea of what the something was. I spent Friday at the Anchorage going over plans for the classes I would begin again in January. Toward the end of the day, one of the young women experienced false labor pains, and I stayed with her while we sent for the doctor. Nothing came of it, though, and before leaving I stopped by Hilda's office to wish her a happy New Year.

"And to you, Johanna. I'm glad you're with us. We all appreciate your energy and intelligence. It's hard to believe you've been here only eight months. It seems much longer than that."

"I hope that's a compliment," I answered, smiling.

"A very heartfelt compliment. Take next week off if you'd like. Aside from Melody's baby I don't anticipate anything out of the ordinary, and Eulalie and I can handle that situation when the time comes. The pantry's stocked and there's coal in the basement. I promise to call if we need you unexpectedly."

"Are you hinting that I'm not needed?"

"I'm *telling* you you're not needed—at least for the next few days. I never like to think of your taking the train when it's so cold, so stay home where it's warm. We'll see you bright and early the Monday after New Year's. The women are already looking forward to your new classes. You've become famous."

"Infamous, more like, but thank you, Hilda." She made the offer as a gift and a compliment, but I heard her words with dismay. Time on my hands again, rattling around the large house with Crea and Grandmother and making more of a nuisance of myself than usual. Idleness did not become me.

As it turned out, the time was not so heavy, after all. Peter visited on Saturday to offer an apology for the Christmas Eve scene and stayed long enough to tell me that his mother remained unappeased.

"I apologized to her for raising my voice, but I will not allow her to speak of Crea disrespectfully, so we're at an impasse. I'll be relieved to leave for school next Thursday. I put Jennie on the train to Boston to spend the New Year holiday with Carl and his parents, so Mother has nothing else to occupy her mind and her displeasure hovers over our house like a large, dark cloud. If I don't leave, I'll say something even stronger and what good will it do? Mother's never going to change." I felt a pang of sympathy for Peter as he stood in front of me, clearly upset by the discord in his family but resolved not to be browbeaten into submission. He glanced up the stairs.

"I don't suppose—"

"Crea won't see you, Peter. We had a brief talk about it last night. She came to tell me she was moving out."

"What?!"

"Don't panic. She and I reached a compromise that allows her to remain here and still keep her self-respect, but it involves not being thrown into situations where you're present. I promised her that if she stayed, there would be no more ambushes or surprises."

"I didn't ambush her!"

"Crea doesn't agree. She's convinced that you and I colluded to throw the two of you together and she's adamant that she won't be a party to it. I hate to admit it, but I think she's more right than wrong, and I'm going to respect her wishes. She's a grown woman and it's what she wants. I'm sorry." Peter didn't argue.

"What am I going to do, Johanna?" His tone held such misery I had to put my arms around him in a hug, no small accomplishment, he taller than I by half a head and much broader in chest and shoulder.

"I don't know, my dear. Give it some time, I suppose. Finish your degree so you have an independent living and continue to send letters. Crea seems to consider correspondence acceptable."

"Crea will never have me without Mother's approval, will she?"

I shook my head. "You know her as well as I, Peter, so you know she wants to do the right thing."

"And Mother will never give her approval," he continued. "It seems hopeless, Johanna, and I don't know what to do right now. I'm not giving up, though, because I know as sure as I'm standing here that there will never be anyone else for me but

Crea O'Rourke. Tell her that, will you?" He took a deep breath. "I'm not one to despair. I'll just trust that when I'm home again in February, something will have changed."

Weeks later I would remember those words as an unintended prophecy, one fulfilled with such horror and grief that its culmination was simply unimaginable.

Sunday night I sat with Grandmother next to the fireplace. She had her feet propped up on an ottoman, wrapped in the woolen shawl Drew had given her for her birthday and reading the travel book he had given her for Christmas. I wanted to accuse her of flaunting Drew Gallagher in front of me but knew that was ridiculous. It was clear she honestly liked him and appreciated his gifts, both purchased with his usual impeccable taste. Some day I would wear the amber earrings he gave me but not in the near future. I had been incredibly stirred by the intimacy of his comparison to my eyes and lips, and the earrings still held too much emotion for me to put them on. It was enough to take them out of their box, to finger the smooth gems, to hold them up and explore the gold flecks in their liquid depths. I wanted to believe they meant more than just the next move in a sophisticated game of seduction, but I could not dismiss my doubts.

"Scowling like that will give you premature wrinkles," Grandmother commented, and I looked away from the fire to find her gaze on me.

"Wrinkles are the least of my worries. Are you warm enough?" Outside I could hear the bitterly cold wind rattling around the eaves, but we still had no snow on the ground. "Green Christmas, full cemetery," someone once told me, and I shivered at the memory of the words. Grandmother, despite improved color and regained strength, remained too frail for my peace of mind.

"At my age it seems a person is never warm enough, not

even in August. What were you frowning over so intently?"

"Everything. Jennie and Carl. Peter and Crea. I sent a note of apology to Aunt Kitty, though I wasn't exactly sure what I should apologize for. I haven't heard a word in return. Is it just my imagination or is she growing more inflexible and unreasonable every year?"

Grandmother laid her book in her lap. "Kitty is the exact image of her mother—in face, form, and temperament. She was raised a certain way, and it's unreasonable to imagine she is capable of changing now."

"Everyone is capable of change."

"No, Johanna. That's just not true. When Harry announced he wanted to marry Kitty, I told him how she would be in twenty years, but he wouldn't listen. Your grandfather and I had agreed years before that once our children were grown, we would trust their judgment and interfere as little as possible in their lives, so we did not press the issue of Harry's choice of a spouse—or your mother's, for that matter—but Kitty tried our resolve."

"Did you disapprove of Father, too?"

"A man with a passion always has a certain element of danger about him. We would not have chosen him for our daughter, but Nettie loved him and he her, and I couldn't disapprove of someone who made her so happy. He treasured your mother as much for the woman she would become as for the girl she was, and I appreciated that he realized the difference. David Swan was a man without an ounce of guile or greed in him, the most genuinely charitable man I ever met." I had never heard her compliment my father before or speak so openly about him and Mother, and I was enthralled.

"I wish I could remember him better. Being with you and Uncle Hal makes me feel closer to Mother, but I feel I've lost Father. He's not here anywhere, not in this house or in this city."

"No. He wasn't a man of the city. He was a man who looked like his roots—with the prairie in his eyes." Amazingly, after a moment she said, "You should plan a trip to Kansas this spring, Johanna, after the threat of snow has past, see your father's hometown, and visit his family. I've forgotten the name of the little place he was from."

"Blessing," I volunteered quickly.

"That's right, Blessing, Kansas. It would be a good trip for you. No doubt your father's family would be happy to see you." I stared at her and then quickly looked away. I never thought to hear those words from her and later would have to take the time to mull over the significance of her change of heart.

"I know I'd be welcome. My Aunt Mary sent a Christmas letter and invited me for a visit again. She invites me every year."

"Then you should go."

"I never felt you wanted me to go."

Grandmother smiled faintly before picking up her book again. "I have it on very good authority that everyone is capable of change," she said.

On the afternoon of New Year's Eve, it began to snow fat, sodden flakes from a dark and weighted sky. Allen came by for a brief visit, ostensibly to wish Grandmother and me a happy New Year. As we chatted I noticed new lines along his forehead and an expression in his eyes I could not fathom and thought he might have something more serious than New Year's Eve plans on his mind. After Grandmother left the room, I asked Allen bluntly if something else had brought him to Hill Street besides the desire to pass along wishes for the new year.

"I don't see you very often anymore, Johanna," was his oblique reply.

"I'm either here or at the Anchorage," I pointed out. "You're the one who's frequently unavailable."

"What do you mean?"

"I came to the dedication at St. Michael's expecting to see you, but you were nowhere to be found."

"I was there briefly."

"So briefly that I never caught a glimpse of you, and I was there for the entire service. I sent an invitation to your apartment last Friday, too, inviting you to Sunday supper, but I never heard a word in response." He had the grace to flush slightly.

"I was out of town, Johanna. I didn't get back until yesterday. I'm sorry." I laid my hand on his as we sat together on the sofa.

"I'm not scolding you, Allen, only pointing out that you're the one who's been elusive lately. I know I've asked you this more than once but is anything wrong?"

In answer he leaned toward me, brushed his lips against mine, then moved closer and put both arms around me. For a moment I was so surprised I couldn't say or do anything, but as he kissed me, more passionately than I anticipated, I pushed him away with an equal fervor.

"Allen, stop that!" I commanded, more astonished than anything else. He let go of me instantly and sat back against the cushions. I expected an apology, I suppose, or at least an explanation, but when he finally spoke that wasn't what I heard.

"You said you were spending this evening at Drew Gallagher's. Is he the reason I've missed my chance with you, Johanna? While I was working hard, trying to make something of myself, were you slipping away to someone else?"

"Don't be ridiculous, Allen! We've been friends several years but only friends. You know you don't care for me in any other way, and I know you never wanted more than that."

"How could you possibly know that? You're always busy, always with a cause. It's hard to keep up with you, Johanna."

"Those words don't rate a response. Really, Allen, what is this all about? I'll never believe you care for me in any significant way or that you've ever thought of me as anything other than a friend or sister. You certainly don't love me."

"You've become an expert on the subject of love, have you?" His question held a touch of bitterness and something gentler besides, a wish, perhaps, or an unarticulated grief.

"Hardly, but I know what we feel for each other is friendly affection and nothing more."

"Someday," he told me, rising, "you'll find out you're not always right, Johanna."

"I'm right about this," I insisted, following him out into the hallway.

"It must be wonderful to be so certain all the time and able to disregard other people's feelings because they don't agree with yours."

"Allen, don't take that tone. When have I ever been other than transparent with you? When did I ever lead you to believe that I would welcome anything besides friendship from you? Don't turn me into a flirt or a villain. That's not fair."

The pleading in my tone must have reached him, for he put a hand under my chin and said gently, "So even you can't read minds. I'm sorry if I distressed you, Johanna. It won't happen again. You're the farthest thing from a villain I can imagine." I watched him walk out into the early evening dusk, snow falling so heavily by then that it quickly hid him from view.

Something had not rung true in that whole exchange, something missing from Allen's voice or something there that shouldn't have been. I couldn't decide which. By the time he left, however, it was late enough that I had to hurry to get ready for Drew's party, so I pushed the unexpected and slightly repellent incident to the back of my mind to bring out later when I could give it more thought.

Crea came to see me off for the night, silently fastening the buttons up the back of my dress and then stepping back to look at me.

"I don't think I've seen you in black before, Johanna. It's very becoming. Is the dress new?"

"No. I've worn it before and with Drew, but I thought the shawl would hide the fact that it's a repeat. Not that anyone would care, I suppose, and Drew Gallagher is much too polite to point it out even if he noticed."

"I don't think he misses much about you."

"He likes to give that impression, but I don't know if it's true or not."

"You think he's only acting a part? Why would he do that?"

"Because it's part of the game."

"What game? What are you talking about, Johanna?"

"Drew Gallagher has pretty manners but by his own admission he sometimes enjoys doing the unexpected or the outrageous in order to shock people. I fear he sees women as fair game so I'm left to wonder if he means anything he says."

"Don't try to convince me you aren't drawn to him. I can tell by the sparkle in your eyes and the color in your cheeks that you enjoy his company."

I arranged a brightly striped silk shawl around me like a sash, the jeweled tones of emerald and sapphire and ruby in brilliant contrast to the black dress.

"That is very true, Crea. More true than I wish sometimes, but I can't let down my guard with him. He's too apt to read it as weakness and pounce when I least expect it."

"You make it sound like a hunter and his prey." I smiled at that but didn't respond. "I know about these things the hard way, Johanna," Crea continued, "and I'd guess you can trust Drew Gallagher."

"Are you suggesting I should let down my guard with him then, and find out what happens?" Crea hesitated.

"When you wear black, you turn into a stranger, so maybe not tonight, not looking like that."

I grinned as I slipped into my shoes and picked up my bag. "We'll see. If it is a contest, I'd like to come out the winner."

"In Drew Gallagher you may have found someone you can't beat. Love has its own rules."

"I never mentioned love."

This time Crea grinned. "You didn't have to."

When Levi pulled up in front of Drew's house on Prairie Avenue, light from every window spilled out onto the accumulating snow, the party already in full swing. A man and a woman went up the front walk together, her laughter shrill and loud in the crisp night air, the unmistakable sound of someone who'd consumed too much alcohol.

"I could wait, Johanna," Levi said, his expression disapproving as he came around to help me out.

"Thank you, Levi, but I'll beg a ride home later. I'm sure Mr. Gallagher's Fritz will bring me home, and if not, I'll call. Crea will hear the phone and let you know." Levi still stood with one hand on my arm.

"I don't know if your grandmother would approve of my leaving you."

I laughed as I pulled the hood of my cape over my head to protect my hair from the wet snowflakes and said, "Grandmother thinks the sun rises and sets on Drew Gallagher. She'd be here with me if her health allowed it, so don't worry." Then, as an afterthought, I added, "Happy New Year to you and May, Levi. I don't know what we'd do without either of you. You both deserve a wonderful 1913." I went up the walk, knocked on the front door, and as the door opened, turned to see the motorcar creep slowly away from the curb and disappear into the falling snow. Oddly and for just a brief moment, I felt abandoned and had to resist the extraordinary impulse to turn and run after Levi. Then at the sound of Drew's voice, the unsettled feeling passed, and I stepped over the threshold into warmth and light.

"You came." Drew lifted the cape from my shoulders and held it as I turned to face him.

"Wouldn't have missed it for the world. Who could resist a house full of peculiar and eccentric people?" I looked past his shoulder to the room beyond where I could hear conversation and laughter against a backdrop of a piano. "You must have a great many friends, Drew. The house seems bursting."

"I have more friends now than I ever did when Douglas was alive." His dry statement brought my attention back to him.

"Because you've settled into a more traditional and acceptable life? Because you won the Starr Award?"

"Because I inherited a great deal of money." He gave a smile and good-natured shrug. "But come and meet my guests and make your own decisions. They're a lively group so I know you won't be bored."

To my mind Drew's earlier description of his guests as *peculiar* and *eccentric* was not an accurate representation of the people I met that evening. Witty and intelligent perhaps or urbane and cosmopolitan or even selfish and unkind. Depending on the persons I conversed with at the time, any of those word pairs would have been more correct, whether the actress whom I recognized from her picture on the theater marquee as she sat drinking from a long-stemmed glass in solitude or the debonair black man fingering a tune on the piano or the small group engaged in heated argument about the value of abstract art. People wandered in and out of rooms, smoked, ate and drank, argued and laughed, all of it a far cry from a traditional McIntyre family gathering or a communal meal at the Anchorage. I was fascinated and entertained for most of the evening.

Drew did his best to introduce me all around, but his duties as host often pulled him away and left me to my share of solitary wandering, which suited me because I was as interested in the house as the guests. On previous visits, I had managed to see only a few specific areas, but tonight most rooms of the house were open and lit, a buffet table set up in the dining room and drinks flowing freely from a well-stocked cabinet in the library. I found my way to a small room that might have done duty as a proper parlor in any other residence but was bland in tone and furnishings in order, I guessed, to provide a neutral backdrop for the gorgeous paintings displayed on the walls.

As I examined one of the paintings, a man behind me commented, "Impressionism is old hat now, I'm afraid, but I'm sure these are Douglas's acquisitions, not Drew's. Drew would enjoy the shock of a Picasso or a Duchamp, not the banality of flowers in a vase."

"But I don't find these particular flowers banal. Perhaps the old adage about beauty being in the eye of the beholder is true."

The man, who held a glass of clear liquid in one hand, stepped next to me to study the painting before us before responding, "Perhaps, but still not Drew's style."

"And you would know because—"

"Because Drew and I go back several years and have enjoyed the kind of common experiences that forge friendship." His tone was slightly mocking and his words slurred enough to support the fact that it was gin in his glass. He turned toward me. "I saw you come in and have been trying to get your attention ever since."

I found the man attractive in a brittle way, his speech clipped and British, dark brown hair, matching eyes, and a pencil-thin mustache.

"Why?"

"Do you believe in love at first sight?"

"Only in works of fiction."

"How cynical. I didn't expect that from a woman with eyes like yours. I'm Byron Stanhope, by the way."

"Johanna Swan."

"*Miss* Swan, I hope."

"Yes. You sound British."

"Expatriate, I'm afraid, with no plans to return."

"No?"

"The authorities would be waiting at the dock. The London police have a long memory."

"That sounds serious."

"Not really. British society is too stuffy for its own good. Americans are more open-minded about life. But let's not talk about me. I'm much more interested in Johanna Swan."

He was a smooth man, in some ways a dark version of Drew Gallagher but lacking Drew's warmth and, I guessed, Drew's honesty.

"How do you know Drew?" he asked.

"Mutual business interests."

"A woman of means then. I don't suppose it could be my good fortune that you're an heiress."

"You're right, it has nothing to do with your good fortune at all." Stanhope slipped my hand under his arm.

"Miss Swan, I'm in love. Let me get you a drink."

"I'd prefer food, thank you."

"I can arrange that as well." He kept up an amusing commentary as we walked toward the dining room. At the sound of a woman's singing voice coming from another room, we stopped to listen. "Viola both looks and sounds beautiful," Stanhope remarked.

My heart sank. "Viola?"

"You know her?"

"We've never been introduced. Brunette and beautiful?"

"And a longtime friend of Drew's. Yes, that's Viola." I didn't expect to feel so lost and hurt at the news. Hadn't I told Crea earlier this evening that my interactions with Drew might be part of a game and contest? "Drew's taste in art may be questionable, but never his taste in women." We stepped into the room where Viola lounged against the piano, singing in a low, beautiful voice to the accompaniment of the black man I'd seen there earlier. "Sit down, Miss Swan, and I'll bring you something from the dining room. Any requests?"

A man too poised to please, I thought critically, and suddenly wished him—or me—elsewhere.

"I'll let you surprise me."

Stanhope quickly returned with a heaped plate. "I hope you really are hungry and weren't just trying to get rid of me." He set the plate carefully on my lap, retrieved his glass from the table, then sat down beside me, his right thigh pressing purposefully against my leg.

"You're not eating?" I asked.

"Love is the food of the gods," he answered, watching me over the rim of his glass as he sipped. "Now tell me about Johanna Swan. Why haven't I ever seen you before?"

"We probably move in different circles," I observed.

Viola, dressed in a sleek white gown with black fur trim at neck and wrists, stopped singing and moved slowly in our direction. Her elegant languor fascinated me, something sensual and catlike about her that would draw any man's attention, and of course there was that red slash of a mouth. Beside her I felt childish, gauche, and provincial.

"Byron, I didn't see you arrive."

"I'm not surprised," my companion answered easily, "with

such a crowd of admirers cluttering your view. Have you met Miss Swan?"

She gave me a long and unblinking look before favoring me with a slight smile. "I've heard the name but not had the pleasure. Be careful with this one, Miss Swan. He eats little girls like you for breakfast."

I knew she patronized me and I wanted to dislike her for any number of reasons, but her brown eyes had a flicker of humor in them and she was so incredibly attractive, I couldn't work up any real aversion.

"Then he must like them fattened up because he just brought me enough supper for the Turkish army. You have a striking voice. I wish you hadn't stopped singing." My compliment surprised her, I think. At least it made her pause before replying.

"Thank you. I dabble, but it's New Orleans Joe at the piano who has the talent. If you stay late enough, he'll loosen up and give you a show of ragtime and jazz." Of Stanhope she asked, "Byron, have you seen Drew? He owes me a drink in exchange for the entertainment." Then looking past us, she answered her own question. "There he is by the fireplace, glaring at us. One of us must have done something very naughty for Drew to look like that but don't worry. I'll protect you." She drifted off.

"I don't think I'm hungry any more," I stated, setting the plate to one side and rising. "You should circulate, Mr. Stanhope. I bet there are all sorts of heiresses present this evening."

Still seated, he took my hand and raised it to his lips. "The name Byron from your lips would sound like music." The words made me laugh out loud.

"Do men really talk like that in England? I can't believe the country that gave us Shakespeare, Keats, and Browning can't do better." He laughed, too, the first natural and unaffected thing he'd done in my presence all evening.

"I thought it was pretty good for being spontaneous."

"It wasn't pretty good and it wasn't spontaneous."

He laughed again and, still holding my hand, said, "I do like you, Johanna Swan. You're not leaving before midnight, are you?"

"No."

"Good. When we ring in the New Year, I'll be in line for the obligatory midnight kiss."

I didn't answer, just pulled my hand free, gave him a genial look, and walked out into the hallway, forgetting Byron Stanhope almost immediately. I had other matters on my mind. Drew had every right to ask anyone he chose to his own party, but Viola's presence still cast a shadow over the evening. Jealousy on top of everything else, I thought with disappointment. How humbling to accept that I was so typically and unremarkably human. I found the kitchen at the end of the hall and entered without invitation.

"Johanna!" An aproned Yvesta, busy filling trays with sweets, looked up with a smile on her face. Beside her Fritz was stacking glasses on more trays and in the background, sitting at one of the tables, was Yvesta's elder daughter wiping cutlery.

"A family affair I see," I said, smiling. "Hello, Yvesta. I hoped I'd get to see you. Happy New Year."

"And to you, Johanna, but I don't have much time to visit right now."

"I can see that, and I promise not to get in the way, only I have to report back to Hilda and Eulalie that you're doing well. Are you?"

Yvesta stopped what she was doing long enough to smile and nod.

"Ya. Very well."

"You're treated fairly, I hope, not overworked, and you're

paid a decent wage, too, aren't you? How are your living quarters?"

Behind me, Drew said, "Paid! You mean I'm supposed to pay Yvesta? I don't recall that was part of the arrangement." I heard more exasperation than teasing in his tone, but Yvesta and Fritz both grinned, so perhaps I misread him.

Turning, I said, "I was only asking, and if you didn't sneak up behind people and listen in on their private conversations, you wouldn't run the risk of having your feelings hurt."

"My feelings are remarkably impervious to insult." From his voice, I decided I wasn't mistaken. For some reason, Drew was out of temper with me.

"Well, good for you. That undoubtedly spares you from the small pains and easy griefs the rest of us mere mortals are forced to endure. I was only saying hello to Yvesta."

"And accusing me of—what?—white slavery?"

"I wasn't accusing you of anything. I was—" But Yvesta intervened, lifting one of the trays and shouldering past both of us.

"Johanna, I am glad to see you, but I have work to do, so please, both of you, go away." She threw a quick glance in Drew's direction and added, "Sir," before she exited the kitchen. Drew took hold of my forearm and tugged me inelegantly out into the hallway.

"It's never wise to cross Yvesta when she gives a direct order. Come along, Johanna." I pulled loose.

"I'm perfectly capable of walking under my own power, thank you. I didn't mean anything by what I said to Yvesta and you know it. Why are you in such a bad temper? Your home is beautiful, and the party's going famously."

"House," he replied brusquely.

"I beg your pardon."

"House, not home. It's just a house." I was surprised by his abrupt words.

"But it's a beautiful house, Drew, one you can be proud of. I've heard people admire it all evening."

"Beauty is rare and counts for very little in life, Johanna. You should know that." I knew he didn't mean the words as they sounded, but they still hurt.

"Yes, you'd think I would have learned that by now with my unbeautiful but ostensibly remarkable face, but I can be a slow student. Sometimes you have to beat me with a stick before I finally get it." The stunning Viola with her rich brown hair and mouth like cherries continued to bother me, whether I chose to admit it or not.

"I didn't mean—" He made no effort to hide his exasperation and I interrupted with similar irritation.

"I know what you meant, but now there are two of us bad-tempered. Go take care of your guests, Drew."

"That's what I'm doing."

"Your other guests then. I can manage just fine without you."

"So I noticed earlier."

"What does that mean?" I shrugged off my question before he could explain and continued, "Never mind. I have no idea why we're arguing and if it was my fault, I apologize. Now, to quote Yvesta, 'Go away. Sir.'" He didn't want to smile, but one corner of his mouth gave an involuntary twitch, and I knew his dark mood had passed.

"I will for now, but don't go too far, Johanna. Remember, you owe me."

"For what?"

"One word: pies."

I remembered Thanksgiving. "Oh. That's right."

"I'll collect payment this evening, so go find a quiet spot and stay out of trouble until I can get rid of some of these people. I don't recall inviting all of them."

Despite myself, I said, "Surely you remember inviting Viola."

Drew gave me a speculative look before he responded, "I invited Charles Montgomery."

"The artist? The one everyone's talking about?"

"The very same. He's painting Viola, or so she says, and he brought her."

"Is that right?" I tried for a skeptical tone but felt suddenly lighter and happier.

"Yes, that's right. Viola moved on to a man of artistic temperament, one who would feed her soul, she said. I can't say I blame her. I have never excelled at soul feeding."

More fool she, I thought, but said only, "A woman has to look out for herself."

From down the hall someone called Drew's name, but before he walked away he repeated, "Don't go too far, Johanna."

Not tonight, I won't, I thought. The evening had become interesting again.

As midnight neared, the party grew even livelier, the man at the piano playing something spirited and loud and the guests, by now well and truly inebriated, dancing, laughing, and chattering at top speed. I liked the eclectic mix of people and enjoyed listening in on multiple conversations that took up everything from the war in the Balkans to a Massachusetts textile strike, from the merits of Jung versus Freud to Amundsen's courageous trip to the South Pole. As I leaned against a shadowed wall, sipped on diluted champagne, and eavesdropped on a unanimous chorus of heated outrage at the federal government's unrelenting proposal to tax everyone's income, Byron Stanhope propped himself next to me.

"So this is where you've hidden yourself, Johanna, my love." By the shine in his eyes and the alcohol on his breath, I could tell he'd spent more than enough time at the beverage sideboard.

"Not hidden, Mr. Stanhope."

"Byron."

"Not hidden, Byron. Just listening. Will we have a federal income tax, do you think?"

"I haven't the slightest idea and I can't say I care. I'm still a British citizen so the old USA only gets the money I choose to give it." He leaned closer. "Now if you'd like me to spend some money on you, I would do so without question. What would you like? Furs? Jewels? What could I offer that would bring you into my arms?"

"Can you arrange universal suffrage for women?"

"Alas, no."

"Then I'm afraid I'm forced to stay out of your arms."

"That's not sporting."

"I don't have to be sporting. Isn't there someone else you'd rather play with?"

"No. Just you." He turned toward me more quickly than I would have thought possible for man under the influence and planted both palms against the wall on either side of me. "Did you hear that?" I was annoyed by his proximity and the uncomfortable feeling of being trapped and unable to move without making a scene.

"Hear what?"

"The clock strike midnight. Happy New Year, Johanna." He leaned to kiss me.

"Will you stop?" I retorted with annoyance. "It isn't midnight yet and even if it were, I have a very short list of men I choose to kiss. Have I mentioned you're not on it?" I gave Stanhope a little shove, not threatened, just irritated, but was still relieved when Drew stepped beside us.

"Byron," Drew said lightly, "go away. You're annoying Miss Swan and, trust me, that's not something you want to do."

Without moving and with his face very close to mine

Stanhope murmured, "Why? Does she bite? I'd love to find out. The thought of it makes me shiver."

"No, Johanna won't bite, but I will. Now go away." I didn't notice anything different in Drew's tone, but Stanhope apparently did for he slowly straightened and turned to give Drew a surprised look. After a moment spent examining Drew's face, Stanhope shoved both hands into his pockets.

"Take it easy, Drew. No harm intended. You should have told me." To me, he said, "I thought you were too good to be true, my love. Please accept my apologies. I didn't realize."

I watched him wander off and then turned back to ask impatiently, "What was he talking about? Realize what?" At that moment both the large grandfather clock in the hallway and the more delicate porcelain mantel clock in the room where we stood began their midnight chimes. Around us, the room filled with even more people, everyone coming together to welcome the new year with laughter and loud greetings that gradually silenced as all the inhabitants found someone to embrace. Drew took my hand and pulled me around the corner into the empty hallway.

"Never mind. I hope I'm on your short list," he said gruffly and kissed me. Then as the clocks stopped chiming and the chatter in the room beyond slowly resumed, he pulled me hard into his arms and kissed me again, very thoroughly, lingering on my mouth and the lobe of one ear in a way that caused wholly new sensations in several parts of my body.

"Johanna," he whispered, "will there be hell to pay if you don't go home tonight?"

To give myself time to think, I pulled away just enough to draw his head back down to mine and kiss him again, which, of course, was not conducive to clear thought at all.

"If I don't go home, where will I go?" I whispered in return. That we felt compelled to lower our voices didn't make sense because from behind us the piano music was uptempo and loud and people once again laughed and talked, the brief intervention of a new year seemingly forgotten.

"To paradise. If you trust me. Straight to paradise, Johanna." When I didn't respond, Drew continued, a depth to his tone I'd never heard before, "I can get rid of all these people very quickly so it would be just you and me. Why not, Johanna? Don't try to tell me you don't recognize there's something special between us, that you don't feel what I feel or aren't as eager as I am. We'll start with just one night, and I promise you won't regret it." Taking unfair advantage of my hesitation, Drew began simultaneously to run his hands up and down my back and kiss me along the base of my throat.

All right, I wanted to say, one night or a lifetime. I'll take whatever you give me. This may be as close to love as either of us gets. But I didn't say anything like that. I was too afraid of being the one not loved, too proud to be just another Flora or Betsy. Instead, I managed to imbue my words with light, almost mocking, amusement and ask, "Will we be even then?"

Drew ceased all movement and his words came out wary and slow. "What did you say?"

"I asked if my spending the night with you would even up the score between us."

He pulled both hands away from me as if I were suddenly hot to the touch and stepped back. "Is that what you think?"

"Why would I think anything else? You're the one who made it a point to say I owed you. Aren't you just telling me the price you expect me to pay? Don't misunderstand me, Drew. You make it very attractive and I might be perfectly willing."

His quiet, steady gaze unnerved me, but by then I felt mired in the need to continue the charade and went on with brittle words that weren't what I wanted to say at all. Pride or self-protection or vanity or the need to hold the upper hand continued to propel me to a place I did not want to go. Once begun, I couldn't stop and I wouldn't take anything back. How could I? I'd look the fool in front of him and shuddered at the thought of being so exposed.

With unintended irony I continued, "I'm just being candid, Drew. You know I like things out in the open. It's not like you care for me in any lasting or meaningful way. You enjoy variety in women, you said. Marriage wasn't an option for your future. I just want to be sure I understand the terms of the agreement before I sign. Isn't that plain good business sense?"

Drew Gallagher eyed me with an intensity that gave the impression I'd turned into a stranger he couldn't quite place. His face had lost all animation, his eyes guarded and still, the last ten minutes—his arms around me, his lips against the pulse in my throat, and my eager hands pulling his head down to mine with a willingness he couldn't have missed—something that had never happened.

He took a deep breath, a touch of humanity creeping back into his eyes, and put both his hands into his pockets. "Yes, I suppose it is."

It took me a moment to return to reality, remember the question, and ask, "Then why are you acting like I'm a child who just threw a tantrum at church? Surely you don't disapprove of a person getting the facts straight."

"I've changed my mind, Johanna. Sometimes you have the same effect as being doused with a bucket of cold water."

"You made a business offer and I'm considering it. I once told you I was willing and able to pay all my debts in full and I meant it. I don't understand why what I said or did should change the mood." But I did understand, of course. I recognized—more from the depth of feeling in his tone than the few words—that he had divulged more than he'd intended, had made himself as close to vulnerable as he was able. And I had spurned, even mocked, the effort.

"I changed my mind, Johanna," he repeated. "My timing was wrong."

"I don't think timing had anything to do with it," I said.

"No?"

"You act like you're disappointed with me, Drew, or surprised by my reaction, but that's disingenuous on your part. We both know you can't resist the challenge of trying to entice a woman into your bed. What goes on between the sexes is a competition to you, and I became part of the game. How many points would you have scored for complete capitulation?"

"I'm not the one who makes everything a contest," he replied shortly.

"Are you saying I do?

His face reflected the scorn I heard in his voice. "'Be nice to Drew so you get what you want. Do this for me and I'll do that for you.' I'd rather have life a competition than a scale, Johanna, with every little gesture weighed in the balance. Nothing given without an expectation of return. I learned that from you, you know. You always expect the worst of men and you always credit them with the worst possible motives. You tar every member of the opposite sex with the same brush, yet if I did that with women, you'd be harping on my unenlightened attitude and lack of fair play. No matter how hard a man tries, he just can't make it past the barriers you've set up to protect yourself." He was close enough to the truth that I flushed.

"Well, you might have made it past my barriers tonight, but you gave up too soon. Now I'm going home. It's late." I marched past him down the hallway before I stopped abruptly and turned around. "What a trite ending! I forgot I don't have a way home so I either have to borrow Fritz or your telephone."

Drew went to the end of the hallway and pushed open the

kitchen door. "Fritz, do you mind taking Miss Swan home?" To me he added, "I'll get your wrap." We stood by the front door wordlessly until Fritz brought the motorcar around to the curb. I was distressed enough that I could have walked home just to use up my excess energy, and it was all I could do to stand next to Drew without fidgeting, fruitlessly wondering if my speculations about his intentions were as accurate as his observations about my character. Snow had fallen steadily the past few hours and still descended without interruption. Everything was blanketed, and I had to step carefully to keep the wet snow from soaking my thin slippers and stockings.

"I could carry you to the curb." Drew made an attempt to retrieve the conversation, but I would have none of it.

"I don't need you to do me any more favors. Your favors are as suspect as mine."

As I picked my way down the walk, I thought I heard Drew say my name, but he could just as well have been cursing me as calling me. Welcome, 1913.

Then the figure of the maiden
Sleeping, and the lover near her,
Whispering to her in her slumbers,
Saying, "Though you were far from me
In the land of Sleep and Silence,
Still the voice of love would reach you!"

Chapter Fifteen

For a woman not given to introspection, I spent the first week of 1913 indulging in nothing but, and with hindsight I realize that everyone with whom I came in contact must have noticed my unnatural state. I snapped short answers to Crea's innocent questions about the party at Drew's house and refused to be drawn out by Grandmother's more oblique inquiries. Once back at the Anchorage, I found it difficult to concentrate and would find myself in Hilda's office asking the same questions I'd asked the day before.

I could not get Drew's comments out of my mind, and once I made it past the illogical expectation of his heartfelt and humble apology arriving at my door, I began to examine his observations about my behavior and character. If what he'd said was valid, then in many ways we were two of a kind, both of us using others to get what we wanted. But surely my objectives were worthy and if so, did the end justify the means? How many of my goals stemmed from a truly selfless desire to help others, and how many from a need to prove that I knew best and had the answers? My attempts at serious thought inevitably became clouded by the memory of being in Drew

Gallagher's arms and the absolute pleasure of his touch. How remarkable, really, that Allen Goldwyn's embrace had aroused in me only a charitable distaste while similar efforts from Drew Gallagher seemed to melt flesh and bone. Love accounted for that and gave me a more sympathetic understanding of many of the girls at the Anchorage. The new year began with a humbling week and month. Character building perhaps but painful nevertheless.

I met Jennie for tea one January afternoon. The snow of New Year's Eve had long stopped falling, but the first two weeks of the month had been so frigid none of it had melted. Dirty mounds of snow sat at every street corner, making a bleak month even bleaker. I wondered if the gray sky and gray snow accounted for Jennie's pallid complexion but didn't mention it. Her mood was low enough without my assistance.

"I had my fitting for my wedding gown yesterday," Jennie volunteered suddenly.

"Eight weeks until the wedding," I commented.

"Yes."

She imbued the single word with such despair that I said impulsively, "Jennie, if this isn't what you want, call it off. I'll support you, and I know your father doesn't want you to be unhappy. I could talk to Uncle Hal if you don't feel up to it. Perhaps Grandmother would intervene with your mother if you talked the situation over with her. You don't have to martyr yourself on the altar of matrimony if it's not what or who you want."

"I need to be married, Johanna," Jennie said quietly, and at the odd choice of words, I paused.

"I don't understand. Is it because of Aunt Kitty or are you feeling pressure from Carl or his family?"

Jennie nodded. "Yes, pressure from all of them," but I thought her tone and expression were evasive. "Carl's parents will be in town the second weekend of February and they're hosting a party for Carl and me at the Chicago Yacht Club."

"I've been there. The way the clubhouse is built over the water offers a beautiful view."

"Of a vast and frozen lake," Jennie responded. "I would have suggested a more congenial setting, something with a little warmth and color, but of course, there's business connected with the reception. I've learned there are ulterior motives attached to everything the Milfords do, so it shouldn't surprise me. The engagement is a good excuse for the family to make alliances with select members of Chicago's business community and where better than the Yacht Club? The Milfords build ships after all. Carl's already bought his club membership and he's making plans to keep one of the family's yachts in Chicago."

"One of the yachts?" I asked. "Are the Milfords really that rich, Jennie?"

She didn't answer at first, only sipped her tea. Finally, "Go ahead and tell me what a lucky girl I am, Johanna. Everyone else does."

"The Milfords are the lucky ones. How could they find anyone as bright and beautiful as you?"

Unexpectedly, my words brought tears to Jennie's eyes, and she quickly wiped the tears away with her fingertips. I hadn't seen my cousin cry since childhood, and the sight so unnerved me that I impulsively reached across the table to her.

"Love, if you're so miserable, let me help you. You know I'd do whatever I can." Jennie took a deep breath to fortify herself, and then the tears were gone, replaced by her familiar smile.

"Sorry. Wedding jitters. Invitations to the February reception are going out to all the family, Johanna. Promise me you'll come."

"Of course. I wouldn't miss it."

"Promise?" Jennie repeated insistently.

"Promise," I replied and some semblance of a cheerful mood restored, she began to describe her wedding dress.

As Jennie gathered up her gloves and bag, she said, "You know I welcomed in the new year with Carl in Boston, but I heard you were with your Mr. Gallagher."

"Where did you hear that?"

She smiled mischievously. "Haven't I told you there are no secrets in the McIntyre family? Did you manage to stay out of trouble?"

"Yes." Jennie gave me an amused look.

"Hmmm. Your tone tells me that maybe you didn't stay out of trouble at all. Good for you. I can't think of any man more tempting than Drew Gallagher. He has an air of promise about him to tempt any woman with blood in her veins. How far did you stray?" I glared, then was forced to smile at her innocent expression.

"Jennie, you are incorrigible. I did not stray." After a pause I added, "Unfortunately. We got into a huge argument, and I haven't heard from him since that night. There. Satisfied?"

"Poor Johanna. Don't worry. He's so smitten with you, I guarantee he's already forgotten the whole incident regardless of what it was about."

"I don't think either of us will forget. We weren't very kind to each other."

"You're too alike, that's the problem."

"We're nothing alike!" I responded indignantly, secretly dismayed that Jennie had arrived so easily at a conclusion with which I still struggled.

"What an innocent you are! A man sees the same promise in you that a woman imagines in Drew Gallagher. Something not quite respectable but with the potential for pleasure and a little fun thrown in besides."

"Jennie!"

"It's true. You're not the same woman who left for England. You were always a woman of energy and accomplishment, but since you came back, you look for challenges and you relish confrontation. Maybe it was your experience on the *Titanic*, I don't know, but now it seems like you have to be in the middle of life. You might as well scrawl *Look at me* across your chest because that's the attitude people sense when you walk into a room."

"You're wrong," I answered, more appalled than flattered but afraid she was right. "I'm not like that."

"Yes, you are, and don't look so horrified. What's wrong with it? You're the one who says it's a new century and women have new roles now. That vigor is what I admire most about you, Johanna, and it's part of what makes you so attractive to Drew Gallagher that he can't keep his eyes off you. He's accustomed to a different kind of woman and you've set him on his ear. He'll come around. I guarantee it. Lucky you."

"Lucky?"

"I wouldn't be surprised if he loved you, and if that's the case, count your blessings. There's nothing to keep the two of you apart except your own stubborn nature. Even if Grandmother didn't allow you to do whatever you pleased, it's clear she approves of Mr. Gallagher. He's so obviously perfect for you. Some of us have to settle for second."

If I hadn't been caught up in Jennie's comments about Drew and totally self-absorbed with my own life, I might have heard the wistful tone in her last words, heard and followed up on it, asked the right questions, pursued the moment, and perhaps been able to stop what happened later. But to my lasting regret I did none of those things. Instead, I stood up quickly.

"He is not perfect for me," I retorted. "Really, Jennie, don't you have enough romantic drama in your own life without invading mine?" She shrugged and stood, too.

"Forget I said anything," she said and easily turned the conversation to something else as we left the tearoom.

By the time February arrived, I had resigned myself to the fact that I would never hear from Drew Gallagher again. It crossed my mind that I could make the first overture of apology or conciliation, but—in Jennie's words—my stubborn nature couldn't or wouldn't make the gesture. Both Crea and Grandmother carefully avoided Drew's name—neither of them was slow-witted and I had snapped at them earlier for perfectly innocent comments.

Once Crea tried to pose a careful question, and I answered ungraciously, "I'm not allowed to mention Peter, so I can't imagine why you think it's acceptable to pry into my personal life." The hurt look on Crea's face made me regret the words as soon as I said them, but the point was made and the damage done. No one tried to interfere any longer in my misery and bad temper. Oddly, I didn't dream of Drew either. He might never have been in my life at all. I imagined him back with the beautiful Viola, the two of them made for each other, enjoying the paradise he had promised me. Fortunately, an unseasonably warm January thaw had interrupted the deep and unremitting freeze Chicago had experienced, and I was able to take daily, brisk walks. Without those unexpected springlike days, I'm convinced I would have exploded.

I made a return visit to Claudette's dress shop to plan a gown for the engagement party. "Something in red," I requested of the owner, "but it's an afternoon occasion, so nothing revealing or too formal. My cousin Jennie is the belle of the afternoon so my dress should be decorous, tasteful, and simple. But red. Definitely red." I planned to wear the same gown with appropriate alterations to the city's Sweetheart Ball held every

St. Valentine's Day, the same ball where three years before I had seen Douglas Gallagher dancing with a beautiful woman in a green satin dress and had tried to imagine what it would be like to be that woman in that particular man's arms.

"Coincidences do not exist," my father once told me. "Everything is at the plan of divine Providence, nothing too small and nothing too big to be excluded from God's good will." Because my father's belief was not to be questioned, I could only wonder what plan had been set in motion by my shipboard meeting with Douglas Gallagher. Did Providence really push me back into the Gallagher orbit so I could meet and love Drew and then be miserable the rest of my life? That hardly seemed reasonable or fair.

Claudette's attempt at keeping me in the background was not quite as successful as I hoped because the dress she created was dazzling in its simplicity and very, very red.

"You'll have to raise the neckline," I requested regretfully, "and maybe if you created an overskirt—" My voice trailed off at the look she gave me. "I'm sorry, Claudette, really. The gown is beautiful just as it is, and it would be perfect for the Sweetheart Ball, but I'll never get away with it for my cousin's engagement party." In the end despite her disapproval, Claudette threw a three-quarter-length overskirt of the same red silk over the narrow, hip-hugging skirt and added a fashionable fur-trimmed jacket to conceal the bodice, pieces I could remove when I attended the February Ball. The compromise satisfied both of us.

I needn't have worried about outshining Jennie. What had I been thinking? When I arrived with Grandmother at the Yacht Club and first saw my cousin in the center of the grand ballroom, I stood literally open-mouthed in admiration before going forward.

"Jennie, you look magnificent!"

Jennie gave a small turn, the ice-blue velvet of her winter gown swirling elegantly around her ankles. "You're not Claudette's only patron, you know." With her gold-streaked hair piled on her head and tiny diamonds dangling from her ears, it seemed a fairy queen had stepped out of the pages of a children's book.

Seeing the bright color in her cheeks, I went closer to whisper, "No more jitters?"

"No, Johanna. No jitters whatsoever. That's all past now." She said the words and followed up with a bland smile before she turned away to greet new arrivals. If her tone was suspect because of its purposeful coolness, I accepted that the present time was hardly the moment for confidences. That will come later, I thought, and made a promise to myself to meet her again soon for tea, somewhere the two of us could talk in confidence. Jennie was like a sister to me, friendly and precocious since the day I crossed my grandparents' threshold, and I loved her. With her bright eyes and quick mind and unexpected kindnesses, she deserved to be happy.

When Jennie said the party was more a business meeting than a festivity, she wasn't far from the truth. Many of Chicago's commercial and industrial elite were present, and Mr. Milford, Senior, moved easily from person to person, introducing himself and his son, supposedly celebrating Carl's engagement but undoubtedly making contacts and forming relationships he hoped would be more pragmatically useful later. Jennie had given me advance warning about the party's business aspect, but it never crossed my mind that Drew might be present until I found him looking at me from across the room. I turned abruptly away, more to catch my breath than anything else, only to find him at my side.

"What are you doing here?" I demanded.

His adorable smile made a brief appearance before he

replied, "I own banks, Johanna. I'm sorry if I neglected to mention that. Your future in-laws are always on the lookout for a low interest rate. Did you think I manipulated an invitation so I could see you?"

"Of course not." I snapped the words and followed up with what I hoped was a disdainful sniff.

"Then you'd be wrong because that's the only reason I agreed to come. Do you honestly think my idea of a good time is talking business with strangers?"

Caught off guard, I said, "I have no idea what you consider a good time."

"Oh, yes, you do," he responded gently. "You know that better than anyone else," and gave me a look that literally made my knees weak, the first time I realized the words could be more than a figure of speech. Made mute by everything his look and his words implied, I could only stare, so that he was forced to say, "This isn't the time and place I would have chosen, but please forgive me for all my bad behavior and promise we can be friends again."

Friends? I wanted to say. Is that what you think I want? Perhaps because I hesitated, Drew put a hand to my arm.

"Johanna, can't we at least talk about it?"

I found my tongue. "Of course, we can. I was struck dumb by your assumption that your behavior was somehow worse than mine. On second thought maybe it was, I don't know, but it would certainly be worth a conversation."

Drew gave me the full force of his grin. "I think so, too."

"But not now. Now I have to do familial duty. My aunt expects me to be the dark foil to Jennie and because Jennie's the one being feted, I don't begrudge the contrast."

"You shouldn't. Your cousin is a lovely girl but next to you in red, she fades into the woodwork. I say that with all due respect."

"You're just complimenting me because red was your idea," I tossed back, but at his words my heart started to sing some nameless, joyful song that threatened to drown out all the other sounds in the room. I love this man, I thought, and whether he loves me in return doesn't matter at the moment. It's enough to be with him on any terms. Maybe that won't do forever, but forever's a long time, and I'm not one to live in the future. All I've ever needed for happiness is today. Drew began a reply, but I saw Grandmother raise a hand for me. "I have to go, Drew. I'm being summoned and it's Jennie's party, after all. I really am along only for contrast." I slipped regretfully away from the warmth of his touch on my arm and went over to where Grandmother sat, one hand resting lightly on her cane. She'd made wonderful progress the last six weeks but still seemed too frail.

"I'm worried about Jennie," she told me. "Kitty and Harry are busy with the crowd and Carl's been in his father's shadow all afternoon. I thought Jennie looked pale and then I saw her head for the ladies' lounge. Make sure she's well, Johanna." I could tell from Grandmother's tone that she was serious in her concern, and knowing that she was not one to be alarmed over trifles, I slipped out of the room.

Jennie wasn't in the nearer lounge, and I went farther down the hall to the second, smaller ladies' area. I didn't think she would have passed the former to come to this plainer and more common lounge, but I stepped inside anyway to take a brief look. On the wall of the foyer hung a full-length mahogany-framed mirror and standing sideways before the mirror, both hands splayed on her abdomen, was Jennie. The click of the outer door interrupted her reverie, and she turned her head slowly away from the mirror to look directly at me. I don't know how I knew. Perhaps because I recognized something intangible in her that I had seen before in a number of the girls at the Anchorage, or perhaps it was the expression on her face, tender and despairing all at once. Whatever the clue, I was immediately certain.

"Jennie." When she moved, the original illusion disappeared, but I knew, for better or worse, that I was right. "How far along?"

She didn't bother to deny anything. "Four months." I didn't know what to say and Jennie went on, "I've known for weeks. I think I knew from the very moment of conception. I should have done something about it, but I didn't know what to do or who to ask. I couldn't ask you."

"You can ask me anything."

"Would you have helped me get rid of it? Would you?"

"No."

"I didn't think so, and it doesn't matter, anyway. I'm such a coward about pain, I never could have gone through with it even if I'd found someone willing. Now I'm glad I didn't. Poor little thing, why should it have to die alone when I'm the one at fault?" I should have caught the implication of her words, but I didn't, too intent on my response.

"Jennie, you don't have to think or talk like that. These things happen in all families." I went forward so I stood closer to her. "I'm sure Carl will do the honorable thing."

At my words, Jennie began to laugh, one hand over her mouth to control the sound, her shoulders shaking, tears forming in her eyes, laughing in a way that wasn't laughter at all, until I was forced to put both hands on her shoulders and give her a firm shake.

"Stop now. Stop, Jennie." I put my arms around her and held her close, her laughter turning into hiccups and her whole body trembling in a way that broke my heart. "It will be all right, love. We'll move the wedding up. It's no one's business but yours and Carl's anyway." I was overwhelmed with tenderness and a desire to protect and comfort her.

My words or perhaps the affection in my tone galvanized her into an unexpected reaction. With surprising force, Jennie broke free and pushed away from me, bumping into a small loveseat that sat against the wall. The heavy skirts of her gown tangled around her feet and she lost her balance enough to drop heavily onto the cushions. Jennie being Jennie, though, she made even that ungainly action look graceful.

"You don't understand, Johanna."

"I understand more than you know."

"No. No, you don't. This has nothing to do with Carl." It took me a moment to understand the full implication of her words, but when her meaning finally dawned on me, I needed to sit down, too.

"Then who?" I finally managed to ask.

Seeming to take strength from my shock, Jennie answered in a firm voice, "I won't tell you. You especially don't need to know; it would only make matters worse." I wondered about that comment—"you especially"—and sensing my disquiet, she quickly added, "It doesn't matter, Johanna. Not any more. For the past two months I've been doing my best to arrange it so Carl would think it was his. That would have made it so much simpler, but Carl's a Milford and a Milford man expects his blushing bride to wait until her wedding night. Stupid, stupid man. I made a fool of myself on more than one occasion and all it did was make the idiot think I was beside myself with desire for him. He's not the brightest star in the sky, but even if I can still fit into my wedding gown, Carl will manage to figure out that a baby born four months after the wedding night isn't his."

"Oh, Jennie."

"If I go through with the wedding, Carl will divorce me."

"He wouldn't, Jennie, not if he loves you."

"Of course, he would. If it's a son, do you think he'll turn the Milford fortune and the Milford name over to a child that's not his? Even if he loved me that much, which, believe me, he doesn't, his parents certainly don't. They'd have me out of the family in a heartbeat, and if Carl didn't agree, they'd disinherit him and pass everything along to his brother. I know them and I know him. Carl won't risk that."

"What about the baby's father?" Jennie's face softened at my words, one hand moving without conscious intent to rest gently on her stomach.

"Mother would never allow it."

I wasn't sure what she meant, whether she was talking about marrying the father of her child or following through with the pregnancy, but I responded grimly, "She may not have much to say about it now. Is he someone who'll do the right thing? He must be someone you care for."

"Care for," Jennie repeated. She managed to color the two simple words with a myriad of emotions—longing, despair, a wisp of tenderness—before she shook her head decidedly back to reality.

"It doesn't matter, Johanna. I can't tell Mother. I can't. My whole life all she's ever dreamed of, all she's ever hoped for and talked about, is a great society wedding, our name linked with the right kind of family and our pictures on the society page. And here it is, just within her grasp, an east coast name, a family fortune, everything she hoped for. You saw her today. I've never seen her so happy, and I can't tell her. I can't face her. I can't."

"Well, I can," I said, but when I started to rise, Jennie grasped my hand and pulled me back down beside her.

"It's not your business, Johanna. Promise me you won't say anything."

"I can't promise that."

Jennie examined my face with desperate intensity. I don't know what she saw there, but the tension in her suddenly deflated and she said softly, "I know you can't, but just for a little while, Johanna. Promise you won't say anything for a little while. Let the party go on as it is. Let the Milfords finish their visit. Let Mother have her time in the spotlight. Promise, Johanna." At my continued hesitation, she went on, "Promise. For me."

"But, Jennie, what will we do?"

"I don't know. I'll think of something. I always do. And in the meanwhile, why spoil the party and the Milfords' visit for Mother? What will another few days hurt? Promise it will be our secret."

Against my better judgment, I nodded. "Only for today, though. We'll take it one day at a time. Tomorrow I'm taking you to tea and we'll figure something out. I know there's a way through this, Jennie. Everything will be all right."

She stood to face the mirror, pinned up the stray hairs that had fallen loose, and smoothed away traces of tears from her cheeks.

"When you say that, Johanna, I can almost believe it." Before I could respond, she turned toward me and said, "I've been so crazy with worry—like a creature caught in a trap— that telling someone was a relief. I'm glad it was you, Johanna. I see things more clearly now. Thank you." Before we walked out into the hallway together to return to the main ballroom, Jennie kissed me gently on the cheek. "I admire you so much. I wish I could have been just like you." In hindsight, I believe the words should have alarmed me, something in their phrasing or tense should have given me pause, but how could I have known? Instead, touched by her words but back among guests and family, I only squeezed her hand in reply.

The afternoon stretched on interminably. For a while I

watched Jennie covertly, but she seemed herself again, accepting congratulations with an unaffected smile, moving among
the guests with an ease that came naturally and becomingly to
her. When the caterers began to set out refreshments, I retreat-
ed to the large windows that overlooked the lake and stopped
long enough to rest my warm forehead against the cold glass.
All I could think about was Jennie, poor girl, and facing Aunt
Kitty with the news. I couldn't begin to imagine my aunt's reaction, and I knew a moment's pity for her, too. She'd spent the
past twenty years devoted to her children, loving them in her
own way and picturing success for them on her terms, a perfect
matrimonial match for Jennie, an influential and prestigious
position for Peter, her own dreams, whatever they once were,
submerged in her hopes for her children. Now all that would
change forever. Despite the claims of progress, once word got
out about Jennie's condition, her prospects for any kind of
prominent marriage would disappear. What had Grandmother
told me on Christmas Eve when I proclaimed the freedoms of
a new century? "Not really as different a world as you like to
think, nor ever will be as far as I'm concerned." I hated to admit it, but maybe she was right. Maybe nothing really changed.
Maybe people couldn't forgive or forget because people never
changed, not inside, not where it mattered.

I turned away from the window and its view of the broad
expanse of frozen lake to face Drew, who stood quietly next to
me, waiting for me to notice him.

"I've been watching you for the past hour and something's wrong. Your glow has dimmed, but I don't believe it's
something as ordinary as being tired. Is it your grandmother's
health?"

I was grateful for his calm interest and wanted nothing
more than to find a quiet spot, somewhere far away from the
milling, chattering group of guests, where I could sit very close

to him and tell him the reason for my sudden heartsickness. But that wouldn't have been fair to Jennie, who demanded and deserved my confidence.

"No, Grandmother's doing fine; though it's clear to me she'll never be strong again, not as she once was. Time goes by so fast, doesn't it, and there's no constant in it."

"It's the surprises that give time meaning and make life worth living."

Thinking of Jennie, I replied, "Not all surprises are good ones, Drew."

"No, but they're all necessary. You of all people wouldn't want the same day repeated over and over. What would you do without new causes and new worlds to conquer?" I started to tell him that I had enough causes for the time being, thank you very much, when over his shoulder and through the window I spied a spot of blue at the shoreline. At first I couldn't believe what I saw and then, knowing it to be true, I gasped and quickly turned away.

"What is it?" Drew asked, sharp and observant.

"Excuse me," I answered. "Jennie needs me," and slipped away from him, moving along the edge of the room and out the door, trying not to draw attention to myself. The weather had warmed significantly over the past week, but it was still unwise for Jennie to be out in the cold, wandering along the lakeshore, of all places, and without a coat. She could be seen clearly from the Club's windows besides. What was she thinking? Jennie must have been more distressed than I thought and anger at my own lack of awareness made me pick up speed. By the time I was outside, I was running, afraid of something nameless and terrible, afraid I would be too late. I didn't grab a coat, either, and the wind off the lake was biting, but as I drew closer to the shoreline, I never gave the temperature a thought. All I could see, all I could think about or focus on was the spot of blue that moved slowly and methodically out onto the frozen lake. It was impossible to run in the hobble skirt I wore, so I stopped at the shore to hike it above my knees before venturing onto the ice. The soft layer of snow gave me some traction, but I still was unable to hurry as fast as I wished for fear of taking a fall. Jennie, perhaps a hundred yards ahead of me and walking at a steady, relaxed pace, had no idea I was there until I called her name. My voice carried clearly in the cold air but except for a tiny hesitation, Jennie didn't turn or acknowledge my presence.

"Jennie," I called again, "come back. This won't solve anything. Stop and come back." She did pause then, turning to face me across the expanse of snow-covered ice but too far away for me to read her expression. I stopped, too, and called her name once more. I thought she shook her head. Then, her posture suddenly regal, head high and back straight, Jennie began to back away from me, her arms wrapped around her stomach, an unconsciously protective gesture for the child she carried. I started to move forward and as the folds of her heavy velvet dress flapped in the lake wind, Jennie simply disappeared from sight. One moment she was there and the next not. At the last, all I really saw were her two arms extended above her head as she dropped into the icy water, then just her hands showing briefly, and then nothing. Nothing but a gaping dark hole in the ice.

I screamed her name and jerked forward but slipped on the ice and fell to my knees. As I rose, I was conscious of a roaring behind me, a loud and furious voice roaring my name like thunder, like the voice of God that cannot be disobeyed.

"Johanna, stop! Stop! Johanna, stop where you are!" The words an order, the voice demanding, Drew's voice calling my name in a powerful rage over and over. "Johanna, stop where you are right now!" The potent command of his voice halted me immediately. I stood perfectly still, listening, then turned away from the terrible place where Jennie had disappeared into the dark lake and faced Drew where he stood along the shoreline.

In a voice that shook just a little, I called, "Don't try to come any closer, Drew. I can hear the ice cracking. There's no use both of us going in." I heard the sibilant hum of the ice, dangerous and teasing, its gentle cracking racing toward me with every step, every movement I made. In the background I was vaguely conscious of a stream of people rushing down the steps of the clubhouse, but I didn't take my eyes from Drew. He stopped moving and stood very still.

"Listen to me, Johanna. In a minute I'm going to ask you to walk toward me."

"I can't move. I'll fall in. Jennie fell in. Did you see?" For a moment I wasn't myself. Something foreign and hysterical crept into my voice. I could hear it and I knew Drew did, too.

"Yes, I saw. Now listen to me. Can you take off that over-skirt and your jacket?"

"Yes."

"Do it now, slowly and carefully. Toss it all very gently to the side and don't move your feet."

With stiff, ungainly fingers I fumbled with the hooks and fasteners without asking why, unaware of the chill of wind and ice, my gaze fixed on Drew. I had slowly grown calmer, could feel the panic gradually dissolving and my heartbeat slowing, all because I trusted him. I trusted him. The sound of Drew's voice was steady and conversational in tone with not a touch of rush or panic in it—we could have been enjoying a cup of tea at the kitchen table.

"Listen now," he went on easily. "When you start walking, walk straight toward me. Don't look right or left, just look at me. If you go into the water—" he repeated the words more slowly for emphasis "—remember to grab for the edge of the ice. No matter what, no matter how cold the water is or how frightened you are, keep your head, reach for the broken edge of the ice, and hold on. You'll bob back up and I'll be there. I'll get you. I promise. I'm not going to lose you, Johanna. I promise. Do you trust me?"

I will not die in water, I thought fiercely, with Drew's confidence seeping into my bones. I did not escape the *Titanic* to drown in an icy lake with the man I love only a few hundred feet away. I intend to live a long time with him and I don't care if we fight like cat and dog and he stops loving me and brings dancing girls home every night. I don't care. I'm the one he'll see every morning at the breakfast table.

"Yes," I said. "I do trust you. May I move now? I'm cold."

He took off his jacket, tossed it behind him, and held out both arms toward me. "You bet, my darling. Come here."

At first I thought I'd make it. The ice groaned but held, and each step brought me closer to Drew standing at the shore's edge, arms outstretched and waiting. The reverberations from Jennie's fall were all around me, the ice cracking in a dreadful kind of race, a relay race, each snap of the ice connecting with another and rushing ever closer toward me. I felt the surface under my feet begin to shift and tremble and resisted the overwhelming impulse to break into a run. Instead, I carefully put one foot in front of the other and with my eyes focused on Drew's face stepped methodically, purposefully forward.

And then, just like that, as suddenly as I saw Jennie disappear, the ice gave way beneath me. I knew I was going in, heard Drew shout, "Hold on," had time to quickly inhale, and then experienced the inhuman, frigid shock of the water. I felt one moment of sheer terror, was briefly immobilized by the cold, and almost opened my mouth to gasp or cry out. I'll never find the hole in the ice again, I thought. I'll be imprisoned beneath, tapping, tapping against it but unable ever to escape, searching endlessly and aimlessly for the opening. Then, so clearly that Drew might have been swimming beside me, I heard his words, "Keep your head, reach for the broken edge of ice, and hold on," so that's what I did. I clamped my mouth shut firmly and without the heavy jacket and overskirt that would have dragged me down too far, I bobbed back up to the surface, gasped another quick breath as my chin rose above the water and reached with numb fingers to find the edge of the ice. My stiffening hands scrabbled along the ice as I sobbed for breath, trying to grasp the slick, glassy surface and drag myself out of that painfully cold water, all the while absolutely sure that Drew was there somewhere reaching for me, too.

With relief and no surprise, I felt Drew's hands clamp onto my wrists and heard him shout, "I have you, Johanna! I have you! Stop struggling!" He grasped my wrists relentlessly, then moved to clasp my forearms. My hands took hold of his arms; it seemed we had suddenly fused together. "Hold onto me the best you can, love. I won't let you go." In an even louder voice directed to someone else, he shouted, "Pull now but slow." When my shoulders heaved out of the water, Drew was able to get one arm and then the other under my arms and around my back. "Pull again," he shouted, and I realized, dead weight that I was from the cold and completely incapable of helping at all, that Drew was stretched out on his stomach across the ice. Two figures held his feet and pulled him back toward the shore as he continued to hold on to me. When my knees came out of the water, they buckled onto the ice and I longed to rest for a moment, at least long enough to catch my breath and stop the terrible gasping sounds emanating from my throat, but Drew would have none of it. Still lying on the ice with our arms around each other, he turned slightly, trying to make us both a little more comfortable.

"We're almost on solid ground, Johanna. Hang on to me if you can. I won't lose you." And then, somehow ignoring the fact that we were both being pulled along the ice like two frozen carcasses of meat, wrapped around each other in an awkward and ungainly embrace, he whispered in my ear, "It took me a lifetime to find you, Johanna. I have no intention of losing you anytime soon."

And although my teeth chattered involuntarily and with enough force to give me a headache, I replied, "You're confused. I found you. Remember?" By then we were both lying on the solid ground of the shore. As people rushed forward, Drew pushed himself to his knees and gathered me against his chest.

"Like it was yesterday," he said and stood, wobbling a moment before he tightened his arms around me and headed for the steps that led to the Yacht Club. When someone offered to take me from him, he never slowed.

"I have her. Maybe you can help with the other one."

The other one, I thought. Jennie. And began to tremble so violently I was afraid I would cause Drew bodily harm. "I'm sorry. I can't stop shaking. I'm sorry."

In answer Drew pulled me even closer, willing his own warmth into me, and moved more quickly up the steps. Someone must have stepped into his path because Drew, in a voice so savage I didn't recognize it, snarled, "Get out of the way," and shouldered inside. I believe people separated before us, but by then every part of me shook and my hands and feet tingled painfully, so I don't really remember much of our entrance. I recall that it was silent except for a disquieting sound in the distance I could not quite place.

Once we reached the women's lounge, Drew placed me onto the nearest couch and without a word stripped off the sopping red dress and every stitch of clothing I was wearing. I was past caring about anything except the cold. The shock of the air on my skin made the sensation of cold even worse, and when I tried to help Drew unfasten and unbutton, my fingers twitched and trembled so badly I had to stop. He rubbed me down with a handful of small finger towels from the lounge and then wrapped me tightly in my own cape that someone handed him. Grandmother. She stood just behind Drew, looking pale and very old. I met her eyes and felt tears suddenly well in mine, spill over, and run down my cheeks.

"I couldn't save Jennie," I cried. "I tried but I couldn't. It was my fault. I'm so sorry."

Tears filled her eyes, too, and coursed down the parchment skin of her face. She made no attempt to stop them so that they fell as small dark spots onto the light gray of her dress.

"No one could save her, Johanna, not even you." I thought that in her usual way, Grandmother was right in more ways than either of us really understood, but I was dumb with horror and cold and unable to say anything more.

Drew, a man on a mission and not to be caught up in sentiment or grief, ordered, "Stay with her while I get my coat. She could use another layer of warmth." After he left, Grandmother sat next to the couch where I lay and placed a hand to my shoulder. I reached up a shaking hand from the folds of my wrap and placed my fingertips over hers. We stayed like that, wordlessly, until Drew returned.

This time he stopped in front of Grandmother and said gently, "I'm sorry about your granddaughter. It's a terrible loss for you and your family."

"Thank you." She sounded old and ill, the words whispered because courtesy demanded it but with a quaver I had never heard from her before, not even when Grandfather died.

The moment passed and Drew was all business again. He took his own coat and wrapped it around me.

"You need it," I protested, trying to push it away. "You were out there, too, and you're soaked. I can't take your coat."

"Be quiet, Johanna." Even if I hadn't run out of the energy to argue, his perfunctory tone would have quieted me. Anyway, clearly he wasn't the one trembling furiously enough to shake the sofa on which I lay. I was responsible for that phenomenon, and the extra layer of coat did feel marvelously warm and comforting. It smelled like Drew besides, which was even better. I gave up the fight easily and completely.

Drew picked me up, stopping before Grandmother long enough to say, "She'll be at my house. I'll take care of her."

"I know you will," Grandmother answered quietly. "I'll have Levi drive Crea over to help you. I won't need Crea's assistance for a while."

The three of us moved out of the lounge and into the hallway. By then, I'd thrown one arm loosely around Drew's neck and leaned my head against his chest, the steady thump of his heart in my ear as beautiful as any sonata. My shaking slowly subsided to be replaced by the oddest lethargy, every limb of my body suddenly lead and so heavy I couldn't lift as much as a finger. Even my mouth refused to work at normal speed. My lips felt swollen and numb and I thought if I tried to speak, the words would come out thick and unintelligible. All I could do was lie in Drew's arms with the steady drum of his heart beating against me. Unaccustomed to being so powerless and with the image of Jennie disappearing into the water lurking behind my closed eyes, I was more frightened than I had ever been. Only the even rhythm of Drew's heartbeat comforted and reassured.

Grandmother still spoke. "I'll be staying with Kitty and Hal. I don't know for how long. Kitty will need someone— perhaps not me but she'll need someone."

We went down the hallway, past the doors to the ballroom

and toward the entrance. The unfamiliar, vaguely alarming background sound I remembered hearing when Drew first carried me inside seemed clearer and louder. I stirred enough to lift my head.

"Oh, God," I whispered, the words more moan than prayer. "Oh, God, poor woman." Drew pulled me against him to block out the sound on my behalf, but that was impossible. The raw and terrible noise followed us and cut to the heart, a keening, high, and constant wail. A woman's grief-stricken, wordless howl of unbearable pain and disbelief. Aunt Kitty, raging uncontrollably for Jennie.

I sat cocooned and quiet next to Drew in the motorcar, swathed in my cape and his coat but still frozen to the bone even with the hood pulled over my wet head for warmth. For a long while I was content neither to move nor speak. Then, in a voice that sounded remarkably calm and normal, I asked, "Do you think there's a chance Jennie didn't die? That someone got to her as you got to me and saved her, too?"

Watching the street as he drove and in a voice as calm as mine, Drew replied, "No, Johanna. No one could get to her. She was out too far and she went in before you. Some of the club members scrambled to find a small boat to push across the ice toward her, but to my knowledge they were unsuccessful."

"But Jennie's young and strong. Maybe she was able to hang on to the edge until they got to her."

"A human being can't survive very long in water that temperature, Johanna." Drew hesitated before adding, "And from where I stood, I wouldn't have guessed she wanted to be rescued. Her actions seemed quite deliberate." Hearing his words made me remember Jennie's and my last conversation.

"Do you care very much that she's dead?" I asked him. I recalled the odd tone of Jennie's voice when she refused to reveal her baby's father: "I won't tell you. You especially don't need to know; it would only make matters worse." I'd heard defiance and a touch of guilt there, and something else she wanted to hide from me. I couldn't help my thoughts.

My words caused him to turn and give me quick, intense look, both brows drawn together in concentration. "I think there's more to your question, but I'll take it at face value. Of course, I care. Your cousin was young with her whole life ahead of her. Why wouldn't I care about such a senseless and need-less death? I care because she was your cousin and because you care, but," he concluded deliberately, "I would care much, much more if it had been you. Is that enough for you?" He returned to his driving and I settled myself more comfortably into my layers of wraps. I was convinced he was not a good enough actor to hide any depth of grief or loss from me.

"For now," I answered and began to shake again, from the cold automobile and from the unbidden picture of Jennie's hands uplifted above the water, clasped together in a final prayer.

I remembered Drew's house the first time I saw it—I'd been drenched then, too—how it had seemed lit from within by something almost mystical and how charmed I was by all the windows and the uncluttered, spacious look and feel of it. I'd admired the house from the beginning, but now, pulling up to the curb in the dusky early evening and seeing all its win-dows filled with welcoming light, I loved that house like it was a person. Nothing cold and dark and icy anywhere. Instead, in a magical way, I thought it had somehow soaked up sun dur-ing the day and now radiated the light and warmth back to all the people who crossed its threshold. I'm going to live here someday, I thought. I love the house because I love the man. We'll be happy at least some of the time and that's happier than Jennie will ever be.

Drew scooped me out of the car and went up the walk,

awkwardly pushing open the front door and calling Yvesta's name as he did so. She came down the hall from the kitchen, followed by her daughters and Fritz bringing up the rear, a happy, well-fed, content little parade.

"Go turn down the bed in the guest room and bring as many extra blankets as you can find. Do we have a hot water bottle somewhere? Get that, too. And make a pot of hot tea and bring it upstairs. Fritz, go get Dr. Shannon and don't come back without him."

"I don't need a doctor," I protested. "I'm just cold, and I could probably walk if you'd put me down."

Following Yvesta through a door that led into the rear wing of the house, Drew gave me a little shake.

"For once, just do what I say, Johanna. The aftereffect of immersion in frigid water is unpleasant at best and very serious at worst. The doctor is just a precaution." He laid me inelegantly onto the bed. "Yvesta, underneath those wraps Miss Swan is naked as a newborn babe. I'm going to get one of my nightshirts which you should help her change into."

"I can dress myself." My attempt at independence was spoiled by my short, unbecoming gasps and chattering teeth. Drew simply shook his head at me as Yvesta pushed back my hood and quickly began to unfasten the layers of coat and cape.

"Johanna, what were you doing to get so soaked?" Yvesta asked. For no reason obvious to Yvesta, her question brought quick tears to my eyes. I think seeing them alarmed her because she patted my shoulder, saying gruffly, "Never mind. It doesn't matter." Yvesta took the nightshirt Drew brought and slid it over my head, then disappeared from the room a moment and came back with a thick towel with which she dried my hair. After pulling the covers up to my chin, she told me, "I'm going to get hot tea, and I wouldn't be surprised if a little whiskey came along with it."

Left alone, I turned on my side and pulled my knees up against my chest, growing warm at last and afraid to move once I'd cozied into a ball. I thought I would sleep but didn't, just lay there, unable to focus on any one thought. My mind seemed as slippery as the ice on the lake—and as treacherous.

Yvesta returned with a tray and a teapot, followed by Drew with the whiskey bottle, two minds apparently working as one. I resisted being moved from my warm spot but they both ignored my wishes and propped me up against the headboard. Drew had changed into a warm sweater over a shirt and dark flannel trousers. Looking at him, his hair becomingly tousled and a perfectly starched collar showing above the latest fashion in men's sweaters, I could hardly believe that a few hours ago he'd been bumped and pulled by his heels over the ice, holding on to me so tightly we must have looked like two sacks of feed corn tied together.

After a well-placed hot water bottle and two cups of hot tea doctored with Drew's best whiskey, my teeth no longer chattered. Yvesta gave me a critical look.

"I don't like those two spots of color in her cheeks. Something's not right there. I'll go watch for the doctor."

When she was gone, I snuggled back down under the covers, sleepy and much warmer. I felt odd, though, warm on the inside yet surrounded by a chilling coat of ice that made me think I must be stiff and cold to the touch. I was conscious, too, of a dull ache in my arms and legs, hands and feet. Probably just bruised, I told myself, and no use making a fuss about it. At least I was alive to feel pain unlike my poor Jennie, one moment there and the next gone, enveloped by the black, cold water and shrouded in ice. Poor lost Jennie. My eyes grew heavy and I knew I was falling asleep but felt there was something I needed to say to Drew, something urgent enough to make me fight sleep and push back the covers to go find him.

I don't recall making any sound, but I must have said his name because Drew replied, "I'm right here, Johanna." He sat in a chair next to the bed, relaxed with one leg thrown over the other and a glass of whiskey held loosely in one hand. I fell back onto the pillow and turned my head to the side so I could see him clearly.

"Thank you for saving my life, Drew. Thank you."

He set down the glass, uncrossed his legs, and leaned forward. "You're welcome," adding conversationally, "I once heard that when one person saves another person's life, the saved life belongs to the rescuer. Is that true, do you think?"

By then I could hardly keep my eyes open, but there was something I wanted Drew to know. I pulled my hand out from under the blankets and reached for his. I love you, I wanted to say. I understand it's not about getting even or owing somebody something or being in another's debt. Love isn't about that. And although I don't belong to anybody, I know I belong with you. I was too exhausted and lethargic, too heartsick, to say any of that, however. Instead, for answer I lifted his hand to my face and rested my cheek against his palm. He unfurled his fingers and cradled the side of my face. With a last push of energy and will, I turned my head enough to drop a light kiss into the palm of Drew's hand.

"Yes, it's true," I murmured before falling deeply and darkly asleep.

Even as rivulets twain, from distant and separate sources,
Seeing each other afar, as they leap from the rocks, and pursuing
Each one its devious path, but drawing nearer and nearer,
Rush together at last, at their trysting-place in the forest;
So these lives that had run thus far in separate channels,
Coming in sight of each other, then swerving and flowing asunder,
Parted by barriers strong, but drawing nearer and nearer,
Rushed together at last, and one was lost in the other.

Chapter Sixteen

The dream, inevitable and vivid and horrific, appeared that first night at Drew's. I am walking on the frozen, snow-covered lake, the ice and the sky the same pewter gray color, so I cannot make out the line of horizon. The world is shrouded in gray. In my dream I am walking barefoot in my nightdress, but I am not at all surprised to feel warm and comfortable. I know I'm looking for Jennie, but as far as I can see there is only gray, whether lake or heavens I can't tell, with no spot of life or color to be seen anywhere. Then to my amazement, I feel a tapping against the ice under my feet. I drop to my knees and begin to scrape away the snow urgently because I know it's Jennie under there and I don't have much time to save her. I crouch down and peer at the spot I've cleared on the ice. Under the ice, now a window into the frigid water, someone looks back at me, eyes wide, lips mouthing words I can't hear, palms pressed up against the ice. I realize with shock that it's not Jennie under the ice. It's Drew. Drew trapped there, Drew's mouth forming unintelligible syllables, Drew's strong, long-fingered hands pounding against the ice, Drew's eyes staring into mine begging for rescue. I begin to scrape at the ice with my hands so violently that blood from my torn fingers begins to streak the snow and then it's not blood but the hem of a red dress. I turn and look up at the figure that suddenly stands beside me on the ice, a still figure who only watches, making no attempt to help. Jennie stands there, wearing my red silk dress.

"Help me, Jennie!" I cry. "It's Drew! Look, it's Drew!" But Jennie won't help. She continues to stand immobile, watching me with a pitying look on her face. I realize suddenly that she cannot help me. Jennie cannot move for she is totally encased in ice, frozen stiff and solid. Trapped, too. Only her eyes are alive. I sob out her name, but it's Drew's name I'm saying because I'm confused and horrified and helpless. Then I awaken.

I have a vague memory of the dream's first occurrence because of Drew, because of his sitting at the edge of my bed and saying calmly against my gasping sobs, "I'm here, Johanna, and everything's all right. It's just a dream. Nothing can hurt you. I'm here." And because of his gathering me into his arms and holding me against his chest, just holding me until I fell back to sleep. I think I remember that.

When I truly awoke, I was amazed to see Crea standing over the bed. I knew I was in Drew's guest room and I remembered everything that happened, but it didn't seem possible that Crea would get here before the doctor.

"Crea," I asked, my voice a little raspy, "did you have time to pack?"

She looked at me suspiciously. "Johanna?"

"Of course, I'm Johanna. Why are you looking at me like that?" My question made her laugh and brightened her face.

"Like what exactly?" Crea filled a glass with water from a pitcher by the bed and lifted it to my lips.

After I took a long, gulping drink, I answered, "Like I'm

crazy or like you've never seen me before. Unless—" I reached up a tentative hand to my face. "Just tell me. Did I freeze something on my face? Am I disfigured? I promise I won't have hysterics if I am. Just tell me."

"No, Johanna. Your face is perfectly fine. Here." She brought me a hand mirror from the bureau. Crea was right. Although too pale and topped by a wild disarray of black, springy curls, my face looked its usual self.

"Then what caused that expression on your face? I know something surprised you."

Seated, Crea asked, "Do you know what day it is, Johanna?"

I shrugged. "I don't really feel in the mood for puzzles, but yesterday's party was on a Saturday and I feel like I've had a good long sleep, so is it Sunday?" At Crea's silence, I continued, "Monday then? Did I sleep a whole day away?"

"Try a whole week."

"No."

"Yes. You've been ill. The doctor said that sometimes a person who's been immersed in cold water feels fine at first, only to run into serious circulation problems afterwards. I've forgotten what he called the condition, but you had it. We weren't sure if you were going to live or if you did live, if you'd keep all your limbs."

I immediately moved my arms and legs under the covers. "I think I have them all."

Crea smiled. "You do, every one of them, and I think you're going to live, besides. We're all relieved."

"We?"

"Your grandmother, for one. She's doing fine," Crea continued quickly at my look. "Don't look so worried. She's staying at your Uncle Hal's for the time being, but she's visited here every day."

Thinking of Grandmother made me think of Jennie. "Did they find Jennie?"

Crea's face sobered. "No. They looked all Saturday afternoon and then went back on Sunday and broke the ice away with picks, but there was no trace of her." The picture of Jennie floating beneath the ice was more horrible than I could express, and Crea grasped my hand in sympathy. "I know. It's awful. Don't think about it."

"How's Aunt Kitty?"

"Peter says," Crea began, and I watched her lovely, porcelain skin color a bright rose as she realized the implication of her words.

To spare her, I ignored the inference and the blush. "Peter says what?"

"That she won't believe Jennie's gone, won't accept it. He says she gets up in the night and goes outside looking for her, that they've found her standing along the shoreline outside their house calling Jennie's name. She insists they set a place for Jennie at the table and she's still planning the wedding."

"Oh, no! How awful! Poor Uncle Hall!" We were both quiet and I felt a surge of fatigue. It was the first I believed I must have been ill a whole week because I was not one to be exhausted from simple conversation. "Crea, don't get stiff and formal with me if I tell you something." When she didn't respond, I went on, "Don't let pride get in the way of being happy. Don't ruin Peter's life and your own through some misguided sense of propriety."

I saw Jennie seated across from me, saying of Drew, "I wouldn't be surprised if he loved you, and if that's the case, count your blessings."

"Don't make Peter settle for second, Crea, or let Aunt Kitty make your decisions. Life's too short to waste love. There. I just needed to say that." She didn't answer, but she didn't lift her chin and tell me to mind my own business, either. Instead, Crea hopped up from her seat.

"I'm going to get Drew. I should have gone first thing. He's been beside himself with worry."

"I can't picture that."

"I can."

"You can't always tell with him, you know, Crea."

"We've shared several nights sitting across your bed. I think I can tell."

I felt a sharp and unbecoming pang of jealousy, completely ridiculous and out of place, but I couldn't help it. I didn't want Drew Gallagher sharing his nights with anyone but me. Crea left the room and despite my desperate intention to stay awake to see Drew, I fell asleep almost before she closed the door behind her.

I awoke later, alone this time, in a darkened room that was dimly lit by a small lamp on the bureau. I swung my feet around to the floor and slowly stood, found my own slippers and warm wool robe that Crea must have brought, and decided to go exploring. Somewhere outside my room was a kitchen and I was starving. A good sign, I thought to myself, and except for a momentary weakness in my knees that dropped me back down onto the bed the first time I stood, I felt clear-headed, healthy, and very hungry. Along the way, I discovered a small room equipped with modern conveniences where I washed my face and ran my hands through my hair. I gave up on an effort to straighten curls that had been slept on for a week. Crea must have tried her best to keep me clean and presentable, but even in the best of times, my hair had a mind of its own.

The house was quiet and at first I thought everyone must be settled and asleep, but spying light under one of the doors along the hall, I revised my opinion. I lost my bearings in the dim interior but felt fairly confident I was outside the kitchen.

Yvesta was still up, perhaps, finishing supper or readying breakfast, and just the person I needed to point me toward something, anything, edible. Once I pushed open the door and stepped inside, however, I realized it wasn't Yvesta and it wasn't the kitchen.

The door gave a soft creak and Drew, seated behind his desk in the library, looked up. The room was bright and warm, with flames crackling in the fireplace. A fleeting look crossed Drew's face when he saw me, surprise or relief or a stronger emotion still, but the handsome domed lamp behind his chair threw an assortment of shadows across both him and the desk, so I couldn't decide whether all I really saw was a simple play of light. He certainly didn't leap to his feet and rush to grab me into his arms. More's the pity.

Instead, seated and wearing the charming smile of which I'd grown inordinately fond, he asked, "What on earth are you doing here, Johanna?"

I suddenly and vividly remembered our first meeting, me sopping wet and standing in this very doorway, dripping onto the same wool rug.

"'The look on your face tells me you think I am some kind of vision, but please don't elaborate,'" I quoted, stepping farther into the room. I could tell my response puzzled him but then knew from his broadened smile that he finally recalled our first exchange, too.

"There is something about you and water, apparently. Should you be up?"

"I'm hungry. I thought this was the kitchen."

"Yes, but should you be up?" he repeated.

I sat down in the chair across from his desk before I answered. "I don't think you need to baby me any more," then hastened to add, "not that I mean to sound ungrateful. You've been very kind and I appreciate everything you've done more than I can say."

His expression looked briefly forbidding, and he moved his hand to brush away my words with a wave. "You don't have to be polite with me, Johanna."

"You didn't let me finish. I only meant it as perfunctory courtesy. There was a *but* coming." Drew waited for me to finish, eyes warm and mouth so inviting I almost lost my train of thought.

"That's all right, then," he conceded, "because perfunctory courtesy is the only kind I allow in this house."

"I was going to add, 'but where is the kitchen?' Do you think Yvesta is still up?" Drew peered at the small clock on his desk.

"Since it's nearly midnight, I hope not, but I am not her keeper, only her employer. Let's go see." Pushing back his chair, he stood up and stretched. "I know where the kitchen is, and I imagine that even without Yvesta we can find something safe for you to eat. I can bring it to your room, if you'd like."

"No, no, no. I don't want you to wait on me any more than you already have and besides I need a change of scenery." I had risen without taking his outstretched hand and we walked side by side into the hallway without touching.

"You sound like your old self again. That's a sure sign you're feeling better."

"I've always had the constitution and the appetite of a horse. Was I very sick?"

"Very."

"It's odd that I don't remember any of it, though." By then we had entered the dark kitchen and Drew turned on lights and began to rummage for plates and utensils.

"None of it?" He stopped his exploration of cupboards to focus on my answer.

"Only the dream and your being there." I remember the

safety of your arms, I wanted to add, the way we fit together, and the words you murmured against my hair. I remember those things, too. But I didn't say any of that. He was too coolly self-possessed, a different man from the one who held me night after night, trying to keep the nightmare at bay.

Drew turned his back to bring down mugs and plates from the shelves, so I couldn't see his face. "Tea and bread, I think," he said aloud. "I'm not a doctor, but I'd guess anything more than that might unsettle your stomach." He put on the kettle for tea.

"I am a nurse, don't forget, and professionally speaking, I'm sure I can handle something with more substance than tea and bread."

"Here's a slice of roast chicken, then, but don't say I didn't warn you."

In a way he was right. I went from a ravenous need for food to feeling full after only a few bites—but those few bites were heavenly while they lasted. As I ate, Drew left the kitchen to return with a small woolen blanket that he draped across my shoulders. I felt him behind me, felt his hands on my shoulders as he arranged the blanket and then felt his hands cease their movement and simply rest there, gentle, warm, protective. For a few seconds, I leaned my head back against him, content and comfortable, aware of that same sensation of fitting together I'd experienced before. It was an odd moment, wordless and unacknowledged, the casual, amused Drew replaced by the man I remembered from my bedside. Coming back to sit across from me at the kitchen worktable, he nursed a shot glass of some liquid while I sipped tea.

"Crea said they weren't able to recover Jennie's body," I volunteered.

"No, and the temperature's dropped again. The ice is solid. They won't find her until spring." Drew paused. "Do you know why she was out there, Johanna?"

"Yes, I think so. She felt overwhelmed by life and was running away."

"Overwhelmed?"

I pulled the blanket more tightly around my shoulders. "Jennie was pregnant and not by Carl. She couldn't face what that meant, which in her eyes was a ruined future. If she went through with the marriage, she believed Carl would divorce her when he discovered the truth, and she was sure he would. If she called off the wedding, she'd have to face her mother's disappointment and society's scorn. Neither alternative was bearable to her. She didn't understand that a woman could live through all that. For her it was the end of the world. The end of her world. I don't know who the father of her child was because she wouldn't tell me, so I don't know if he was unwilling to do the right thing or if she was unable to have a life with him. Perhaps he was married, I don't know. She was purposefully evasive with me that day. She said the man's name wasn't important and that I especially didn't need to know, that knowing would make matters worse." When I stopped talking, Drew sat back in his chair and idly swirled the liquid in his glass, clearly digesting everything I had just said.

"Is that why you asked me if I cared very much about your cousin's death?"

"Did I?"

"Driving back from the Yacht Club."

I remembered then. "I don't know. I wasn't myself." At his continuing steady gaze, I added reluctantly, "I suppose it was." Drew set his glass down and rested folded hands on the tabletop.

"Johanna, I was not the father of your cousin's child." I started to protest that the thought never crossed my mind, but of course, I would have been lying and he would have known, so I said nothing. "Do you believe me?"

Instead of answering his question, I commented, "Jennie was young and beautiful with a wild side to her many men would find hard to resist. It would be understandable if a man acted on the attraction." My response did not satisfy Drew.

"I was not the father of your cousin's child. Do you believe me?" he repeated.

I wanted to, more than anything, and in fact at that moment, sitting across from him with the force of his personality and his hazel glare both directed at me, I did believe him. But once apart from him and alone with my own thoughts, I wasn't sure the confidence would last. Whatever he saw on my face made him unfold his hands and lean forward. Were it not for the expanse of the table, I believe he would have grabbed me by the shoulders.

"Johanna, since the evening of the Starr Award, I have not been alone with any woman but you and Yvesta. In any capacity for any reason. Period. And please remove that skeptical expression from your face. It irritates me."

"I just find it hard to believe, generally speaking. You told me you liked women and preferred a variety of them."

"Are you always going to throw my words back into my face?"

"I'm not the one who prided himself on his feminine conquests. You did say that, didn't you?"

"I said a lot of things that were all your fault."

"My fault?! How is your masculine braggadocio my fault?"

"If you were in a boat overloaded with cargo, Johanna, and it started to sink, what would you do?"

"I hope there's a good reason for this digression. I'd throw items overboard, of course."

"So do you understand now?"

I stared at him. Had he lost his mind? "Understand what, for heaven's sake? I have no idea what you're talking about." My frustrated response made him grin.

"I know you don't. That's one of the reasons I find you so damned delightful. Such an intelligent woman and still so dense! I've been sinking, Johanna, in one way or another since the afternoon you invaded my house and dripped rainwater all over the floor of the library, and I've been throwing all my excess baggage overboard ever since. Yes, it's true I like women, and I imagine I'll always look twice at a beautiful one. But I love you." His good-humored tone and easy smile were not how I expected to receive a declaration of love.

"Aren't you supposed to be down on one knee when you say that? Aren't you supposed to snatch me into your arms and cover me with kisses?"

"I don't think it's humanly possible to do all those things simultaneously or even consecutively. Think about it."

"You know what I mean."

"Yes, my darling, I do, and while the thought of covering you with kisses has its own inherent attraction, I'm not going to take advantage of a sick woman." I could only stare at him, so that he reached even farther across the table and took my hands in his. "Johanna, your cousin was a beautiful woman, but she paled next to you, as every woman inevitably does—at least to me. I never touched her. The only woman I want to touch is you. You."

"Oh." The look he gave me was having an effect on my heartbeat, my ability to maintain coherent thought, and my emotions. Even worse, out of nowhere I began to cry, tears filling my eyes and overflowing down my cheeks. "I'm sorry. I don't know why I'm crying. I never cry."

"You've been sick and you're still tired. It's all right to cry." He stood and came around the table. "And it's all right if you don't love me. That's all right, too."

"But—"

"Don't say anything in your weakened condition that you might later regret. Wait until you feel better and you're yourself again."

"Preachy and annoying, you mean?"

He laughed out loud. "No. Headstrong and confident and feisty."

I dabbed at my eyes with a table napkin before I stood. "You say the sweetest things to turn a girl's head."

At that he stepped closer and took me by the shoulders. "If you want sweet things, all you have to do is ask. I didn't think they'd hold any weight with you." Looking down into my face, he smiled and said, more gently, "Poor girl. All you really wanted was tea and toast, wasn't it? You need to go back to bed. Crea will have my head for letting you sit in this cold kitchen." He cupped my face between his hands. "But first I want to be sure you know that everything I told you tonight is true. Everything. I will never lie to you, Johanna."

"I know," I said, turning my face so I could lightly kiss each finger of his left hand, "but you're right, my illness gives you an unfair advantage. I'm teary and tired and I don't like that. I need to get stronger so I can think clearly, and I need to find out the state of my family. I want to go home tomorrow, Drew. Thank you for everything, but I want to go home."

"I wish this house on Prairie Avenue was your home."

I backed away, smiling, and shook my head. "It's not, though." Then softening my words, I added deliberately, "Not yet, anyway."

Crea and I left for Hill Street the next day. Seated behind Levi, I waved at Drew as he stood in the doorway and felt a pang of loneliness and loss as the automobile pulled away and Drew faded from sight. It was a necessary move, though, both practically and emotionally. I needed to get away from Drew long enough to catch an emotional breath, and I was anxious to see Grandmother. She was back from her stay at Uncle Hal's, and seeing her at the front door, I felt an immeasurable relief. If anything, she looked more robust than I remembered and her limp was hardly noticeable.

Peter visited that same afternoon and I was pleased to see that Crea didn't retreat. Instead, they sat together on the love-seat, not touching but each comfortable with the other, two people who belonged together and had finally accepted it. He didn't have any good news about Aunt Kitty, whose delusions continued, to the grief and disruption of her family.

"We've brought in a nurse to stay with her so she doesn't wander outside again. She's determined to go looking for Jennie on the lake." Peter hesitated, the memory of the terrible afternoon showing in his eyes, and then asked, "Do you know why Jennie did what she did, Johanna?"

"She was unhappy about the wedding," I answered, a half-truth that would have to do as explanation. I was not going to share any more with the family. What purpose would be served by revealing the whole sad story? "She felt trapped between Carl's parents and your mother, and she didn't have the ability or the strength to say no. I don't think she cared very much for Carl, and she couldn't bear the idea of a lifetime spent with someone she didn't love. Jennie was confused, Peter, confused and running away. I know she never meant it to end as it did."

Without realizing it, Peter reached for Crea's hand and clasped it in his. "She should have told me. I would have helped her." I had no response to that. Of all people, Peter understood the inexorable strength of his mother's will and purpose. And, of course, he did not know the whole story. Crea may have guessed there was more, but she and I never spoke of it. Ever.

"I'm going upstairs to rest a while. No, don't get up. I can manage fine on my own."

I wanted the two of them to have the opportunity to talk about their own future, hopefully to conclude that finding a life partner was more than a match of families and fortunes. Amid all the intricacies and the unknowns of life, discovering a person with whom to share the future was the finest of miracles and should be recognized and appreciated as such. What power could society's disapproval have against so rare and so precious an encounter?

That line of thought always brought me to Drew saying he loved me and the conflicting emotions that declaration stirred inside me: my wanting it to be so with all my heart and loving him in return but also a shadow of doubt I could not banish. I believed him about Jennie, I did, except for an unbidden thought first thing in the morning or an unvoiced question just before I fell asleep. Too many Floras, Betsys, and Henriettas in my past. Too much deception and grief.

Yet warring with that cautious past was the feel of Drew's hands clamped firmly on my wrists as I scrabbled to find the edge of the ice, his arms around me, rocking me, talking to me after a nightmare, the calm sincerity of his voice when he said, "I will never lie to you, Johanna." I thought I would get to the point where I believed him completely but feared it might take longer than he was willing to wait. Drew would not be content with even the smallest doubt about his veracity, I could not convincingly lie to him, and I could not imagine life without him. For several days I struggled with the conundrum of truth and desire, grew stronger, and gradually regained my energy.

When Uncle Hal visited at the end of the week, my heart went out to him. He looked all his age and then some, tired, thin, and sad. Grandmother was resting, but he and I sat together in the front room and I told him the same story of

Jennie I'd shared with Peter.

When I finished, he said, "I should have seen what was happening. I should have known."

"You can't blame yourself. Jennie didn't share her misery easily, and Carl seemed to be—perhaps is—a nice enough young man."

"She never loved me, you know." For a minute I thought he was talking about Jennie and opened my mouth to protest, but then I realized he wasn't talking about Jennie at all. "You never knew Kitty as a girl. Jennie was her exact image. She was a beauty and I fell hard the first time I met her. Kitty had other plans, though. She had her heart set on another young man and until her parents got involved, I didn't stand a chance. But I was the better catch—old family, old money, prestigious law firm. Poor Kitty. Like Jennie she didn't have the will or the words to refuse. I knew it all along, knew there was someone else, but a young man in love can't see anything but his own need. I thought she'd grow to love me in time but she never did. I was always a duty to her. I shut my eyes and my ears to her plans for Jennie because it was the first I'd seen Kitty happy in years. Now I've lost them both and it's no one's fault but my own."

"That's not true. People are responsible for their own decisions. Aunt Kitty could have refused you. Jennie could have spoken up. Women aren't children at the mercy of a man's stronger will and higher intelligence. We're adults who must make our own thoughtful choices." My vigorous, spontaneous response made me realize how profoundly some of my own beliefs about women had changed over the past months, fault harder to place and roles more ambiguous. Without articulating the words, for years I'd assumed most women were victims, helpless and ultimately passive in their own lives. Now I saw things differently, saw the power of accountability and self-respect. I would have to rework my own assumptions to fit this new century of promise.

"I was blind to what was happening in my own house," Uncle Hal repeated doggedly. "I failed them both." He straightened in his chair, the sharing at an end. "We're not having any kind of service for Jennie, not yet. Maybe in the spring." When her body washes ashore, I thought, and in case Aunt Kitty regains her faculties. That's what he's thinking.

"Jennie loved light and color," I commented. "She was like springtime, bright and beautiful." Uncle Hal blinked back tears, patted my hand, and rose.

"Jennie admired you, Johanna. She often said she wanted to be like you. As strong and brave as Johanna, she said. In a way you were her hero. She never would have done what she did if she'd known you would be endangered, too. She would never have done anything to hurt you—you, especially, Johanna."

I saw Uncle Hal to the front door and after he was gone went to sit by the fire. His departing words, similar to Jennie's enigmatic response to my questions about her baby's father— "You especially don't need to know; it would only make matters worse"—struck me with the force of a blow. Of course, Drew and Jennie were not involved in any way. What was I thinking? They could have seen each other publicly and openly if they'd wished. There was no need for subterfuge. Even more than that, I knew neither one would willingly hurt me with such a deceit. But then what did her words mean? Compared to everyone else, why should I especially be kept in ignorance? Why would my knowing the father of Jennie's make matters worse? I sat deep in thought for a long time, mentally retraced my steps from the moment I arrived home last April, pictured parties, envisioned faces, tried to recapture Jennie's presence on all the occasions I was with her. When I was done, I could draw only one conclusion. How had Uncle Hal phrased it? "I was blind to what was happening in my own house. I failed them both." I felt a similar frustrated regret but mixed with that regret was a surge of selfishly pure joy. Drew Gallagher said he loved me and I believed he did, believed it with all my heart, sat amazed at the extraordinary gift I'd been given, wanted him to know I could match him love for love and was prepared to do just that—if he hadn't changed his mind through this past silent week. I would have to risk his change of feeling, however, because before I went to Drew and offered him myself and my future, I had someone else I needed to see. I sat down and wrote a note that Levi delivered the next day.

The following morning I dressed for a trip on the train much as Amundsen must have dressed en route to the South Pole. It was the last week of February and surprisingly warm and sunny, but I retained a horror of being cold that I imagined would stay with me my whole life.

"Johanna, you're not fully recovered. I don't know why you feel you have to go out at all, but at least let Levi drive you to your destination." Crea fussed over me so annoyingly that I had to shake loose.

"I am recovered. At least recovered enough to go to church. I'll be fine." As a distraction, I added, "Isn't Peter leaving for school tomorrow?" and had the satisfaction of seeing her annoyed look.

"Peter has nothing to do with this discussion and you know it. You did that to take the attention off you, a ploy that has lost its effectiveness."

I smiled. "It worked fine just now," then added affectionately, "You will make a wonderful cousin-in-law someday. I won't have to break you in to all my tricks." From Crea's expression, it was clear I found the remark more entertaining than she did. There was nothing of the victim about Crea, I thought, and we will do well together through the years. She won't take any nonsense from me and that's healthy for both of us. Despite the seriousness of the meeting I'd set up at St. Michael's Cathedral, my heart felt released from a burden. God willing, I had a future with Drew Gallagher and although that future might turn out to be many things, I knew for certain it would never be boring. I can't abide tedium.

The first thing I noticed upon entering St. Michael's were those glorious windows, the turquoise, purple and scarlet glass gleaming like gemstones. The late morning sun lit the windows, burnished their trim, and splashed color on the pale orange walls. A breathtakingly beautiful extravagance of color. I saw the bent shoulders of the man I sought and went to sit next to him, no words at first. We sat side by side in a back corner pew, where I was content to soak up the brilliant color of the windows and their implied warmth.

"It's always like summer in here," I said finally, breaking the stillness. "In its own way as bright and beautiful as Jennie. I can tell she was your inspiration for this."

At those words Allen Goldwyn turned toward me. His face was the dull color of concrete and his eyes red from sleeplessness, a haggard man consumed by grief. "She was my inspiration for everything," he told me simply. "For everything. The world is dim and gray now and it always will be." I laid a calming hand over his trembling one that clutched the pew in front of us.

"I'm so sorry, Allen. I didn't realize until yesterday."

"She worried that you cared for me. I told her you and I were friends and nothing more, but she said she wasn't so sure."

"Surely you didn't hide your relationship because of me!" I exclaimed. "Please don't let that be the reason."

"I never meant for anything to happen. I could have loved her in secret all my life, I think, content to be somewhere in her orbit. That's all I needed. Just to be near her."

"You would have courted me to stay near her."

"Is that so terrible? I didn't think it was."

I couldn't answer. What would I be willing to do to keep Drew in my life? What dignity would I sacrifice?

Allen continued, "One afternoon we met downtown, purely by chance, and I could tell she was upset. I don't think she even remembered my name then, just knew I was your friend. I asked her for tea and while she talked, I listened. After that, nothing was the same, not for either of us."

"Allen, did you know—" I started and then stopped. Was it kind or necessary to mention Jennie's condition?

"Did I know about the baby? Not right away, but I guessed. At first she said it was Carl's but I knew. I knew she didn't care for him. I knew I was the only one. A man knows when a woman loves him, and Jennie loved me. Me."

"Then if you both cared for each other, what kept you apart? You have a good job with a good firm, you're talented and making a name for yourself, and you'll be comfortably situated someday. I don't understand."

"Goldwyn," he said bleakly. "Jennie Goldwyn. Do you honestly think your aunt would let her daughter marry a Jew and a working class Jew at that?"

"Oh, Allen, I never thought about that. It shouldn't matter."

"It does matter, though. You know it does. I begged Jennie. I told her we could handle anything together. I told her we could have a life together and what did anything else matter? But I couldn't convince her to confront her mother. She said we could continue to see each other after she was married, that it would be safer and easier for both of us, and by then I was desperate not to lose her. I would have done anything she asked. I followed her on the train to Boston after Christmas.

I begged her to marry me, begged her to take the chance, but she said she couldn't do it. She just couldn't. She sobbed like a child, Johanna." The words brought such excruciating pain to him that he leaned his forehead onto his hands that grasped the pew before us.

I placed an arm across his shoulders. "My dear, I'm so sorry. So sorry."

Allen shook off my arm and turned his face toward me. "You don't understand. Jennie was my inspiration, perfect in face and form. Every part of her was pleasing to look at. She was light and color and silk to the touch. She was everything to me. Everything. I don't understand why she couldn't take the chance. Why wasn't I enough for her? I need her, Johanna. Without her I can't find anything beautiful in the world. I'm nothing but a blind man." He began to cry in hoarse, desperate sobs that echoed in the empty church. I put my arms around him and held him against me muffling the sound, his head on my breast and both of us shaking from the force of his weeping. I cried, too, for all the lives touched and changed and lost, grieving especially for my Jennie, only a step away from happiness but a step she could not take.

After a while Allen pulled away, taking long, shuddering breaths in an attempt to regain his composure.

We were both silent until I asked, "What can I do for you?" His eyes, dark in an ashen face, brimming with misery and even more red-rimmed than before, met mine.

"Be happy, Johanna. Be happy for all of us. You have the power." Then he stood shakily. "Just be happy." He walked to the end of the pew and down the center aisle to the back doors without looking back. I sat in the cathedral a while longer, exhausted from Allen's raw grief, until the sun splashed through the windows again and dappled the walls with more vivid color. Like Jennie's smile, I thought, and was comforted.

Her spirit lived on in this bright and beautiful place.

Jennie was gone, but for a reason known only to God, I was alive, spared death more than once while other lives disappeared around me. Humbled and exhilarated, I realized that without my deserving it and through no effort of my own, life and hope were still mine and with them, love and beauty and light and joy. Grief and tears and loss, too, all in their time, but that was life as well, and they were all gifts too precious to be wasted or sacrificed because of fear or indecision. Allen was right. I had the power to be happy. I had the will for it, too. The recollection of Drew's voice came soft as a sigh, so real that for a moment I thought he'd come to sit beside me: "Johanna, what on earth are you doing?" The whisper was all I needed to hurry out and catch the next train for Prairie Avenue.

In any popular novel of the time, I would have hurried to Drew's house, he would have thrown open the front door, and we would have rushed into each other's arms. Unfortunately, real life is more pragmatic than fiction. Yvesta answered the door, not Drew.

"He's at his office, Johanna. Why would you think he'd be home in the middle of the afternoon? And what are you doing out by yourself? You still look too pale, if you ask me." She ushered me inside and took my coat. "Of course, you can stay, but it may be a long wait. He hasn't been getting home until after dark. 'Johanna hurt Mr. Gallagher's feelings and he's unhappy,' I told Fritz."

"Me?" I protested. "I didn't do anything."

"You went home. You left him alone when he liked having you here."

I followed Yvesta down the hallway and into the kitchen, still exonerating myself. "I have a home, too, Yvesta. Drew Gallagher can't go through life getting everything he wants whenever he wants it."

She poured me a cup of tea and set out a platter of cookies. "He doesn't want everything. He only wants you, but he's too much the gentleman to tell you in a way that will hold your attention."

"Too much a gentleman, my foot," I replied, but the words came out garbled because my mouth was full of oatmeal cookie. Then, more hesitantly, "Are you sure?"

"I know about these things. Mr. Gallagher is a good man, Johanna. You could do worse." She wrapped two cookies in a napkin and handed them to me. "But you already know that. Now go wait for him in the library. He'll be home for supper tonight."

"May I use the telephone to let Grandmother know I'll be back late?" I asked meekly and at Yvesta's nod went to take care of that task.

"I'm at Drew's," I told Crea, who picked up the other end, "and I don't know when or if I'll be home tonight. Don't worry."

After a silence, Crea said, "Congratulations, Johanna. It's about time," and hung up without a good-bye.

Fritz came in to kindle a fire in the library hearth and then left me alone to wander aimlessly until I spied the small volume of Longfellow's sonnets I gave Drew at Christmas lying on the corner of his desk. I kicked off my shoes and curled up in a soft, wing-backed chair with the book. The library reminded me of Drew, too, handsome and intelligent; like the books that crowded the shelves Drew hid behind a cover. He concealed himself purposefully, I thought, for protection, afraid someone might actually uncover the little boy whose parents hadn't loved him, fearful, as well, that he had inherited his brother's demons. No demons for you, love, I thought with a smile. They won't be allowed in our house.

Drew had marked several of the sonnets, made notes in

the margins, underscored and circled, scrawled the letter J here and there. I was more engrossed in his comments than in the poems themselves when he pushed open both library doors and stood arms akimbo in the doorway.

Looking up, I said, "This is more beautiful than I remember. Listen," and read, "'The white drift of worlds o'er chasms of sable / The star-dust that is whirled aloft and flies / From the invisible chariot-wheels of God.' You quoted those words the night we kissed for the first time. Do you remember? I do. It's one of my 'secret anniversaries of the heart.'"

He came in farther and tossed his jacket on a chair. "Does anyone know you're here?"

"Yvesta knows and Fritz and Crea and Grandmother by now, I assume. Why?"

Drew leaned casually against the desk, arms folded across his chest, observing me with narrowed eyes. "Because I can't believe anyone allowed you out by yourself. You're still too thin and pale."

"Compliments, again. I think I will request sweet things if my alternative is to be criticized for the rest of my life." At my words he moved to sit across from me in the matching hearth chair, the fire's warmth between us.

"What are you up to, Johanna?"

"I've been thinking."

"That makes me nervous."

"No, it doesn't. I don't think anything makes you nervous. That's one of the things I find most tempting about you, the way you stay so calm and slightly amused regardless of the circumstances. It makes me want to say and do things just to get you stirred up."

"That's easy enough." He patted his lap. "Come and sit here." I eyed him and then shook my head, making him grin. "I'm disappointed to discover you're all talk, my love." We looked at each other wordlessly, the fire crackling and Drew's smile slowly fading, replaced by an intense, searching expression. "Why are you here, Johanna?"

"I thought you might want to marry me. You've never put it in those words, so I may have it wrong—I get things wrong sometimes—but I certainly want to marry you. And if not marriage, then I'll settle for some other arrangement. I warn you, however, that Grandmother will be a hard sell. She is very—"

"Johanna, be quiet." I stopped obediently. "What is going on?"

"I'm proposing. I've never done it before so I may be going about it all wrong, and of course, in novels the woman isn't allowed to propose. She has to be wooed properly and then act reluctant and shy, but that's not me and it never will be. I don't have a coy bone in my body, and when it comes to you, I am as far from reluctant as a woman can be."

Drew sat with a hand splayed on each arm of his chair and feet flat on the floor, watching me in the still and focused way I thought I could never grow tired of. Please God that I would have many, many years to test my theory.

"Why would you want to marry me?"

"Because I love you, of course," I answered simply. "I flat out love you. I even love you when I'm annoyed with you, when you're acting like a typical man, who always has to know everything and get his own way. It's pathetic, I suppose, but I love you even then. Sometimes, God help me, I think I especially love you then."

He stood, took one long step, grabbed both my wrists and pulled me to my feet. "This is acting like a typical man," he said and kissed me roughly, thoroughly, and for a long time. My response gave proof to the words I'd just spoken.

Later, sitting on his lap despite my earlier refusal, I commented, "You can act like a typical man any time and I promise never to get annoyed." His arms tightened around me and I continued, "This is what I remember from the nightmare. You holding me and the two of us fitting together so perfectly we might have been created for each other. I know that sounds fanciful, but I believe it somehow." After a moment and more to myself than to him, I asked in a low voice, "Why should I be allowed to be happy like this?"

"Because you make other people happy," a lift at the end to make the words more suggestion than fact.

"I don't, though. You of all people understand how annoying I can be, how I force others to do what they don't want to do, how I want my own way, and how I hate compromise because I think I'm always right."

"Let me revise my words, then. You make me happy." A fact this time.

"I don't know why." Drew pushed me away to look straight into my eyes, a message in his glance that he hoped I'd understand without further elaboration.

"That's why," he said.

But I had to sigh and respond, "I'm sorry, Drew. Please believe me when I tell you I'm done with game playing. I really can't understand what you're trying to tell me."

My words gave him pause, and he fumbled for the right words as he said, "I like the way I look in your eyes, Johanna. I like the man you think you see when you look at me, and while I know I'm not that man, you make me want to be him. I like you thinking I'm generous and kind when I'm neither of those things."

"Yes, you are," I protested vehemently. "Look at Cox's."

"You know why I started Cox's? Because I wanted to get as far with you as I could, so I thought to myself, what can I do to get Johanna Swan's attention? And Cox's was born just like that. There wasn't a noble goal anywhere in sight."

"So what? You know all I care about are actions and results," I retorted and took a little time to clarify which actions I was particularly interested in at the moment.

"I liked holding you like this when you were ill," he went on softly a while later. "I liked being able to comfort you when no one else could. I liked how you called for me when you were frightened. I've never been that important to anyone before. I like it when you leap to my defense. No one's ever done that before either. Just the opposite, in fact. I like the way you run at life full tilt, Johanna. In a way I can't quite grasp, I seem to come alive with you. Without you nothing has meaning or joy. There. Does that help you understand what I'm trying to tell you?"

For a fleeting moment I recalled Allen Goldwyn's grief-contorted face before I answered Drew's question in a way he would understand. He is not a man for ambiguity.

Much later, after words that only Drew and I need to know, I found myself in a deliciously precarious position on the sofa. I had placed both my palms up against his chest and said breathlessly, "I'm all right with this whatever you answer, but you never did accept my proposal, and I'd just like to know— for curiosity's sake—if you plan to make an honest woman of me afterwards."

My words stopped him cold. He pulled away and looked down at me, handsome but flushed and decidedly preoccupied, tie gone and shirt open, his hair ruffled because I'd just spent considerable time running my hands through it, hazel eyes slightly glazed, breaths coming as short and shallow as mine. I watched the reckless, primitive emotion fade from his eyes to be replaced by a more sedate and rueful expression, and then with a sigh he disentangled himself and stood up.

"You, Miss Swan, are already the most honest woman I know. Yes, I accept your proposal." He began to button his shirt.

I stood, too, talking as I tried to rearrange my skirts. "Marriage, you mean? Or some other arrangement?"

"Marriage, Johanna. What else would I dare offer the daughter of missionaries?"

"I'm not going to change, Drew," I warned, suddenly struck by the enormity of the words we'd just exchanged. "I'm still going to work at the Anchorage and walk in suffrage demonstrations and bully people to get what I want. If that matters to you, you should say something now because if you don't, you've got me for life."

Drew put both hands on my shoulders and pulled me close. "Promises, promises," he whispered before he found the hollow of my throat. "Work and demonstrate and bully all you want, my love. I wouldn't have it any other way."

Like a French poem is Life; being only
Perfect in structure
When with the masculine rhymes mingled
The feminine are.

Epilogue, 1938

With my usual self-absorption and because I was young and in love, I thought my marriage concluded the story. I scribbled down the details of 1912 and tucked the telling away in an old hatbox. I'll read it again when I'm old and gray, I thought, and moved on with my life. Of course, with years between then and now, I realize our wedding was a beginning and not an ending at all. Theo, our youngest son, is at an age of curiosity, fourteen and one to pester both Drew and me with questions about life, so I recently pulled out the manuscript I wrote twenty-five years ago and reread it over several evenings.

During that time Drew periodically stopped to read over my shoulder. Sometimes he read in silence, remembering, as I did, the joy and the grief of that time. Other times, he dropped a kiss lightly on the back of my neck and whispered something into my ear I will not repeat but that warms me in a way that has not changed from our wedding night. In all respects, Drew Gallagher was a man of pleasant surprises from the start.

The morning after accepting my marriage proposal, Drew appeared at the front door of the house on Hill Street, smiled at me as one casual acquaintance to another, and asked to see Grandmother.

"Why?" I asked, following him into the parlor.

"Johanna, my business is with your grandmother."

"If you plan to ask her for my hand in marriage, you needn't bother. In two weeks I'll be twenty-four years old. I can decide what to do with my own hand."

"So I noticed last night," he commented and in spite of my best intentions, I blushed like a schoolgirl, which I could tell delighted him. He had pity on me, though, and continued, "I'm going to do everything properly if it kills both of us. Besides, what can it hurt? It may be an outdated custom to you, but it's still respectful, and the gesture will please your grandmother."

"One of the reasons I love you," I said over my shoulder as I left to tell Grandmother of Drew's presence, "is that you are right more often than I am. I can't say that about many other men."

Grandmother was both unsurprised and approving. What she actually said, according to Drew, was, "That's very courteous of you, Mr. Gallagher, and for the record, you have my blessing. I knew the two of you would suit from the first moment I met you, so I feel some vindication. But even if I loathed you, we both know that if Johanna wants to marry you, neither your wishes nor mine hold any weight in the matter whatsoever."

Drew came downstairs and immediately bent on one knee in front of me.

"Get up right now," I ordered, horrified. "You don't have to do that."

"Yes, I do. You told me I did."

"Did I?" I stopped, arrested midthought with remembering. "Well, I was wrong. That's not important. The other part, though—"

"The part about covering you with kisses, you mean?"

"Exactly. Now that part is important."

— 408 —

Sometime later, after comfortably picking up where we'd left off the night before, Drew set me away from him, started to speak, cleared his throat because his voice had gone husky, and reached into an inside pocket for a small black velvet box. The ring it contained was gloriously beautiful, its large center diamond stone surrounded by a circle of amber, all in a setting of gold. Spectacular.

"I love it, but it's too expensive, Drew. Is it right to spend this kind of money when there are so many needy people?" I didn't take the ring off, however, despite my pang of conscience, just kept staring at it on my finger, mesmerized by the radiant depth of color.

"Yes, it is right, my love. Very right. But knowing your love of barter, I contacted a man this morning to begin work on the second phase of the Cox Experiment. Another building exactly like the first. Will you let that be a fair trade for the ring?"

I blinked back tears (apparently not completely recovered yet, I thought in self-defense) and murmured, "Yes. That seems equitable. Thank you."

He grinned at my tone of concession, brushed a tear from my cheek with his thumb, and asked, "May we set a wedding date now? Tomorrow would be fine with me or this afternoon if we could arrange it. With spring around the corner, the nights are getting shorter. We're losing valuable time."

Tears gone, I smiled and promised, "We'll have to wait a little longer than a day but don't despair. I'll make it up to you." With my natural predilection to skip any wordy parts and get straight to the action, Drew would be the first to concede that I kept my promise.

The lake returned Jennie to us the first Sunday in May, her remains snagged on an old pier along the northern coast and only recognizable by her long, fair hair and a few tattered remains of her ice-blue velvet dress. The news of her body's recovery was meaningless to Aunt Kitty, who lived out her years in a state of delusion, telling anyone who would listen that her daughter was marrying into the Boston Milfords, turning down Jennie's bed every night, and setting a place for her at the table. My Uncle Hal played his part in the charade, loved Aunt Kitty until the day she died and even after, always believing it was his fault she didn't love him in return, always blaming himself for her disappointment and sad life, forever carrying the burden of a debt he did not know how to repay. Uncle Hal's gone now, that good and faithful man. I miss him. Peter and Crea named their first son after him and with a natural willingness to please, Harry Rourke McIntyre turned out to be as good-natured and affectionate as both his father and his grandfather. I think the boy and his sisters were a joy and comfort to Uncle Hal during his last years. Certainly I saw him laugh more in their presence than during any other time of his life I could recall.

I married Andrew Gallagher June 21, 1913, in a small ceremony in our parlor on Hill Street. Because we were a family in mourning, the ceremony and the guest list were modest. It was not I, after all, who was expected to wed that year. I chose a plain wedding dress of deep cream edged in delicate brown lace so I could also wear the amber earrings Drew gave me for Christmas. To match your eyes and your mouth, he told me, and I wore the earrings that day as a promise of everything I willingly gave him. He did not miss the message.

In his way of always keeping me just a little off balance, Drew announced that he had found the perfect sermon text for the wedding and asked if I thought the officiating minister would be offended by the suggestion. "Song of Solomon, chapter eight, verse seven." He paused, then hastily added, "If you agree, Johanna. It is your wedding, too, of course."

"Thank you for that concession, but that's not why I was taken aback. I had no idea you studied the Scriptures."

"I didn't, but I'm marrying the daughter of missionaries so I'm sure that will have to change"

"What is Song of Solomon, chapter eight, verse seven?"

When he quoted the passage, my heart gave a twist and I saw a sudden, jumbled procession of faces in my mind's eye: Douglas Gallagher was there, and Jennie and Allen, Aunt Kitty and Uncle Hal, my parents, my little brother Teddy, and my grandparents. All of them, in body or in spirit, would be with us on our wedding day.

"Does it suit you?" Drew asked gently.

I blinked back tears to respond, "Yes. No wonder I love you."

Song of Songs, chapter eight, verse seven: *Many waters cannot quench love.*

I worried that my black eye wouldn't fade before the ceremony, but fortunately I was able to cover the residual discoloration with face powder. Drew was in better shape because the scrape on his cheek gave him the look of a roguish Caribbean pirate. Still, we were a rough looking pair on our wedding day.

I had headed off for New York City to join the largest suffrage parade ever planned, scheduled for the tenth of May. As I traveled on the eastbound train, someone wordlessly sat down beside me. When I turned to greet my new seat partner, there sat my beloved smiling at me.

"I thought you had business that couldn't wait," I said, taking a brusque tone because as always I was stirred by his proximity, one reaction that has not changed one little bit all these years later.

"Why should you get to have all the fun?" He picked up my gloved hand and kissed the back of it. "Besides, I have some sympathy for the cause. Do you think only women believe in equality and justice?" I didn't answer, just snuggled my shoulder closer to his and sat, content. In an odd sort of contradiction, I am always content when I'm with Drew, even when we argue or when he encourages me to slow down and think things through and I am hell-bent for action and will not listen. Even then he satisfies me. Especially then.

The march down Fifth Avenue began peacefully, thousands of women and by newspaper accounts almost five hundred men besides, until some of the hooting observers on the sidelines became hostile and then violent. One rough man leaped out in front of me and when I moved to push past him, he twirled me around. His rude handling of me made me lose my temper. I reached a hand to brush him off and he apparently thought I meant him some harm, never mind that he was at least eight inches taller and a hundred pounds heavier than I. He swung his arms forward, hit me squarely in the eye, and knocked me down—an accident, I believe now, but all Drew needed to tear into the man like an avenging and furious tornado. By then our entire side of the street was engaged in a shameful but invigorating melee and the police elbowed their way through, breaking up altercations, and arresting anyone suspicious, which—incredibly—included Drew and me. We sat in a paddy wagon on our way to the police station, both of us trying to nurse the other until almost simultaneously and without warning we began to laugh, one of those wonderfully cathartic and exhausting laughs that makes a person cry and ends in edgy hiccups, just a tenuous moment away from starting up all over again. We spent the night in a jail cell with other suffrage supporters and some of their roughest protesters all locked together in common misery. In the morning, released and out in the street, I gave Drew a critical look.

"How do you always manage to look so darned presentable? You were in a knock-down fight and just spent the night in a crowded and repulsive holding cell, yet you look like a man on his way to the opera. I on the other hand—" I looked down at my torn skirt and tried ineffectively to smooth down my hair "—am a mess. Look at me."

Drew put both hands on my shoulders. "I am looking at you and you aren't a mess. You are a beautiful sight. Every moment with you is such an adventure, Johanna! You're the only woman who can make me feel completely alive." He laughed out loud, then kissed me passionately right there in the middle of the sidewalk, people excusing themselves around us and more than a few ribald comments made in passing. None of that mattered. In his usual predictably accurate way, our life together has been and is an adventure still.

Grandmother died in the influenza epidemic of 1917, ill one day and literally gone the next, her weakened constitution unable to fight off the deadly illness. Her spirit stayed strong, but her body could not do the same. May grieved her passing even more than I. I was pregnant that year and had awful dreams of losing both Grandmother and the baby to the terrible pandemic of that time, but despite my secret fears, our Richard was born healthy, strong-willed, and vocal. His great-grandmother's spirit lives on in him, and I don't believe the proximity of her death and my son's birth was an accident.

Following the ratification of the nineteenth amendment on August 26, 1920, I cast my first vote in a presidential election. My candidate lost, but that was hardly the point. That first time the action itself mattered more than the result. Perhaps women would have had the vote sooner, but The Great War interrupted the suffrage movement and rightly so. Life is about priorities after all. Thousands of young men died in the mud of Europe's forests and fields, and the vote for women could wait for world peace.

I have to thank women's suffrage for a more delicate gift besides. Our David was conceived at the Mediterranean villa where our family vacationed following the election, the holiday we had promised each other years before to celebrate the momentous occasion. A warm and loving child from the start, David seemed to reflect the sun and blue waters of his beginning.

In the last year of the war, the papers reported Carl Milford's death. Apparently he abandoned his heritage of water and ships because he died in air combat as a flying ace over the skies of Germany. Unmarried, the paper said. Perhaps I had wronged Carl. Perhaps he loved Jennie more than I suspected and water became a horror and a reminder to him of what he had lost. Perhaps like Uncle Hal he was at the mercy of a woman unable—for all his heartfelt devotion—to love him in return.

Now I think, as unbelievable as it seems, that a second war threatens world peace, and this war strikes closer to home. Our Theo, fourteen as I write and a boy of energy and adventure, will soon be an age ripe for soldiering. Sometimes at night I think about my sons going off to war and it is almost more than I can bear. I turn and pull myself against Drew so I can hear the sound of his heartbeat in my ear, the same comforting sound I remember as he held my soaked, shivering, and freezing body, the same steady rhythm that still keeps nightmares at bay.

A man of surprises, that Drew Gallagher. He argues with the statement but it is obvious he is a better father than I am a mother. His consistent, calm, good-natured, and loving parenting was a necessary balance to my prosing on passionately about the need for tolerance and justice and personal integrity. I once overheard young David ask his older brother Richard if he thought it was a sin that he didn't like wax beans since Mother said many people didn't have enough to eat. I felt an instant and dreadful guilt at the little boy's troubled question.

David, our middle child, the one with the tender conscience and now in divinity school, always took everything to heart, the only one of our three sons as troubled by dreams as his mother.

"I'm ruining our children," I had said to Drew later that day, dropping onto the hassock next to his feet. "I wish I were more like you. You let the boys be boys." Drew pulled me into his lap at the comment and held me against him, a comfortable place to which I had by then grown accustomed.

"Perhaps I do," he responded, "but you teach them to be men, and you're the one they'll thank someday. You bring the passion, Johanna."

"Well," I told him thoughtfully, "there's passion— and then there's passion. You do very nicely on your own accord." He did, too. Who would have thought that a man so fond of the company of women, who once said he preferred variety in his female companions and stated with unequivocal firmness that he contemplated a wife with horror, would turn out to be such a tender, loving, faithful husband? I take no credit for the phenomenon, only enjoy its benefits.

Originally I prepared for daughters, anticipated my own little army of suffragettes, and planned to encourage them to scale new heights on behalf of women everywhere, but in the ironic way of divine Providence, we were blessed instead with sons.

When our first child Richard was born, I felt a small and shameful pang of disappointment that he was not a daughter until Drew came in, the baby in his arms.

"A son," he said and then stopped, unable to continue. I saw on my husband's face something of the little boy he once had been, a wistful remnant of the unloved Drew in the cold San Francisco mansion, an unguarded expression that spoke of redemption and unbelievable second chances. At that moment the gender of our children became totally irrelevant.

In private moments Drew reminds me that none of our sons was conceived domestically.

"Not," I usually answer with a half smile, "for want of trying," which always brings a wicked grin to his face and a predictable and enjoyable response. He's right, though. Richard followed a visit on behalf of the Red Cross to the war zone in the south of France, David arrived after our Mediterranean holiday, and Theo was born nine months after Drew and I traveled to China for an emotional search for the three Swan graves and reconnection with my old friend Dinah Hudson in the process. Obviously, the tourist sites were not all we explored when we were out of the country.

We have certainly seen the world and continue to do so. I have run the Swan-Gallagher Philanthropic Organization for the last twenty years and travel both nationally and internationally on its behalf. Gallagher Enterprises grew to include banks and businesses on both coasts and in Europe as well. When the American stock market crashed in 1929, our diverse foreign investments helped keep our banks open and ensure the safety of all the funds. Because of Drew's personal and financial commitment and with my complete support, none of our investors lost a cent and our employees did not lose their jobs. Not many could say the same during those difficult years, and it was the primary reason Drew received the Starr Award an unprecedented second time.

From time to time, our paths cross Allen Goldwyn's. When that occurs, we never make more than cursory and courteous conversation. I know he married, but I have never met his wife. He's still in the building business, constructing practical train stations and warehouses around the city, plain rectangular buildings, close to the ground and finished in grays and browns. He makes a good living, I'm told.

Drew and I could have honeymooned anywhere. Money was no object and Drew was expansive in his urging. "Moscow," he suggested. "A villa in Tuscany. Paris. Africa. Choose Johanna. Let me take you somewhere you've always dreamed of visiting."

When I told him my preference, he scrutinized my face to be sure I wasn't joking, realized I wasn't, gave a sigh, and left to buy train tickets. We spent the bulk of our honeymoon in Blessing, Kansas, reserved the best room of the Hansen House for our nights and spent our days getting to know the family I had never met. My fears that Drew would be bored or uncomfortable with people from the Kansas countryside were presumptuous, unnecessary, and unfounded. He was as easy discussing hog futures as he was the latest price of feed corn with Uncle Pete, the husband of my father's sister, Mary. My Uncle Carl owned and operated the Hansen House with his wife Louisa, so he and Drew were thick as thieves about investments and interest rates from the start. I had a bevy of cousins, too, and cousins-in-law and children of cousins, enough that I had to write down names and try to memorize them in the evenings. I found the graves of my father's parents and felt an unexpected rush of emotion and connection as I stood by the plain markers that showed the resting places of Johanna and Theodore Swan. My honeymoon trip was a journey of discovery and delight, in some ways I had anticipated and others accompanied by an unexpected twist of the heart.

I remember awakening late one morning in our room at the Hansen House, reaching next to me for Drew and finding his place and pillow empty and cold. I sat up suddenly to discover my husband fully dressed and seated cross-legged at the foot of the bed, apparently engrossed in watching me sleep.

"Have you been out already?" I asked. As a woman of energy and industry, I was embarrassed to sleep late.

"Out and about, yes."

"You should have awakened me."

"You didn't get enough sleep last night," he said and grinned.

I decided not to pursue that particular subject and asked, "Where did you go?"

"There's an auction at that big stone house on the south end of town. Do you remember seeing it? A beautiful old place right across from the department store. I went to take a look."

I reached for my robe and yawned unglamorously. "Didn't Aunt Mary say that was the banker's house?"

"The banker's widow's house. A Mrs. Fairchild. Since there weren't any children, the estate is auctioning off her belongings. Carl told me there were some fine old furnishings and to get there early if I wanted to have a chance at anything."

"I saw several markers for Fairchilds in the cemetery. How sad to see one's personal and private mementoes given to strangers." Changing my posture to mimic Drew's, I sat cross-legged with my back against the headboard and asked, "So? Did you buy something? Do we have to make room in the parlor? Will you expect me to wear some fashion find that's caught your fancy even if it's thirty years out of date?"

"Would you do that if I asked, Johanna?" I couldn't tell if he were teasing or serious.

"I would do anything for you," I answered evenly. "Haven't you figured that out by now?"

We sat as still as two bookends with rows of dreams and memories yet to make propped between us. Finally, Drew held out his hand to show a worn velvet box resting on his palm.

"I found something that made me think of you." he said. In a queer way the moment reminded me of the first time we had talked face to face, when he'd held his hand outstretched between us tightly clenching Douglas's returned jewelry.

Without a word I rose, tied my robe around me, and went to sit on the edge of the bed next to Drew. I took the box from his hand and opened it. Inside, on yellowed satin lining, lay an unusual and antique piece of woman's jewelry, intricately crafted, delicate, and very feminine. A petite round timepiece set in rich butter-gold and surrounded by small amber stones dangled from a graceful, golden, lily-shaped brooch. I had never seen anything like it.

"It's beautiful," I breathed, "but is it right for us to have so private a token of one man's love for his wife?" I recognized it as the kind of gift a husband would choose—one-of-a-kind, distinctive, expensive—and wondered about the woman who had worn the gorgeous thing. Had she also been one-of-a-kind, distinctive, expensive?

"From what I've heard of the Fairchilds, I doubt if love was an integral part of their relationship, but if it was and this object represents Gordon Fairchild's devotion to his wife, then yes, it is right, exactly right, for you to have it. There would be no difference in the giving."

I understood Drew's meaning, heard his unspoken words, and reached for his hand. "Thank you," I said and did not mean the watch.

"I saw it and thought of you," Drew explained, his voice suddenly low and ragged. "The amber is the exact color of your eyes. I saw it right away and had to have it because of what it is and what it means to me."

"I don't understand."

"It's all about time, Johanna, about filling meaningless, endless minutes and hours just to make it through to the next meaningless, endless day. A sad progression of wasted, wasteful time. Until you came along and suddenly time had an edge to it in a way I never imagined it could. It's not that you give meaning to my life as much as you give meaning to my time. That's what I thought when I saw it." Drew spoke with unusual hesitancy, searching for the right words and still, I could see by his face, not satisfied with the results. "Do you understand anything I just said to you?"

I held the amber watch in my hand, gently caressed the stones and stroked the smooth gold, wondering what heartfelt meaning, if any, it had once held for another man and his wife, both now gone. The golden lily, no longer coldly metallic and inanimate, slowly warmed to my skin and seemed to take comfort and welcome from my touch. Somehow, I thought, this lovely ornament knows that it will be worn over my heart for all the years to come, knows and approves and is satisfied. Was it enchanted? Or did it simply reflect the emotion I felt for my husband?

I watched gold flecks in the amber take on a life of their own, watched the stones begin to move, sparkle, and deepen in burnished color, a display of happiness I could not misread. Enchanted, indeed, I decided, and caught in its golden gleam a brief but unobstructed glimpse into my future. I saw the man Drew Gallagher was and the man he would grow to be, saw the depth and the intensity of his feeling for me. That look into the future generated a profound sense of well-being, a feeling of overflowing gratitude, and a humbling knowledge of strength that remain with me to this day. I recalled Allen's words, "Be happy for all of us. You have the power" and understood their meaning.

We're all surrounded by time, overwhelmed by it, eventually drowned in it, each of us a small circle of humanity with the same inherent qualities of those amber jewels to move and sparkle. Only for most of us, it takes another's warmth and touch and the certainty of belonging to make that happen. Every day of our lives we're given opportunities to intersect with others but for a multitude of reasons, because of fear or anger or pride, because of our own frailties or the weaknesses of others, because of past pain or the possibility of future hurt, we don't risk the connection. We don't take the chance and so forfeit the opportunity for something marvelous. We lose any hope for the prospect of joy—and more than love it's joy that gives lasting meaning to whatever time we're given.

Drew sat next to me on the bed, watching my face and waiting with uncharacteristic indecision for some kind of reassurance. He had tried to share something that he was only beginning to understand himself, had exposed an inner part of himself to me that he had kept hidden for many years, and I understood that being vulnerable was new to him and not altogether comfortable.

I was filled with such tenderness for my husband that I hesitated for a moment, longing to make the right response. My darling, I thought, I don't have the words to say what I need to say. The only thing I know for sure is that if we don't take advantage of the moment, we could lose out on everything. I am as vulnerable as you, I wanted to tell him, my heart just as exposed and because of you, I am all at risk. But I refuse to be afraid. I have exchanged fear for joy and I won't let you be afraid either.

I didn't say any of those words, however. I could not get them out and even if I had, they wouldn't have sounded right. Not then. We were both so new at sharing.

But my husband had asked me a question—"Do you understand anything I just said to you?"—and still waited for my reply, so I gave him a simple answer, offered trust and truth with every syllable and warmed each word with my love as my hands had warmed the amber lily and brought it to life. It was all I could say and would have to do for the time being. Drew deserved more from me but, God willing, I would have years to elaborate.

"Yes," was all I said. "I understand perfectly."

All quoted poems are from the collections of American poet Henry Wadsworth Longfellow (1807-1882)

Dedication page, from "Footsteps of Angels"
Frontispiece, from "The Song of Hiawatha"
Chapter one, from "God's-Acre"
Chapter two, from "Something Left Undone"
Chapter three, from "Holidays"
Chapter four, from "Haunted Houses"
Chapter five from "The Haunted Chamber"
Chapter six from "The Two Rivers"
Chapter seven, from "The Sound of the Sea"
Chapter eight, from "Endymion"
Chapter nine, from "A Summer Day by the Sea"
Chapter ten, from "Maidenhood"
Chapter eleven, from "It Is Not Always May"
Chapter twelve, from "Dedication"
Chapter thirteen, from "The Goblet of Life"
Chapter fourteen, from "Snow-Flakes"
Chapter fifteen, from "The Song of Hiawatha"
Chapter sixteen, from "The Courtship of Miles Standish"
Epilogue, from "Elegaic Verse VII"